Leonora Christina Ulfeldt

Memoirs of Leonora Christina

Outlook

Leonora Christina Ulfeldt

Memoirs of Leonora Christina

1. Auflage | ISBN: 978-3-73262-151-4

Erscheinungsort: Frankfurt am Main, Deutschland

Erscheinungsjahr: 2018

Outlook Verlag GmbH, Frankfurt.

Reproduction of the original.

Henry S. King & Co., 65, Cornhill

MEMOIRS OF
LEONORA CHRISTINA

DAUGHTER of CHRISTIAN IV. of DENMARK

WRITTEN DURING HER
IMPRISONMENT IN THE BLUE
TOWER AT COPENHAGEN
1663—1685

TRANSLATED BY F. E. BUNNÈTT

LONDON
HENRY S. KING & CO., 65 CORNHILL
1872

LONDON: PRINTED BY
SPOTTISWOODE AND CO., NEW-STREET SQUARE
AND PARLIAMENT STREET

PREFACE.

In placing the present translation of LEONORA CHRISTINA ULFELDT's Memoirs before the English reading public, a few words are due from the Publishers, in order to explain the relation between this edition and those which have been brought out in Denmark and in Germany.

The original autograph manuscript of Leonora Christina's record of her sufferings in her prison, written between the years 1674 and 1685, belongs to her descendant the Austrian Count Joh. Waldstein, and it was discovered only a few years ago. It was then, at the desire of Count Waldstein, brought to Copenhagen by the Danish Minister at Vienna, M. Falbe, in order that its authenticity might be thoroughly verified by comparison with documents preserved in the Danish archives and libraries, and known to be in the hand-writing of the illustrious authoress. When the existence of this interesting historic and literary relic had become known in Denmark, a desire to see it published was naturally expressed on all sides, and to this the noble owner most readily acceded.

Thus the first Danish edition came to light in 1869, promoted in every way by Count Waldstein. The editor was Mr. Sophus Birket-Smith, assistant librarian of the University Library at Copenhagen, who enriched the edition with a historical introduction and copious notes. A second Danish edition appeared a few months later; and in 1871 a German translation of the Memoir was edited by M. Ziegler, with a new introduction and notes, founded partly on the first Danish edition, partly on other printed sources, to which were added extracts from some papers found in the family archives of Count Waldstein, and which were supposed to possess the interest of novelty.

The applause with which this edition was received in Germany suggested the idea of an English version, and it was at first intended merely to translate M. Ziegler's book into English. During the progress of the work, however, it was found preferable to adopt the second Danish edition as the basis of the English edition. The translation which had been made from M. Ziegler's German, has been carefully compared with the Danish original, so as to remove any defects arising from the use of the German translation, and give it the same value as a translation made direct from the Danish; a new introduction and notes have been added, for which the Danish editor, Mr. Birket-Smith has supplied the materials; and instead of the fragments of Ulfeldt's Apology and of an extract from Leonora Christina's Autobiography found in the German edition, a complete translation of the Autobiography to the point where Leonora's Memoir of her sufferings in prison takes up the thread of the narrative, has been inserted, made from the original French text, recently published by Mr. S. Birket-Smith. As a matter of course the preface of Count Waldstein, which appears in this edition, is the one prefixed to the Danish edition. The manuscript itself of the record of Leonora Christina's sufferings in prison was commenced in 1674, and was at first intended to commemorate only what had happened during the preceding ten years of her captivity; it was afterwards extended to embrace the whole period down to 1685, and subjected to a revision which resulted in numerous additions and alterations. As, however, these do not seem to have been properly worked in by the authoress herself, the Memoir is here rendered, as in the Danish edition, in its original, more perfect shape, and the subsequent alterations made the subject of foot notes.

PREFACE
TO
THE DANISH EDITION.

When, in the summer of 1858, I visited the graves of my Dani
the family of Ulfeldt, in the little village church at Quærndrup,
of Egeskov, on the island of Fyn, I resolved to honour the memo
ancestress Leonora Christina, and thus fulfil the duty of a
publishing this autograph manuscript which had come to me
heirlooms left by my father.

It is well known that the last male representative of the family
Chancellor of the Court and Realm of Her Majesty the Er
Theresia, had only two daughters. One of them, Elizabeth, m
Christian, Count Waldstein, while the younger married Count Th

Out of special affection for her younger son Emanuel (my late
grandmother bequeathed all that referred to the Ulfeldts to h
manuscript which I now—in consequence of requests from vari
also from high places—give to publicity by the learned assist
Sophus Birket-Smith, thus came to me through direct descent from

'Corfitz, Count of Ulfeldt of the holy Roman Empire, Lord of tl
Költz-Jenikau, Hof-Kazof, Brödlich, Odaslowitz, and the fief Zinlt
of the Golden Vliess, First Treasurer of the hereditary lands in
Ambassador at the Ottoman Porte, afterwards Chancellor of the C
Empire, sworn Privy Councillor and first Lord Steward of his In
Royal Majesty Carolus VI., as well as of His Imperial Roman
Majesty of Hungary, Bohemia,' &c.

We add: the highly honoured paternal guide of Her Majesty
Empress Maria Theresia, of glorious memory, during the first y
government, until the time when the gifted Prince Kaunitz, who
sometimes even was too much for this, morally noble lady, be
successor.

I possess more than eleven imposing, closely written folio volume
contain the manuscripts of the Chancellor of the Empire, his negociat
the Sublime Porte, afterwards with the States-General of the Nether
well as the ministerial protocols from the whole time that he held the
Imperial Chancellor; all of which prove his great industry and love
while the original letters and annotations of his exalted

istress, which are inserted in these same volumes, testify to the sincere, almost childlike confidence with which she honoured him.

But this steady and circumspect statesman was the direct grandson of the restless and proud

CORFITZ, first Count of Ulfeldt of the Roman Empire, High Steward of the Realm in Denmark, &c., and of his devoted and gifted wife LEONORA CHRISTINA, through their son

LEO, Imperial Count Ulfeldt, Privy Councillor, Field-marshal, and Viceroy in Catalonia of the Emperor Carl VI., and his wife, a born Countess of Zinzendorf.

I preserved, therefore with great care this manuscript, as well as all other relics and little objects which had belonged to my Danish ancestress, whose exalted character and sufferings are so highly calculated to inspire sympathy, interest, and reverence. Amongst these objects are several writings, such as fragments of poems, prayers, needlework executed in prison (some embroidered with hair of a fair colour); a christening robe with cap worked in gold, probably used at the christening of her children; a very fine Amulet of Christian IV. in blue enamel, and many portraits; amongst others the original picture in oil of which a copy precedes the title page, &c. &c.

Considering that the manuscript has been handed down directly from my ancestors from generation to generation in direct line, I could not personally have any doubt as to its genuineness. Nevertheless I yielded to the suggestions of others, in order to have the authenticity of the manuscript thoroughly tested. In what way this was done will be seen from the Introduction of the Editor.

Though the final verdict of history may not yet have been given on Corfitz Ulfeldt, yet—tempus omnia sanat—yon ominous pillar, which was to perpetuate the memory of his crime into eternity, has been put aside as rubbish and left to oblivion. Noble in forgetting and pardoning, the great nation of the North has given a bright example to those who still refuse to grant to Albert, Duke of Friedland—the great general who saved the Empire from the danger that threatened it from the North—the place which this hero ought to occupy in the Walhalla at Vienna.

But as to the fiery temper of Corfitz and the mysterious springs which govern the deeds and thoughts of mankind, it may be permitted to me, his descendant, to cherish the belief, which is almost strengthened into a conviction, that a woman so highly gifted, of so noble sentiments, as Leonora appears to us, would never have been able to cling with a love so true, and so enduring through all the changes of life, to a man who was unworthy of it.

JOH. COUNT WALDSTEIN.

CAIRO: *December 8, 1868.*

CONTENTS.

MEMOIRS
OF
LEONORA CHRISTINA.

INTRODUCTION.

Amongst the women celebrated in history, Leonora Christina, the heroine as well as the authoress of the Memoirs which form the subject of this volume, occupies a conspicuous place, as one of the noblest examples of every womanly virtue and accomplishment, displayed under the most trying vicissitudes of fortune. Born the daughter of a King, married to one of the ablest statesmen of his time, destined, as it seemed, to shine in the undisturbed lustre of position and great qualities, she had to spend nearly twenty-two years in a prison, in the forced company—more cruel to her than solitary confinement—of male and female gaolers of the lowest order, and for a long time deprived of every means of rendering herself independent of these surroundings by intellectual occupation. She had to suffer alone, and innocently, for her husband's crimes; whatever these were, she had no part in them, and she endured persecution because she would not forsake him in his misfortune. Leonora Christina was the victim of despotism guided by personal animosity, and she submitted with a Christian meekness and forbearance which would be admirable in any, but which her exalted station and her great mental qualities bring out in doubly strong relief.

It is to these circumstances, which render the fate of Leonora so truly tragic, as well as to the fact that we have her own authentic and trustworthy account before us, that the principal charm of this record is due. Besides this, it affords many incidental glimpses of the customs and habits of the time, nor is it without its purely historical interest. Leonora and her husband, Corfits Ulfeldt, were intimately connected with the principal political events in the North of Europe at their time; even the more minute circumstances of their life have, therefore, a certain interest.

No wonder that the history of this illustrious couple has formed, and still forms, the theme both of laborious scientific researches and of poetical compositions. Amongst the latter we may here mention in passing a well- known novel by Rousseau de la Valette,[1] because it has had the undeserved honour of being treated by a modern writer as an historical source, to the great detriment of his composition. Documents which have originated from these two personages are of course of great value. Besides letters and public documents, there exist several accounts written by both Corfits Ulfeldt and Leonora referring to their own life and actions. Ulfeldt published in 1652 a defence of his political conduct, and composed, shortly before his death, another, commonly called the 'Apology of Ulfeldt,' which has not yet been printed entirely, but of which an extract was published in 1695 in the supplement of the English edition of Rousseau de la Valette's book. Some extracts from an incomplete copy discovered by Count Waldstein in 1870, in the family archives at the Castle of Palota, were published with the German edition of Leonora's Memoir; complete copies exist in Copenhagen and elsewhere. Leonora Christina, who was an accomplished writer, has composed at least four partial accounts of her own life. One of them, referring to a journey in 1656, to be mentioned hereafter, has been printed long ago; of another, which treated of her and Ulfeldt's imprisonment at Bornholm, no copy has yet been discovered. The third is her Autobiography, carried down to 1673, of which an English version follows this Introduction; it was written in the Blue Tower, in the form of a letter to the Danish antiquarian, Otto Sperling, jun., who wished to make use of it for his work, 'De feminis doctis.'[2]

About a century ago a so-called Autobiography of Leonora was published in Copenhagen, but it was easily proved to be a forgery; in fact, the original of her own work existed in the Danish archives, and had been described by the historian Andreas Höier. It has now been lost, it is supposed, in the fire which destroyed the Castle of Christiansborg in 1794, but a complete copy exists in Copenhagen, as well as several extracts in Latin; another short extract in French belongs to Count Waldstein. Finally, Leonora Christina wrote the memoir of her sufferings in the prison of the Blue Tower from 1663-1685, of which the existence was unknown until discovered by Count Waldstein, and given to the public in the manner indicated in the Preface.

In introducing these memoirs to the English public, a short sketch of the historical events and the persons to whom they refer may not be unwelcome, particularly as Leonora herself touches only very lightly on them, and principally describes her own personal life.

Leonora Christina was a daughter of *King Christian IV.* of Denmark and *Kirstine Munk.* His Queen, Anna Catherine, born a princess of Brandenburg, died in 1612, leaving three princes (four other children died early), and in 1615 the King contracted a morganatic marriage with Kirstine Munk, a lady of an ancient and illustrious noble family. Leonora was born July 18 (new style), 1621, at the Castle of Fredriksborg, so well known to all who have visited Denmark, which the King had built twenty miles north of Copenhagen, in a beautiful part of the country, surrounded by smiling lakes and extensive forests. But little is known of her childhood beyond what she tells herself in her Autobiography. Already in her eighth year she was promised to her future husband, Corfits Ulfeldt, and in 1636 the wedding was celebrated with great splendour, Leonora being then fifteen years old. The family of Ulfeldt has been known since the close of the fourteenth century. Corfits' father had been Chancellor of the Realm, and somewhat increased the family possessions, though he sold the ancient seat of the family, Ulfeldtsholm, in Fyen, to Lady Ellen Marsvin, Kirstine Munk's mother. He had seventeen children, of whom Corfits was the seventh; and so far Leonora made only a poor marriage. But her husband's great talents and greater ambition made up for this defect. Of his youth nothing is known with any certainty, except that he travelled abroad, as other young noblemen of his time, studied at Padua, and acquired considerable proficiency in foreign languages.[3] He became a favourite of Christian IV., at whose Court he had every opportunity for displaying his social talents. At the marriage of the elected successor to the throne, the King's eldest son, Christian, with the Princess Magdalene Sibylle of Saxony, in 1634, Corfits Ulfeldt acted as maréchal to the special Ambassador Count d'Avaux, whom Louis XIII. had sent to Copenhagen on that occasion, in which situation Ulfeldt won golden opinions,[4] and he was one of the twelve noblemen whom the King on the wedding-day made Knights of the Elephant. After a visit to Paris in 1635, in order to be cured of a wound in the leg which the Danish physicians could not heal, he obtained the sanction of the King for his own marriage with Leonora, which was solemnised at the Castle of Copenhagen, on October 9, 1636, with as much splendour as those of the princes and princesses. Leonora was the favourite daughter of Christian IV., and as far as royal favour could ensure happiness, it might be said to be in store for the newly-married pair.

As we have stated, Ulfeldt was a poor nobleman; and it is characteristic of them both that one of her first acts was to ask him about his debts, which he could not but have incurred living as he had done, and to pay them by selling her jewels and ornaments, to the amount of 36,000 dollars, or more than 7,000*l.* in English money—then a very large sum. But the King's favour soon procured him what he wanted; he was made a member of the Great Council, Governor of Copenhagen, and Chancellor of the Exchequer.

He executed several diplomatic missions satisfactorily; and when, in 1641, he was sent to Vienna as special Ambassador, the Emperor of Germany, Ferdinand III., made him a Count of the German Empire. Finally, in 1643, he was made Lord High Steward of Denmark, the highest dignity and most responsible office in the kingdom. He was now at the summit of power and influence, and if he had used his talents and opportunities in the interests of his country, he might have earned the everlasting gratitude of his King and his people.

But he was not a great man, though he was a clever and ambitious man. He accumulated enormous wealth, bought extensive landed estates, spent considerable sums in purchasing jewels and costly furniture, and lived in a splendid style; but it was all at the cost of the country. In order to enrich himself, he struck base coin (which afterwards was officially reduced to its proper value, 8 per cent. below the nominal value), and used probably other unlawful means for this purpose, while the Crown was in the greatest need of money. At the same time he neglected the defences of the country in a shameful manner, and when the Swedish Government, in December 1643, suddenly ordered its army, which then stood in Germany, engaged in the Thirty Years' War, to attack Denmark without any warning, there were no means of stopping its victorious progress. In vain the veteran King collected a few vessels and compelled the far more numerous Swedish fleet to fly, after a furious battle near Femern, where he himself received twenty-three wounds, and where two of Ulfeldt's brothers fell fighting at his side; there was no army in the land, because Corfits, at the head of the nobility, had refused the King the necessary supplies. And, although the peace which Ulfeldt concluded with Sweden and Holland at Brömsebro, in 1645, might have been still more disastrous than it was, if the negotiation had been entrusted to less skilful hands, yet there was but too much truth in the reproachful words of the King, when, after ratifying the treaties, he tossed them to Corfits saying, 'There you have them, such as you have made them!'

From this time the King began to lose his confidence in Ulfeldt, though the latter still retained his important offices. In the following year he went to Holland and to France on a diplomatic mission, on which occasion he was accompanied by Leonora. Everywhere their personal qualities, their relationship to the sovereign, and the splendour of their appearance, procured them the greatest attention and the most flattering reception. While at the Hague Leonora gave birth to a son, whom the States-General offered to grant a pension for life of a thousand florins, which, however, Ulfeldt wisely refused. In Paris they were loaded with presents; and in the Memoirs of Madame Langloise de Motteville on the history of Anna of Austria (ed. of Amsterdam, 1783, ii. 19-22) there is a striking *récit* of the appearance and reception of Ulfeldt and Leonora at the French Court. On their way home Leonora took an opportunity of making a short trip to London, which capital she wished to see, while her husband waited for her in the Netherlands.

If, however, this journey brought Ulfeldt and his wife honours and presents on the part of foreigners, it did not give satisfaction at home. The diplomatic results of the mission were not what the King had hoped, and he even refused to receive Ulfeldt on his return. Soon the turning-point in his career arrived. In 1648 King Christian IV. died, under circumstances which for a short time concentrated extraordinary power in Ulfeldt's hands, but of which he did not make a wise use.

Denmark was then still an elective monarchy, and the nobles had availed themselves of this and other circumstances to free themselves from all burdens, and at the same time to deprive both the Crown and the other Estates of their constitutional rights to a very great extent. All political power was virtually vested in the Council of the Realm, which consisted exclusively of nobles, and there remained for the king next to nothing, except a general supervision of the administration, and the nomination of the ministers. Every successive king had been obliged to purchase his election by fresh concessions to the nobles, and the sovereign was little more than the president of an aristocratic republic. Christian IV. had caused his eldest son Christian to be elected successor in his own lifetime; but this prince died in 1647, and when the King himself died in 1648, the throne was vacant.

As Lord High Steward, Ulfeldt became president of the regency, and could exercise great influence on the election. He did not exert himself to bring this about very quickly, but there is no ground for believing that he meditated the election either of himself or of his brother-in-law, Count Valdemar, as some have suggested. The children of Kirstine Munk being the offspring of a morganatic marriage, had not of course equal rank with princes and princesses; but in Christian IV.'s lifetime they received the same honours, and Ulfeldt made use of the interregnum to obtain the passage of a decree by the Council, according them rank and honours equal with the princes of the royal house.

But as the nobles were in nowise bound to choose a prince of the same family, or even a prince at all, this decree cannot be interpreted as evidence of a design to promote the election of Count Valdemar. The overtures of the Duke of Gottorp, who attempted to bribe Ulfeldt to support his candidature, were refused by him, at least according to his own statement. But Ulfeldt did make use of his position to extort a more complete surrender of the royal power into the hands of the nobility than any king had yet submitted to, and the new King, Fredrik III., was compelled to promise, amongst other things, to fill up any vacancy amongst the ministers with one out of three candidates proposed by the Council of the Realm. The new King, Fredrik III., Christian IV.'s second son, had never been friendly to Ulfeldt. This last action of the High Steward did not improve the feelings with which he regarded him, and when the coronation had taken place (for which Ulfeldt advanced the money), he expressed his thoughts at the banquet in these words: 'Corfitz, you have to-day bound my hands; who knows, who can bind yours in return?' The new Queen, a Saxon princess, hated Ulfeldt and the children of Kirstine Munk on account of their pretensions, but particularly Leonora Christina, whose beauty and talents she heartily envied.

Nevertheless Ulfeldt retained his high offices for some time, and in 1649 he went again to Holland on a diplomatic mission, accompanied by his wife. It is remarkable that the question which formed the principal subject of the negotiation on that occasion was one which has found its proper solution only in our days—namely, that of a redemption of the Sound dues. This impost, levied by the Danish Crown on all vessels passing the Sound, weighed heavily on the shipping interest, and frequently caused disagreement between Denmark and the governments mostly interested in the Baltic trade, particularly Sweden and the Dutch republic.

It was with especial regard to the Sound dues that the Dutch Government was constantly interfering in the politics of the North, with a view of preventing Denmark becoming too powerful; for which purpose it always fomented discord between Denmark and Sweden, siding now with the one, now with the other, but rather favouring the design of Sweden to conquer the ancient Danish provinces, Skaane, &c., which were east of the Sound, and which now actually belong to Sweden. Corfits Ulfeldt calculated that, if the Dutch could be satisfied on the point of the Sound dues, their unfavourable interference might be got rid of; and for this purpose he proposed to substitute an annual payment by the Dutch Government for the payment of the dues by the individual ships. Christian IV. had never assented to this idea, and of course the better course would have been the one adopted in 1857—namely, the redemption of the dues by all States at once for a proportionate consideration paid once for all. Still the leading thought was true, and worthy of a great statesman.

Ulfeldt concluded a treaty with Holland according to his views, but it met with no favour at Copenhagen, and on his return he found that in his absence measures had been taken to restrict his great power; his conduct of affairs was freely criticised, and his enemies had even caused the nomination of a committee to investigate his past administration, more particularly his financial measures.

At the same time the new Court refused Leonora Christina and the other children of Kirstine Munk the princely honours which they had hitherto enjoyed. Amongst other marks of distinction, Christian IV. had granted his wife and her children the title of Counts and Countesses of Slesvig and

Holstein, but Fredrik III. declined to acknowledge it, although it could have no political importance, being nothing but an empty title, as neither Kirstine Munk nor her children had anything whatever to do with either of these principalities. Ulfeldt would not suffer himself to be as it were driven from his high position by these indications of disfavour on the part of the King and the Queen (the latter was really the moving spring in all this), but he resolved to show his annoyance by not going to Court, where his wife did not now receive the usual honours.

This conduct only served to embolden those who desired to oust him from his lucrative offices, not because they were better patriots, but because they hoped to succeed him. For this purpose a false accusation was brought against Ulfeldt and Leonora Christina, to the effect that they had the intention of poisoning the King and the Queen. Information on this plot was given to the Queen personally, by a certain Dina Vinhowers, a widow of questionable reputation, who declared that she had an illicit connection with Ulfeldt, and that she had heard a conversation on the subject between Corfits Ulfeldt and Leonora, when on a clandestine visit in the High Steward's house. She was prompted by a certain Walter, originally a son of a wheelwright, who by bravery in the war had risen from the ranks to the position of a colonel, and who in his turn was evidently a tool in the hands of other parties. The information was graciously received at Court; but Dina, who, as it seems, was a person of weak or unsound mind, secretly, without the knowledge of her employers, warned Ulfeldt and Leonora Christina of some impending danger, thus creating a seemingly inextricable confusion.

At length Ulfeldt demanded a judicial investigation, which was at once set on foot, but in which, of course, he occupied the position of a defendant on account of Dina's information. In the end Dina was condemned to death and Walter was exiled. But the statements of the different persons implicated, and particularly of Dina herself at different times, were so conflicting, that the matter was really never entirely cleared up, and though Ulfeldt was absolved of all guilt, his enemies did their best in order that some suspicion might remain. If Ulfeldt had been wise, he might probably have turned this whole affair to his own advantage; but he missed the opportunity. Utterly absurd as the accusation was, he seems to have felt very keenly the change of his position, and on the advice of Leonora, who did not doubt that some other expedient would be tried by his enemies, perhaps with more success, he resolved to leave Denmark altogether.

After having sent away the most valuable part of his furniture and movable property, and placed abroad his amassed capital, he left Copenhagen secretly and at night, on July 14, 1651, three days after the execution of Dina. The gates of the fortress were closed at a certain hour every evening, but he had a key made for the eastern gate, and ere sunrise he and Leonora, who was disguised as a valet, were on board a vessel on their way to Holland. The consequences of this impolitic flight were most disastrous. He had not laid down his high offices, much less rendered an account of his administration; nothing was more natural than to suppose that he wished to avoid an investigation. A few weeks later a royal summons was issued, calling upon him to appear at the next meeting of the Diet, and answer for his conduct; his offices, and the fiefs with which he had been beneficed, were given to others, and an embargo was laid on his landed estates.

Leonora Christina describes in her Autobiography how Ulfeldt meanwhile first went to Holland, and thence to Sweden, where Queen Christina, who certainly was not favourably disposed to Denmark, received Ulfeldt with marked distinction, and promised him her protection. But she does not tell how Ulfeldt here used every opportunity for stirring up enmity against Denmark, both in Sweden itself and in other countries, whose ambassadors he tried to bring over to his ideas. On this painful subject there can be no doubt after the publication of so many authentic State Papers of that time, amongst which we may mention the reports of Whitelock, the envoy of Cromwell, to whom Ulfeldt represented that Denmark was too weak to resist an attack, and that the British Government might easily obtain the abolition of the Sound dues by war.

It seems, however, as if Ulfeldt did all this merely to terrify the Danish King into a reconciliation with him on terms honourable and advantageous to the voluntarily exiled magnate. Representations were several times made with such a view by the Swedish Government, and in 1656 Leonora Christina herself undertook a journey to Copenhagen, in order to arrange the matter. But the Danish Government was inaccessible to all such attempts.

This attitude was intelligible enough, for not only had Ulfeldt left Denmark in the most unceremonious manner, but in 1652 he published in Stralsund a defence against the accusations of which he had been the subject, full of gross insults against the King; and in the following year he had issued an insolent protest against the royal summons to appear and defend himself before the Diet, declaring himself a Swedish subject. But, above all, the influence of the Queen was too great to allow of any arrangement with Ulfeldt. The King was entirely led by her; she, from her German home, was filled with the most extravagant ideas of absolute despotism, and hated the free speech and the independent spirit prevailing among the Danish nobility, of which Ulfeldt in that respect was a true type. Leonora Christina was compelled to return in 1656, without even seeing the King, and as a fugitive. It is of this journey that she has given a Danish account, besides the description in the Autobiography.

It may be questioned whether it would not have been wise, if possible, to conciliate this dangerous man; but at any rate it was not done, and Ulfeldt was, no doubt, still more exasperated. Queen Christina had then resigned, and her successor, Carl Gustav, shortly after engaged in a war in Poland. The Danish Government, foolishly overrating its strength, took the opportunity for declaring war against Sweden, in the hope of regaining some of the territory lost in 1645. But Carl Gustav, well knowing that the Poles could not carry the war into Sweden, immediately turned his whole force against Denmark, where he met with next to no resistance. Ulfeldt was then living at Barth, in Pommerania, an estate which he held in mortgage for large sums of money advanced to the Swedish Government. Carl Gustav summoned Ulfeldt to follow him, and Ulfeldt obeyed the summons against the advice of Leonora Christina, who certainly did not desire her native country to be punished for the wrongs, if such they were, inflicted upon her by the Court.

The war had been declared on June 1, 1657; in August Ulfeldt issued a proclamation to the nobility in Jutland, calling on them to transfer their allegiance to the Swedish King. In the subsequent winter a most unusually severe frost enabled the Swedish army to cross the Sounds and Belts on the ice, Ulfeldt assisting its progress by persuading the commander of the fortress of Nakskov to surrender without resistance; and in February the Danish Government had to accept such conditions of peace as could be obtained from the Swedish King, who had halted a couple of days' march from Copenhagen. By this peace Denmark surrendered all her provinces to the east of the Sound (Skaane, &c.), which constituted one-third of the ancient Danish territory, and which have ever since belonged to Sweden, besides her fleet, &c.

But the greatest humiliation was that the negotiation on the Swedish side was entrusted to Ulfeldt, who did not fail to extort from the Danish Crown the utmost that the neutral powers would allow. For himself he obtained restitution of his estates, freedom to live in Denmark unmolested, and a large indemnity for loss of income of his estates since his flight in 1651. The King of Sweden also rewarded him with the title of a Count of Sölvitsborg and with considerable estates in the provinces recently wrested from Denmark. Ulfeldt himself went to reside at Malmö, the principal town in Skaane, situated on the Sound, just opposite Copenhagen, and here he was joined by Leonora Christina.

In her Autobiography Leonora does not touch on the incidents of the war, but she describes how her anxiety for her husband's safety did not allow her to remain quietly at Barth, and how she was afterwards called to her mother's sick-bed, which she had to leave in order to nurse her husband, who fell ill at

Malmö. We may here state that Kirstine Munk had fallen into disgrace, when Leonora was still a child, on account of her flagrant infidelity to the King, her paramour being a German Count of Solms. Kirstine Munk left the Court voluntarily in 1629,[5] shortly after the birth of a child, whom the King would not acknowledge as his own; and after having stayed with her mother for a short time, she took up her residence at the old manor of Boller, in North Jutland, where she remained until her death in 1658.

Various attempts were made to reconcile Christian IV. to her, but he steadily refused, and with very good reason: he was doubtless well aware that Kirstine Munk, as recently published diplomatic documents prove, had betrayed his political secrets to Gustav Adolf, the King of Sweden, and he considered her presence at Court very dangerous. Her son-in-law was now openly in the service of another Swedish king, but the friendship between them was not of long duration. Ulfeldt first incurred the displeasure of Carl Gustav by heading the opposition of the nobility in the newly acquired provinces against certain imposts laid on them by the Swedish King, to which they had not been liable under Danish rule. Then other causes of disagreement arose. Carl Gustav, regretting that he had concluded a peace, when in all probability he might have conquered the whole of Denmark, recommenced the war, and laid siege to Copenhagen. But the Danish people now rose as one man; foreign assistance was obtained; the Swedes were everywhere beaten; and if the Dutch, who were bound by treaty to assist Denmark, had not refused their co- operation in transferring the Danish troops across the Sound, all the lost provinces might easily have been regained.

The inhabitants in some of these provinces also rose against their new rulers. Amongst others, the citizens of Malmö, where Ulfeldt at the time resided, entered into a conspiracy to throw off the Swedish dominion; but it was betrayed, and Ulfeldt was indicated as one of the principal instigators, although he himself had accepted their forced homage to the Swedish King, as his deputy. Very probably he had thought that, if he took a part in the rising, he might, if this were successful, return to Denmark, having as it were thus wiped out his former crimes, but having also shown his countrymen what a terrible foe he could be. As it was, Denmark was prevented by her own allies from regaining her losses, and Ulfeldt was placed in custody in Malmö, by order of Carl Gustav, in order that his conduct might be subjected to a rigorous examination.

Ulfeldt was then apparently seized with a remarkable malady, a kind of apoplexy, depriving him of speech, and Leonora Christina conducted his defence. She wrote three lengthy, vigorous, and skilful replies to the charges, which still exist in the originals. He was acquitted, or rather escaped by a verdict of Not Proven; but as conscience makes cowards, he contrived to escape before the verdict was given. Leonora Christina describes all this in her Autobiography, according to which Ulfeldt was to go to Lubeck, while she would go to Copenhagen, and try to put matters straight there. Ulfeldt, however, changed his plan without her knowledge, and also repaired to Copenhagen, where they were both arrested and sent to the Castle of Hammershuus, on the island of Bornholm in the Baltic, an ancient fortress, now a most picturesque ruin, perched at the edge of perpendicular rocks, overhanging the sea, and almost surrounded by it.

The Autobiography relates circumstantially, and no doubt truthfully, the cruel treatment to which they were here subjected by the governor, a Major-General Fuchs. After a desperate attempt at escape, they were still more rigorously guarded, and at length they had to purchase their liberty by surrendering the whole of their property, excepting one estate in Fyen. Ulfeldt had to make the most humble apologies, and to promise not to leave the island of Fyen, where this estate was situated, without special permission. He was also compelled to renounce on the part of his wife the title of a Countess of Slesvig-Holstein, which Fredrik III. had never acknowledged. She never made use of that title afterwards, nor is she generally known by it in history. Corfits Ulfeldt being a Count of the German Empire, of course Leonora and her children were, and remained, Counts and Countesses of Ulfeldt. This compromise was effected in 1661.

Having been conveyed to Copenhagen, Ulfeldt could not obtain an audience of the King, and he was obliged, kneeling, to tender renewed oath of allegiance before the King's deputies, Count Rantzow, General Hans Schack, the Chancellor Redtz, and the Chancellor of the Exchequer, Christofer Gabel, all of whom are mentioned in Leonora's account of her subsequent prison life.

A few days after, Corfits Ulfeldt and Leonora Christina left Copenhagen, which he was never to see again, she only as a prisoner. They retired to the estate of Ellensborg, in Fyen, which they had still retained. This was the ancient seat of the Ulfeldts, which Corfits' father had sold to Ellen Marsvin, Leonora Christina's grandmother, and which had come to Leonora through her mother. In the meanwhile it had been renamed and rebuilt such as it stands to this day, a picturesque pile of buildings in the Elizabethan style. Here Ulfeldt might have ended his stormy life in quiet, but his thirst for revenge left him no peace. Besides this, a great change had taken place in Denmark. The national revival which followed the renewal of the war by Carl Gustav in 1658 led to a total change in the form of government.

It was indisputable that the selfishness of the nobles, who refused to undertake any burden for the defence of the country, was the main cause of the great disasters that had befallen Denmark. The abolition of their power was loudly called for, and the Queen so cleverly turned this feeling to account, that the remedy adopted was not the restoration of the other classes of the population to their legitimate constitutional influence, but the entire abolition of the constitution itself, and the introduction of hereditary, unlimited despotism. The title 'hereditary king,' which so often occurs in Danish documents and writings from that time, also in Leonora's Memoir, has reference to this change. Undoubtedly this was very little to Ulfeldt's taste. Already, in the next year after his release, 1662, he obtained leave to go abroad for his health. But, instead of going to Spaa, as he had pretended, he went to Amsterdam, Bruges, and Paris, where he sought interviews with Louis XIV. and the French ministers; he also placed himself in communication with the Elector of Brandenburg, with a view of raising up enemies against his native country. The Elector gave information to the Danish Government, whilst apparently lending an ear to Ulfeldt's propositions.

When a sufficient body of evidence had been collected, it was laid before the High Court of Appeal in Copenhagen, and judgment given in his absence, whereby he was condemned to an ignominious death as a traitor, his property confiscated, his descendants for ever exiled from Denmark, and a large reward offered for his apprehension. The sentence is dated July 24, 1663. Meanwhile Ulfeldt had been staying with his family at Bruges. One day one of his sons, Christian, saw General Fuchs, who had treated his parents so badly at Hammershuus, driving through the city in a carriage; immediately he leaped on to the carriage and killed Fuchs on the spot. Christian Ulfeldt had to fly, but the parents remained in Bruges, where they had many friends.

It was in the following spring, on May 24, 1663, that Leonora Christina, much against her own inclination, left her husband—as it proved, not to see him again alive. Ulfeldt had on many occasions used his wealth in order to gain friends, by lending them money—probably the very worst method of all. It is proved that at his death he still held bonds for more than 500,000 dollars, or 100,000*l.*, which he had lent to various princes and noblemen, and which were never paid. Amongst others he had lent the Pretender, afterwards Charles II., a large sum, about 20,000 patacoons, which at the time he had raised with some difficulty. He doubted not that the King of England, now that he was able to do it, would recognise the debt and repay it; and he desired Leonora, who, through her father, was cousin of Charles II., once removed, to go to England and claim it. She describes this journey in her Autobiography.

The Danish Government, hearing of her presence in England, thought that Ulfeldt was there too, or hoped at any rate to obtain possession of important documents by arresting her, and demanded her extradition. The British Government ostensibly refused, but underhand it gave the Danish minister, Petcum, every assistance. Leonora was arrested in Dover, where she had arrived on her way back, disappointed in the object of her journey. She had obtained enough and to spare of fair promises, but no money; and by secretly giving her up to the Danish Government, Charles II. in an easy way quitted himself of the debt, at the same time that he pleased the King of Denmark, without publicly violating political propriety. Leonora's account of the whole affair is confirmed in every way by the light which other documents throw upon the matter, particularly by the extracts contained in the Calendar of State Papers, Domestic Series, of the reign of Charles II., 1663-64.

Leonora was now conducted to Copenhagen, where she was confined in the Blue Tower—a square tower surmounted by a blue spire, which stood in the court of the royal castle, and was used as a prison for grave offenders (see the engraving). At this point the Memoir of her sufferings in the prison takes up the thread of her history, and we need not here dwell upon its contents.

As soon as Ulfeldt heard that the Brandenburg Government had betrayed him, and that sentence had been passed on him in Copenhagen, he left Bruges. No doubt the arrest of Leonora in England was a still greater blow to him. The Spanish Government would probably have surrendered him to the Danish authorities, and he had to flee from place to place, pursued by Danish agents demanding his extradition, and men anxious to earn the reward offered for his apprehension, dead or alive. His last abode was Basle, where he passed under a feigned name, until a quarrel between one of his sons and a stranger caused the discovery of their secret. Not feeling himself safe, Ulfeldt left Basle, alone, at night, in a boat descending the Rhine; but he never reached his destination. He was labouring under a violent attack on the chest, and the night air killed him. He breathed his last in the boat, on February 20, 1664. The boatmen, concluding from the gold and jewels which they found on him that he was a person of consequence, brought the body on shore, and made the matter known in Basle, from whence his sons came and buried him under a tree in a field— no one knows the spot.

Meanwhile the punishment of beheading and quartering had been executed on a wooden effigy in Copenhagen. His palace was demolished, and the site laid out in a public square, on which a pillar of sandstone was erected as an everlasting monument of his crimes. This pillar was taken away in 1842, and the name was changed from Ulfeldt Square to Greyfriars Square, as an indication of the forgetting and forgiving spirit of the time, or perhaps rather because the treason of Ulfeldt was closely connected with the ancient jealousy between Danes and Swedes, of which the present generation is so anxious to efface the traces.

His children had to seek new homes elsewhere. Christian, who killed Fuchs, became a Roman Catholic and died as an abbé; and none of them continued the name, except the youngest son Leo, who went into the service of the German Emperor, and rose to the highest dignities. His son Corfits likewise filled important offices under Charles VI. and Maria Theresa, but left no sons. His two daughters married respectively a Count Waldstein and a Count Thun, whose descendants therefore now represent the family of Ulfeldt.

Leonora Christina remained in prison for twenty-two years—that is, until the death of Sophia Amalia, the Queen of Fredrik III. This King, as well as his son Christian V., would willingly have set her at liberty; but the influence of the Queen over her husband and son was so strong that only her death, which occurred in 1685, released Leonora.

The Memoir of her life in prison terminates with this event, and her after-life does not offer any very remarkable incidents. Nevertheless, a few details, chiefly drawn from a MS. in the Royal Library at Copenhagen, recently published by Mr. Birket Smith, may serve to complete the historical image of this illustrious lady. The MS. in question is from the hand of a Miss Urne, of an ancient Danish family, who managed the household of Leonora from 1685 to her death in 1698. A royal manor, formerly a convent, at Maribo, on the island of Laaland, was granted to Leonora shortly after her release from the Blue Tower, together with a sufficient pension for a moderate establishment.

'The first occupation of the Countess,' says Miss Urne, 'was devotion; for which purpose her household was assembled in a room outside her bed-chamber. In her daily morning prayer there was this passage: "May the Lord help all prisoners, console the guilty, and save the innocent!" After that she remained the whole forenoon in her bedchamber, occupied in reading and writing. She composed a book entitled the "Ornament of Heroines," which Countess A. C. Ulfeldt and Count Leon took away with them, together with many other rare writings. Her handiwork is almost indescribable, and without an equal; such as embroidering in silk, gold embroidery, and turning in amber and ivory.'

It will be seen from Leonora's own Memoir that needlework was one of her principal occupations in her prison. Count Waldstein still possesses some of her work; in the Church of Maribo an altar-cloth embroidered by her existed still some time ago; and at the Castle of Rosenborg, in Copenhagen, there is a portrait of Christian V. worked by Leonora in silk, in return for which present the King increased her annual pension. Miss Urne says that she sent all her work to Elizabeth Bek, a granddaughter of Leonora, who lived with her for some years. But she refused to send her Leonora's Postille, or manual of daily devotion, which had been given Leonora on New Year's Day, in the last year of her captivity, by the castellan, Torslev, who is mentioned in Leonora's Memoir, and who had taught her to turn ivory, &c. This book has disappeared; but amongst the relics of Leonora Christina, the Royal Library at Copenhagen preserves some leaves which had been bound up with it, and contain verses, &c., by Leonora, and other interesting matter.

Her MS. works were taken to Vienna after her death. It is not known what has become of some of them. A copy of the first part of the book on heroines exists in Copenhagen. Miss Urne says that she possessed fragments of a play composed by her and acted at Maribo Kloster; also the younger Sperling speaks of such a composition in Danish verse; but the MS. seems to be lost now.

Several of Leonora's relations stayed with her from time to time at Maribo; amongst them the above-mentioned Elizabeth Bek, whose mother, Leonora Sophie, famous for her beauty, had married Lave Bek, the head of an ancient Danish family in Skaane. After Ulfeldt's death Lave Bek demanded of the Swedish Government the estates which Carl Gustav had given to Ulfeldt in 1658, but which the Swedish Government had afterwards confiscated, without any legal ground. Leonora Christina herself memorialised the Swedish King on the subject, and at least one of her memorials on the subject, dated May 23, 1693, still exists; but it was not till 1735 that these estates were given up to Lave Bek's sons. Leonora's eldest daughter, Anne Catherina, lived with her mother at Maribo for several years, and was present at her death. She had married Casetta, a Spanish nobleman, mentioned by Leonora Christina in her Memoir, who was with her in England when she was arrested. After the death of Casetta and their children, Anne Catherina Ulfeldt came to live with her mother. She followed her brother to Vienna, where she died. It was she who transmitted the MS. of Leonora's Memoir of her life in the Blue Tower to the brother, with the following letter, which is still preserved with the MS.:—

'This book treats of what has happened to our late lady mother in her prison. I have not been able to persuade myself to burn it, although the reading of it has given me little pleasure, inasmuch as all those events concern her miserable state. After all, it is not without its use to know how she has been treated; but it is not needful that it should come into the hands of strangers, for it might happen to give pleasure to those of our enemies who still remain.'

The letter is addressed 'A Monsieur, Monsieur le Comte d'Ulfeldt,' &c., but without date or signature. The handwriting is, however, that of Anne Catherina Ulfeldt, and she had probably sent it off to Vienna for safety immediately after her mother's death, before she knew that her brother would come to Maribo himself. Miss Urne says, in the MS. referred to, that the King had ordered that he was to be informed immediately of Leonora's demise, in order that she might be buried according to her rank and descent; but she had beforehand requested that her funeral might be quite plain. Her coffin, as well as those of three children who had died young, and whose coffins had been provisionally placed in a church at Copenhagen, was immured in a vault in the church of Maribo; but when this was opened some forty years ago, no trace of Leonora's mortal remains could be found, though those of the children were there: from which it is concluded that a popular report, to the effect that the body had been secretly carried abroad, contains more truth than was formerly supposed. Count Waldstein states that in the family vault at Leitsmischl, there is one metal coffin without any inscription, and which may be hers. If so, Leonora has, as it were, after her death followed her husband into exile. At any rate, the final resting-place of neither of them is known with certainty.

AUTOBIOGRAPHY
OF
LEONORA CHRISTINA
1673.

AUTOBIOGRAPHY.

Sir,[6]—To satisfy your curiosity, I will give you a short account of the life of her about whom you desire to be informed. She was born at Fredericksborg, in the year 1621, on June 11.[7] When she was six weeks old her grandmother took her with her to Dalum, where she remained until the age of four years; her first master there being Mr. Envolt, afterward a priest at Roeskild. About six months after her return to the Court, her father sent her to Holland to his cousin, a Duchess of Brunswick, who had married Count Ernest of Nassau, and lived at Lewarden.

Her sister Sophia, who was two years and a half older than herself, and her brother, who was a year younger, had gone to the aforesaid Duchess nearly a year before. I must not forget to mention the first mischances that befell her at her setting out. She went by sea in one of the royal ships of war; having been two days and a night at sea, at midnight such a furious tempest arose that they all had given up any hope of escaping. Her tutor, Wichmann Hassebart (afterwards Bishop of Fyn), who attended her, woke her and took her in his arms, saying, with tears, that they should both die together, for he loved her tenderly. He told her of the danger, that God was angry, and that they would all be drowned. She caressed him, treating him like a father (after her usual wont), and begged him not to grieve; she was assured that God was not angry, that He would see they would not be drowned, beseeching him again and again to believe her. Wichmann shed tears at her simplicity, and prayed to God to save the rest for her sake, and for the sake of the hope that she, an innocent girl, reposed in Him. God heard him, and after having lost the two mainmasts, they entered at dawn of day the harbour of Fleckeröe,[8] where they remained for six weeks.

Having received orders to proceed by sea, they pursued their route and arrived safely. Her sister being informed of her arrival, and being told that she had come with a different retinue to herself—with a suite of gentlemen, lady preceptor, servants and attendants, &c.—she burst into tears, and said that she was not surprised that this sister always insinuated herself and made herself a favourite, and that she would be treated there too as such. M. Sophia was not mistaken in this; for her sister was in greater favour with the Duchess, with her governess, and with many others, than she was herself. Count Ernest alone took the side of M. Sophia, and this rather for the sake of provoking his wife, who liked dispute; for M. Sophia exhibited her obstinacy even towards himself. She did all the mischief she could to her sister, and persuaded her brother to do the same.

To amuse you I will tell you of her first innocent predilections. Count Ernest had a son of about eleven or twelve years of age; he conceived an affection for her, and having persuaded her that he loved her, and that she would one day be his wife, but that this must be kept secret, she fancied herself already secretly his wife. He knew a little drawing, and by stealth he instructed her; he even taught her some Latin words. They never missed an opportunity of retiring from company and conversing with each other.

This enjoyment was of short duration for her; for a little more than a year afterwards she fell ill of small-pox, and as his elder brother, William, who had always ridiculed these affections, urged him to see his well-beloved in the condition in which she was, in order to disgust him with the sight, he came one day to the door to see her, and was so startled that he immediately became ill, and died on the ninth day following. His death was kept concealed from her. When she was better she asked after him, and she was made to believe that he was gone away with his mother (who was at this time at Brunswick), attending the funeral of her mother. His body had been embalmed, and had been placed in a glass case. One day her preceptor made her go into the hall where his body lay, to see if she recognised it; he raised her in his arms to enable her to see it better. She knew her dear Moritz at once, and was seized with such a shock that she fell fainting to the ground. Wichmann in consequence carried her hastily out of the hall to recover her, and as the dead boy wore a garland of rosemary, she never saw these flowers without crying, and had an aversion to their smell, which she still retains.

As the wars between Germany and the King of Denmark had been the cause of the removal of his aforesaid children, they were recalled to Denmark when peace was concluded. At the age of seven years and two months she was affianced to a gentleman of the King's Chamber. She began very early to suffer for his sake. Her governess was at this time Mistress Anne Lycke, Qvitzow's mother. Her daughter, who was maid of honour, had imagined that this gentleman made his frequent visits for love of her. Seeing herself deceived, she did not know in what manner to produce estrangement between the lovers; she spoke, and made M. Sophia speak, of the gentleman's poverty, and amused herself with ridiculing the number of children in the family. She regarded all this with indifference, only declaring once that she loved him, poor as he was, better than she loved her rich gallant.[9]

At last they grew weary of this, and found another opportunity for troubling her—namely, the illness of her betrothed, resulting from a complaint in his leg; they presented her with plaisters, ointments, and such like things, and talked together of the pleasure of being married to a man who had his feet diseased, &c. She did not answer a word either for good or bad, so they grew weary of this also. A year and a half after they had another governess, Catharina Sehestedt, sister of Hannibal.[10] M. Sophia thus lost her second, and her sister had a little repose in this quarter.

When our lady was about twelve years old, Francis Albert, Duke of Saxony, [11] came to Kolding to demand her in marriage. The King replied that she was no longer free, that she was already betrothed; but the Duke was not satisfied with this, and spoke to herself, and said a hundred fine things to her: that a Duke was far different to a gentleman. She told him she always obeyed the King, and since it had pleased the King to promise her to a gentleman, she was well satisfied. The Duke employed the governess to persuade her, and the governess introduced him to her brother Hannibal, then at the Court, and Hannibal went with post-horses to Möen, where her betrothed was, who did not linger long on the road in coming to her. This was the beginning of the friendship between Monsieur and Hannibal, which afterwards caused so much injury to Monsieur. But he had not needed to trouble himself, for the Duke never could draw from her the declaration that she would be ready to give up her betrothed if the King ordered her to do so. She told him she hoped the King would not retract from his first promise. The Duke departed ill satisfied, on the very day the evening of which the betrothed arrived. (Four years afterwards they quarrelled on this subject in the presence of the King, who appeased them with his authority.)

It happened the following winter at Skanderborg that the governess had a quarrel with the language-master, Alexandre de Cuqvelson, who taught our lady and her sisters the French language, writing, arithmetic, and dancing. M. Sophia was not studious; moreover, she had very little memory; for her heart was too much devoted to her dolls, and as she perceived that the governess did not punish her when Alexandre complained of her, she neglected everything, and took no trouble about her studies. Our lady imagined she knew enough when she knew as much as her sister. As this had lasted some time, the governess thought she could entrap Alexandre; she accused him to the King, said that he treated the children badly, rapped their fingers, struck them on the hand, called them bad names, &c., and with all this they could not even read, much less speak, the French language. Besides this, she wrote the same accusations to the betrothed of our lady. The betrothed sent his servant Wolff to Skanderborg, with menaces to Alexandre. At the same time Alexandre was warned that the King had sent for the prince,[12] to examine his children, since the father-confessor was not acquainted with the language.

The tutor was in some dismay; he flattered our lady, implored her to save him, which she could easily do, since she had a good memory, so that he could prove by her that it was not his fault that M. Sophia was not more advanced. Our lady did not yield readily, but called to his remembrance how one day, about half a year ago, she had begged him not to accuse her to the governess, but that he had paid no attention to her tears, though he knew that the governess treated them shamefully. He begged her for the love of Jesus, wept like a child, said that he should be ruined for ever, that it was an act of mercy, that he would never accuse her, and that from henceforth she should do nothing but what she wished. At length she consented, said she would be diligent, and since she had yet three weeks before her, she learnt a good deal by heart.[13] Alexandre told her one day, towards the time of the examination, that there was still a great favour she could render him: if she would not repeat the little things which had passed at school-time; for he could not always pay attention to every word that he said when M. Sophia irritated him, and if he had once taken the rod to hit her fingers when she had not struck her sister strongly enough, he begged her for the love of God to pardon it. (It should be mentioned that he wished the one to strike the other when they committed faults, and the one who corrected the other had to beat her, and if she did not do so strongly enough, he took the office upon himself; thus he had often beaten our lady.)

She made excuses, said that she did not dare to tell a lie if they asked her, but that she would not accuse him of herself. This promise did not wholly satisfy him; he continued his entreaties, and assured her that a falsehood employed to extricate a friend from danger was not a sin, but was agreeable to God; moreover, it was not necessary for her to say anything, only not to confess what she had seen and heard. She said that the governess would treat her ill; so he replied that she should have no occasion to do so, for that he would never complain to her. Our lady replied that the governess would find pretext enough, since she was inclined to ill-treat the children; and anyhow, the other master who taught them German was a rude man, and an old man who taught them the spinette was a torment, therefore she had sufficient reason for fear. He did not give way, but so persisted in his persuasion that she promised everything.

When the prince arrived the governess did not forget to besiege him with her complaints, and to beg him to use his influence that the tutor might be dismissed. At length the day of the examination having come, the governess told her young ladies an hour before that they were to say how villanously he had treated them, beaten them, &c. The prince came into the apartments of the ladies accompanied by the King's father-confessor (at that time Dr. Ch(r)estien Sar); the governess was present the whole time.

They were first examined in German. M. Sophia acquitted herself very indifferently, not being able to read fluently. The master Christoffre excused her, saying that she was timid. When it came to Alexandre's turn to show what his pupils could do, M. Sophia could read little or nothing. When she stammered in reading, the governess looked at the prince and laughed aloud. There was no difference in the gospel, psalms, proverbs, or suchlike things. The governess was very glad, and would have liked that the other should not have been examined. But when it came to her turn to read in the Bible, and she did not hesitate, the governess could no longer restrain herself, and said, 'Perhaps it is a passage she knows by heart that you have made her read.' Alexandre begged the governess herself to give the lady another passage to read. The governess was angry at this also, and said, 'He is ridiculing me because I do not know French.' The prince then opened the Bible and made her read other passages, which she did as fluently as before. In things by heart she showed such proficiency that the prince was too impatient to listen to all.

It was then Alexandre's turn to speak, and to say that he hoped His Highness would graciously consider that it was not his fault that M. Sophia was not more advanced. The governess interrupted him saying, 'You are truly the cause of it, for you treat her ill!' and she began a torrent of accusations, asking
M. Sophia if they were not true. She answered in the affirmative, and that she could not conscientiously deny them. Then she asked our lady if they were not true. She replied that she had never heard nor seen anything of the kind. The governess, in a rage, said to the Prince, 'Your highness must make her speak the truth; she dares not do so, for Alexandre's sake.'

The Prince asked her if Alexandre had never called her bad names—if he had never beaten her. She replied, 'Never.' He asked again if she had not seen nor heard that he had ill-treated her sister. She replied, 'No, she had never either heard or seen it.' At this the governess became furious; she spoke to the prince in a low voice; the prince replied aloud, 'What do you wish me to do? I have no order from the King to constrain her to anything.' Well, Alexandre gained his cause; the governess could not dislodge him, and our lady gained more than she had imagined in possessing the affection of the King, the goodwill of the Prince, of the priest, and of all those who knew her. But the governess from that moment took every opportunity of revenging herself on our lady.

At length she found one, which was rather absurd. The old Jean Meinicken, who taught our lady the spinette, one day, in a passion, seized the fingers of our lady and struck them against the instrument; without remembering the presence of her governess, she took his hand and retaliated so strongly that the strings broke. The governess heard with delight the complaints of the old man. She prepared two rods; she used them both, and, not satisfied with that, she turned the thick end of one, and struck our lady on the thigh, the mark of which she bears to the present day. More than two months elapsed before she recovered from the blow; she could not dance, nor could she walk comfortably for weeks after. This governess did her so much injury that at last our lady was obliged to complain to her betrothed, who had a quarrel with the governess at the wedding of M. Sophia, and went straight to the King to accuse her; she was at once dismissed, and the four children, the eldest of which was our lady, went with the princess[14] to Niköping, to pass the winter there, until the king could get another governess. The King, who had a good opinion of the conduct of our lady, who at this time was thirteen years and four months old, wrote to her and ordered her to take care of her sisters. Our lady considered herself half a governess, so she took care not to set them a bad example. As to study, she gave no thought to it at this time; she occupied herself in drawing and arithmetic, of which she was very fond, and the princess, who was seventeen years of age, delighted in her company. Thus this winter passed very agreeably for her.

At the approach of the Diet, which sat eight days after Pentecost, the children came to Copenhagen, with the prince and princess, and had as governess a lady of Mecklenburg of the Blixen family, the mother of Philip Barstorp who is still alive. After the Diet, the king made a journey to Glückstad in two days and a half, and our lady accompanied him; it pleased the King that she was not weary, and that she could bear up against inconveniences and fatigues. She afterwards made several little journeys with the King, and she had the good fortune occasionally to obtain the pardon of some poor criminals, and to be in favour with the king.

Our lady having attained the age of fifteen years and about four months, her betrothed obtained permission for their marriage, which was celebrated (with more pomp than the subsequent weddings of her sisters), on October 9, 1636. The winter after her marriage she was with her husband at Möen, and as she knew that her husband's father had not left him any wealth, she asked him concerning his debts, and conjured him to conceal nothing from her. He said to her, 'If I tell you the truth it will perhaps frighten you.' She declared it would not, and that she would supply what was needful from her ornaments, provided he would assure her that he had told her everything. He did so, and found that she was not afraid to deprive herself of her gold, silver, and jewels, in order to pay a sum of thirty-six thousand rix-dollars. On April 21, 1637, she went with her husband to Copenhagen in obedience to the order of the king, who gave him the post of V.R.[15] He was again obliged to incur debt in purchasing a house and in setting up a larger establishment.

There would be no end were I to tell you all the mischances that befell her during the happy period of her marriage, and of all the small contrarieties which she endured; but since I am assured that this history will not be seen by anyone, and that you will not keep it after having read it, I will tell you a few points which are worthy of attention. Those who were envious of the good fortune of our lady could not bear that she should lead a tranquil life, nor that she should be held in esteem by her father and King; I may call him thus, for the King conferred on her more honours than were due to her from him. Her husband loved and honoured her, enacting the lover more than the husband.

She spent her time in shooting, riding, tennis, in learning drawing in good earnest from Charles v. Mandern, in playing the viol, the flute, the guitar, and she enjoyed a happy life. She knew well that jealousy is a plague, and that it injures the mind which harbours it. Her relations tried to infuse into her head that her husband loved elsewhere, especially M. Elizabet, and subsequently Anna, sister of her husband, who was then in her house. M. Elizabet began by mentioning it as a secret, premising that no one could tell her and warn her, except her who was her sister.

As our lady at first said nothing and only smiled, M. Elis… said: 'The world says that you know it well, but that you will not appear to do so.' She replied with a question: 'Why did she tell her a thing as a secret, which she herself did not believe to be a secret to her? but she would tell her a secret that perhaps she did not know, which was, that she had given her husband permission to spend his time with others, and when she was satisfied the remainder would be for others; that she believed there were no such jealous women as those who were insatiable, but that a wisdom was imputed to her, which she did not possess; she begged her, however, to be wise enough not to interfere with matters which did not concern her, and if she heard others mentioning it (as our lady had reason to believe that this was her own invention) that she would give them a reprimand. M. Elis… was indignant and went away angry, but Anna, Monsieur's sister, who was in the house, adopted another course. She drew round her the handsomest women in the town, and then played the procuress, spoke to her brother of one particularly, who was a flirt, and who was the handsomest, and offered him opportunities, &c. As she saw that he was proof against it, she told him (to excite him) that his wife was jealous, that she had had him watched where he went when he had been drinking with the King, to know whether he visited this woman; she said that his wife was angry, because the other woman was so beautiful, said that she painted, &c.

The love borne to our lady by her husband made him tell her all, and, moreover, he went but rarely afterwards to his sister's apartments, from which she could easily understand that the conversation had not been agreeable to him; but our lady betrayed nothing of the matter, visited her more than before, caressed this lady more than any other, and even made her considerable presents. (Anna remained in her house as long as she lived.)

All this is of small consideration compared with the conduct of her own brother. It is well known to you that the Biel... were very intimate in our lady's house. It happened that her brother made a journey to Muscovy, and that the youngest of the Biel... was in his suite. As this was a very lawless youth, and, to say the truth, badly brought up, he not only at times failed in respect to our lady's brother, but freely expressed his sentiments to him upon matters which did not concern him; among other things, he spoke ill of the Holstein noblemen, naming especially one, who was then in waiting on the King, who he said had deceived our lady's brother. The matter rested there for more than a year after their return from this journey. The brother of our lady and Biel... played cards together, and disputed over them; upon this the brother of our lady told the Holstein nobleman what Biel... had said of him more than a year before, which B. did not remember, and swore that he had never said. The Holstein nobleman said insulting things against Biel....

Our lady conversed with her brother upon the affair, and begged him to quiet the storm he had raised, and to consider how it would cause an ill-feeling with regard to him among the nobility, and that it would seem that he could not keep to himself what had been told him in secret; it would be very easy for him to mend the matter. Her brother replied that he could never retract what he had said, and that he should consider the Holstein nobleman as a villain if he did not treat B. as a rogue.

At length the Holstein nobleman behaved in such a manner as to constrain B. to send him a challenge. B. was killed by his adversary with the sword of our lady's brother, which she did not know till afterwards. At noon of the day on which B. had been killed in the morning, our lady went to the castle to visit her little twin sisters; her brother was there, and came forward, laughing loudly and saying, 'Do you know that Ran... has killed B...?' She replied, 'No, that I did not know, but I knew that you had killed him. Ran... could do nothing less than defend himself, but you placed the sword in his hand.' Her brother, without answering a word, mounted his horse and went to seek his brother-in-law, who was speaking with our old friend,[16] told him he was the cause of B.'s death, and that he had done so because he had understood that his sister loved him, and that he did not believe that his brother-in-law was so blind as not to have perceived it. The husband of our lady did not receive this speech in the way the other had imagined, and said, 'If you were not her brother, I would stab you with this poniard,' showing it to him. 'What reason have you for speaking thus?' The good-for-nothing fellow was rather taken aback at this, and knew not what to say, except that B… was too free and had no respect in his demeanour; and that this was a true sign of love. At length, after some discussion on both sides, the brother of our lady requested that not a word might be said to his sister.

As soon as she returned home, her husband told her everything in the presence of our old friend, but ordered her to feign ignorance. This was all the more easy for her, as her husband gave no credence to it, but trusted in her innocence. She let nothing appear, but lived with her brother as before. But some years after, her brother ill-treated his own mother, and her side being taken by our lady, they were in consequence not good friends.

In speaking to you of the occupations of our lady, after having reached the age of twenty-one or thereabouts, I must tell you she had a great desire to learn Latin. She had a very excellent master,[17] whom you know, and who taught her for friendship as well as with good will. But she had so many irons in the fire, and sometimes it was necessary to take a journey, and a yearly accouchement (to the number of ten) prevented her making much progress; she understood a little easy Latin, but attempted nothing difficult; she then learnt a little Italian, which she continued studying whenever an opportunity presented itself.

I will not speak of her short journeys to Holstein, Jutland, &c.; but in the year 1646 she made a voyage with her husband by sea, in the first place to Holland, where she gave birth to a son six weeks after her arrival at the Hague. From thence she went with her husband to France, first to Paris and afterwards to Amiens; there they took leave of the King and of the Queen Mother, Regent, and as they were returning by Dunkirk she had the curiosity to see England, and begged her husband to permit her to cross over with a small suite, to which he consented, since one of the royal vessels lay in the roads. She took a nobleman with her who knew the language, our old friend, a servant, and the valet of the aforesaid nobleman, and this was the whole of her retinue. She embarked, and her husband planned to pass through Flanders and Brabant, and to await her at Rotterdam. As she was on the vessel a day and night, and the wind did not favour them, she resolved to land and to follow her husband, fancying she could reach him in time to see Flanders and Brabant; she had not visited these countries before, having passed from Holland by sea to Calais.

She found her husband at Ostend, and travelled with him to Rotterdam; from thence she pursued her former plan, embarked at Helvoot-Sluys, and arrived at Duns, went to London, and returned by Dover, making the whole voyage in ten days, and she was again enceinte. She was an object of suspicion in London. The Prince Palatine, then Elector of Heidelberg,[18] belonged to the party opposed to the beheaded King, who was then a prisoner; and they watched her and surrounded her with spies, so she did not make a long sojourn in London. Nothing else was imagined, when it was known she had been there, but that she had letters from the King of Dan… for the King of Engl…. She returned with her husband to Dan….

In the year 1648 fortune abandoned our lady, for on February 28 the King was taken from her by death. She had the happiness, however, of attending upon him until his last breath. Good God, when I think of what this good King said to her the first day, when she found him ill in bed at Rosenborg, and wept abundantly, my heart is touched. He begged her not to weep, caressed her, and said: 'I have placed you so securely that no one can move you.' Only too much has she felt the contrary of the promise of the King who succeeded him, for when he was Duke and visited her at her house, a few days after the death of the King, finding her in tears, he embraced her, saying: 'I will be a father to you, do not weep.' She kissed his hand without being able to speak. I find that some fathers have been unnatural towards their children.

In the year 1649 she made another voyage with her husband to Holland, and at the Hague gave birth to a daughter. When her husband returned from this journey, he for the first time perceived the designs of Hannibal, of Gerstorp, and Wibe, but too late. He absented himself from business, and would not listen to what his wife told him. Our old friend shared the opinion of our lady, adducing very strong reason for it, but all in vain; he said, that he would not be a perpetual slave for the convenience of his friends. His wife spoke as a prophet to him, told him that he would be treated as a slave when he had ceased to have authority, that they would suspect him, and envy his wealth; all of which took place, though I shall make no recital of it, since these events are sufficiently known to you.

We will now speak a little of the events which occurred afterwards. When they had gained their cause,[19] our lady feared that the strong party which they had then overcome would not rest without ruining them utterly at any cost; so she advised her husband to leave the country, since he had the King's permission to do so,[20] and to save his life, otherwise his enemies would contrive some other invention which would succeed better. He consented to this at length, and they took their two eldest children with them, and went by sea to Amsterdam. At Utrecht they left the children with the servants and a female attendant, and our lady disguised herself in male attire and followed her husband, who took the route to Lubeck, and from thence by sea to Sweden, to ask the protection of Queen Christina, which he received; and as the Queen knew that his wife was with him in disguise, she requested to see her, which she did.

The husband of our lady purposed to remain some time in Pomerania, and the Queen lent him a vessel to convey him thither. Having been three days at sea, the wind carried them towards Dantzig, and not being able to enter the town, for it was too late, they remained outside the gates at a low inn. An adventure fit for a novel here happened to our lady. A girl of sixteen, or a little more, believing that our lady was a young man, threw herself on her neck with caresses, to which our lady responded, and played with the girl, but, as our lady perceived what the girl meant, and that she could not satisfy her, she turned her over to Charles, a man of their suite, thinking he would answer her purpose; he offered the girl his attentions, but she repelled him rudely, saying, she was not for him, and went again to our lady, accosting her in the same way. Our lady got rid of her, but with difficulty however, for she was somewhat impudent, and our lady did not dare to leave her apartment. For the sake of amusing you, I must tell you, what now occurs to me, that in the fort before Stade, the name of which has escaped me, our lady played with two soldiers for drink, and her husband, who passed for her uncle, paid the expenses; the soldiers, willing to lose for the sake of gaining the beer, and astonished that she never lost, were, however, civil enough to present her with drink.

We must return to Dantzig. The husband of our lady, finding himself near Thoren, desired to make an excursion there, but his design was interrupted by two men, one who had formerly served in Norway as Lieutenant-Colonel, and a charlatan who called himself Dr. Saar, and who had been expelled from Copenhagen. They asked the Mayor of the town to arrest these two persons, believing that our lady was Ebbe Wl....[21] They were warned by their host that these persons said they were so-and-so, and that these gentlemen were at the door to prevent their going out. Towards evening they grew tired of keeping guard, and went away. Before dawn the husband of our lady went out of the house first, and waited at the gate, and our lady with the two servants went in a coach to wait at the other gate until it was opened; thus they escaped this time.

They went by land to Stralsund, where our lady resumed her own attire, after having been in disguise twelve weeks and four days, and having endured many inconveniences, not having gone to bed all the time, except at Stockholm, Dantzig, and Stettin. She even washed the clothes, which inconvenienced her much. The winter that they passed at Stralsund, her husband taught her, or rather began to teach her, Spanish. In the spring they again made a voyage to Stockholm, at the desire of Queen Chr…. This good Queen, who liked intrigue, tried to excite jealousy and to make people jealous, but she did not succeed. They were in Sweden until after the abdication of the Queen, and the wedding and coronation of King Charles and Queen Hedevig, which was in the year 1654. They returned to Pomerania for a visit to Barth, which they possessed as a mortgage. There, our lady passed her time in study, sometimes occupied with a Latin book, sometimes with a Spanish one. She translated a small Spanish work, entitled *Matthias de los Reyos*; but this book since fell into the hands of others, as well as the first part of *Cleopatre*, which she had translated from the French, with matters of greater value.

In the year 1657,[22] her husband persuaded her to make a voyage to Dannem… to try and gain an audience with the King, and see if she could not obtain some payment from persons who owed them money. Our lady found various pleas for not undertaking this voyage, seeing a hundred difficulties against its successful issue; but her husband besought her to attempt it, and our old friend shared her husband's opinion that nothing could be done to her, that she was under the protection of the King of Sweden, and not banished from Dan… with similar arguments. At length she yielded, and made the journey in the winter, travelling in a coach with six horses, a secretary, a man on horseback, a female attendant, a page and a lacquey—that was all. She went first to see her mother in Jutland, and remained there three days; this was immediately known at the Court.

When she had passed the Belt, and was within cannon-shot of Corsör, she was met by Uldrich Chr. Guldenl…,[23] who was on the point of going to Jutland to fetch her. He returned with his galley and landed; she remained in her vessel, waiting for her carriage to be put on shore. Guld… impatient, could not wait so long, and sent the burgomaster Brant to tell her to come ashore, as he had something to say to her. She replied that if he had anything to say to her, he ought to show her the attention of coming to her. Brant went with this answer; awaiting its issue, our lady looked at her attendants and perceived a change in them all. Her female attendant was seized with an attack from which she suffers still, a trembling of the head, while her eyes remained fixed. The secretary trembled so that his teeth chattered. Charles was quite pale, as were all the others. Our lady spoke to them, and asked them why they were afraid; for her they had nothing to fear, and less for themselves. The secretary answered, 'They will soon let us know that.' Brant returned with the same message, with the addition that Gul… was bearer of the King's order, and that our lady ought to come to him at the Castle to hear the King's order. She replied that she respected the King's order there as well as at the castle; that she wished that Gul… would please to let her know there the order of His Majesty; and when Brant tried to persuade her, saying continually, 'Oh! do give in, do give in!' she used the same expression, and said also, 'Beg Gul… to give in,' &c. At length she said, 'Give me sufficient time to have two horses harnessed, for I cannot imagine he would wish me to go on foot.'

When she reached the castle she had the coach pulled up. Brant came forward to beg her to enter the castle; she refused, and said she would not enter; that if he wished to speak to her he must come to her, that she had come more than half-way. Brant went, and returned once again, but she said the same, adding that he might do all that seemed good to him, she should not stir from the spot. At length the good-for-nothing fellow came down, and when he was ready to speak to her, she opened the coach and got out. He said a few polite words to her, and then presented her with an order from the King, written in the chancery, the contents of which were, that she must hasten to depart from the King's territory, or she would have to thank herself for any ill that might befall her. Having read the order she bowed, and returned him the order, which was intended to warn her, saying, 'That she hoped to have been permitted to kiss the King's hand, but as her enemies had hindered this happiness by such an order, there was nothing left for her but to obey in all humility, and thanking His Majesty most humbly for the warning, she would hasten as quickly as possible to obey His Majesty's commands. She asked if she were permitted to take a little refreshment, for that they had had contrary winds and had been at sea all day. Gul… answered in the negative, that he did not dare to give her the permission; and since she had obeyed with such great submission, he would not show her the other order that he had, asking her at the same moment if she wished to see this other order? She said, no; that she would abide by the order that she had seen, and that she would immediately embark on board her ferry-boat to return. Gul… gave her his hand, and begged her to make use of his galley.

She did so. They went half the way without speaking; at length Gul… broke the silence, and they entered into conversation. He told her that the King had been made to believe that she had assembled a number of noblemen at her mother's house, and that he had orders to disperse this cabal. They had a long conversation together, and spoke of Dina's affair; he said the King did not yet know the real truth of it. She complained that the King had not tried to know it. At length they arrived by night at Nyborg. Gul… accompanied her to her hostelry, and went to his own, and an hour afterwards sent Scherning[24] to tell her that at dawn of day she must be ready, in order that they might arrive at Assens the next evening, which it was impossible to do with her own horses, as they did not arrive till morning. She assented, saying she would act in obedience to his orders, began talking with Scherning, and conversed with him about other matters. I do not know how, but she gained his good graces, and he prevailed so far with Gul… that Gul… did not hasten her unduly. Towards nine o'clock the next morning he came to tell her that he did not think it necessary to accompany her further, but he hoped she would follow the King's order, and begged her to speak with Kay v. Ahlefeld at Haderslef, when she was passing through; he had received orders as to what he had to do. She promised this, and Gul… returned to Copenhagen, placing a man with our lady to watch her.

Our lady did not think it necessary to speak to Kay v. Ahlefeld, for she had nothing to say to him, and she did not want to see more orders; she passed by Haderslef, and went to Apenrade, and awaited there for ten days[25] a letter from Gul… which he had promised to write to her; when she saw that he was not going to keep his word she started on her way to Slesvig, halting half way with the intention of dining. Holst, the clerk of the bailiwick of Flensborg, here arrived in a coach with two arquebuses larger and longer than halberds. He gave orders to close the bar of Boy…, sent to the village, which is quite close, that the peasants should hold themselves ready with their spears and arms, and made four persons who were in the tavern take the same arms, that is, large poles. Afterwards he entered and made a long speech, with no end of compliments to our lady, to while away the time. The matter was, that the governor[26] desired her to go to Flensborg, as he had something to say to her, and he hoped she would do him the pleasure to rest a night at Flensborg.

Our lady replied that she had not the pleasure of his acquaintance, and therefore she thought he took her for someone else; if she could oblige him in anything she would remain at Slesvig the following day, in order to know in what she could serve him. No, it was not that; he repeated his request. She ordered Charles to have the horses put to. Holst understood this, which was said in French, and begged her for the love of God not to set out; he had orders not to let her depart. 'You,' said she, in a somewhat haughty tone, 'who are you? With what authority do you speak thus?' He said he had no written order, but by word of mouth, and that his governor would soon arrive; he begged her for the love of God to pardon him. He was a servant, he was willing to be trodden under her feet. She said: 'It is not for you to pay me compliments, still less to detain me, since you cannot show me the King's order, but it is for me to think what I ought to do.'

She went out and ordered her lacquey, who was the only determined one of her suite, to make himself master of Holst's chariot and arquebuses. Holst followed her, begging her a hundred times, saying, 'I do not dare to let you pass, I do not dare to open the bar.' She said, 'I do not ask you to open;' she got into the coach. Holst put his hand upon the coach-door and sang the old song. Our lady, who had always pistols in her carriage when she travelled, drew out one and presented it to him saying, 'Draw back, or I will give you the contents of this.' He was not slow in letting go his hold; then she threw a patacoon to those who were to restrain her, saying, 'Here is something for drink; help in letting the carriage pass the fosse!' which they immediately did.

Not a quarter of an hour after she had gone, the governor arrived with another chariot. There were two men and four guns in each chariot. Our lady was warned of the pursuit; she begged her two coachmen, whom she had for herself and her baggage, to dispute them the road as much as they could; she ordered Charles always to remain at the side of her carriage, in order that she might throw herself upon the horse if she saw that they gained ground. She took off her furred robe. They disputed the road up to the bridge, which separated the territory of the King from that of the Duke.

When she had passed the bridge she stopped, put on her robe, and alighted. The others paused on the other side of the bridge to look at her, and thus she escaped again for this time.[27] But it was amusing to see how the secretary perspired, what fright he was in; he did not afterwards pretend to bravery, but freely confessed that he was half dead with fear. She returned to Barth, and found her husband very very ill. Our old friend had almost given up all hope of his recovery, but her presence acted as a miracle; he was sufficiently strong in the morning to be taken out of bed, to the great surprise of our old friend.

Just as our lady was thinking of passing some days in tranquillity, occupied in light study, in trifling work, distillations, confectionery, and such like things, her husband mixed himself in the wars. The King of Sweden sent after him to Stettin; he told his wife that he would have nothing to do with them. He did not keep his word, however; he did not return to Barth, but went straight off with the King. She knew he was not provided with anything; she saw the danger to which he was exposed, she wished to share it; she equipped herself in haste, and, without his sending for her, went to join him at Ottensen. He wished to persuade her to return to Hamburgh, and spoke to her of the great danger; she said the danger was the reason why she wished to bear him company, and to share it with him; so she went with him, and passed few days without uneasiness, especially when Friderichsodde was taken; she feared for both husband and son. There she had the happiness of reconciling the C. Wrangel and the C. Jaques,[28] which her husband had believed impossible, not having been able to succeed. She had also the good fortune to cure her eldest son and eight of her servants of a malignant fever named Sprinckeln; there was no doctor at that time with the army, our old friend having left.

When her husband passed with the King to Seeland, she remained at Fyen. The day that she had resolved to set out on the following to return to Schone, a post arrived with news that her mother was at the point of death and wished to speak to her; she posted to Jutland, found Madame very ill and with no hope of life. She had only been there one night, when her husband sent a messenger to say that if she wished to see him alive she must lose no time. Our lady was herself ill; she had to leave her mother, who was already half dead; she had to take her last farewell in great sorrow, and to go with all speed to seek her husband, who was very ill at Malmöe. Two days afterwards she received the tidings of her mother's death, and as soon as the health of her husband permitted it, she went to Jutland to give the necessary orders for her mother's funeral. She returned once more to Schone before the burial; after the funeral[29] she went to Copenhagen and revisited Malmöe one day before the King of Sweden began the war for the second time and appeared before Kopenh....

In the year 1659 the King of Sweden ordered her husband to be arrested at Malmöe. She went immediately to Helsingör to speak to the King, but had not the happiness of speaking to him; on the contrary, the King sent two of his counsellors to tell her that she was free to choose whether she would return to her estates and superintend them, or go back to Malmöe and be arrested with her husband. She thanked His Majesty very humbly for the favour of the choice; she chose to suffer with her husband, and was glad to have the happiness of serving him in his affliction, and bearing the burden with him which would lighten it to him.

She returned to Malmöe with these news; her husband exhibited too much grief that she was not permitted to solicit on his behalf, and she consoled him as well as she was able. A few days after, an officer came to their house and irritated her husband so much by his impertinent manner that he had a fit of apoplexy. Our lady was overwhelmed with sorrow; she sent for the priest the next morning, made her husband receive the holy communion, and received it herself. She knew not at what hour she might be a widow; no one came to see her, no one in consequence consoled her, and she had to console herself. She had a husband who was neither living nor dead; he ate and drank; he spoke, but no one could understand him.

About eight months after, the King began to take proceedings against her husband, and in order to make her answer for her husband they mixed her up in certain points as having asked for news: whence the young lady was taken whom her husband brought to Copenhagen? who was Trolle? and that she had kept the property of a Danish nobleman in her house.[30] Since her husband was ill, the King graciously permitted her to answer for him; thus they proceeded with her for nine weeks in succession; she had no other assistance in copying her defence than her eldest daughter, then very young. She was permitted to make use of Wolff, for receiving the accusations and taking back the replies, but he wrote nothing for her. If you are interested in knowing the proceedings, Kield[31] can give you information respecting them.

When the proceedings had lasted so many weeks, and she had answered with regard to the conversations which it was said her husband had had with one and another, they fancied that her husband feigned illness. Four doctors were sent with the commandant to visit the sick man, and they found that he was really ill; not content with this, they established the Court in his house, for they were ashamed to make her come to them. They caused the city magistrate to come, placing him on one side of the hall, and on the other the Danish noblemen who were under arrest, all as witnesses; eight Commissioners sat at a round table, the lawyer in front of the table and two clerks at another table; having made these arrangements, our lady was desired to enter.

We must mention, in the first place, that two of the delinquents who were executed afterwards, and another, together with one of the servants of her husband, were brought there. The principal delinquents were summoned first, and afterwards the others, to take an oath that they would speak the truth. We must mention that these gentlemen were already condemned, and were executed a few days afterwards. When the lawyer had said that they had now taken their oaths according to the law, our lady said, 'Post festum! After having proceeded against my husband so many weeks, having based everything on the tattle of these delinquents, you come, after they are condemned to suffer for their trespasses, and make them take an oath. I do not know if this is conformable to law!'

The lawyer made no reply to this, and, thinking to confuse our lady, said that he found things contrary the one to the other, cited passages, leaves, lines, and asked her if she could make these things agree. She, having at that time a good memory, remembered well what her own judgment had dictated to her, and said that they would not find her replies what the lawyer said, but so-and- so, and asked that they should be read openly, which was done. The lawyer made three attempts of the same kind; when they saw there was nothing to be gained by this, the Commissioners attacked her three at a time, one putting one question and another, another. She said to them quietly, 'Messieurs, with your permission, let one speak at a time, for I am but one, and I cannot answer three at once!' At which they were all a little ashamed.

The principal point to which they adhered was, that her husband was a vassal by oath, and a servant of the King, with which assertion they parried every objection. She proved that it was not so, that her husband was neither vassal nor a servant; he had his lands under the King just as many Swedes had elsewhere, without on that account being vassals; that he had never taken an oath of fidelity to the King of Sweden, but that he had shown him much fidelity; that he owed him no obligation—this she showed by a letter from the King, in which he thanked him for his services, and hoped so to act that he would render him still more. She shut the mouth of the delinquent,[32] and begged the Commissioners to reflect on what she had said.

When all was over, after the space of three hours, she requested that the protocol might be read before her. The President said that she need have no doubt the protocol was correct, that she should have a copy of it, that they now understood the matter, and would make a faithful report of it to the King. No sentence was passed, and they remained under arrest. The King of Sweden died, and peace was concluded, but they remained under arrest. A friend came to inform them, one day, that there was a vessel of war in the roads, which was to take them to Finland. When she saw her husband a little recovered, that he could use his judgment, she advised him to escape and go to Lubeck. She would go to Copenhagen and try to arrange the matter. He consented to it, and she contrived to let him out in spite of all the guards round the house (thirty-six in number).

When she received the news that he had passed and could reckon that he was on his way to Lubeck, she escaped also, and went straight to Copenh…. Having arrived there, she found her husband arrived before her; she was much surprised and vexed, fearing what happened afterwards, but he had flattered himself so with the comfortable hope that he would enter into the good graces of the King. The next day they were both arrested and brought to Borringh… [33]; her husband was ill; on arriving at Borr… they placed him on a litter and brought him from the town to the castle, a distance of about two leagues.

It would weary you to tell you of all that passed at Borr… If you take pleasure in knowing it, there is a man in Hamburgh who can tell it you.[34] I will tell you, however, a part and the chief of what I remember concerning it. At Rönne, the town where they disembarked at Borringh——, our lady wrote to the King and to the Queen in the name of her husband, who was ill, as I have already said, and gave the memorials to Colonel Rantzou, who promised to deliver them, and who gave hopes of success.[35] There Fos arrived and conveyed them to the Castle of Hammershuus. The governor Fos saw that our lady had a small box with her, and was seized with the desire to know what was in it and to possess himself of it. He sent one Dina, the wife of the warder to our lady, to offer to procure a boat for their escape. There is no doubt she accepted the offer, and promised in return five hundred crowns. This was enough for Fos; he went one night with the Major to their apartment, thundered like a madman, said that they wished to betray him, &c.; the end of the farce was, that he took the box, but, for the sake of a little ceremony, he sealed it with her husband's seal, promising to keep it for its safety.

About three weeks after, he took the two prisoners to walk a little in the fields; the husband would not go, but the wife went out to take the air. The traitor gave her a long history of his past adventures, how many times he had been in prison, some instances of how great lords had been saved by the assistance of those they had gained over, and made their fortune. He thought they would do the same. She said she had not much to dispose of, but besides that, they would find other means for rewarding such a service. He said he would think of it, that he had nothing to lose in Dan....

After various discussions from day to day, her husband wished her to offer him 20,000 rix-dollars; this sum seemed to him too little, and he asked 50,000 dollars. She said that she could easily promise it, but could not keep her word, but provided it was twenty she would pay it. He asked for a security; her husband had a note which would give security, but our lady did not think it good that he should see this note, and told Fos that in her box there was a letter that could secure it; she did not know that he had already opened the box. Some days after, she asked him if he had made up his mind? He said, 'I will not do it for less than 50,000, and there is no letter in your box which would secure it to me. I have opened it; to-morrow I will send it to Copenh....' She asked him quietly if he had done right in breaking her husband's seal; he answered rudely that he would take the responsibility.

Towards autumn, Hannibal and the other heirs of our lady's mother sent to her husband to notify to him that they could not longer delay dividing the inheritance, and since they knew that he had in his possession papers of importance, they requested to be informed of them. Her husband stated in his reply that Fos had taken his letters, and that in a rude manner. This answer having been read in the presence of Fos, he flew in a thundering rage, used abusive language first to the husband and then to the wife, her husband having firmly promised our lady not to dispute with this villain, for she feared some evil might result, but to leave her to answer, for Fos would be answered.

She was not angry; she ridiculed him and his invectives. At length he told her that she had offered him 20,000 dollars to induce him to become a traitor; she replied with calmness, 'If it had been 50,000, what then?' Fos leapt into the air like an enraged animal, and said that she lied like a ———, &c. She was not moved, but said 'You speak like an ass!' Upon this he loaded her with abuse, and then retracted all that he had just said. She said quite quietly, 'I am not going to appeal to these gentlemen who are present (there were four) to be witnesses, for this is an affair that will never be judicially settled, and nothing can efface this insult but blood.' 'Oh!' said he, seizing his sword, and drawing it a little out of the scabbard, 'this is what I wear for you, madam.' She, smiling, drew the bodkin from her hair, saying, 'Here are all the arms at present which I have for you.' He manifested a little shame, and said that it was not for her but her sons, if she still had four.[36] She, moreover, ridiculed him, and said that it was no use his acting the brave there. In short, books could be filled with all the quarrels between these two persons from time to time. He shouted at times with all his might, he spoke like a torrent, and foamed at the mouth, and the next moment he would speak low like another man. When he shouted so loudly, our lady said, 'The fever is attacking him again!' He was enraged at this.

Some weeks afterwards he came to visit them, and assumed a humble manner. Our lady took no notice of it, and spoke with him on indifferent subjects; but her husband would not speak to him, and never afterwards was he able to draw from him more than a few words. Towards Christmas, Fos treated the prisoners very ill, more so than formerly, so that Monsieur sent the servant to beg him to treat him as a gentleman and not as a peasant. Fos went to them immediately, after having abused Monsieur's servant; and as he entered, Monsieur left the apartment and went into another, and refused to give him his hand. Fos was enraged at this, and would not remain, nor would he speak a word to our lady, who begged him to hear her. A moment after, he caused the door to be bolted, so that they could not go out to take the air, for they before had free access to a loft. At every Festival he devised means of annoying them; he closed all the windows, putting to some bars of iron, and to others wooden framework and boxes; and as to their food, it was worse than ever. They had to endure that winter in patience; but as they perceived that Fos's design was that they should die of hunger, they resolved to hazard an escape, and made preparation through the winter, in order to escape as soon as the thaw would set in.

Our lady, who had three pairs of sheets that her children had sent her, undid some articles of clothing and made cordage and a sail; she sewed them with silk, for she had no thread. Her husband and the servant worked at the oars. When the moon was favourable to them in the month of April, they wished to carry out the plan they had been projecting for so long a time. Our lady was the first to make the descent: the height was seventy-two feet; she went on to the ravelin to await the others. Some time elapsed before her husband came, so she returned, and at last she heard a great noise among the ropes, her husband having lost a shoe in his descent. They had still to wait for the valet; he had forgotten the cord, and said that he could not carry it with him.

It was necessary to descend the rampart into the moats, which were dry; the height is about forty feet. Our lady was the first to descend; she helped her husband, for his strength was already failing. When they were all three in the fosse, the moon was obscured and a little rain fell. This was unfortunate, as they could not see which road to take. Her husband said it would be better to remain where they were till daylight, for they might break their necks in descending the rocks. The servant said he knew the way, as he had observed it when the window was free; that he would go in front. He went in advance, gliding in a sitting position, after him our lady, and then her husband; they could not see an inch before them; the man fell from an incredible height, and did not speak; our lady stopped, shouted to him, and asked him to answer if he was alive.

He was some time before he answered, so she and her husband considered him dead; at length he answered, and said he should never get out of this ravine; our lady asked him if he judged the depth to be greater than one of the cords could reach? She would tie two together, and throw the end to him to draw him up. He said that one cord would be sufficient, but that she could not draw him up, that she would not be strong enough; she said she could, she would hold firm, and he should help himself with his knees. He took courage, and she drew him up; the greatest marvel was, that on each side of her there was a precipice deeper than that over which he fell, and that she had nothing by which to support herself, except a small projection, which they believed to be of earth, against which she placed her left foot, finding no resting-place for the right one.

We can truly say that God had granted her his protection, for to escape from such a danger, and draw another out of it, could not have been done by unaided man. Our fool Fos explained it otherwise, and used it for his own purposes, saying that without the assistance of the devil it would have been impossible to stand firm in such a place, still less to assist another; he impressed this so well on the Queen, that she is still of the opinion that our lady exercises sorcery. Fos would take the glory from God to give it to the devil, and this calumny has to be endured with many others. But let us return to our miserable fugitives, whom we left in the fosse. Our lady, who had shouted to her husband not to advance, as soon as she heard the valet fall, called to him to keep back, turn quietly, and to climb upwards, for that there was no passage there; this was done, and they remounted the fosse and kept themselves quiet. Her husband wished that they should remain there, since they did not know which road to take.

While they were deliberating, the moon shone forth a little, and our lady saw where she was, and she remembered a good passage which she had seen on the day when she walked out with the governor; she persuaded her husband to follow her; he complained of his want of strength; she told him that God would assist him, and that he did not require great strength to let himself glide down, that the passage was not difficult, and that in ascending on the opposite side, which was not high, the valet and herself could assist him. He resolved, but he found it difficult enough; at length, however, they succeeded; they had then to go half a quarter of a league to reach the place where the boats were.

Her husband, wearied out, could not walk, and begged her, for the love of God, to leave him where he was; he was ready to die; she consoled him, and gave him restoratives, and told him that he had but a little step to make; he begged her to leave him there, and to save herself with the servant: she would find means afterwards to rescue him from prison. She said no, she would not abandon him; that he knew well the opportunities she had had to escape before, if she had wished to forsake him; that she would never quit him nor leave him in the hands of this tyrant; that if Fos ventured to touch him, she was resolved on avenging herself upon him.

After having taken a little breath, he began again to proceed. Our lady, who was loaded with so many ropes and clothes, could scarcely walk, but necessity gave her strength. She begged her husband to lean on her and on the valet, so he supported himself between them, and in this way arrived where the boats were; but too late, for it was already day. As our lady saw the patrol coming in the distance, she begged her husband to stop there with the valet, saying that she would go forward in advance, which she did. She was scarcely a musket-shot distant from a little town where the major lodged, when she spoke with the guard, and asked them after the major. One of them went for the major, whose name was Kratz.

The major saw our lady with great consternation; he asked after her husband. She told him where he was, and in a few words she requested that he would go to the castle and tell Major-General Fos that his ill-treatment had been the cause of the desperate resolution they had taken, and to beg him not to ill-treat them; they were at present sick at heart; they could not endure anything; she begged him to consider that those who had resolved to face more than one form of death, would not fear it in any shape. Kratz conducted the prisoners to his house, mounted his horse, and went in search of the governor, who was still in bed, and told him the affair.

The governor got out of bed like a furious creature, swore, menaced; after having recovered a little, the major told him what our lady had begged him to say. Then he was for some time thoughtful, and said, 'I confess it; they had reason to seek their liberty, for otherwise they would never have had it.' He did not immediately come for the prisoners, for he had another apartment prepared for them. As he entered, he assumed a pleasant manner, and asked if they ought to be there; he did not say an unkind word, but, on the contrary, said he should have done the same. They were conducted to the Royal Hall to warm themselves, for they were all wet with the rain; our lady had then an opportunity of speaking to the valet, and of taking from him the papers that he had, which contained all that had passed during the time of their imprisonment,[37] and she counselled the valet to lay aside the arms that he had upon him, and that if he had anything which he wished to secure that he would deliver it up to her keeping. The valet gave her what she asked, followed her orders, threw away his arms, but as regarded his own papers he would not give them up, for he did not share her fears; but he knew afterwards, for Fos caused him to be entirely stripped, and took away everything from him, and made him pay well for having noted down the dishes that they had on the first day of the Festivals, and on the rest.

At length towards evening our lady and her husband were conveyed into another apartment, and the valet into the body-guard loaded with irons. They were there together thirteen weeks, until Fos received orders from the Court to separate them; meanwhile, he encased the prisons in iron. I may well use such a term, for he caused plates of iron to be placed on the walls, double bars and irons round the windows.[38] When he had permission to separate them, he entered one day to begin a quarrel, and spoke of the past; our lady begged him not to say more, but he would go on; he was determined to quarrel. He said to her, 'Madame, you are so haughty, I will humble you; I will make you so—so small,' and he made a measurement with his hand from the floor. 'You have been lifted up and I will bring you down.' She laughed, and said, 'You may do with me whatever you will, but you can never humble me so that I shall cease to remember that you were a servant of a servant of the King my father;' at last, he so forgot himself as to hold his fist in her face. She said to him, keeping her hand on her knife which she had in her pocket, 'Make use of your foul mouth and accursed tongue, but keep your hands quiet.' He drew back, and made a profound bow in ridicule, calling her 'your grace,' asked her pardon, and what he had to fear. She said, 'You have nothing to fear; if you take liberties, you will meet with resistance—feeble enough, but such as I have strength to give you.'

After some further invectives, he said farewell, and begged they might be good friends; he came once more and conducted himself in the same manner, but less violently. He said to a captain who was present, of the name of Bolt, that he did it expressly in order to have a quarrel with her husband, that he might revenge himself for her conduct upon him, but that her husband would not speak to him. At length the unhappy day of their separation came, and Fos entered to tell them that they must be prepared to bid each other a final farewell, for that he had orders to separate them, and in this life they would never see each other again; he gave them an hour to converse together for the last time. You can easily imagine what passed in this hour; but as they had been prepared for this separation weeks before, having been warned of it by their guard with whom they could talk, it did not surprise them. Our lady had gained over four of the guards, who were ready to let them escape easily enough, but her husband would not undertake it, always saying that he had no strength, but that she might do it. Well, they had to abide by it; after this sad day[39] they were separated, he in one prison below and she in another above, one above another, bars before the windows, he without a servant, and she without a waiting woman.

About three weeks after, our lady fell ill; she requested a woman or girl to wait upon her, and a priest. Fos sent answer, with regard to a woman or girl to wait upon her, he did not know anyone who would do it, but that there was a wench who had killed her child, and who would soon be beheaded, and if she wished for her, she could have her. As to a priest, he had no orders, and she would have no priest even if death were on her lips. Our lady said nothing but 'Patience; I commend it to God.' Our lady had the happiness of being able to give her husband signs daily, and to receive such, and when the wind was not too strong they could speak to one another. They spoke Italian together, and took their opportunity before the reveille. Towards the close of the governorship of this villain, he was informed of this. He then had a kind of machine made which is used to frighten the cattle from the corn in the summer, and which makes a great noise, and he desired the sentinel to move this machine in order to hinder them hearing each other.

Fifteen days before Count Rantzow came to Borringholm to treat with them, Fos had news of it from Copenhagen from his intimate friend Jaques P…; he visited our lady, told her on entering that her children had been expelled from Skaane by the Swedes; our lady said, 'Well, the world is wide, they will find a place elsewhere.' He then told her that Bolt had come from Copenhagen with the tidings that they would never be let at liberty; she replied, 'Never is a long time; this imprisonment will not last a hundred years, much less an eternity—in the twinkling of an eye much may change; the hand of God, in whom are the hearts of kings, can change everything.' He said, 'You have plenty of hope; you think perhaps if the King died, you would be free?' She replied, 'God preserve the King. I believe that he will give me liberty, and no one else.' He chatted about a great many things, and played the flatterer.

At length Count Rantzow came and made a stay at Borringh… of eleven weeks. He visited the prisoners, and did them the favour of having the husband to dine with him, and in the evening our lady supped with him, and he conferred with them separately. Our lady asked him of what she was accused; he replied, 'Will you ask that? that is not the way to get out of Borringholm; do you know that you have said the King is your brother? and kings do not recognise either sisters or brothers.' She replied, 'To whom had I need to say that the King is my brother? who is so ignorant in Denmark as not to know that? I have always known, and know still, the respect that is due to the King; I have never given him any other title than my King and Lord; I have never called him my brother, in speaking of him; kings are gracious enough to recognise their sisters and brothers as such; for example, the King of England gives the title of sister to his brother's wife, although she is of very mediocre extraction.[40] Rantzow replied, 'Our King does not wish it, and he does not know yet the truth about Dina's affair.' She said, 'I think the King does not wish to know.' He replied, 'Indeed, by God he desires with all his heart to be informed of it.' She answered, 'If the King will desire Walter to tell him, and this with some earnestness, he will be informed of it.' Rantzow made no reply.

When he had concluded everything with her husband, whom he had obliged to yield up all his possessions, Rantzow acquainted our lady with the fact; she said that her husband had power to give up what was his, but that the half belonged to her, and that this she would not give up, not being able to answer for it before God nor before her children; she had committed no crime; liberty should be given to her husband for the half of their lands, and that if the King thought he could retain her with a good conscience she would endure it. Rantzow with a serious air replied, 'Do not think that your husband will ever be set at liberty, if you do not sign with him.' She said that the conditions were too severe; that they should do better for their children to die as prisoners, God and all the world knowing their innocence, than to leave so many children beggars. Rantzow said, 'If you die in prison, all your lands and property are forfeited, and your children will have nothing; but at this moment you can have your liberty, live with your husband; who knows, the King may still leave you an estate, and may always show you favour, when he sees that you yield to his will.' Our lady said that since there was no other prospect for her husband's liberty, she would consent. Rantzow ordered her husband and herself separately to place in writing the complaints they had to bring forward against Fos, and all that had happened with regard to their attempt at escape;

which was done. Our lady was gracious in her demeanour to Fos, but her husband could not make up his mind even to speak to him. Rantzow returned to Copenh… and eighteen days afterwards the galley of Gabel came with orders to the new governor (Lieutenant-Colonel Lytkens, a very well-bred man and brave soldier, his wife a noble lady of the Manteuffel family, very polite and pretty), that he should make the prisoners sign the papers sent, and when the signature was done, should send them on together.

The governor sent first to the husband, as was befitting, who made difficulties about signing because they had added points here and there, and among other things principally this, that they were never to plead against Fos. The husband said he would rather die. The good governor went in search of the wife and told her everything, begging her to speak to her husband from the window; when he knew that she had spoken to him, he would return. She thanked the governor, and when he had gone out she spoke to her husband, and persuaded him to sign. Then the governor made her sign also; and after that, towards nine o'clock in the evening, her husband came to her, having been separated just twenty-six weeks.[41] They were separated on a Saturday, and they met again on a Saturday. Fos was still at the castle; it is easy to believe that he was in great rage. Time does not permit to dwell on it. Two days afterwards they embarked and came to Copenhagen, and were received on the Custom-house pier by C. Rantzow and Gabel. The Queen knew nothing of it. When she was told of it she was so angry that she would not go to table. In a few words the King held his ground, and as she would not accept the thanks of Monsieur and his wife, the King ordered her to receive them in writing. They spent the Christmas of 1660 in the house of C. Rantzow. Afterwards they went to Fyen, to the estate of Ellensborg, which was graciously left to them.[42]

Her husband having permission to go to France to take the waters for eighteen months, left Ell… with his family in the month of June 1662, and landed at Amsterdam. Our lady went from thence to Bruges to hire a house, and returned to Amsterdam. Her daughter Helena fell ill of the small-pox; she remained with her, and her husband and the other children went to Bruges. When her daughter had recovered, she went to rejoin her husband and children. She accompanied her husband, who went to France. Having arrived at Paris, the doctors did not find it advisable that he should take the waters, and he returned to Bruges. Her husband begged our lady to make a journey to England, and to take her eldest son with her. She raised obstacles, and showed him plainly that she should obtain nothing; that she should only be at great expense. She had examples before her which showed her that the King of England would never pay her husband. He would not have been turned from his purpose at this time but for their son's rencontre with Fos, which prevented the journey that winter, and postponed the misfortunes of our lady, though it did not ultimately prevent them.

But towards the spring the same design was again brought forward; our lady was assisted by the nobleman who followed her afterwards[43] in dissuading her husband; but no reasoning could avail; he believed the King could not forget the benefits received, and refuse to pay his cousin. Our lady prepared for her departure, since her husband wished it. The day that she bade him her last farewell—a fatal day, indeed—her husband's heart did not tell him that these would be the last embraces he would give her, for he was so satisfied and so full of joy that she and all were astonished. She, on the contrary, was sad. The last day of their intercourse was May 24, 1663. She had many contretemps at first, and some time elapsed before she had the honour of speaking to the King.

The King greeted her after the fashion of the country, treated her as his cousin,[44] and promised her all sorts of satisfaction; that he would send his secretary[45] to her to see her papers, which he did. The secretary made her fine promises, but the time was always postponed. The minister resident, Petkum, minister of the King of Danem…, came to visit her (he had placed some obstacles in the way of her demands, from what was told her). She showed him her papers, informed him of the affair, told him that the King of Denmark had had all the papers in his hands, and had graciously returned them. The traitor made a semblance of understanding the affair, and promised that he would himself help in securing the payment of her demands. But this Judas always intended to betray her, asking her if she did not like to make excursions, speaking to her of beautiful houses, gardens and parks, and offering her his coach. But our lady was not inclined to make excursions.

When he saw that he could not catch her in this way, he obtained an order to arrest her. Our poor lady knew nothing of all this; she had letter upon letter from her husband requesting her return. She took leave of the King by letter, gave her papers to a lawyer[46] upon a receipt, and set out from London. Having arrived at Dover, and intending to embark the same evening for Flanders, a lieutenant of the name of Braten[47] appeared, who came to show her an order from the King of Anglet… which she read herself, the purport of which was that the governor was to arrest such a lady, and to place her in the castle till further orders. She asked the reason why. He said that she had left without permission from the King. She told him that she had taken leave of the King by letter, and had spoken the day before her departure with the Prime Minister and Vice-Admiral Aschew,[48] who had bade her farewell.[49]

When she came to the castle, the emissary of Petkum presented himself, by name Peter Dreyer. Then the Lieutenant said, 'It is the King of Danemarc who has ordered you to be arrested.' She asked the cause. He replied, 'You undoubtedly set out incognito from Danemarck.' She replied to this that the King of Danem… had given her husband leave of absence for a term of eighteen months, which had not yet expired. They ordered her boxes and those of the nobleman who accompanied her to be opened, and they took all the papers. Afterwards Dreyer spoke to her, and she asked him why she was treated thus? He said he did not know the real cause, but that he believed it was for the death of Fos, and that she was believed to have been the cause of his death. They always mentioned this to her, and no other cause.

This double traitor Braten enacted the gallant, entertained her, made her speak English (as she was bolder in speaking this language than any other), for she had just begun to learn it well, having had a language-master in London. One day he told that they intended conducting her to Danemarck. She told him there was no need to send her to Danem…; she could go there very well by herself. He said, 'You know yourself what suits you; if you will not go there willingly, I will manage so that you may go to Flanders.' She did not see that this was feasible, even if he was willing; she spoke with him as to the means, saw that he did not satisfy her, and did not trust his conversation; as he was cunning, he made her believe that the King wished her to go secretly, and that he would take it all upon himself; that the King had his reasons why he did not wish to deliver her into the hands of the King of Danem….

This deception had such good colouring, for she had written several times to the King during her arrest, and had begged him not to reward her husband's services by a long arrest, only speaking of what she had done at the Hague for him: she had taken her jewels and rings and given them to him, when his host would not any longer supply him with food.[50] Her claim was not small; it exceeded 20,000 patacoons.[51]

Our lady allowed herself to be persuaded that the King of England wished her to leave secretly. The traitor Braten told her that he thought it best that she should disguise herself as a man. She said that there was no necessity she should disguise herself; that no one would pursue her; and even if it were so, that she would not go in disguise with any man who was not her husband. After having been detained seventeen days at Dover, she allowed herself to be conducted by Braten, at night, towards the ramparts, descended by a high ladder which broke during her descent, passed the fosse, which was not difficult; on the other side there was a horse waiting for her, but the nobleman, her attendant, and the nobleman's valet, went on foot; they would not allow her valet to go with them; Braten made an excuse of not being able to find him, and that time pressed; it was because they were afraid that there would be an effort at defence.

When she arrived where the traitors were, her guide gave a signal by knocking two stones one against another. At this, four armed men advanced; Petkum and Dreyer were a little way off; one held a pistol to her breast, the other a sword, and said, 'I take you prisoner.' The other two traitors said, 'We will conduct you to Ostend.' She had always suspected treachery, and had spoken with her companion, in case it happened, what it would be best to do, to give herself up or to defend herself? She decided on allowing herself to be betrayed without a struggle, since she had no reason to fear that her life would be attempted because her son had avenged the wrong done to his parents. Thus she made no resistance, begged them not to take so much trouble, that she would go of herself; for two men held her with so much force that they hurt her arm. They came with a bottle of dry wine to quench her thirst, but she would not drink; she had a good way to go on foot, for she would not again mount the horse.

She showed some anger towards her guide, begged him in English to give her respects to the governor,[52] but to convey to the traitor Braten all the abuse that she could hurriedly call to mind in this language, which was not quite familiar to her. She advanced towards the boat; the vessel which was to convey her was in the roads, near the Downs. She bade farewell to the nobleman. She had two bracelets with diamonds which she wished to give him to convey to her children; but as he feared they would be taken from him, she replaced them without troubling him with them. She gave a pistol to her servant, and a mariner then carried her to the boat; she was placed in an English frigate that Petkum had hired, and Dreyer went with her.[53] She was thirteen days on the road, and arrived near the Custom-house pier on August 8, 1663, at nine o'clock in the morning.

[The remaining part of the Autobiography treats of the commencement of her imprisonment in the Blue Tower, which forms the subject of the following Memoir.]

A RECORD
OF
THE SUFFERINGS OF THE IMPRISONED
COUNTESS
LEONORA CHRISTINA.

PREFACE.
TO MY CHILDREN.

Beloved children, I may indeed say with Job, 'Oh, that my grief were thoroughly weighed, and my calamity laid in the balances together! For now it would be heavier than the sand of the sea.' My sufferings are indeed great and many; they are heavy and innumerable. My mind has long been uncertain with regard to this history of my sufferings, as I could not decide whether I ought not rather to endeavour to forget them than to bear them in memory. At length, however, certain reasons have induced me, not only to preserve my sorrow in my own memory, but to compose a record of it, and to direct it to you, my dear children.[54]

The first of these reasons is the remembrance of the omnipotence of God; for I cannot recall to mind my sorrow and grief, my fears and distresses, without at the same time remembering the almighty power of God, who in all my sufferings, my misery, my affliction, and anxiety, has been my strength and help, my consolation and assistance; for never has God laid a burden upon me, without at the same time giving me strength in proportion, so that the burden, though it has weighed me down and heavily oppressed me, has not overwhelmed me and crushed me; for which I praise and extol through eternity the almighty power of the incomprehensible God.

I wish, therefore, not alone to record my troubles and to thank God for His gracious support in all the misfortunes that have befallen me, but also to declare to you, my dear children, God's goodness to me, that you may not only admire with me the inconceivable help of the Almighty, but that you may be able to join with me in rendering Him thanks. For you may say with reason that God has dealt wonderfully with me; that He was mighty in my weakness and has shown His power in me, the frailest of His instruments. For how would it have been possible for me to resist such great, sudden, and unexpected misfortunes, had not His spirit imparted to me strength? It was God who Himself entered with me into the Tower-gate; it was He who extended to me His hand, and wrestled for me in that prison cell for malefactors, which is called 'the Dark Church.'

Since then, now for almost eleven years, He has always been within the gate of my prison as well as of my heart; He has strengthened me, comforted me, refreshed me, and often even cheered me. God has done wonderful things in me, for it is more than inconceivable that I should have been able to survive the great misfortunes that have befallen me, and at the same time should have retained my reason, sense, and understanding. It is a matter of the greatest wonder that my limbs are not distorted and contracted from lying and sitting, that my eyes are not dim and even wholly blind from weeping, and from smoke and soot; that I am not short-breathed from candle smoke and exhalation, from stench and close air. To God alone be the honour!

The other cause that impels me is the consolation it will be to you, my dear children, to be assured through this account of my sufferings that I suffer innocently; that nothing whatever has been imputed to me, nor have I been accused of anything for which you, my dear children, should blush or cast down your eyes in shame. I suffer for having loved a virtuous lord and husband, and for not having abandoned him in misfortune. I was suspected of being privy to an act of treason for which he has never been prosecuted according to law, much less convicted of it, and the cause of the accusation was never explained to me, humbly and sorrowfully as I desired that it should be. Let it be your consolation, my dear children, that I have a gracious God, a good conscience, and can boldly maintain that I have never committed a dishonourable act. 'This is thankworthy,' says the apostle St. Peter, 'if a man for conscience toward God endure grief, suffering wrongfully.' I suffer, thank God, not for my misdeeds, for that were no glory to me; yet I can boast that from my youth up I have been a bearer of the cross of Christ, and had incredibly secret sufferings, which were very heavy to endure at such an early age.

Although this record of my sufferings contains and reveals nothing more than what has occurred to me in this prison, where I have now been for eleven years, I must not neglect in this preface briefly to recall to your minds, my dear children, my earlier misfortunes, thanking God at the same time that I have overcome them.

Not only you, my dear children, know, but it is known throughout the whole country, what great sorrow and misfortune Dina and Walter, with their powerful adherents, inflicted on our house in the year 1651.

Although I will not mention the many fatiguing and difficult journeys, the perils by sea, and various dangers which I have endured in foreign countries, I will only remind you of that journey which my lord requested me to undertake to Denmark, contrary to my wish, in the year 1657.[E1] It was winter time, and therefore difficult and dangerous. I endured scorn and persecution; and had not God given me courage and taken it from him who was to have arrested me, I should not at that time have escaped the misery of captivity.

You will remember, my dear children, what I suffered and endured during fourteen months in custody at Malmöe; how the greatest favour which His Majesty, King Charles X. of Sweden, at that time showed me, was that he left it to my free will, either to remain at liberty, taking care of our property, or to be in prison with my lord. I acknowledged the favour, and chose the latter as my duty, esteeming it a happiness to be allowed to console and to serve my anxious husband, afflicted as he subsequently was by illness. I accepted it also as a favour that I was allowed (when my lord could not do it himself on account of illness) to appear before the tribunal in his stead. What anxiety and sorrow I had for my sick lord, what trouble, annoyance and distress, the trial caused me (it was carried on daily for more than nine weeks), is known to the most high God, who was my consolation, assistance, and strength, and who inspired me with heart and courage to defend the honour of my lord in the presence of his judges.

You will probably not have forgotten how quickly one misfortune followed another, how one sorrow was scarcely past when a greater one followed in its track; we fared, according to the words of the poet:

> Incidit in Scyllam, qui vult vitare Charibdin.

We escaped custody and then fell into strict captivity, without doubt by the dispensation of God, who inspired my lord with the idea of repairing, contrary to our agreement, to Copenhagen instead of Lübeck. No pen can describe how sorrowful I was when, contrary to all expectation, I met my lord in Copenhagen, when I had imagined him escaped from the power and violence of all his enemies. I expected just that which my lord did not believe would happen, but which followed immediately—namely, our arrest. The second day after my arrival (which they had waited for) we were apprehended and conveyed to Bornholm, where we were in close imprisonment for seventeen months. I have given a full description of what I suffered, and this I imagine is in your keeping, my dear children; and from it you see what I and my sick lord endured; how often I warded off greater misery, because my lord could not always brook patiently the bad treatment of the governor, Adolf Foss, who called himself Fux.

It was hard and bitter indeed to be scorned and scoffed at by a peasant's son; to have to suffer hunger at his will, and to be threatened and harassed by him; but still harder and more bitter was it to be sick beneath his power, and to hear from him the words that even if death were on my lips no minister of God's word should come to me. Oh monstrous tyranny! His malice was so thoroughly beyond all bounds, that he could not endure that we should lighten each other's cross; and for this reason he contrived, after the lapse of eleven months, to have us separated from each other, and to place us each in the hardest confinement.

My husband (at that time already advancing in years) without a servant, and I without an attendant, was only allowed a light so long as the evening meal lasted. I cannot forbear bitterly recalling to mind the six months of long and hard separation, and the sad farewell which we took of each other; for to all human sight there was no other prospect than that which the governor announced to us—namely, that we were seeing and speaking with each other for the last time in this world. God knows best how hard our sufferings were, for it was He who consoled us, who gave us hope contrary to all expectation, and who inspired me with courage when the governor visited me and endeavoured to fill me with despair.

God confirmed my hope. Money and property loosened the bonds of our captivity, and we were allowed to see and speak with each other once more. Sad as my lord had been when we were separated at Borringholm, he was joyous when two years afterwards he persuaded me to undertake the English journey, not imagining that this was to part us for ever. My lord, who entertained too good an opinion of the King of England, thought that now that he had come to the throne he would remember not only his great written and spoken promises, but that he would also bear in mind how, at the time of his need and exile, I had drawn the rings from my fingers and had pawned them for meals for him and his servants. But how unwillingly I undertook this journey is well known to some of you, my dear children, as I was well aware that from an ungrateful person there is nothing else to be expected but ingratitude. I had the example of others by whom to take warning; but it was thus destined to be.

Bitter bread was in store for me, and bitter gall was to fill my cup in the Blue Tower of Copenhagen Castle; thither was I to go to eat it and drink it out. It is not unknown to you how falsely the King of England acted towards me; how well he received me on my arrival; how he welcomed me with a Judas kiss and addressed me as his cousin; and how both he himself and all his high ministers assured me of the royal favour, and promised me payment of the money advanced. You know how cunningly (at the desire of His Majesty the King of Denmark) he had me arrested at Dover, and subsequently sent me word through the traitor Lieutenant Braten that he would let me escape secretly, at the same time delivering me into the hand of the Danish Minister Simon Petcon, who had me arrested by eight armed men; keeping aloof, however, himself, and never venturing to come near me. They held sword and pistol to my breast, and two of them took me between them and placed me in a boat, which conveyed me to a vessel held in readiness by the said Minister; a man of the name of Peter Dreyer having received orders to conduct me to Copenhagen.

From this period this record of my suffering begins. It contains all that happened to me within the gates of the Blue Tower. Reflect, my dear children, on these hard sufferings; but remember also God's great goodness towards me. Verily, He has freed me from six calamities; rest assured that He will not leave me to perish in the seventh. No! for the honour of His name, He will mightily deliver me.

The narrative of my sufferings is sad to hear, and must move the hardest heart to pity; yet in reading it, do not be more saddened than can be counterbalanced by joy. Consider my innocence, courage, and patience; rejoice over these.

I have passed over various petty vexations and many daily annoyances for the sake of brevity, although the smallest of them rankled sore in the wounds of my bitter sorrow.

I acknowledge my weaknesses, and do not shrink from confessing them to you. I am a human being, and am full of human imperfections. Our first emotions are not under our own power; we are often overhasty before we are able to reflect. God knows that I have often made myself deaf and blind, in order not to be carried away by passion. I am ashamed to mention and to enumerate the unchaste language, bad words and coarse invectives, of the prison governor Johan Jaeger, of Kresten Maansen, the tower warder, of Karen the daughter of Ole, and of Catharina Wolff; they would offend courtly ears. Yet I can assure you they surpass everything that can be imagined as indecent, ugly, churlish and unbecoming; for coarse words and foul language were the tokens of their friendliness and clemency, and disgusting oaths were the ornament and embellishment of their untruthfulness; so that their intercourse was most disagreeable to me. I was never more glad than when the gates were closed between me and those who were to guard me. Then I had only the woman alone, whom I brought to silence, sometimes amicably, and at others angrily and with threats.

I have also had, and have still, pleasant intercourse with persons whose services and courtesies I shall remember as long as I live. You, my dear children, will also repay them to every one as far as you are able.

You will find also in this record of my sufferings two of the chief foes of our house, namely Jörgen Walter and Jörgen Skröder,[E2] with regard to whom God has revenged me, and decreed that they should have need of me, and that I should comfort them. Walter gives me cause to state more respecting him than was my intention.

Of the psalms and hymns which I have composed and translated, I only insert a few, in order that you, my dear children, may see and know how I have ever clung steadfastly to God, who has been and still is my wall of defence against every attack, and my refuge in every kind of misfortune and adversity. Do not regard the rhymes; they are not according to the rules which poets make; but regard the matter, the sense, and the purport. Nor have I left my other small pastime unmentioned, for you may perceive the repose of my mind from the fact that I have had no unemployed hours; even a rat, a creature so abominable to others, affording me amusement.

I have recorded two observations, which though they treat of small and contemptible animals, yet are remarkable, and I doubt whether any naturalist hitherto has observed them. For I do not think it has been recorded hitherto that there exists a kind of caterpillar which brings forth small living grubs like itself, nor either that a flea gives birth to a fully-formed flea, and not that a nit comes from a nit.[55]

In conclusion, I beg you, my dear children, not to let it astonish you that I would not avail myself of the opportunity by which I might have gained my freedom. If you rightly consider it, it would not have been expedient either for you or me. I confess that if my deceased lord had been alive, I should not only have accepted the proposal, but I should have done my utmost to have escaped from my captivity, in order to go in quest of him, and to wait on him and serve him till his last breath; my duty would have required this. But since he was at that time in rest and peace with God, and needed no longer any human service, I have with reason felt that self-obtained liberty would have been in every respect more prejudicial than useful to us, and that this would not be the way to gain the possessions taken from us, for which reason I refused it and endeavoured instead to seek repose of mind and to bear patiently the cross laid upon me. If God so ordains it, and it is His divine will that through royal mercy I should obtain my freedom, I will joyfully exert myself for you, my beloved children, to the utmost of my ability, and prove in deed that I have never deviated from my duty, and that I am no less a good and right-minded mother than I have been a faithful wife. Meanwhile let God's will be your will. He will turn and govern all things so that they may benefit you and me in soul and body, to whose safe keeping I confidently recommend you all, praying that He will be your father and mother, your counsellor and guide. Pray in return for me, that God may direct me by His good spirit, and grant me patience in the future as heretofore. This is all that is requested from you by,

My dearly beloved children, your affectionate mother,

LEONORA CHRISTINA, V.E.G.

Written in the Blue Tower, anno 1674, the 18th of July, the eleventh year of imprisonment, my birthday, and fifty-third year of my age.[56]

I bear also in mind, with the greatest humility and gratitude, our gracious hereditary King's favour towards me, immediately after His Majesty came to the throne. I remember also the sympathy of our most gracious Queen Regent, and of Her Highness the Electoral Princess of Saxony in my unfortunate fate; also the special favour of Her Majesty the Queen.

I have also not forgotten to bear duly in mind the favour shown towards me by Her Majesty the Queen Mother, the virtuous Landgravine of Hesse.

I have also recorded various things which occurred in my imprisonment during the period from the year 1663 to the year 1674, intending with these to conclude the record of my sufferings; as I experienced a pleasure, and often consoled myself, in feeling that it is better to remain innocently in captivity than to be free and to have deserved imprisonment. I remember having read that captivity has served many as a protection from greater dangers, and has guarded them from falling into the hands of their enemies. There have been some who have escaped from their prison and immediately after have been murdered. There have also been some who have had a competence in prison and afterwards have suffered want in freedom. Innocent imprisonment does not diminish honour, but rather increases it. Many a one has acquired great learning in captivity, and has gained a knowledge of things which he could not master before. Yes, imprisonment leads to heaven. I have often said to myself: 'Comfort thyself, thou captive one, thou art happy.'

Since the year 1674 constituted only half the period of my captivity, I have added in this record of my sufferings some facts that occurred since that time within my prison-gates. I am on the eve of my liberty, May 19, 1685. To God alone be the honour, who has moved His Royal Majesty to justice! I will here mention those of whose death I have been informed during my captivity.

1. The Prime Minister of His Majesty, Count Christian of Rantzow[E3], died in the month of September, 1663. He did not live to drink the health of our Princess and of the Electoral Prince of Saxony at the feast of their betrothal. Still less did he live long enough to see a wooden effigy quartered in mockery of my lord, according to his suggestion. Death was very bitter to him.

2. The Mistress of the Robes of the Queen Dowager, who was so severe on me in my greatest sorrow, had a long and painful illness; she said with impatience that the pain of hell was not greater than her pain. Her screams could often be heard in the tower. She was carried on a bed into the town, and died there.

3. The death of Able Catherine was very painful. As she had formerly sought for letters on the private parts of my person, so she was afterwards herself handled by the surgeons, as she had boils all over her. She was cut and burnt. She endured all this pain, hoping to live, but neither the art of the surgeons nor the visits of the Queen could save her from death.[E4]

4. Secretary Erich Krag, who had displayed the malice of his heart in my imprisonment in the 'Dark Church,' was snatched away by death in a place of impurity. He was lively and well, had invited guests to dinner, sat and wrote at his table, went out to obey the necessities of nature, and was found dead by his attendants when they had waited some time for him.

5. Major-General Fridrich von Anfeldte,[E5] who had more than once manifested his delight at my misfortunes, died as he had lived. He was a godless man and a blasphemer. He fell a victim to jealousy, and went mad, because another obtained an honorary title which he had coveted; this was indeed little enough to deprive him of sense and reason. He would hear nothing of God, nor would he be reconciled with God. Both Queens, the Queen Dowager and the Queen Regent, persuaded him at length to be so. When he had received the sacrament, he said, 'Now your Majesties have had your desire; but what is the good of it?' He continued to curse and to swear, and so died.

6. General Schak died after a long illness.

7. Chancellor Peter Retz likewise.

8. His Royal Majesty King Friedrich III.'s death accelerated the death of the Stadtholder Cristoffer Gabel. He felt that the hate of the Queen Dowager could injure him greatly, and he desired death. God heard him.[E6]

9. It has pleased God that I should be myself a witness of Walter's miserable death; indeed, that I should compassionate him. When I heard him scream, former times came to my mind, and I often thought how a man can allow

himself to be led to do evil to those from whom he had only received kindness and honour.

10. Magister Buch, my father-confessor, who acted so ill to me, suffered much pain on his bed of languishing. He was three days speechless before he died.

11. When the rogue and blasphemer, Christian, who caused me so much annoyance in my captivity, had regained his liberty and returned to his landlord, Maans Armfeld in Jutland, he came into dispute with the parish priest, who wanted him to do public penance for having seduced a woman. The rogue set fire to the parsonage; the minister's wife was burnt to death in trying to save some of her property, and all the minister's possessions were left in ashes. The minister would not bring the rogue to justice. He commended him to the true Judge, and left vengeance to Him. The incendiary's conscience began to be awakened; for a long time he lived in dread, and was frightened if he saw anyone coming at all quickly, and he would call out and say tremblingly, 'Now they are going to take me!' and would run hither and thither, not knowing where to go. At length he was found dead on the field, having shot himself; for a long rifle was found lying between his legs, the barrel towards his breast, and a long ramrod in his hand, with which he had touched the trigger. He did not, therefore, die in as Christian a manner as if he had perished under the hand of the executioner, of which he had so lightly said that he should not care for it at all, so long as he could bring someone else into trouble.

⸻⸻⸻⸻⸻

A RECORD OF SUFFERING;

OR, A REMINISCENCE OF ALL THAT OCCURRED TO ME, LEONORA CHRISTINA, IN THE BLUE TOWER, FROM AUGUST 8 OF THE YEAR 1663, TO JUNE 1 [57] OF THE YEAR 1674.

The past is rarely remembered without sorrow, for it has been either better or worse than the present. If it was more joyous, more happy, and full of honour, its remembrance justly saddens us, and in proportion as the present is full of care, unhappiness, and dishonour. If past times were sadder, more miserable, and more deplorable than the present, the remembrance of them is equally sorrowful, for we recover and feel once more all the past misfortunes and adversities which have been endured in the course of time. But all things have, as it were, two handles by which they may be raised, as Epictetus says.

The one handle, he says, is bearable; the other is not bearable; and it rests with our will which handle we grasp, the bearable or the unbearable one. If we grasp the bearable one, we can recall all that is transitory, however sad and painful it may have been, rather with joy than with sorrow.[E7] So I will seize the bearable handle, and in the name of Jesus I will pass rapidly through my memory, and recount all the wretchedness and misery, all the grief, scorn and suffering, contempt and adversity, which have befallen me in this place, and which I have overcome with God's help. I will, moreover, in no wise grieve over it; but, on the contrary, I will remind myself at every step of the goodness of God, and will thank the Most High who has been constantly near me with His mighty help and consolation; who has ruled my heart, that it should not depart from God; who has preserved my mind and my reason, that it has not become obscured; who has maintained my limbs in their power and natural strength, and even has given, and still gives me, repose of mind and joyfulness. To Thee, incomprehensible God, be honour and praise for ever!

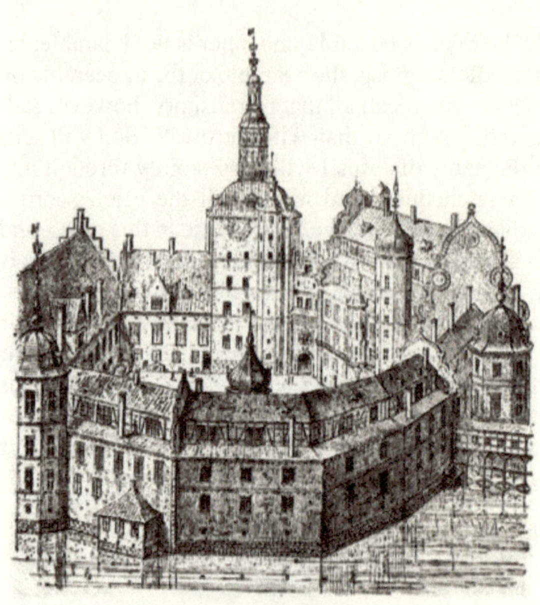

DAS ALTE SCHLOSS IN COPENHAGEN
MIT DEM BLAUEN THURM.

THE OLD CASTLE OF COPENHAGEN.
SHOWING THE BLUE TOWER IN THE MIDDLE OF THE BACK-GROUND.

And now to proceed with my design. I consider it necessary to begin the record of my sufferings with the commencement of the day which concluded with the fatal evening of my captivity, and to mention somewhat of that which befell me on the vessel. After the captain had cast anchor a little outside the pier of St. Anna, on August 8, 1663, at nine o'clock in the forenoon, he was sent on shore with letters by Peter Dreyer, who was commissioned by Petcon, at that time the minister resident in England, of his Majesty the King of Denmark, to take charge of me. I dressed myself and sat down in one of the cabins of the sailors on the deck, with a firm resolution to meet courageously all that lay before me;[58] yet I in no wise expected what happened; for although I had a good conscience, and had nothing evil with which to reproach myself, I had at various times asked the before-mentioned Peter Dreyer the reason why I had been thus brought away. To this question he always gave me the reply which the traitor Braten had given me at Dover (when I asked of him the cause of my arrest); namely, that I was, perhaps, charged with the death of Major-General Fux, and, that it was thought I had persuaded my son to slay him; saying, that he knew of no other cause. At twelve o'clock Nils Rosenkrantz, at that time Lieutenant-Colonel, and Major Steen Anderson Bilde, came on board with some musketeers. Lieutenant-

Colonel Rosenkrantz did not salute me. The Major walked up and down and presently passed near me. I asked him, en passant, what was the matter? He gave me no other answer than, 'Bonne mine, mauvais jeu;' which left me just as wise as before. About one o'clock Captain Bendix Alfeldt came on board with several more musketeers, and after he had talked some time with Peter Dreyer, Dreyer came to me and said, 'It is ordered that you should go into the cabin.' I said, 'Willingly;' and immediately went. Soon after, Captain Alfeldt came in to me, and said he had orders to take from me my letters, my gold, silver, money, and my knife. I replied, 'Willingly.' I took off my bracelets and rings, gathered in a heap all my gold, silver, and money, and gave it to him. I had nothing written with me, except copies of the letters which I had addressed to the King of England, notes respecting one thing or another relating to my journey, and some English vocabularies; these I also gave up to him. All these Alfeldt placed in a silver utensil which I had with me, sealed it in my presence, and left the vessel with it. An hour, or somewhat more, afterwards, Major-General Friderich von Anfeldt,[59] Commandant in Copenhagen, arrived, and desired that I should come to him outside the cabin. I obeyed immediately. He greeted me, gave me his hand, and paid me many compliments, always speaking French. He was pleased to see me in health, he feared the sea might have inconvenienced me; I must not allow the time to seem long to me; I should soon be accommodated otherwise. I caught at the last word and said, smiling, 'Monsieur says otherwise, but not better.' 'Yes, indeed,' he replied, 'you shall be well accommodated; the noblest in the kingdom will visit you.' I understood well what he meant by this, but I answered: 'I am accustomed to the society of great people, therefore that will not appear strange to me.' Upon this, he called a servant and asked for the before-mentioned silver utensil (which Captain Alfeldt had taken away with him). The paper which Captain Alfeldt had sealed over it was torn off. The Major-General turned to me, and said: 'Here you have your jewels, your gold, silver, and money back; Captain Alfeldt made a mistake—they were only letters which he had orders to demand, and these only have been taken out, and have been left at the Castle; you may dispose of the rest as you wish yourself.' 'In God's name,' I answered, 'am I, therefore, at liberty to put on again my bracelets and rings?' 'O Jesus,' he said, 'they are yours; you may dispose of them as you choose.' I put on the bracelets and rings, and gave the rest to my attendant. The Major-General's delight not only appeared in his countenance, but he was full of laughter, and was overflowing with merriment. Among other things he said that he had had the honour of making the acquaintance of two of my sons; that he had been in their society in Holland; and he praised them warmly. I complimented him in return, as was proper, and I behaved as if I believed that he was speaking in good faith. He indulged in various jokes, especially with my attendant; said that she was pretty, and that he wondered I could venture to keep such a pretty maiden; when Holstein ladies kept pretty maids it was only to put their husbands in good humour; he held a long discourse on how they managed, with other unmannerly jests which he carried on with my attendant. I answered nothing else than that he probably spoke from experience. He said all kinds of foolish jokes to my servant, but she did not answer a word. Afterwards the prison governor told me that he (von Anfeldt) had made the King believe, at first, that my attendant was my daughter, and that the King had been long of that opinion. At length, after a long conversation, the Major-General took his leave, saying that I must not allow the time to seem long to me; that he should soon come again; and he asked what he should say to his Majesty the King. I begged him to recommend me in the best manner to their Majesties' favour, adding that I knew not well what to say or for what to make request, as I was ignorant of what intentions they had with regard to me. Towards three o'clock Major-General von Anfeldt returned; he was full of laughter and merriment, and begged me to excuse him for being so long away. He hoped the time had not appeared long to me; I should soon get to rest; he knew well that the people (with this he pointed to the musketeers, who stood all along both sides of the vessel) were noisy, and inconvenienced me, and that rest would be best for me. I answered that the people did not inconvenience me at all; still I should be glad of rest, since I had been at sea for thirteen days, with rather bad weather. He went on with his compliments, and said that when I came into the town his wife would do herself the honour of waiting on me, and, 'as it seems to me,' he continued, 'that you have not much luggage with you, and perhaps, not the clothes necessary, she will procure for you whatever you require.' I thanked him, and said that the honour was on my side if his wife visited me, but that my luggage was as much as I required at the time; that ifI needed anything in the future, I hoped she might be spared this trouble; that I had not the honour of knowing her, but I begged him, nevertheless, to offer her my respects. He found various subjects of discourse upon Birgitte Speckhans[E8] and other trifles, to pass away the time; but it is not worth the trouble to recall them to mind, and still less to write them down. At last a message came that he was to conduct me from the vessel, when he said to me with politeness: 'Will it please you, madame, to get into this boat, which is lying off the side of the ship?' I answered, 'I am pleased to do anything that I must do, and that is commanded by His Majesty the King.' The Major- General went first into the boat, and held out his hand to me; the Lieutenant- Colonel Rosenkrantz, Captain Alfeldt, Peter Dreyer, and my attendant, went with me in the boat. And as a great crowd of people had assembled to look at the spectacle, and many had even gone in boats in order to see me as they wished, he never took his eyes off me; and when he saw that I turned sometimes to one side and sometimes to another, in order to give them this pleasure, he said, 'The people are delighted.' I saw no one truly who gave any signs of joy, except himself, so I answered, 'He who rejoices to-day, cannot know that he may not weep to-morrow; yet I see, that, whether for joy or sorrow, the people are assembling in crowds, and many are gazing with amazement at one human being.' When we were advanced a little further, I saw the well-known wicked Birgitte Ulfeldt,[E9] who exhibited great delight. She was seated in an open carriage; behind her was a young man, looking like a student. She was driving along the shore. When I turned to that side, she was in the carriage and laughed with all her might, so that it sounded loudly. I looked at her for some time, and felt ashamed of her impudence, and at the disgrace which she was bringing on herself; but for the rest, this conduct did not trouble me more than the barking of the dogs, for I esteemed both equally. [60] The Major-General went on talking incessantly, and never turned his eyes from me; for he feared (as he afterwards said) that I should throw myself into the water. (He judged me by himself; he could not endure the change of fortune, as his end testified, for it was only on account of an honorary title which another received in his stead that he lost his mind. He did not know that I was governed by another spirit than he, which gave me strength and courage, whilst the spirit he served led him into despair.[61]) When the boat arrived at the small pier near the office of the Exchequer, Captain Alfeldt landed and gave me his hand, and conducted me up towards the castle bridge. Regiments of horse and foot were drawn up in the open place outside the castle; musketeers were standing on both sides as I walked forwards. On the castle bridge stood Jockum Walburger, the prison governor, who went before me; and as the people had placed themselves in a row on either side up to the King's Stairs, the prison governor made as if he were going thither; but he turned round abruptly, and said to Alfeldt, 'This way,' and went to the gate of the Blue Tower; stood there for some time and fumbled with the key; acted as if he could not unlock it, in order that I might remain as long as possible a spectacle to the people. And as my heart was turned to God, and I had placed all my confidence in the Most High, I raised my eyes to heaven, sought strength, power, and safety from thence, and it was graciously vouchsafed me. (One circumstance I will not leave unnoticed—namely, that as I raised my eyes to heaven, a screaming raven flew over the Tower, followed by a flock of doves, which were flying in the same direction.) At length, after a long delay, the prison governor opened the Tower gate, and I was conducted into the Tower by the before-mentioned Captain Alfeldt. My attendant, who was preparing to follow me, was called back by Major-General von Anfeldt, and told to remain behind. The prison governor went up the stairs, and showed Alfeldt the way to a prison for malefactors, to which the name of the 'Dark Church' has been given. There Alfeldt quitted me with a sigh and a slight reverence. I can truly say of him that his face expressed pity, and that he obeyed the order unwillingly. The clock was striking half-past five when Jockum closed the door of my prison. I found before me a small low table, on which stood a brass candlestick with a lighted candle, a high chair, two small chairs, a fir-wood bedstead without hangings and with old and hard bedding, a night-stool and chamber utensil. At every side to which I turned I was met with stench; and no wonder, for three peasants who had been imprisoned here, and had been removed on that very day, and placed elsewhere, had used the walls for their requirements. Soon after the door had been closed, it was opened again, and there entered Count Christian Rantzow, Prime Minister, Peter Zetz, Chancellor, Christoffer von Gabel, at that time Chancellor of the Exchequer, and Erich Krag, at that time Secretary, all of whom gave me their hands with civility. The Chancellor spoke and said: 'His Royal Majesty, my gracious master and hereditary king, sends you word, madame, that His Majesty has great cause for what he is doing against you, as you will learn.' I replied: 'It is much to be regretted by me, if cause should be found against me; I will, however, hope that it may not be of such a kind that His Majesty's displeasure may be lasting. When I know the cause I can defend myself.' Count Rantzow answered: 'You will obtain permission to defend yourself.' He whispered something to the Chancellor, upon which the Chancellor put a few questions: first, Whether on my last journey I had been in France with my husband? To which I answered in the affirmative. Then, What my husband was doing there? To which I replied, that he was consulting physicians about his health, whether it would be serviceable to him to use the warm baths in the country, which no one would advise him to do; he had even been dissuaded from trying them by a doctor in Holland of the name of Borro,[E10] when he had asked his opinion. Thirdly, What I had purposed doing in England? To this I replied that my intention had been to demand payment of a sum of money which the King of England owed us, and which we had lent him in the time of his misfortune. Fourthly, Who had been in England with me? I mentioned those who were with me in England—namely, a nobleman named Cassetta, my attendant who had come hither with me, a lacquey named Frantz, who had remained in England, and the nobleman's servant. Fifthly, Who visited my husband in Bruges? I could not exactly answer this, as my lord received his visits in a private chamber, where I was not admitted. Count Rantzow said, 'You know, I suppose, who came to him oftenest?' I answered, that the most frequent visitors among those I knew were two brothers named Aranda,[E11] the before-mentioned Cassetta, and a nobleman named Ognati. Sixthly the Chancellor asked, With whom I had corresponded here in the country? To which I answered, that I had written to H. Hendrick Bielcke, to Olluff Brockenhuuss, Lady Elsse Passberg, and Lady Marie Ulfeldt;[E12] I did not remember any more. Count Rantzow enquired if I had more letters than those which I had given up? To which I answered in the negative, that I had no more. He asked further, Whether I had more jewels with me than those he had seen? I answered that I had two strings of small round pearls on my hat, and a ring with a diamond, which I had given a lieutenant named Braten in Dover (it was he who afterwards betrayed me). Count Rantzow asked, How much the pearls might have been worth? This I could not exactly say. He said, that he supposed I knew their approximate value. I said they might be worth 200 rix-dollars, or somewhat more. Upon this they were all silent for a little. I complained of the severity of my imprisonment, and that I was so badly treated. Count Rantzow answered, 'Yes Madame, His Royal Majesty has good cause for it; if you will confess the truth, and that quickly, you may perhaps look for mercy. Had Maréchal de Birron[E13] confessed the matter respecting which he was interrogated by order of the King, when the royal mercy was offered to him if he would speak the truth, it would not have fared with him as it did. I have heard as a truth that the King of France would have pardoned him his crime, had he confessed at once; therefore, bethink yourself, madame!' I answered, 'Whatever I am asked by order of His Majesty, and whatever I am cognizant of, I will gladly say in all submission.' Upon this Count Rantzow offered me his hand, and I reminded him in a few words of the severity of my imprisonment. Count Rantzow promised to mention this to the King. Then the others shook hands with me and went away. My prison was closed for a little. I therefore profited by the opportunity, and concealed here and there in holes, and among the rubbish, a gold watch, a silver pen which gave forth ink and was filled with ink, and a scissor-sheath worked with silver and tortoiseshell. This was scarcely done when the door was again opened, and there entered the Queen's Mistress of the Robes, her woman of the bed-chamber, and the wife of the commissariat clerk, Abel Catharina. I knew the last. She and the Queen's woman of the bed-chamber carried clothes over their arm; these consisted of a long dressing-gown stitched with silk, made of flesh-coloured taffeta and lined with white silk, a linen under- petticoat, printed over with a black lace pattern, a pair of silk stockings, a pair of slippers, a shift, an apron, a night-dress, and two combs. They made me no greeting. Abel Cath. spoke for them, and said: 'It is the command of Her Majesty the Queen that we should take away your clothes, and that you should have these in their place.' I answered, 'In God's name!' Then they removed the pad from my head, in which I had sown up rings and many loose diamonds. Abel Cath. felt all over my head to see if anything was concealed in my hair; then she said to the others, 'There is nothing there; we do not require the combs.' Abel Cath. demanded the bracelets and rings, which were a second time taken from me. I took them off and gave them to them, except one small ring which I wore on the last joint of my little finger, and which could not be worth more than a rix-dollar, this I begged to be allowed to keep. 'No,' said the Mistress of the Robes, 'You are to retain nothing.' Abel Cath.

said, 'We are strictly forbidden to leave you the smallest thing; I have been obliged to swear upon my soul to the Queen that I would search you thoroughly, and not leave you the smallest thing; but you shall not lose it; they will all be sealed up and kept for you, for this I swear the Queen has said.' 'Good, good, in God's name!' I answered. She drew off all my clothes. In my under-petticoat I had concealed some ducats under the broad gold lace; there was a small diamond ornament in my silk camisole, in the foot of my stockings there were some Jacobuses', and there were sapphires in my shoes. When she attempted to remove my chemise, I begged to be allowed to retain it. No; she swore upon her soul that she dared not. She stripped me entirely, and the Mistress of the Robes gave Abel Cath. a nod, which she did not at once understand; so the Mistress of the Robes said: 'Do you not remember your orders?' Upon this, Abel Cath. searched my person still more closely, and said to the lady in waiting: 'No, by God! there is nothing there.' I said: 'You act towards me in an unchristian and unbecoming manner.' Abel Cath. answered: 'We are only servants; we must do as we are ordered; we are to search for letters and for nothing else; all the rest will be given back to you; it will be well taken care of.' After they had thus despoiled me, and had put on me the clothes they had brought, the servant of the Mistress of the Robes came in and searched everywhere with Abel Cath., and found every thing that I had concealed. God blinded their eyes so that they did not observe my diamond earrings, nor some ducats which had been sown into leather round one of my knees; I also saved a diamond worth 200 rix-dollars; while on board the ship I had bitten it out of the gold, and thrown the gold in the sea; the stone I had then in my mouth.[62]

The Mistress of the Robes was very severe; they could not search thoroughly enough for her. She laughed at me several times, and could not endure that I sat down, asking whether I could not stand, and whether anything was the matter with me. I answered, 'There is only too much the matter with me, yet I can stand when it is necessary.' (It was no wonder that the Mistress of the Robes could so well execute the order to plunder, for she had frequently accompanied her deceased husband. Colonel Schaffshaussen[E14], in war.) When she had searched every part thoroughly, they took all my clothes, except a taffeta cap for the head, and went away. Then the prison governor came in with his hat on, and said, 'Leonora, why have you concealed your things?' I answered him not a word; for I had made the resolution not to answer him, whatever he might say; his qualities were known to me; I was aware that he was skilful in improving a report, and could twist words in the manner he thought would be acceptable, to the damage of those who were in trouble. He asked again with the same words, adding 'Do you not hear?' I looked at him over my shoulder, and would not allow his disrespect to excite me. The table was then spread, and four dishes were brought in, but I had no appetite, although I had eaten little or nothing the whole day.

An hour afterwards, when the dishes had been carried away, a girl came in named Maren Blocks, and said that she had orders from the Queen to remain the night with me. The prison governor joked a good deal with the before-mentioned Maren, and was very merry, indulging in a good deal of loose talk. At last, when it was nearly ten o'clock, he said good night and closed the two doors of my prison, one of which is cased with copper. When Maren found herself alone with me, she pitied my condition, and informed me that many, whom she mentioned by name (some of whom were known to me) had witnessed my courage with grief and tears, especially the wife of H. Hendrick Bielcke[E12b], who had fainted with weeping. I said, 'The good people have seen me in prosperity; it is no wonder that they deplore the instability of fortune;' and I wished that God might preserve every one of those from misfortune, who had taken my misfortune to heart. I consoled myself with God and a good conscience; I was conscious of nothing wrong, and I asked who she was, and whom she served? She said she was in the Queen's private kitchen, and had the silver in her keeping (from which I concluded that she had probably to clean the silver, which was the case). She said that the Queen could get no one who would be alone with me, for that I was considered evil; it was said also that I was very wise, and knew future events. I answered, 'If I possessed this wisdom, I scarcely think that I should have come in here, for I should then have been able to guard myself against it.' Maren said we might know things and still not be able to guard against them.

She told me also that the Queen had herself spoken with her, and had said to her, 'You are to be this night with Leonora; you need not be afraid, she can now do no evil. With all her witchcraft she is now in prison and has nothing with her; and if she strikes you, I give you leave to strike her back again till the blood comes.' Maren said also, 'The Queen knows well that my mind has been affected by acute illness, and therefore she wished that I should be with you.' So saying she threw her arms round my neck as I was sitting, and caressed me in her manner, saying, 'Strike me, dear heart, strike me!' 'I will not,' she swore, 'strike again.' I was rather alarmed, fearing that the frenzy might come on. She said further that when she saw me coming over the bridge, she felt as if her heart would burst. She informed me with many words how much she loved me, and how the maid of honour, Carisius, who was standing with her in the window, had praised me, and wished to be able to do something for my deliverance, with many such words and speeches. I accepted the unusual caress, as under the circumstances I could not help it, and said that it would be contrary to all justice to offer blows to one who manifested such great affection as she had done, especially to one of her sex;

adding, that I could not think how the Queen had imagined that I struck people, as I had never even given a box on the ears to a waiting-woman. I thanked her for her good opinion of me, and told her that I hoped all would go well, dark as things looked; that I would hold fast to God, who knew my innocence, and that I had done nothing unjustifiable; that I would commend my cause to Him, and I did not doubt that He would rescue me: if not immediately He would do so some day, I was well assured.

Maren began to speak of different things; among others of my sister Elizabeth Augusta[E15], how she had sat in her porch as I had been conveyed past as a prisoner, and had said that if I were guilty there was nothing to say against it, but that if I were innocent they were going too far. I said nothing to this, nor did I answer anything to much other tittle-tattle. She began to speak of her own persecution, which she did with great diffuseness, interspersing it with other stories, so that the conversation (in the present circumstances) was very wearisome to me; I was besides very tired, and worn out with care, so I said I would try to sleep and bid her good-night. My thoughts prevented me from sleeping. I reflected on my present condition, and could in no wise reconcile myself to it, or discover the cause of such a great misfortune. It was easy to perceive that somewhat besides Fux's death was imputed to me, since I was treated with such disrespect.

When I had long lain with my face to the wall, I turned round and perceived that Maren was silently weeping, so I asked her the reason of her tears. She denied at first that she was crying, but afterwards confessed that she had fallen into thinking over this whole affair. It had occurred to her that she had heard so much of Lady Leonora and her splendour, &c., of how the King loved her, and how every one praised her, &c., and now she was immured in this execrable thieves' prison, into which neither sun nor moon shone, and where there was a stench enough to poison a person only coming in and out, far more one who had to remain in it. I thought the cause of her weeping was that she should be shut up with me in the terrible prison; so I consoled her, and said that she would only remain with me until another had been fixed upon, since she was in other service; but that I for my part did not now think of past times, as the present gave me sufficient to attend to; if I were to call to mind the past, I would remember also the misfortunes of great men, emperors, kings, princes, and other high personages, whose magnificence and prosperity had far exceeded mine, and whose misfortunes had been far greater than mine; for they had fallen into the hands of tyrants, who had treated them inhumanly, but this king was a Christian king, and a conscientious man, and better thoughts would occur to him when he had time to reflect, for my adversaries now left him no leisure to do so. When I said this, she wept even more than before, but said nothing, thinking in herself (as she declared to me some days afterwards) that I did not know what an infamous sentence had been pronounced upon my late lord,[E16] and weeping all the more because I trusted the King so firmly. Thus we went on talking through the night.

On the morning of August 9, at six o'clock, the prison governor came in, bade me good morning, and enquired whether we would have some brandy. I answered nothing. He asked Maren whether I was asleep; she replied that she did not know, came up to my bed, and put the same question to me. I thanked her, adding that it was a kind of drink which I had never tasted. The prison governor chattered with Maren, was very merry considering the early hour, told her his dreams, which he undoubtedly invented merely for the sake of talking. He told her, secretly, that she was to come to the Queen, and ordered her to say aloud that she wished to go out a little. He said that he would remain with me in the meanwhile, until she returned, which he did, speaking occasionally to me, and asking me whether I wished for anything? whether I had slept? whether Maren had watched well? But he got no answer, so that the time seemed very long to him. He went out towards the stairs and came back again, sang a morning psalm, screamed out sometimes to one, and sometimes to another, though he knew they were not there.

There was a man named Jon who helped to bring up the meals with Rasmus the tower warder, and to him he called more than forty times and that in a singing tone, changing his key from high to low, and screaming occasionally as loud as he could, and answering himself 'Father, he is not here! by God, he is not here!' then laughing at himself; and then he began calling again either for Jon or for Rasmus, so that it seemed to me that he had been tasting the brandy. About eight o'clock Maren came back, and said that at noon two women would come to relieve her. After some conversation between the prison governor and Maren, he went out and shut the doors. Maren told me how the Queen had sent for her, and asked her what I was doing, and that she answered that I was lying down quietly, and not saying anything. The Queen had asked whether I wept much. Maren replied, 'Yes indeed, she weeps silently.' 'For,' continued Maren, 'if I had said that you did not weep, the Queen would have thought that you had not yet enough to weep for.' Maren warned me that one of the two women who were to watch me was the wife of the King's shoemaker, a German, who was very much liked by the Queen. Her Majesty had employed her to attend Uldrich Christian Gyldenlöwe in the severe and raving illness of which he died, and this woman had much influence with the Queen. With regard to the other woman, Maren had no idea who she might be, but the last-mentioned had spoken with the Queen in Maren's presence, and had said that she did not trust herself to be alone with me. The women did not come before four o'clock in the afternoon. The prison governor accompanied them, and unlocked the door for them. The first was the wife of the shoemaker, a woman named Anna, who generally would not suffer anybody else to speak. The other was the wife of the King's groom, a woman named Catharina, also a German. After greeting me, Anna said that her Majesty the Queen had ordered them to pass a day or two with me and wait upon me. 'In God's name,' I answered.

Anna, who was very officious, asked me, 'Does my lady wish for anything? She will please only say so, and I will solicit it from the Queen.' I thanked her, and said that I should like to have some of my clothes, such as two night-jackets, one lined with silk and another braided with white, my stomacher, something for my head, and above all my bone box of perfume, which I much needed. She said she would at once arrange this, which she did, for she went immediately and proffered my request. The things were all delivered to me by the prison governor at six o'clock, except my box of perfume, which had been lost, and in its place they sent me a tin box with a very bad kind of perfume. When the time arrived for the evening meal, Catharina spread a stool by the side of my bed, but I had no desire to eat. I asked for a lemon with sugar, and they gave it me. The prison governor sat down at the table with the two women, and did the part of jester, so much so that no one could have said that they were in a house of mourning, but rather in one of festivity. I inwardly prayed to God for strength and patience, that I might not forget myself. God heard my prayer, praised be His name. When the prison governor was tired of the idle talking and laughing, he bade good night after ten o'clock, and told the women to knock if they wanted anything, as the tower warder was just underneath. After he had locked both the doors, I got up, and Catharina made my bed. Anna had brought a prayer-book with her, from which I read the evening prayer, and other prayers for them; then I laid down and bid them good night. They laid on a settle-bed which had been brought in for them. I slumbered from time to time, but only for short intervals.

About six o'clock on the morning of August 10 the prison governor opened the door, to the great delight of the women, who were sincerely longing for him, especially Catharina, who was very stout; she could not endure the oppressive atmosphere, and was ill almost the whole night. When the prison governor, after greeting them, had inquired how it fared with them, and whether they were still alive, he offered them brandy, which they readily accepted. When it was seven o'clock, they requested to go home, which they did, but they first reported to the Queen all that had happened during the half-day and the night. The prison governor remained with me.

When it was near nine o'clock, he brought in a chair without saying anything. I perceived from this that visitors were coming, and I was not wrong; for immediately afterwards there entered Count Rantzow, prime minister, chancellor H. Peter Retz, Christoffer Gabel, the chancellor of the exchequer, and secretary Erick Krag, who all shook hands with me and seated themselves by my bed. Krag, who had paper, pen and ink with him, seated himself at the table. Count Rantzow whispered something to the chancellor. The chancellor upon this began to address me as on the previous occasion, saying that his Majesty the King had great cause for his treatment of me. 'His Majesty,' he went on to say, 'entertains suspicion with regard to you, and that not without reason.' I inquired in what the suspicion consisted. The chancellor said, 'Your husband has offered the kingdom of Denmark to a foreign lord.' I inquired if the kingdom of Denmark belonged to my husband, that he could thus offer it, and as no one answered, I continued and said, 'Good gentlemen, you all know my lord; you know that he has been esteemed as a man of understanding, and I can assure you that when I took leave of him he was in perfect possession of his senses. Now it is easy to perceive that no sensible man would offer that which was not in his own power, and which he had no right to dispose of. He is holding no post, he has neither power nor authority; how should he, therefore, be so foolish as to make such an offer, and what lord would accept it?'

Count Rantzow said: 'Nevertheless it is so, madame; he has offered Denmark to a foreign potentate; you know it well.' I answered, 'God is my witness that I know of no such thing.' 'Yes,' said Count Rantzow, 'your husband concealed nothing from you, and therefore you must know it.' I replied, 'My husband certainly never concealed from me anything that concerned us both. I never troubled myself in former days with that which related to his office; but that which affected us both he never concealed from me, so that I am sure, had he entertained any such design, he would not have held it a secret from me. And I can say, with truth, that I am not the least aware of it.' Count Rantzow said: 'Madame, confess it while the King still asks you to do so.'

I answered, 'If I knew it I would gladly say so; but as truly as God lives I do not know it, and as truly am I unable to believe that my husband would have acted so foolishly, for he is a sick man. He urged me to go to England in order to demand the money that had been lent; I undertook the journey, unwillingly, chiefly because he was so very weak. He could not go up a few steps of the stairs without resting to get his breath; how should he, then, undertake a work of such labour? I can say with truth that he is not eight days without an attack, sometimes of one kind sometimes of another.' Count Rantzow again whispered with the chancellor, and the chancellor continued: 'Madame, say without compulsion how the matter stands, and who is privy to it; say it now, while you are asked freely to do so. His Majesty is an absolute Sovereign; he is not fettered by law; he can do as he will; say it.' I answered: 'I know well that his Majesty is an absolute Sovereign, and I know also, that he is a

Christian and a conscientious man; therefore, his Majesty will do nothing but what he can justify before God in heaven. See, here I am! You can do with me what you will; that which I do not know I cannot say.'

Count Rantzow began again to bring forward the Maréchal de Birron, and made a long speech about it. To this I at length replied, that the Maréchal de Birron in nowise concerned me; that I had no answer to make on the matter, and that it seemed to me that it was not a case in point. Count Rantzow asked me why, when I was demanded with whom I had corresponded in the kingdom, I had not said that I had written to him and to the treasurer Gabel. To this I replied that I thought those who asked me knew it well, so that it was not necessary for me to mention it; I had only said that of which they probably did not know. Count Rantzow again whispered to the chancellor, and the chancellor said: 'In a letter to Lady Elsse Passberg you have written respecting another state of things in Denmark,' (as he said this, he looked at Count Rantzow and asked if it was not so, or how it was); 'what did you mean by that, madame?' I replied that I could not recollect what cause her letter had given me to answer it in this way; what came before or what followed, would, without a doubt, explain my meaning; if I might see the letter, it would prove at once that I had written nothing which I could not justify.

Nothing more was said with regard to it. Count Rantzow asked me what foreign ministers had been with my lord in Bruges. 'None,' I answered, 'that I am aware of.' He asked further whether any Holstein noblemen had been with him. I answered, 'I do not know.' Then he enumerated every Prince in Germany, from the Emperor to the Prince of Holstein, and enquired respecting each separately whether any of their Ministers had been with my husband. I gave the same answer as before to each question, that I was not aware that any one of them had been with him. Then he said, 'Now, madame, confess! I beg you; remember Maréchal de Birron! you will not be asked again.' I was somewhat tired of hearing Birron mentioned so often, and I answered rather hastily: 'I do not care about the Maréchal de Birron; I cannot tell what I do not know anything about.'

Secretary Krag had written somewhat hurriedly it seemed, for when at my desire he read aloud what he had written, the answers did not accord with the questions; this probably partly arose from hurry, and partly from malice, for he was not amicably inclined towards my late lord. I protested against this when he read the minutes. The chancellor agreed with me in every item, so that Krag was obliged to re-write it. After this they got up and took their leave. I requested to beg His Majesty the King to be gracious to me, and not to believe what he had been informed with regard to my husband. I could not imagine they would find that he had ever deviated from his duty. 'Yes,' answered Count Rantzow, 'if you will confess, madame, and tell us who is concerned in this business and the details of it, you might perhaps find him a gracious lord and king.' I protested by the living God that I knew nothing of it; I knew of nothing of the kind, much less of accomplices. With this they went away, after having spent nearly three hours with me, and then the prison governor and the women entered. They spread the table and brought up the meal, but I took nothing but a draught of beer. The prison governor sat down to table with the women. If he had been merry before, he was still more so now, and he told one indecent story after another.

When they had had enough of feasting and talking he went away and locked the door; he came as usual again about four o'clock in the afternoon, and let the women go out, staying with me until they returned, which generally was not for two hours. When the women were alone with me, Anna told Catharina of her grief for her first husband, and nothing else was talked of. I behaved as if I were asleep, and I did the same when the prison governor was alone with me, and he then passed the time in singing and humming. The evening meal was also very merry for the women, for the prison governor amused them by telling them of his second marriage; how he had wooed without knowing whom, and that he did not know it until the betrothal. The story was as ludicrous as it was diffuse. I noticed that it lasted an hour and a quarter.

When he had said good night, Anna sat down on my bed and began to talk to Catharina, and said, 'Was it not a horrible story of that treacherous design to murder the King and Queen and the whole royal family?' Catharina answered, 'Thank God the King and Queen and the whole family are still alive!' 'Yes,' said Anna, 'it was no merit of the traitors, though, that they are so; it was too quickly discovered; the King knew it three months before he would reveal it to the Queen. He went about sorrowfully, pondering over it, unable quite to believe it; afterwards, when he was quite certain of it, he told the Queen; then the body-guard were doubled, as you know.' Catherina enquired how they had learnt it. Anna answered, 'That God knows; it is kept so secret that no one is allowed as much as to ask from whom it came.' I could not help putting in a word; it seemed to me a pity that they could not find out the informer, and it was remarkable that no one ventured to confess having given the information. Catherina said, 'I wonder whether it is really true?' 'What do you mean?' answered Anna; 'would the King do as he is doing without knowing for certain that it is true? How can you talk so?' I regarded this conversation as designed to draw some words from me, so I answered but little, only saying that until now I had seen nothing which gave credibility to the report, and that therefore I felt myself at liberty not to believe it until I saw certain proof of it. Anna adhered to her statement, wondered that there could be such evil people as could wish to murder the good King, and was very diffuse on the matter.

[E17] She could be at no loss for material, for she always began again from the beginning; but at last she had to stop, since she spoke alone and was not interrupted either by Catharina or by me.

I got up and requested to have my bed made, which Catharina always did. Anna attended to the light during the night, for she was more watchful than Catharina. I read aloud to them from Anna's book, commended myself to God, and laid down to sleep. But my sleep was light, the promenades of the rats woke me, and there were great numbers of them. Hunger made them bold; they ate the candle as it stood burning. Catharina, moreover, was very uncomfortable all night, so that this also prevented my sleeping. Early on the morning of August 11 the prison governor came as usual with his brandy attentions, although they had a whole bottle with them. Catharina complained a good deal, and said she could not endure the oppressive air; that when she came in at the door it seemed as if it would stifle her; if she were to remain there a week she was certain that she would be carried out dead. The prison governor laughed at this.

The women went away, and he remained with me. He presented me Major-General von Anfeldt's compliments, and a message from him, that I 'should be of good courage; all would now soon be well.' I made no reply. He enquired how I was, and whether I had slept a little; and answered himself, 'I fancy not much.' He asked whether I would have anything, again answering himself, 'No, I do not think you wish for anything.' Upon this he walked up and down, humming to himself; then he came to my bedside and said: 'Oh, the dear King! he is indeed a kind master! Be at peace; he is a gracious sovereign, and has always held you in esteem. You are a woman, a weak instrument. Poor women are soon led away. No one likes to harm them, when they confess the truth. The dear Queen, she is indeed a dear Queen! She is not angry with you. I am sure if she knew the truth from you, she would herself pray for you. Listen! if you will write to the Queen and tell her all about the matter, and keep nothing back, I will bring you pen, ink, and paper. I have no wish, on my soul! to read it. No, God take me if I will look at it; and that you may be sure of this, I will give you wax that you may seal it. But I imagine you have probably no seal?' As I answered him not a word, he seized my hand and shook it rather strongly, saying, 'Do you not hear? Are you asleep?' I raised my head threateningly; I should like to have given him a box on the ears, and I turned round to the wall.

He was angry that his design had failed, and he went on grumbling to himself for more than an hour. I could not understand a word beyond, 'Yes, yes! you will not speak.' Then he muttered somewhat between his teeth: 'You will not answer; well, well, they will teach you. Yes, by God! hum, hum, hum.' He continued thus until the tower warder, Rasmus, came and whispered something to him; then he went out. It seemed to me that there was someone speaking with him, and so far as I could perceive it must have been someone who asked him if the ink and paper should be brought up, for he answered, 'No, it is not necessary; she will not.' The other said, 'Softly, softly!' The prison governor, however, could not well speak softly, and I heard him say, 'She cannot hear that; she is in bed.' When he came in again he went on muttering to himself, and stamped because I would not answer; he meant it kindly; the Queen was not so angry as I imagined. He went on speaking half aloud; he wished the women would come; he did nothing else but beg Rasmus to look for them.

Soon after Rasmus came and said that they were now going up the King's Stairs. Still almost an hour passed before they came in and released him. When they had their dinner (my own meal consisted of some slices of lemon with sugar) the prison governor was not nearly so merry as he was wont to be, though he chattered of various things that had occurred in former times, while he was a quarter-master. He also retired sooner than was his custom. The women, who remained, talked of indifferent matters. I also now and then put in a word, and asked them after their husbands and children. Anna read some prayers and hymns from her book, and thus the day passed till four o'clock, when the prison governor let them out. He had brought a book with him, which he read in a tolerably low tone, while he kept watch by me. I was well pleased at this, as it gave me rest.

At the evening meal the prison governor began amongst other conversation to tell the women that a prisoner had been brought here who was a Frenchman; he could not remember his name; he sat cogitating upon the name just as if he could not rightly hit upon it. Carl or Char, he did not know what he was called, but he had been formerly several years in Denmark. Anna enquired what sort of a man he was. He replied that he was a man who was to be made to sing,[63] but he did not know for a certainty whether he was here or not. (There was nothing in all this.) He only said this in order to get an opportunity of asking me, or to perceive whether it troubled me.

He had undoubtedly been ordered to do this; for when he was gone Anna began a conversation with Catharina upon this same Carl, and at last asked me whether we had had a Frenchman in our employ. I replied that we had had more than one. She enquired further whether there was one among them named Carl, who had long been in our service. 'We had a servant,' I answered, 'a Frenchman named Charle; he had been with us a long time.' 'Yes, yes,' she said, 'it is he. But I do not think he has arrived here yet; they are looking for him.' I said, 'Then he is easy to find, he was at Bruges when I left that town.' Anna said she fancied he had been in England with me, and she added, 'That fellow knows a good deal if they get him.' I answered, 'Then it were to be wished that they had him for the sake of his information.' When she perceived that I troubled myself no further about him she let the conversation drop, and spoke of my sister Elizabeth Augusta, saying that she passed her every day. She was standing in her gateway or sitting in the porch, and that she greeted her, but never uttered a word of enquiry after her sister, though she knew well that she was waiting on me in the Tower. I said I thought my sister did not know what would be the best for her to do. 'I cannot see,' said Anna, 'that she is depressed.' I expressed my opinion that the less we grieved over things the better. Other trifles were afterwards talked of, and I concluded the day with reading, commended myself to the care of Jesus, and slept tolerably well through the night.

August 12 passed without anything in particular occurring, only that Anna tried to trouble me by saying that a chamber next to us was being put in order, for whom she did not know; they were of course expecting someone in it. I could myself hear the masons at work. On the same day Catharina said that she had known me in prosperity, and blessed me a thousand times for the kindness I had shown her. I did not remember having ever seen her. She said she had been employed in the storeroom in the service of the Princess Magdalena Sybille, and that when I had visited the Princess, and had slept in the Castle, I had sent a good round present for those in the storeroom, and that she had had a share in it, and that this she now remembered with gratitude. Anna was not pleased with the conversation, and she interrupted it three times; Catharina, however, did not answer her, but adhered to the subject till she had finished. The prison governor was not in good humour on this day also, so that neither at dinner nor at supper were any indecent stories related.

On August 13, after the women had been into the town and had returned, the prison governor opened the door at about nine o'clock, and whispered something to them. He then brought in another small seat; from this I perceived that I was to be visited by one more than on the previous occasion. At about ten o'clock Count Rantzow, General Skack, Chancellor Retz, Treasurer Gabel, and Secretary Krag entered. They all saluted me with politeness; the four first seated themselves on low seats by my bedside, and Krag placed himself with his writing materials at the table. The Chancellor was spokesman, and said, 'His royal Majesty, my gracious Sovereign and hereditary King, sends you word, madame, that his Majesty has great cause for all that he is doing, and that he entertains suspicions with regard to you that you are an accomplice in the treason designed by your husband; and his royal Majesty had hoped that you would confess without compulsion who have participated in it, and the real truth about it.'

When the Chancellor ceased speaking, I replied that I was not aware that I had
done anything which could render me suspected; and I called God to witness
that I knew of no treason, and therefore I could mention no names. Count
Rantzow said, 'Your husband has not concealed it from you, hence you know
it well.' I replied, 'Had my husband entertained so evil a design, I believe
surely he would have told me; but I can swear with a good conscience, before
God in Heaven, that I never heard him speak of anything of the kind. Yes, I can
truly say he never wished evil to the King in my hearing, and therefore I fully
believe that this has been falsely invented by his enemies.' Count Rantzow and
the Chancellor bent their heads together across to the General, and whispered
with each other for some time. At length the Chancellor asked me whether, if
my husband were found guilty, I would take part in his condemnation. This
was a remarkable question, so I reflected a little, and said, 'If I may know on
what grounds he is accused, I will answer to it so far as I know, and so much as
I can.' The Chancellor said, 'Consider well whether you will.' I replied as
before, that I would answer for him as to all that I knew, if I were informed of
what he was accused. Count Rantzow whispered with Krag, and Krag went
out, but returned immediately.

Soon afterward some one (whom I do not know) came from the Chancellor's
office, bringing with him some large papers. Count Rantzow and the
Chancellor whispered again. Then the Chancellor said, 'There is nothing
further to do now than to let you know what sort of a husband you have, and
to let you hear his sentence.' Count Rantzow ordered the man who had brought
in the papers to read them aloud. The first paper read was to the effect that
Corfitz, formerly Count of Ulfeldt, had offered the kingdom of Denmark to a
foreign sovereign, and had told the same sovereign that he had ecclesiastical
and lay magnates on his side, so that it was easy for him to procure the crown
of Denmark for the before-mentioned sovereign.

A paper was then read which was the defence of the clergy, in which they
protested that Corfitz, Count of Ulfeldt, had never had any communication
with any of them; that he had at no time shown himself a friend of the clergy,
and had far less offered them participation in his evil design. They assured his
royal Majesty of their fidelity and subjection, &c. Next, a paper was read,
written by the Burgomaster and council in Copenhagen, nearly similar in
purport, that they had had no correspondence with Count Corfitz Ulfeldt, and
equally assuring his royal Majesty of their humble fidelity. Next followed the
reading of the unprecedented and illegal sentence which, without a hearing,
had been passed on my lord. This was as unexpected and grievous as it was
disgraceful, and unjustifiable before God and all right-loving men. No
documents were brought forward upon which the sentence had been given.
There was nothing said about prosecution or defence; there was no other

foundation but mere words; that he had been found guilty of having offered the crown of Denmark to a foreign sovereign, and had told him that he had on his side ecclesiastical and lay magnates, who had shown by their signed protestations that this was not the case, for which reason he had been condemned as a criminal.

When the sentence with all the names subjoined to it had been read, the reader brought it to me, and placed it before me on the bed. Everyone can easily imagine how I felt; but few or none can conceive how it was that I was not stifled by the unexpected misery, and did not lose my sense and reason. I could not utter a word for weeping. Then a prayer was read aloud which had been pronounced from the pulpit, in which Corfitz was anathematised, and God was prayed not to allow his gray hair to go to the grave in peace. But God, who is just, did not listen to the impious prayer of the unrighteous, praised be His name for ever.

When all had been read, I bemoaned with sighs and sorrowful tears that I had ever lived to see this sad day, and I begged them, for Jesus' sake, that they would allow me to see on what the hard judgment was based. Count Rantzow answered, 'You can well imagine, madame, that there are documents upon which we have acted: some of your friends are in the council.' 'May God better it!' I said. 'I beg you, for God's sake, to let me see the documents. Les apparences sont bien souvent trompeuses. What had not my husband to suffer from that Swede in Skaane, during that long imprisonment, because he was suspected of having corresponded with his Majesty, the King of Denmark, and with his Majesty's ministers? Now, no one knows better than his Majesty, and you my good lords, how innocently he suffered at that time, and so this also may be apparently credible, and yet may not be so in truth. Might I not see the documents?' To this no answer was given. I continued and said, 'How is it possible that a man who must himself perceive that death is at hand should undertake such a work, and be so led away from the path of duty, when he did not do so at a time when he acknowledged no master, and when such great promises were made him by the Prince of Holstein, as the Prince's letters show, which are now in his Majesty's hands.' Count Rantzow interrupted me and said, 'We did not find those letters.' 'God knows,' I replied, 'they were there; of that I am certain.' I said also, 'At that time he might have done something to gratify a foreign sovereign; at that time he had power and physical vigour, and almost the entire government was in his hands; but he never looked to his own advantage, but pawned his own property to hasten the King's coronation, so that no impediment might come between.[64] This is his reward! Good gentlemen, take an example of me, you who have seen me in prosperity, and have compassion on me. Pray his royal Majesty to be mild, and not to proceed to such severity.'

The Chancellor and Treasurer were moved by this, so that the tears came into their eyes. Count Rantzow said to the General and the Chancellor, 'I think it is a fortnight ago since the sentence was published?' The Chancellor answered, 'It is seventeen days ago.'[E18] I said, 'At that time I was still in England, and now I am asked for information on the matter! Oh, consider this, for God's sake! and that there was no one present to speak on my husband's behalf.' Count Rantzow enquired whether I wished to appeal against it? I replied, 'How am I to appeal against a judicial decree? I only beg for Jesus' sake that what I say may be considered, and that I may have the satisfaction of seeing the documents upon which the sentence is based.'

Count Rantzow answered as before, that there were documents, and that some of my friends had sat in the council, and added that all had been agreed, and that not one had had anything to say against it. I dared not say what I thought. I knew well how matters are done in such absolute governments: there is no such thing as opposition, they merely say, 'Sign, the King wishes it; and ask not wherefore, or the same condemnation awaits thee.'[65] I was silent, and bewailed my unhappiness, which was irremediable. When Krag read aloud the minutes he had written, namely, that when I was asked whether I would participate in my husband's sentence, I had answered that I would consider of it. I asked, 'How was that?' The Chancellor immediately replied, 'No, she did not say so, but she requested to know the accusation brought against her husband.' I repeated my words again,[66] I know not whether Krag wrote them or not; for a great part of that which I said was not written. Krag yielded too much to his feelings in the matter, and would gladly have made bad worse. He is now gone where no false writings avail; God took him away suddenly in an unclean place, and called him to judgment without warning. And Count Rantzow, who was the principal mover and inventor of that illegal sentence, the like of which was never known in Denmark, did not live to see his desire fulfilled in the execution of a wooden image.[E19] When this was done, they rose and shook hands with me. This painful visit lasted more than four hours.

They went away, leaving me full of anxiety, sighing and weeping—a sad and miserable captive woman, forsaken by all; without help, exposed to power and violence, fearing every moment that her husband might fall into their hands, and that they might vent their malice on him. God performed on that day a great miracle, by manifesting His power in my weakness, preserving my brain from bewilderment, and my tongue from overflowing with impatience. Praised be God a thousand times! I will sing Thy praise, so long as my tongue can move, for Thou wast at this time and at all times my defence, my rock, and my shield!

When the gentlemen were gone away, the prison governor came and the women, and a stool was spread by the side of my bed. The prison governor said to me, 'Eat, Leonora; will you not eat?' As he said this, he threw a knife to me on the bed. I took up the knife with angry mind, and threw it on the ground. He picked up the knife, saying, 'You are probably not hungry? No, no! you have had a breakfast to-day which has satisfied you, have you not? Is it not so?' Well, well, come dear little women (addressing the two women), let us eat something! You must be hungry, judging from my own stomach.' When they had sat down to table, he began immediately to cram himself, letting it fall as if inadvertently from his mouth, and making so many jokes that it was sad to see how the old man could not conceal his joy at my unhappiness.

When the meal was finished, and the prison governor had gone away, Anna sat down by my bed and began to speak of the sorrow and affliction which we endure in this world, and of the joy and delights of heaven; how the pain that we suffer here is but small compared with eternal blessedness and joy, wherefore we should not regard suffering, but should rather think of dying with a good conscience, keeping it unsullied by confessing everything that troubles us, for there is no other way. 'God grant,' she added, 'that no one may torment himself for another's sake.' After having repeated this remark several times, she said to me, 'Is it not true, my lady?' 'Yes, certainly it is true,' I replied; 'you speak in a Christian manner, and according to the scriptures.' 'Why will you, then,' she went on to say, 'let yourself be tormented for others, and not say what you know of them?' I asked whom she meant. She answered, 'I do not know them.' I replied, 'Nor do I.' She continued in the same strain, however, saying that she would not suffer and be tormented for the sake of others, whoever they might be; if they were guilty they must suffer; she would not suffer for them; a woman was easily led away, but happiness was more than all kindred and friends.

As she seemed unable to cease chattering, I wished to divert her a little, so I asked whether she were a clergyman's daughter; and since she had before told me of her parentage, she resented this question all the more, and was thoroughly angry; saying, 'If I am not a clergyman's daughter, I am the daughter of a good honest citizen, and not one of the least. In my time, when I was still unmarried, I never thought that I should marry a shoemaker.' I said, 'But your first husband, too, was also a shoemaker.' 'That is true,' she replied, 'but this marriage came about in a very foolish manner,' and she began to narrate a whole history of the matter, so that I was left in peace. Catharina paced up and down, and when Anna was silent for a little, she said, with folded hands, 'O God, Thou who art almighty, and canst do everything, preserve this man for whom they are seeking, and never let him fall into the hands of his enemies. Oh God, hear me!' Anna said angrily to her, 'Catharina, do you know what you are saying? How can you speak so?' Catharina answered, 'Yes, I know well what I am saying. God preserve him, and let him never fall into the hands of his enemies. Jesus, be Thou his guide!' She uttered these words with abundant tears. Anna said, 'I think that woman is not in her senses.' Catharina's kind wish increased my tears, and I said, 'Catharina shows that she is a true Christian, and sympathises with me; God reward her, and hear her and me!' Upon this Anna was silent, and has not been so talkative ever since. O God, Thou who art a recompenser of all that is good, remember this in favour of Catharina, and as Thou heardest her at that time, hear her prayer in future, whatever may be her request! And you, my dear children, know that if ever fortune so ordains it that you can be of any service either to her or her only son, you are bound to render it for my sake; for she was a comfort to me in my greatest need, and often took an opportunity to say a word which she thought would alleviate my sorrow.

The prison governor came as usual, about four o'clock, and let the women out, seating himself on the bench and placing the high stool with the candle in front of him. He had brought a book with him, and read aloud prayers for a happy end, prayers for the hour of death, and prayers for one suffering temporal punishment for his misdeeds. He did not forget a prayer for one who is to be burnt; in reading this he sighed, so religious had he grown in the short time. When he had read all the prayers, he got up and walked up and down, singing funeral hymns; when he knew no more, he began again with the first, till the women released him. Catharina complained that her son had been ill, and was greatly grieved about it. I entered into her sorrow, and said that she ought to mention her son's illness to the Queen, and then another would probably be appointed in her place; and I begged her to compose herself, as the child would probably be better again. During the evening meal the prison governor was very merry, and related all sorts of coarse stories. When he was gone, Anna read the evening prayer. I felt very ill during this night, and often turned about in bed; there was a needle in the bed, with which I scratched myself; I got it out, and still have it.[67]

On August 14, when the prison governor opened the door early, the women told him that I had been very ill in the night. 'Well, well,' he answered, 'it will soon be better.' And when the women were ready to go to the Queen (which they were always obliged to do), Anna said to Catharina, outside the door, 'What shall we say to the Queen?' Catharina answered: 'What shall we say, but that she is silent and will say nothing!' 'You know very well that the Queen is displeased at it.' 'Nevertheless, we cannot tell a lie;' answered Catharina; 'she says nothing at all, so it would be a sin.'[68] Catharina came back to the mid-day meal, and said that the Queen had promised to appoint another in her stead; in the afternoon, she managed secretly to say a word to me about the next chamber, which she imagined was being put in readiness for me and for no one else; she bid me good night, and promised to remember me constantly in her prayers. I thanked her for her good services, and for her kind feeling towards me.

About four o'clock the prison governor let her and Anna out. He sang one hymn after another, went to the stairs, and the time appeared long to him, till six o'clock, when Anna returned with Maren Blocks. At the evening meal the prison governor again told stories of his marriage, undoubtedly for the sake of amusing Maren. Anna left me alone, and I lay quiet in silence. Maren could not find an opportunity of speaking with me the whole evening, on account of Anna. Nothing particular happened on August 15 and 16.

When the prison governor let out Anna in the morning and afternoon, Maren Blocks remained with me, and the prison governor went his own way and locked the door, so that Maren had opportunity of talking with me alone. She told me different things; among others, that the Queen had given my clothes to the three women who had undressed me, that they might distribute them amongst themselves. She asked me whether I wished to send a message to my sister Elizabeth. I thanked her, but said that I had nothing good to tell her. I asked Maren for needles and thread, in order to test her. She replied she would gladly procure them for me if she dared, but that it would risk her whole well-being if the Queen should know it; for she had so strictly forbidden that anyone should give me either pins or needles. I inquired 'For what reason?' 'For this reason,' she replied, 'that you may not kill yourself.' I assured her that God had enlightened me better than that I should be my own murderer. I felt that my cross came from the hand of the Lord, that He was chastising me as His child; He would also help me to bear it; I trusted in Him to do so. 'Then I hope, dear heart,' said Maren, 'that you will not kill yourself; then you shall have needles and thread; but what will you sew?' I alleged that I wished to sew some buttons on my white night-dress, and I tore off a pair, in order to show her afterwards that I had sewn them on.

Now it happened that I had sewn up some ducats in a piece of linen round my knee; these I had kept, as I pulled off the stockings myself when they undressed me, and Anna had at my desire given me a rag, as I pretended that I had hurt my leg. I sewed this rag over the leather. They all imagined that I had some secret malady, for I lay in the linen petticoat they had given me, and went to bed in my stockings. Maren imagined that I had an issue on one leg, and she confided to me that a girl at the court, whom she mentioned by name, and who was her very good friend, had an issue of which no one knew but herself, not even the woman who made her bed. I thought to myself, you keep your friend's secret well; I did not, however, make her any wiser, but let her believe in this case whatever she would. I was very weak on those two days,

and as I took nothing more than lemon and beer, my stomach became
thoroughly debilitated and refused to retain food. When Maren told the prison
governor of this, he answered, 'All right, her heart is thus getting rid of its
evil.' Anna was no longer so officious, but the prison governor was as merry
as ever.

On August 17 the prison governor did not open the door before eight o'clock,
and Anna asked him how it was that he had slept so long. He joked a little;
presently he drew her to the door and whispered with her. He went out and in,
and Anna said so loudly to Maren, that I could hear it (although she spoke as
if she were whispering), 'I am so frightened that my whole body trembles,
although it does not concern me. Jesus keep me! I wish I were down below!'
Maren looked sad, but she neither answered nor spoke a word. Maren came
softly up to my bed and said, 'I am sure some one is coming to you.' I
answered, 'Let him come, in God's name.' Presently I heard a running up and
down stairs, and also overhead, for the Commissioners came always through
the apartments, in order not to cross the square. My doors were closed again.
Each time that some one ran by on the stairs, Anna shuddered and said, 'I quite
tremble.'

This traffic lasted till about eleven. When the prison governor opened the door, he said to me, 'Leonora, you are to get up and go to the gentlemen.' God knows that I could hardly walk, and Anna frightened me by saying to Maren, 'Oh! the poor creature!' Maren's hands trembled when she put on my slippers. I could not imagine anything else than that I was to be tortured, and I consoled myself with thinking that my pain could not last long, for my body was so weary that it seemed as if God might at any moment take me away. When Maren fastened the apron over my long dress, I said: 'They are indeed sinning heavily against me; may God give me strength.' The prison governor hurried me, and when I was ready, he took me by the arm and led me. I would gladly have been free of his help, but I could not walk alone. He conducted me up to the next story, and there sat Count Rantzow, Skack, Retz, Gabel, and Krag, round the table.

They all rose when I entered, and I made them a reverence as well as I was able. A small low seat had been placed for me in the middle, in front of the table. The Chancellor asked me whether I had not had more letters than those taken from me in England. I answered that I had not had more; that all my letters had been then taken from me. He asked further, whether I had at that time destroyed any letters. 'Yes,' I answered, 'one I tore in two, and threw it in a closet.' 'Why did you do so?' enquired Count Rantzow. 'Because' I replied, 'there were cyphers in it; and although they were of no importance, I feared, notwithstanding, that they might excite suspicion.' Count Rantzow said: 'Supposing the pieces were still forthcoming?' 'That were to be wished,' I replied, 'for then it could be seen that there was nothing suspicious in it, and it vexed me afterwards that I had torn it in two.' Upon this the Chancellor drew forth a sheet of paper upon which, here and there, pieces of this very letter were pasted, and handed it to Krag, who gave it to me. Count Rantzow asked me if it were not my husband's handwriting. I answered that it was. He said: 'A part of the pieces which you tore in two have been found, and a part are lost. All that has been found has been collected and copied.' He then asked the Chancellor for the copy, who gave it to Count Rantzow, and he handed it to me, saying, 'See there what is wanting, and tell us what it is that is missing.' I took it, and looked over it and said: 'In some places, where there are not too many words missing, I think I can guess what is lost, but where a whole sentence is wanting, I cannot know.'

Most of the letter had been collected without loss of intervening pieces, and it all consisted of mirth and jest. He was telling me that he had heard from Denmark that the Electoral Prince of Saxony was to be betrothed with the Princess of Denmark;[E20] and he joked, saying that they would grease their throats and puff out their cheeks in order that with good grace and voice they might duly trumpet forth each their own titles, and more of the same kind, all in high colouring. He described the way in which Count Rantzow contrived to let people know his titles; when he had a dinner-party, there was a man employed to read aloud his titles to the guests, asking first each separately, whether he knew his titles; if there was anyone who did not know them, the secretary must forthwith come and read them aloud.

It seemed that Count Rantzow referred all this to himself, for he asked me what my husband meant by it. I replied that I did not know that he meant anything but what he had written; he meant undoubtedly those who did such things. The Chancellor averted his face from Count Rantzow, and his lips smiled a little; Gabel also did the same. Among other things there were some remarks about the Electoral Prince, that he probably cherished the hope of inheriting the Crown of Denmark; 'mais j'espère … cela ne se fera point.' Count Rantzow enquired as to the words which were wanting. I said, if I remembered rightly, the words had been, 'qu'en 300 ans.' He enquired further as to the expressions lacking here and there, some of which I could not remember exactly, though they were of no importance. I expressed my opinion that they could easily gather what was wanting from the preceding and following words; it was sufficiently evident that all was jest, and this was apparent also to Gabel, who said, 'Ce n'est que raillerie.' But Count Rantzow and the General would not allow it to pass as jest.

Skack said: 'One often means something else under the cloak of jest, and names are used when others are intended.' For in the letter there was something said about drinking out; there was also an allusion made to the manners of the Swiss at table, and all the titles of the canton nobles were enumerated, from which Skack thought that the names of the cities might have another signification. I did not answer Skack; but as Count Rantzow continued to urge me to say what my husband had meant by it, I replied that I could not know whether he had had another meaning than that which was written. Skack shook his head and thought he had, so I said: 'I know no country where the same customs are in vogue at meals as in Switzerland; if there are other places where the same customs prevail, he may perhaps have meant these also, for he is only speaking of drinking.'

Gabel said again, 'It is only jest.' The cyphers, for the sake of which I had torn the letter in two, were fortunately complete, and nothing was missing. Count Rantzow gave me a sheet of paper, to which pieces of my lord's letter were pasted, and asked me what the cyphers meant. I replied, 'I have not the key, and cannot solve them out of my head.' He expressed his opinion that I could do it. I said I could not. 'Well, they have been read,' he said, 'and we know what they signify.' 'All the better,' I answered. Upon this, he gave me the interpretation to read, and the purport of it was that our son had written from Rome, asking for money, which was growing short, for the young nobleman was not at home. I gave the paper back to Count Rantzow without saying anything. Count Rantzow requested the Treasurer that he should read the letter, and Rantzow began again with his questions wherever anything was wanting, requesting that I should say what it was. I gave him the same answer as before; but when in one passage, where some words were missing, he pressed me hard to say them, and it was evident from the context that they were ironical (since an ironical word was left written), I said: 'You can add as much of the same kind as pleases you, if one is not enough; I do not know them.' Gabel again said, 'Ce n'est que raillerie.'[E21]

No further questions were then made respecting the letters; but Count Rantzow enquired as to my jewels, and asked where the large diamond was which my husband had received in France.[E22] I replied that it had long been sold. He further asked where my large drop pearls where, which I had worn as a feather on my hat, and where my large pearl head-ornament was. 'All these,' I replied, 'have long been sold.' He asked further whether I had then no more jewels. I answered, 'I have none now.' 'I mean,' he said, 'elsewhere.' I replied, 'I left some behind.' 'Where, then?' he asked. 'At Bruges,' I replied. Then he said: 'I have now somewhat to ask you, madame, that concerns myself. Did you visit my sister in Paris the last time you were there?' I replied, 'Yes.' He asked whether I had been with her in the convent, and what was the name of the convent. I informed him that I had been in the convent, and that it was the Convent des Filles Bleues. At this he nodded, as if to confirm it. He also wished to know whether I had seen her. I said that no one in the convent might be seen by anyone but parents; even brothers and sisters were not allowed to see them.[E23] 'That is true,' he said, and then rose and gave me his hand. I begged him to induce his gracious Majesty to have pity on me, but he made no answer. When the Treasurer Gabel gave me his hand, I begged the same favour of him. He replied, 'Yes, if you will confess,' and went out without waiting for a reply.

For more than three hours they had kept up the interrogation. Then the prison governor came in and said to me: 'Now you are to remain in here; it is a beautiful chamber, and has been freshly whitewashed; you may now be contented.' Anna and Maren also came in. God knows, I was full of care, tired and weary, and had insufferable headache; yet, before I could go to rest, I had to sit waiting until the bedstead had been taken out of the 'Dark Church' and brought hither. Anna occupied herself meanwhile in the Dark Church, in scraping out every hole; she imagined she might find something there, but in vain. The woman who was to remain with me alone then came in. Her pay was two rix-dollars a week; her name is Karen, the daughter of Ole. After the prison governor had supped with the woman and Maren, Anna and Maren

Blocks bade me good night; the latter exhibited great affection. The prison governor bolted two doors before my innermost prison. In the innermost door there is a square hole, which is secured with iron cross-bars. The prison governor was going to attach a lock to this hole, but he forebore at Karen's request, for she said she could not breathe if this hole were closed. He then affixed locks to the door of the outer chamber, and to the door leading to the stairs; he had, therefore, four locks and doors twice a day to lock and unlock.

I will here describe my prison. It is a chamber, seven of my paces long and six wide; there are in it two beds, a table, and two stools. It was freshly whitewashed, which caused a terrible smell; the floor, moreover was so thick with dirt, that I imagined it was of loam, though it was really laid with bricks. It is eighteen feet high, with a vaulted ceiling, and very high up is a window which is two feet square. In front of it are double thick iron bars, besides a wire-work, which is so close that one could not put one's little finger into the holes. This wire-work had been thus ordered with great care by Count Rantzow (so the prison governor afterwards told me), so that no pigeons might bring in a letter—a fact which he had probably read in a novel as having happened. I was weak and deeply grieved in my heart; I looked for a merciful deliverance, and an end to my sorrow, and I sat silent and uncomplaining, answering little when the woman spoke to me. Sometimes in my reverie I scratched at the wall, which made the woman imagine that I was confused in my head; she told this to the prison governor, who reported it to the Queen, and during every meal-time, when the door was open, she never failed to send messengers to enquire how it fared with me, what I said, and what I was doing.

The woman had, however, not much to tell in obedience to the oath she, according to her own statement, had taken in the presence of the prison governor. But afterwards she found some means to ingratiate herself. And as my strength daily decreased, I rejoiced at the prospect of my end, and on August 21 I sent for the prison governor, and requested him to apply for a clergyman who could give me the sacrament. This was immediately granted, and His Majesty's Court preacher, Magister Mathias Foss, received orders to perform for me the duties of his office, and exhorted me, both on behalf of his office and in consequence of the command he had received, not to burden my conscience; I might rest assured, he said, that in this world I should never see my husband again, and he begged me to say what I knew of the treason. I could scarcely utter a word for weeping; but I said that I could attest before God in heaven, from whom nothing is hidden, that I knew nothing of this treason. I knew well I should never see my husband again in this life; I commended him to the Almighty, who knew my innocence; I prayed God only for a blessed end and departure from this evil world; I desired nothing from the clergyman but that he should remember me in his prayers, that God might by death put an end to my affliction. The clergyman promised faithfully to grant my request. It has not pleased God to hear me in this: He has willed to prove my faith still further, by sending to me since this time much care, affliction, and adversity. He has helped me also to bear the cross, and has Himself supported its heaviest end; His name be praised for ever. When I had received the Lord's Supper, M. Foss comforted me and bid me farewell.

I lay silently for three days after this, taking little or nothing. The prison governor often enquired whether I wished for anything to eat or drink, or whether he should say anything to the King. I thanked him, but said I required nothing.

On August 25 the prison governor importuned me at once with his conversation, expressing his belief that I entertained an evil opinion of the Queen. He inferred it from this: the day before he had said to me that His Majesty had ordered that whatever I desired from the kitchen and cellar should be at once brought to me, to which I had answered, 'God preserve His Majesty; he is a good sovereign; may he show clemency to evil men!' He had then said, 'The Queen is also good,' to which I had made no answer. He had then tried to turn the conversation to the Queen, and to hear if he could not draw out a word from me; he had said: 'The Queen is sorry for you that you have been so led away. It grieves her that you have willed your own unhappiness; she is not angry; she pities you.' And when I made no answer, he repeated it again, saying from time to time, 'Yes, yes, my dear lady, it is as I say.' I was annoyed at the talk, and said, 'Dieu vous punisse!' 'Ho, ho!' he said, misinterpreting my words, and calling Karen, he went out and closed the doors. Thus unexpectedly I got rid of him. It was ridiculous that the woman now wanted to oblige me to attend to what the prison governor had said. I begged her to remember that she was now not attending on a child (she had before been nurse to children). She could not so easily depart from her habit, and for a long time treated me as a child, until at length I made her comprehend that this was not required.

When I perceived that my stomach desired food and could retain it, I became impatient that I could not die, but must go on living in such misery. I began to dispute with God, and wanted to justify myself with Him. It seemed to me that I had not deserved such misfortune. I imagined myself far purer than David was from great sins, and yet he could say, 'Verily I have cleansed my heart in vain, and washed my hands in innocency. For all the day long have I been plagued, and chastened every morning.' I thought I had not deserved so exceedingly great a chastisement as that which I was receiving. I said with Job, 'Show me wherefore thou contendest with me. Is it good unto thee that thou shouldest oppress, that thou shouldest despise the work of thine hands?' I repeated all Job's expressions when he tried to justify himself, and it seemed to me that I could justly apply them to myself. I cursed with him and Jeremiah the day of my birth, and was very impatient; keeping it, however, to myself, and not expressing it aloud. If at times a word escaped me, it was in German (since I had generally read the Bible in German), and therefore the woman did not understand what I was saying. I was very restless from coughing, and turned from side to side on the bed. The woman often asked me how I was. I begged her to leave me quiet and not to speak to me. I was never more comfortable than in the night when I observed that she was sleeping; then, unhindered, I could let my tears flow and give free vent to my thoughts. Then I called God to account. I enumerated everything that I had innocently suffered and endured during my life, and I enquired of God whether I had deviated from my duty? Whether I ought to have done less for my husband than I had done? Whether the present was my recompense for not having left him in his adversity? Whether I was to be now tortured, tormented, and scorned for this? Whether all the indescribable misfortunes which I had endured with him were not enough, that I had been reserved for this irremediable and great trouble? I do not wish to conceal my unreasonableness. I will confess my sins. I asked if still worse misfortunes were in store for me for which I was to live? Whether there was any affliction on earth to be compared to mine? I prayed God to put an end to my sufferings, for it redounded in no wise to his honour to let me live and be so tormented. I was after all not made of steel and iron, but of flesh and blood. I prayed that He would suggest to me, or inform me in a dream, what I was to do to shorten my misery.

When I had long thus disputed and racked my brains, and had also wept so bitterly that it seemed as if no more tears remained, I fell asleep, but awoke with terror, for I had horrible fancies in my dreams, so that I feared to sleep, and began again to bewail my misery. At length God looked down upon me with his eye of mercy, so that on August 31 I had a night of quiet sleep, and just as day was dawning I awoke with the following words on my lips: 'My son, faint not when thou art rebuked of the Lord; for whom the Lord loveth he chasteneth, and scourgeth every son whom he receiveth.' I uttered the last words aloud, thinking that the woman was sleeping; possibly she awoke at the moment, and she asked me whether I wished for anything. I answered 'No.' 'You were speaking,' she said, 'and you mentioned your stockings; I could not understand the rest.' I replied, 'It must have been then in my sleep. I wish for nothing.'

I then lay quietly thinking. I perceived and confessed my folly, that I, who am only dust and ashes, and decay, and am only fit for the dunghill, should call

God to account, should dispute with my Creator and his decrees, and should wish to censure and question them. I began to weep violently, and I prayed fervently and from my heart for mercy and forgiveness. While I had before boasted with David, and been proud of my innocence, now I confessed with him that before God there is none that doeth good; no, not one. While before I had spoken foolishly with Job, I now said with him that I had 'uttered that I understood not; things too wonderful for me which I knew not.' I besought God to have mercy on me, relying on his great compassion. I cited Moses, Joshua, David, Jeremiah, Job, Jonah, and others, all highly endowed men, and yet so weak that in the time of calamity they grumbled and murmured against God. I prayed that He would in his mercy forgive me, the frailest of earthen vessels, as I could not after all be otherwise than as He had created me. All things were in his power; it was easy to Him to give me patience, as He had before imparted to me power and courage to endure hard blows and shocks. And I prayed God (after asking forgiveness of my sins) for nothing else than good patience to await the period of my deliverance. God graciously heard me. He pardoned not only my foolish sins, but He gave me that also for which I had not prayed, for day by day my patience increased. While I had often said with David, 'Will the Lord cast off for ever? and will he be favourable no more? Is his mercy clean gone for ever? doth his promise fail for evermore? Hath God forgotten to be gracious? Hath He in anger shut up his tender mercies?' I now continued with him, 'This is my infirmity, but I will remember the years of the right hand of the Most High.' I said also with Psalm cxix.: 'It is good for me that I have been afflicted; that I might learn thy statutes.'

The power of God was working within me. Many consolatory sentences from the Holy Scriptures came into my mind; especially these:—'If so be that we suffer with Christ, that we may be also glorified together.' Also: 'We know that all things work together for good to them that love God.' Also: 'My grace is sufficient for thee, for my strength is made perfect in weakness.' I thought especially often of Christ's words in St. Luke, 'Shall not God avenge his own elect, which cry day and night unto him, though he bear long with them? I tell you that he will avenge them speedily.' I felt in my trouble how useful it is to have learned psalms and passages from the Bible in youth. Believe me, my children, that it has been a great consolation to me in my misery. Therefore, cultivate now in your youth what your parents taught you in childhood; now, while trouble visits you less severely, so that when it comes, you may be ready to receive it and to comfort yourselves with the Word of God.

I began by degrees to feel more at peace, and to speak with the woman, and to answer the prison governor when he addressed me. The woman told me sundry things, and said that the prison governor had ordered her to tell him everything that I spoke or did, but that she was too wise to do such a thing; that she understood now better than she had done at first how to behave. He went out, but she remained shut up with me, and she would be true to me. And as it appeared that I did not at once believe what she said, she swore it solemnly, and prayed God to punish her if ever she acted falsely towards me. She stroked and patted my hand, and laid it against her cheek, and begged that I would believe her, using the words, 'My dearest lady, you can believe me; as truly as I am a child of God, I will never deceive you! Now, is not that enough?' I answered, 'I will believe you;' thinking at the same time that I would do and say nothing but what she might divulge. She was very glad that she had induced me to speak, and said, 'When you lay so long silent, and I had no one with whom I could speak, I was sad, and determined that I would not long lead this life, even if they gave me double as much, for I should have become crazed. I was afraid for you, but still more for myself, that my head would give way.'

She went on talking in this way, introducing also various merry stories. When she was young she had been in the service of a clergyman, who encouraged his domestics in the fear of God, and there she had learned prayers and sentences from the Bible by heart; she knew also the Children's Primer, with the explanatory remarks, and sang tolerably well. She knew in some measure how she should walk before God and behave towards her neighbour; but she acted contrary to her knowledge—for she had a malicious temper. She was an elderly woman, but she liked to reckon herself as middle-aged. It appeared that in her youth she had been pretty and rather dissolute, since even now she could not lay aside her levity, but joked with the tower-warder, and the prison governor's coachman, a man of the name of Peder, and with a prisoner named Christian (more will presently be said with regard to this prisoner; he was free to go about the tower).[69]

Maren Blocks often sent me a message through this coachman, besides various kinds of candied sugar and citron, letting me know from time to time whether anything new was occurring. All this had to be done through the woman. One day she came in when the doors were closed, and brought me a message from Maren Blocks, saying, 'My lady, if you will now write to your children in Skaane, there is a safe opportunity for you to do so.' I answered, 'My children are not in Skaane, yet if I can send a message to Skaane, I have a friend there who will probably let me know how it fares with my children.' She gave me a piece of crumpled paper and a pencil. I wrote a few words to F. Margrete Rantzow,[E24] saying that she probably knew of my miserable condition, but supposing that her friendship was not lessened by it, and begging her to let me know how my children were, and from what cause they had come to Skaane, as I had been informed was the case, though I did not believe it. This was what I wrote and gave to the woman. I heard nothing further of it, and I imagine that she had been ordered to find out to whom I wrote, &c. (They have been busy with the idea that some of you, my dear children, might come to Skaane.) I sewed up the letter or slip of paper in such a manner that it could not be opened without making it apparent. I asked the woman several times if she knew whether the letter had been sent away. She always answered that she did not know, and that with a morose expression, and at last she said (when I once more asked her to enquire of Peder), 'I suppose that the person who ought to have it has got it.' This answer made me reflect, and since then I asked no further.

I remained all this time in bed, partly because I had nothing with which to beguile the time, and partly because of the cold, for no stove was placed in my prison till after the New Year. Occasionally I requested the woman to manage, through Peder, that I should have a little silk or thread, that I might beguile the time by embroidering a piece of cloth that I had; but the answer I received was that he dared not. A long time afterwards it came to my knowledge that she had never asked Peder for it. There was trouble enough, however, to occupy my thoughts without my needing to employ the time in handiwork.

It was on September 2 that I heard some one moving early overhead, so I asked the woman if she knew whether there was a chamber there (for the woman went up every Saturday with the night-stool). She answered that there was a prison there like this, and outside was the rack (which is also the case). She observed that I showed signs of fear, and she said, 'God help! Whoever it is that is up there is most assuredly to be tortured.' I said, 'Ask Peder, when the doors are unlocked, whether there is a prisoner there.' She said she would do so, and meanwhile she kept asking herself and me who it might be. I could not guess; still less did I venture to confess my fear to her, which she nevertheless perceived, and therefore increased; for after she had spoken with Peder, about noon,[70] and the doors were locked, she said, 'God knows who it is that is imprisoned there! Peder would tell me nothing.' She said the same at the evening meal, but added that she had asked him, and that he would give no answer. I calmed myself, as I heard no more footsteps above, and I said, 'There is no prisoner up there.'[71] 'How do you know that?' she asked. 'I gather it from the fact,' I said, 'that since this morning I have heard no one above; I think if there were anyone there, they would probably give him something to eat.' She was not pleased that my mind was quieted, and therefore she and Peder together endeavoured to trouble me.

On the following day, when the doors were being locked after the mid-day dinner (which was generally Peder's task), and he was pulling to my innermost door, which opens inside, he put in his head and said, 'Casset!' She was standing beside the door, and appeared as if she had not rightly understood him, saying, 'Peder spoke of some one who is in prison, but I could not understand who it is.' I understood him at once, but also behaved as if I had not. No one knows but God what a day and night I had. I turned it over in my mind. It often seemed to me that it might be that they had seized him, although Cassetta was a subject of the King of Spain; for if treason is suspected, there is no thought given as to whose subject the man suspected may be. I lay in the night secretly weeping and lamenting that the brave man should have come into trouble for my sake, because he had executed my lord's will, and had followed me to England, where we parted, I should say, when Petcon and his company separated us and carried me away.

I lay without sleep till towards day, then I fell into a dream which frightened me. I suppose my thoughts caused it. It came before me that Cassetta was being tortured in the manner he had once described to me that a Spaniard had been tortured: four cords were fastened round his hands and feet, and each cord was made secure in a corner of the room, and a man sometimes pulled one cord and sometimes another; and since it seemed to me that Cassetta never screamed, I supposed that he was dead, and I shrieked aloud and awoke. The woman, who had long been awake, said: 'O God! dear lady, what ails you? Are you ill? You have been groaning a long time, and now you screamed loudly.' I replied, 'It was in my dream; nothing ails me.' She said further, 'Then you have had a bad dream?' 'That may well be,' I answered. 'Oh, tell me what you have dreamt; I can interpret dreams.' I replied, 'When I screamed I forgot my dream, otherwise no one can interpret dreams better than I.' I thank God I do not regard dreams; and this dream had no other cause than what I have said. When the door was locked after the mid-day meal, the woman said of herself (for I asked no further respecting the prisoners), 'There is no one imprisoned there; shame on Peder for his nonsense!' I asked him who was imprisoned there, and he laughed at me heartily. 'There is no one there, so let your mind be at peace.' I said, 'If my misfortunes were to involve others, it would be very painful to me.'

Thus matters went on till the middle of September, and then two of our servants were brought as prisoners and placed in arrest; one Nils Kaiberg, who had acted as butler, and the other Frans, who had been in our service as a lacquey. After having been kept in prison for a few weeks and examined they were set at liberty. At the same time two Frenchmen were brought as prisoners: an old man named La Rosche, and a young man whose name I do not know. La Rosche was brought to the tower and was placed in the witch- cell; a feather-bed had been thrown down, and on this he lay; for some months he was never out of his clothes. His food consisted of bread and wine;

he refused everything else. He was accused of having corresponded with Corfitz, and of having promised the King of France that he would deliver Crooneborg into his hands.[72] This information had been given by Hannibal Sehested, who was at that time in France, and he had it from a courtesan who was then intimate with Hannibal, but had formerly been in connection with La Rosche, and probably afterwards had quarrelled with him. There was no other proof in favour of the accusation. Probably suspicion had been raised by the fact that this La Rosche, with the other young man, had desired to see me when I was in arrest in Dover, which had been permitted, and they had paid me their respects. It is possible that he had wished to speak with me and to tell me what he had heard in London, and which, it seemed to him, excited no fears in me. But as I was playing at cards with some ladies who had come to look at me, he could not speak with me; so he asked me whether I had the book of plays which the Countess of Pembroke had published.[E25] I replied, 'No'. He promised to send it me, and as I did not receive it, I think he had written in it some warning to me, which Braten afterwards turned to his advantage.

However all this may be, La Rosche suffered innocently, and could prove upon oath that he had never spoken with my lord in his life, and still less had corresponded with him.[73] In short, after some months of innocent suffering, he was set at liberty and sent back to France. The other young man was confined in an apartment near the servants' hall. He had only been apprehended as a companion to the other, but no further accusation was brought against him.[E26] At first, when these men were imprisoned, there was a whispering and talking between the prison governor and the woman, and also between Peder and her; the prison governor moreover himself locked my door. I plainly perceived that there was something in the wind, but I made no enquiries. Peder at length informed the woman that they were two Frenchmen, and he said something about the affair, but not as it really was. Shortly before they were set at liberty the prison governor said, 'I have two parle mi franço in prison; what they have done I know not.' I made no further enquiries, but he jested and said, 'Now I can learn French.' 'That will take time,' said I.

In the same month of September died Count Rantzow. He did not live to see the execution of an effigy, which he so confidently had hoped for, being himself the one who first had introduced this kind of mockery in these countries.[E27]

On October 9 our Princess Anna Sophia was betrothed to the Electoral Prince of Saxony. On the morning of the day on which the festivities were to take place I said to the woman, 'To-day we shall fast till evening.' For I thought they would not think of me, and that I should not receive any of the remains until the others had been treated, at any rate, to dinner. She wished to know the reason why we were to fast. I answered, 'You shall know it this evening.' I lay and thought of the change of fortune: that I, who twenty-eight years ago had enjoyed as great state as the Princess, should now be lying a captive, close by the very wall where my bridal chamber had been; thank God, that it afflicted me but little. Towards noonday, when the trumpets and kettledrums were sounding, I said, 'Now they are conducting the bride across the square to the great hall.' 'How do you know that?' said the woman. 'I know it,' I said; 'my spirit tells me so.' 'What sort of spirit is that?' she asked. 'That I cannot tell you,' I replied. And as the trumpets blew every time that a new course of dishes and sweets were produced, I mentioned it; and before they were served the kettledrums were sounded. And as they were served on the square in front of the kitchen, I said each time, 'We shall have no dinner yet.' When it was nearly three o'clock, the woman said, 'My stomach is quite shrunk up; when shall we have dinner?' I answered, 'Not for a long time yet; the second course is only now on the table; we shall have something at about seven o'clock, and not before.' It was as I said. About half-past seven the prison governor came and excused himself, saying that he had asked for the dinner, but that all hands in the kitchen were occupied. The woman, who had always entertained the idea that I was a witch, was now confirmed in her opinion.[74]

On the following day knights were dubbed, and each time when the trumpets blew I did not only say, 'Now they have made a knight' (for I could hear the herald calling from the window, though I could not understand what he said), but even who had been made a knight; for this I guessed, knowing who were in the Council who were not knights before; and because it was as I said, the woman believed for certain that I was an enchantress. I perceived this, as she put questions to me concerning things which I could not know, and to which I often gave equivocal answers. I thought perhaps that the fear she had that I could know what would happen might hinder her from entangling me with lies. Since then she whispered much less with the prison governor. She told of a person whom she regarded as a witch, whose power, however, consisted in nothing else than in the science of curing French pox, and causing the miscarriage of bad women, and other improprieties. She had had much intercourse with this woman.

Some time after the departure of the Electoral Prince it was determined that a wooden effigy should be subjected to capital punishment, and on the forenoon my chamber was opened, swept, cleaned, and strewed with sand.[75] When it was opened, towards noon, and the woman had been on the stairs, talking with the coachman, she came in, and walking up to my bed, stood as if startled, and said hurriedly, 'Oh, Jesus! Lady, they are bringing your husband!' The news terrified me, which she observed; for as she uttered it, I raised myself in the bed and stretched out my right arm, and was not able to draw it back again at once. Perhaps this vexed her, for I remained sitting in this way and not speaking a word; so she said, 'My dearest lady, it is your husband's effigy.' To this I said, 'May God punish you!' She then gave full vent to her evil tongue, and expressed her opinion that I deserved punishment, and not she, and used many unprofitable words. I was quite silent, for I was very weak, and scarcely knew where I was. In the afternoon I heard a great murmuring of people in the inner palace square, and I saw the effigy brought across the street by the executioner on a wheelbarrow, and placed in the tower below my prison.

The next morning, at about nine o'clock, the effigy was wofully treated by the executioner, but no sound came from it. At the mid-day meal the prison governor told the woman how the executioner had cut off its head, and had divided the body into four quarters, which were then placed on four wheels, and attached to the gallows, while the head was exhibited on the town hall. The prison governor stood in the outer chamber, but he narrated all this in a loud tone, so that I might hear it, and repeated it three times.[E28] I lay and thought what I should do; I could not show that I made but little of it, for then something else perhaps would be devised to trouble me, and in the hurry I could think of nothing else than saying to the woman with sadness, 'Oh, what a shame! speak to the prison governor and tell him to beg the King to allow the effigy to be taken down and not to remain as it is!' The woman went out, and spoke softly with the prison governor; but he answered aloud and said, 'Yes, indeed, taken down! There will be more put up; yes, more up;' and kept on repeating these words a good while.

I lay silently thinking; I said nothing, but indulged in my own reflections. Sometimes I consoled myself, and hoped that this treatment of the effigy was a token that they could not get the man; then again fear asserted its sway. I did not care for the dishonour, for there are too many instances of great men in France whose effigies have been burnt by the executioner, and who subsequently arrived again at great honour.

When the door was unlocked again for the evening meal, there was a whispering between the prison governor and the woman. A lacquey was also sent, who stood outside the outer door and called the prison governor to him (my bed stands just opposite the doors, and thus when all three doors are opened I can see the staircase door, which is the fourth). I do not know what the woman can have told the prison governor, for I had not spoken all day, except to ask her to give me what I required; I said, moreover, nothing more than this for several days, so that the prison governor grew weary of enquiring longer of the woman; for she had nothing to communicate to him respecting me, and she tormented him always with her desire to get away; she could not longer spend her life in this way.

But as she received no other consolation from him than that he swore to her that she would never get away as long as she lived, for some days she did nothing else than weep; and since I would not ask her why she wept, she came one day up to my bedside crying, and said, 'I am a miserable being!' I asked her why? what ailed her? 'I ail enough,' she answered; 'I have been so stupid, and have allowed myself to be shut up here for the sake of money, and now you are cross with me and will not speak with me.' I said, 'What am I to say? you wish perhaps to have something to communicate to the prison governor?' Upon this she began to call down curses on herself if she had ever repeated to the prison governor a word that I had said or done; she wished I could believe her and speak with her; why should she be untrue to me? we must at any rate remain together as long as we lived. She added many implorations as to my not being angry; I had indeed cause to be so; she would in future give me no cause for anger, for she would be true to me. I thought, 'You shall know no more than is necessary.'

I let her go on talking and relating the whole history of her life—such events as occur among peasants. She had twice married cottagers, and after her last widowhood she had been employed as nurse to the wife of Holger Wind, so that she had no lack of stories. By her first husband she had had a child, who had never reached maturity, and her own words led me to have a suspicion that she had herself helped to shorten the child's days; for once when she was speaking of widows marrying again, she said among other things, 'Those who wish to marry a second time ought not to have children, for in that case the husband is never one with the wife.' I had much to say against this, and I asked her what a woman was to do who had a child by her first husband. She answered quickly, 'Put a pillow on its head.' This I could only regard as a great sin, and I explained it to her. 'What sin could there be,' she said, 'when the child was always sickly, and the husband angry in consequence?' I answered as I ought, and she seemed ill at ease. Such conversation as this gave me no good reason to believe in the fidelity which she had promised me.

The woman then took a different tack, and brought me word from the coachman of all that was occurring. Maren Blocks sent me a prayer-book through her, and that secretly, for I was allowed no book of any kind, nor any needles and pins; respecting these the woman had by the Queen's order taken an oath to the prison governor. Thus the year passed away. On New Year's day, 1664, the woman wished me a happy year. I thanked her, and said, 'That is in God's hands.' 'Yes,' she said, 'if He wills it.' 'And if He does not will it,'

I answered, 'it will not be, and then He will give me patience to bear my heavy cross.' 'It is heavy,' she said, 'even to me; what must it not be to you? May it only remain as it is, and not be worse with you!' It seemed to me as if it could not be worse, but better; for death, in whatever form, would put an end to my misery. 'Yes,' she said, 'is it not all one how one dies?' 'That is true,' I answered; 'one dies in despair, another with free courage.' The prison governor did not say a word to me that day. The woman had a long talk with the coachman; she no doubt related to him our conversation.

In the month of March the prison governor came in and assumed a particularly gentle manner, and said, among other things, 'Now you are a widow; now you can tell the state of all affairs.' I answered him with a question, 'Can widows tell the state of all affairs?' He laughed and said, 'I do not mean that; I mean this treason!' I answered, 'You can ask others about it who know of it; I know of no treason.' And as it seemed to him that I did not believe that my husband was dead,[E29] he took out a newspaper and let me read it, perhaps chiefly because my husband was badly treated in it. I did not say much about it— nothing more than, 'Writers of newspapers do not always speak the truth.' This he might take as he liked.

I lay there silently hoping that it might be so, that my husband had by death escaped his enemies; and I thought with the greatest astonishment that I should have lived to see the day when I should wish my lord dead; then sorrowful thoughts took possession of me, and I did not care to talk. The woman imagined that I was sad because my lord was dead, and she comforted me, and that in a reasonable manner; but the remembrance of past times was only strengthened by her consolatory remarks, and for a long time my mind could not again regain repose. Your condition, my dearest children, troubled me. You had lost your father, and with him property and counsel. I am captive and miserable, and cannot help you, either with counsel or deed; you are fugitives and in a foreign land. For my three eldest sons I am less anxious than for my daughters and my youngest son.[E30] I sat up whole nights in my bed, for I could not sleep, and when I have headache I cannot lay my head on the pillow. From my heart I prayed to God for a gracious deliverance. It has not pleased God to grant this, but He gave me patience to bear my heavy cross.

My cross was so much heavier to me at first, as it was strictly forbidden to give me either knife, scissors, thread, or anything that might have beguiled the time to me. Afterwards, when my mind became a little calmer, I began to think of something wherewith to occupy myself; and as I had a needle, as I have before mentioned, I took off the ribands of my night-dress, which were broad flesh- coloured taffeta. With the silk I embroidered the piece of cloth that I had with different flowers worked in small stitches. When this was finished, I drew threads out of my sheet, twisted them, and sewed with them. When this was nearly done, the woman said one day, 'What will you do now when this is finished?' I answered, 'Oh, I shall get something to do; if it is brought to me by the ravens, I shall have it.' Then she asked me if I could do anything with a broken wooden spoon. I answered, 'Perhaps you know of one?' After having laughed a while, she drew one forth, the bowl of which was half broken off. 'I could indeed make something with that,' I said, 'if I had only a tool for the purpose. Could you persuade the prison governor or Peder the coachman to lend me a knife?' 'I will beg for one,' she answered, 'but I know well that they will not.' That she said something about it to the prison governor I could perceive from his answer, for he replied aloud, 'She wants no knife; I will cut her food for her. She might easily injure herself with one.'[76]

What she said to the coachman I know not (this I know, that she did not desire me to obtain a knife, for she was afraid of me, as I afterwards discovered). The woman brought the answer from the coachman that he dared not for his life. I said, 'If I can but have a piece of glass, I will see what I can make that is useful with the piece of spoon.' I begged her to look in a corner in the outermost room, where all rubbish was thrown; this she did, and found not only glass, but even a piece of a pewter cover which had belonged to a jug. By means of the glass I formed the spoon handle into a pin with two prongs, on which I made riband, which I still have in use (the silk for this riband I took from the border of my night-dress). I bent the piece of pewter in such a manner that it afterwards served me as an inkstand. It also is still in my keeping. As a mark of fidelity, the woman brought me at the same time a large pin, which was a good tool for beginning the division between the prongs, which I afterwards scraped with glass.

She asked me whether I could think of anything to play with, as the time was so long to her. I said, 'Coax Peder, and he will bring you a little flax for money and a distaff.' 'What!' she answered, 'shall I spin? The devil may spin! For whom should I spin?' I said, 'To beguile the time, I would spin, if I only had what is necessary for it.' 'That you may not have, dear lady,' said she; 'I have done the very utmost for you in giving you what I have done.' 'If you wish something to play with,' said I, 'get some nuts, and we will play with them.' She did so, and we played with them like little children. I took three of the nuts, and made them into dice, placing two kinds of numbers on each, and we played with these also. And that we might know the ⊙ which I made with the large pin,[77] I begged her to procure for me a piece of chalk, which she did, and I rubbed chalk into it. These dice were lost, I know not how; my opinion is that the coachman got possession of them, perhaps at the time that he cheated the woman out of the candles and sugar left. For he came to her one day at noon quite out of breath, and said she was to give him the candles and the sugar which he had brought her from Maren Blocks, and whatever there was that was not to be seen, as our quarters were to be searched. She ran out with the things under her apron, and never said anything to me about it until the door was locked. I concealed on myself, as well as I was able, my pin, my silk, and the pieces of sewing with the needle and pin. Nothing came of the search, and it was only a *ruse* of the coachman, in order to get the candles that were left, for which she often afterwards abused him, and also for the sugar.

I was always at work, so long as I had silk from my night-dress and stockings, and I netted on the large pin, so that it might last a long time. I have still some of the work in my possession, as well as the bobbins, which I made out of wooden pegs. By means of bags filled with sand I made cords which I formed into a bandage (which is worn out), for I was not allowed a corset, often as I begged for one; the reason why is unknown to me. I often beguiled the time with the piece of chalk, painting with it on a piece of board and on the table, wiping it away again, and making rhymes and composing hymns. The first of these, however, I composed before I had the chalk. I never sang it, but repeated it to myself.

A morning hymn, to the tune, 'Ieg wil din Priiss ud Synge'[E31]:—

I

God's praise I will be singing
    In every waking hour.
My grateful tribute bringing
    To magnify his power;
And his almighty love,
    His angel watchers sending,
    My couch with mercy tending,
And watching from above.

II

In salt drops streaming ever
    The tears flowed from my eyes;
I often thought I never
    Should see the morning rise.
Yet has the Lord instilled
    Sleep in his own good pleasure;
    And sleep in gracious measure
Has his command fulfilled.

III

Oh Christ! Lord of the living,
    Thine armour place on me,
Which manly vigour giving,
    Right valiant shall I be,
'Gainst Satan, death, and sin.
    And every carnal feeling,
    That nought may come concealing
Thy sway my heart within.

IV

Help me! Thy arms extending;
    My cross is hard and sore:
Support its heaviest ending,
    Or I can bear no more.
Too much am I oppressed!
    My trust is almost waning
    With pain and vain complaining!
Thine arrows pierce my breast.

V

In mercy soothe the sorrow
    That weighs the fatherless;
Vouchsafe a happier morrow,
    And all my children bless!
Strength to their father yield,
    In their hard fate respect them,
    From enemies protect them;
My strength, be Thou their shield.

VI

I am but dust and ashes,
    Yet one request I crave:
Let me not go at unawares
    Into the silent grave.
With a clear mind and breast
    My course in this world closing,
    Let me, on Thee reposing,
Pass to Thy land of rest.

I composed the following hymn in German and often sang it, as they did not understand German; a hymn, somewhat to the air of 'Was ist doch auff dieser Welt, das nicht fehlt?' &c.:—

I

Reason speaketh to my soul:
        Fret not Soul,
Thou hast a better goal!
    It is not for thee restricted
        That with thee
        Past should be
All the wrongs inflicted.

II

Why then shouldst thou thus fret thee,
        Anxiously,
Ever sighing, mournfully?
    Thou canst not another sorrow
        Change with this,
        For that is
Which shall be on the morrow.

III

Loss of every earthly gain

Bringeth pain;
Fresh courage seek to obtain!
Much was still superfluous ceded,
Nature's call
After all
Makes but little needed.

IV

Is the body captive here?
Do not fear:
Thou must not hold all too dear;
Thou art free—a captive solely;
Can no tower
Have the power
Thee to fetter wholly?

V

All the same is it at last
When thou hast
The long path of striving past,
And thou must thy life surrender;
Death comes round,
Whether found
On couch hard or tender.

VI

Courage then, my soul, arise!
Heave no sighs
That nought yet thy rest supplies!
God will not leave thee in sorrow:
Well He knows
When He chose
Help for thee to borrow.

Thus I peacefully beguiled the time, until Doctor Otto Sperling[E32] was brought to the tower; his prison is below the 'dark church.' His fate is pitiable. When he was brought to the tower his feet and hands were chained in irons. The prison governor, who had formerly not been friendly with him, rejoiced heartily at the doctor's misfortune, and that he had fallen into his hands, so that the whole evening he did nothing but sing and hum. He said to the woman, 'My Karen, will you dance? I will sing.' He left the doctor to pass the night in his irons. We could hear that a prisoner had been brought in from the murmuring, and the concourse of people, as well as from the locking of the prison, which was below mine (where iron bolts were placed against the door).[78] The joy exhibited by the prison governor excited my fear, also that he not only himself opened and shut my door, but that he prevented the woman from going out on the stairs, by leaning against the outermost door of my prison. The coachman stood behind the prison governor making signs; but as the prison governor turned from side to side, I could not rightly see him.

On the following day, at about eight o'clock, I heard the iron bolts drawn and the door below opened; I could also hear that the inner prison was opened (the doctor was then taken out for examination). The woman said, 'There is certainly a prisoner there; who can it be?' I said: 'It seems indeed that a prisoner has been brought in, for the prison governor is so merry. You will find it out from Peder; if not to-day, another time. I pity the poor man, whoever he may be.' (God knows my heart was not as courageous as I appeared.) When my door was opened at noon (which was after twelve o'clock, for they did not open my door till the doctor had been conveyed to his cell again), the prison governor was still merrier than usual, and danced about and sang, 'Cheer up! courage! It will come to pass!'

When he had cut up the dinner, he leaned against the outer door of my prison and prevented the woman from going out, saying to me, 'I am to salute you from the Major-General von Alfeldt; he says all will now soon be well, and you may console yourself. Yes, yes, all will now soon be well!' I behaved as if I received his words in their apparent meaning, and I begged him to thank the Major-General for his consolation; and then he repeated the same words, and added, 'Yes, indeed! he said so.' I replied with a question: 'What may it arise from that the Major-General endeavours to cheer me? May God cheer him in return! I never knew him before.' To this the prison governor made no answer at all. While the prison governor was talking with me, the coachman was standing behind him, and showed by gestures how the prisoner had been bound hand and foot, that he had a beard and a calotte on his head, and a handkerchief round his neck. This could not make me wiser than I was, but it could indeed grieve me still more. At the evening meal the woman was again prevented speaking with the coachman, and the coachman again made the same signs, for the prison governor was standing in his usual place; but he said nothing, nor did I.[79] On the following morning the Doctor was again brought up for examination, and the prison governor behaved as before. As he stood there ruminating, I asked him who the prisoner below was. He answered that there was no one below. I let the matter rest for the time, and as we proceeded to speak of other things, the woman slipped out to Peder, who told her quickly who it was. Some days went by in the same manner. When sentence had been pronounced on the Doctor, and his execution was being postponed,[80] and I said nothing to the prison governor but when he accosted me, he came in and said: 'I see that you can judge that there is a prisoner below. It is true, but I am forbidden to tell you who it is!' I answered: 'Then I do not desire to know.' He began to feel some compassion, and said: 'Don't fret, my dear lady; it is not your husband, nor your son, nor daughter, nor brother-in-law, nor any relative; it is a bird which ought to sing,[81] and will not, but he must, he must!' I said: 'I ought to be able to guess from your words who it is. If the bird can sing what can ring in their ears, he will probably do so; but he cannot sing a melody which he does not know!' Upon this he was silent, and turned away and went out.

By degrees all became quiet with regard to the Doctor, and no more was said about the matter, and the prison governor came in from time to time when the door was opened, and often made himself merry with the woman, desiring her to make a curtsey to him, and showing her how she should place her feet and carry her body, after the fashion of a dancing-master. He related also different things that had occurred in former times, some of them evidently intended to sadden me with the recollection of my former prosperity: all that had happened at my wedding, how the deceased King had loved me. He gave long accounts of this, not forgetting how I was dressed, and all this he said for the benefit of no one else but myself, for the woman meanwhile stood on the stairs talking with the tower warder, the coachman, and the prisoner Christian.

Maren Blocks, who constantly from time to time sent me messages and kept me informed of what was going on, also intimated to me that she was of opinion that I could practise magic, for she wrote me a slip of paper[82] with the request that I should sow dissension between the Lady Carisse and an Alfelt, explaining at length that Alfelt was not worthy of her, but that Skinckel was a brave fellow (Carisse afterwards married Skinckel). As the letter was open, the coachman knew its contents, and the woman also. I was angry at it, but I said nothing. The woman could easily perceive that I was displeased at it, and she said, 'Lady, I know well what Maren wishes.' I replied, 'Can you help her in it?' 'No,' she declared, and laughed heartily. I asked what there was to laugh at. 'I am laughing,' said she, 'because I am thinking of the clever Cathrine, of whom I have spoken before, who once gave advice to some one desiring to sow discord between good friends.' I enquired what advice she had given. She said that they must collect some hairs in a place where two cats had been fighting, and throw these between the two men whom it was desired to set at variance. I enquired whether the trick succeeded. She replied, 'It was not properly tried.' 'Perhaps,' I said, 'the cats were not both black?' 'Ho, ho!' said she, 'I see that you know how it should be done.' 'I have heard more than that,' I replied; 'show her the trick, and you will get some more sugar-candy, but do not let yourself be again cheated of it by Peder as you were lately. Seriously, however, Peder must beg

Maren Blocks to spare me such requests!' That she as well as Maren believed that I could practise magic was evident in many ways. My own remarks often gave cause for this. I remembered how my deceased lord used to say (when in his younger days he wished to make anyone imagine that he understood the black art), that people feared those of whom they had this opinion, and never ventured to do them harm. It happened one day at the mid-day meal, when the prison governor was sitting talking with me, that the woman carried on a long conversation on the stairs with the others respecting the witches who had been seized in Jutland, and that the supreme judge in Jutland at that time sided with the witches and said they were not witches.[E33] When the door was locked we had much talk about witches, and she said, 'This judge is of your opinion, that it is a science and not magic.' I said, as I had before said, that some had more knowledge than others, and that some used their knowledge to do evil; although it might happen naturally and not with the devil's art, still it was not permitted in God's Word to use nature for evil purposes; it was also not fair to give the devil the honour which did not belong to him. We talked on till she grew angry, laid down and slept a little, and thus the anger passed away.

Some days after she said: 'Your maid is sitting below in the prison governor's room, and asks with much solicitude after you and what you are doing. I have told Peder of what you have sewed, and of the ribbons you have made, but he has promised solemnly not to mention it to anyone except to Maren, Lars' daughter; she would like so much to be here with you.' I replied: 'It would be no good for her to sit with me in prison; it would only destroy her own happiness; for who knows how long I may live?' I related of this same waiting-maid that she had been in my employ since she was eight years old, all that I had had her taught, and how virtuous she was. To this she replied, 'The girl will like to see what you have sewed; you shall have it again directly.' I handed it to her, and the first time the doors were unlocked she gave it to the prison governor, who carried it to the Queen. (Two years afterwards the prison governor told me this himself, and that when the King had said, 'She might have something given her to do,' the Queen had answered, 'That is not necessary. It is good enough for her! She has not wished for anything better.') I often enquired for the piece of sewing, but was answered that Peder was not able to get it back from the girl.

Late in the autumn the prison governor began to sicken: he was ill and could not do much, so he let the coachman frequently come alone to lock and unlock both the doctor's door below and mine. The iron bars were no longer placed before the outermost prison below, but four doors were locked upon me. One day, when Peder was locking up, he threw me a skein of silk,[83] saying, 'Make me some braces for my breeches out of it.' I appeared not to have heard, and asked the woman what it was that he had said. She repeated the same words. I behaved as if I did not believe it, and laughed, saying, 'If I make the braces for him, he will next wish that you should fasten them to his breeches.' A good deal of absurd chatter followed. As meal-time was approaching, I said to the woman, 'Give Peder back his silk, and say that I have never before made a pair of braces; I do not know how they are made.' (Such things I had to endure with smiles.)

At the time that our former palace here in the city (which we had ceded by a deed when we were imprisoned at Borringholm) was pulled down, and a pillar (or whatever it is) was raised to my lord's shame, the prison governor came in when he unlocked at noon, and seated himself on my bed (I was somewhat indisposed at the time), and began to talk of former times (I knew already that they were pulling down the palace), enumerating everything the loss of which he thought might sadden me, even to my coach and the horses. 'But,' he said, 'all this is nothing compared with the beautiful palace!' (and he praised it to the utmost); 'it is now down, and not one stone is left on another. Is not that a pity, my dear lady?' I replied: 'The King can do what he will with his own; the palace has not been ours for some time.' He continued bewailing the beautiful house and the garden buildings which belonged to it. I asked him what had become of Solomon's temple? Not a stone of that beautiful building was now to be found; not even could the place be pointed out where the temple and costly royal palace had once stood. He made no answer, hung his head, and pondered a little, and went out. I do not doubt he has reported what I said. Since that day he began to behave himself more and more courteously, saying even that His Majesty had ordered him to ask me whether I wished for anything from the kitchen, the cellar, or the confectioner, as it should be given me; that he had also been ordered to bring me twice a week confectionery and powdered sugar, which was done.[84] I begged the prison governor to thank the King's Majesty for the favour shown me, and praised, as was proper, the King's goodness most humbly. The prison governor would have liked to praise the Queen had he only been able to find cause for so doing; he said, 'The Queen is also a dear Queen!' I made no answer to this. He came also some time afterwards with an order from the King that I should ask for any clothes and linen I required: this was written down, and I received it later, except a corset, and that the Queen would not allow me. I never could learn the cause of this. The Queen also was not well pleased that I obtained a bottle-case with six small bottles, in which was sprinkling-water, headwater, and a cordial. All this, she said, I could well do without; but when she saw that in the lid there was an engraving representing the daughter of Herod with the head of St. John on a charger, she laughed and said, 'That will be a cordial to her!' This engraving set me thinking that Herodias had still sisters on earth.

The prison governor continued his politeness, and lent me at my desire a

German Bible, saying at the same time, 'This I do out of kindness, I have no order to do so; the Queen does not know it.' 'I believe that,' I replied, and thanked him; but I am of opinion that the King knew it well. Some days afterwards Maren Blocks sent for her prayer-book back again. I had taught the woman a morning and evening prayer by heart, and all the morning and evening hymns, which she repeated to me night and morning. I offered to teach her to read if she would procure an A B C. She laughed at this jeeringly, and said, 'People would think me crazed if I were to learn to read now.' I tried to persuade her by argument, in order that I might thus get something to beguile the time with; but far from it; she knew as much as she needed. I sought everywhere for something to divert my thoughts, and as I perceived that the potter, when he had placed the stove, had left a piece of clay lying outside in the other room, I begged the woman to give it to me.

The prison governor saw that she had taken it, but did not ask the reason. I mixed the clay with beer, and made various things, which I frequently altered again into something else; among other things I made the portraits of the prison governor and the woman, and small jugs and vases. And as it occurred to me to try whether I were able to make anything on which I could place a few words to the King, so that the prison governor should not observe it (for I knew well that the woman did not always keep silence; she would probably some time say what I did), I moulded a goblet over the half of the glass in which wine was brought to me, made it round underneath, placed it on three knobs, and wrote the King's name on the side—underneath the bottom these words ... il y a un ... un Auguste.[E34]

I kept it for a long time, not knowing in what way I could manage to get it reported what I was doing, since the woman had solemnly sworn to me not to mention it: so I said one day: 'Does the prison governor ask you what I am doing?' 'Yes, indeed he does,' she replied, 'but I say that you are doing nothing but reading the Bible.' I said: 'You may ingratiate yourself in his favour and say that I am making portraits in clay; there is no reason that he should not know that.' She did so, and three days after he came to me, and was quite gentle, and asked how I passed my time. I answered, 'In reading the Bible.' He expressed his opinion that I must weary of this. I said I liked at intervals to have something else to do, but that this was not allowed me. He enquired what I had wanted the clay for, which the woman had brought in to me; he had seen it when she had brought it in. I said, 'I have made some small trifles.' He requested to see them. So I showed him first the woman's portrait; that pleased him much, as it resembled her; then a small jug, and last of all the goblet. He said at once: 'I will take all this with me and let the King see it; you will perhaps thus obtain permission to have somewhat provided you for pastime,'[85] I was well satisfied. This took place at the mid-day meal. At supper he did not come in. The next day he said to me: 'Well, my dear lady, you have nearly brought me into trouble!' 'How so?' I asked. 'I took the King a petition from you! the Queen did not catch sight of it, but the King saw it directly and said, "So you are now bringing me petitions from Leonora?" I shrank back with terror, and said, "Gracious King! I have brought nothing in writing!" "See here!" exclaimed the King, and he pointed out to me some French writing at the bottom of the goblet. The Queen asked why I had brought anything written that I did not understand. I asserted that I had paid no attention to it, and begged for pardon. The good King defended me, and the *invention* did not please him ill. Yes, yes, my dear lady! be assured that the King is a gracious sovereign to you, and if he were certain that your husband were dead, you would not remain here!' I was of opinion that my enemies well knew that my husband was dead. I felt that I must therefore peacefully resign myself to the will of God and the King.

I received nothing which might have beguiled the time to me, except that which I procured secretly, and the prison governor has since then never enquired what I was doing, though he came in every evening and sat for some time talking with me; he was weak, and it was a labour to him to mount so many steps. Thus we got through the year together.

The prison governor gradually began to feel pity for me, and gave me a book which is very pretty, entitled 'Wunderwerck.'[E35] It is a folio, rather old, and here and there torn; but I was well pleased with the gift. And as he sat long of an evening with me, frequently till nine o'clock, talking with me, the malicious woman was irritated.[86] She said to Peder, 'If I were in the prison governor's place, I would not trust her in the way he does. He is weak; what if she were now to run out and take the knife which is lying on the table outside, and were to stab him? She could easily take my life, so I sit in there with my life hanging on a thread.'

Absurd as the idea was, the knife was not only in consequence hidden under the table, but the prison governor for a long time did not venture to come to me, but sat outside by my outermost door and talked there just as long as before, so that I was no gainer.[87] (I did not know what the woman had said till three years afterwards, when it was mentioned by the prisoner Christian, who had heard the woman's chatter.)

One day when the prison governor intended to go to the holy communion, he stood outside my outermost door and took off his hat, and begged for my forgiveness; he knew, he said, that he had done much to annoy me, but that he was a servant. I answered, 'I forgive you gladly!' Then he went away, and Peder closed the door. The woman said something to Peder about the prison governor, but I could not understand what. Probably she was blaming the prison governor, for she was so angry that she puffed; she could not restrain her anger, but said: 'Fye upon the old fool! The devil take him! I ought to beg pardon too? No' (she added with an oath), 'I would not do it for God's bitter death! No! no!' and she spat on the ground. I said afterwards: 'What does it matter to you that the prison governor asks me for my friendship? Do you lose anything by it? If you will not live like a Christian and according to the ordinances of the Church, do not at any rate be angry with one who does. Believe assuredly that God will punish you, if you do not repent of what evil you have done and will not be reconciled with your adversaries before you seek to be reconciled with God!'

She thought that he had done nothing else than what he was ordered to do. I said, 'You good people know best yourselves what has been ordered you.' She asked, 'Do I do anything to you?' I answered, 'I know not what you do. You can tell any amount of untruths about me without my knowing it.' Upon this she began a long story, swearing by and asserting her fidelity; she had never lied to anyone nor done anyone a wrong. I said: 'I hear; you are justifying yourself with the Pharisee.' She started furiously from her seat and said, 'What! do you abuse me as a Pharisee?' 'Softly, softly!' I said; 'while only one of us is angry, it is of no consequence; but if I get angry also, something may come of it!' She sat down with an insolent air, and said, 'I should well imagine that you are not good when you are angry! It is said of you that in former days you could bear but little, and that you struck at once. But now'——(with this she was silent). 'What more?' I said. 'Do you think I could not do anything to anyone if I chose, just as well as then, if anyone behaved to me in a manner that I could not endure? Now much more than then! You need not refuse me a knife because I may perhaps kill you; I could do so with my bare hands. I can strangle the strongest fellow with my bare hands, if I can seize him unawares, and what more could happen to me than is happening? Therefore only keep quiet!'

She was silent, and assumed no more airs; she was cast down, and did not venture to complain to the prison governor. What she said to the others on the stairs I know not, but when she came in, when the room was locked at night, she had been weeping.[88]

On Sunday at noon I congratulated[E36] the prison governor and said: 'You are happy! You can reconcile yourself with God, and partake of His body and blood; this is denied to me (I had twice during two years requested spiritual consolation, but had received in answer that I could not sin as I was now in prison; that I did not require religious services). And as I talked upon this somewhat fully with the prison governor, I said that those who withheld from me the Lord's Supper must take my sins upon themselves; that one sinned as much in thought as in word and deed; so the prison governor promised that he would never desist from desiring that a clergyman should come to me; and asked whom I wished for. I said: 'The King's Court preacher, whom I had in the beginning of my troubles.' He said: 'That could scarcely be.' I was satisfied whoever it was.

A month afterwards I received the holy communion from the German clergyman, M. Hieronimus Buk, who behaved very properly the first time, but spoke more about the law than the gospel. The prison governor congratulated me, and I thanked him, for he had brought it about.

1665. In this year, on Whitsun-eve, the prison governor ordered May-trees to be placed in my inner prison, and also in the anteroom. I broke small twigs from the branches, rubbed off the bark with glass, softened them in water, laid them to press under a board, which was used for carrying away the dirt from the floor, and thus made them flat, then fastened them together and formed them into a weaver's reed. Peder the coachman was then persuaded to give me a little coarse thread, which I used for a warp. I took the silk from the new silk stockings which they had given me, and made some broad ribbons of it (The implements and a part of the ribbons are still in my possession.) One of the trees (which was made of the thick end of a branch which Peder had cut off) was tied to the stove, and the other I fastened to my own person. The woman held the warp: she was satisfied, and I have no reason to think that she spoke about it, for the prison governor often lamented that I had nothing with which to beguile the time, and he knew well that this had been my delight in former times, &c.[89]

He remained now again a long time with me after meals, for his fear had passed away, or he had, perhaps, forgotten, as his memory began to fail him. He said then many things which he ought not. He declined perceptibly, and was very weak; he would remain afterwards sitting outside, reading aloud, and praying God to spare his life. 'Yes,' he would say, 'only a few years!' When he had some alleviation, he talked unceasingly. Creeping along the wall to the door, he said, 'I should like to know two things: one is, who will be prison governor after me? The other is, who is to to have my Tyrelyre?' (That was Tyre, his wife.) I replied: 'That is a knowledge which you cannot obtain now, especially who will woo your wife. You might, perhaps, have already seen both, but at your age you may yet have long to live.' 'Oh!' said he, 'God grant it!' and looked up to the window. 'Do you think so, my dear lady?' 'Yes, I do,' I replied. A few days afterwards, he begged me again to forgive him, if he had done me any wrong since the last time, for he wished to make reconciliation with God before he became weaker, and he wept and protested, saying, 'It indeed grieves me still that I should have often annoyed you, and you comfort me.' On Sunday at noon I congratulated him on his spiritual feast.

Thus he dragged on with great difficulty for about fourteen days, and as I heard that two men were obliged almost to carry him up the stairs, I sent him word that he might remain below on the ground floor of the tower, and that he might rest assured I would go nowhere. He thanked me, crawled up for the last time to my door, and said, 'If I did that and the Queen heard of it, my head would answer for it.' I said: 'Then confess your weakness and remain in bed. It may be better again; another could meanwhile attend for you.' He took off his cap in recognition of my advice, and bade me farewell. I have never seen him again since then. One day afterwards he crawled up in the tower- chamber, but came no farther.

A man of the name of Hans Balcke was appointed in his place to keep watch over the prisoners. He was very courteous. He was a cabinet-maker by trade; his father, who had also been a cabinet-maker, had worked a good deal for me in the days of my prosperity. This man had travelled for his trade both in Italy and Germany, and knew a little Italian. I found intercourse with him agreeable, and as he dined in the anteroom outside, in the tower, I begged him to dine with me, which he did for fourteen days. One day, when he carved the joint outside, I sent him word requesting him to come in. He excused himself, which appeared strange to me.

After he had dined, he said that Peder the coachman had jeered at him, and that he had been forbidden to dine with me. When he afterwards remained rather long with me talking, I begged him myself to go, so that this also might not be forbidden. He had on one occasion a large pin stuck in his sleeve, and I begged him for it. He said, 'I may not give it you, but if you take it yourself, I can't help it.' So I took it, and it has often been of use to me. He gave me several books to read, and was in every way courteous and polite. His courtesy was probably the reason why the prisons were not long entrusted to him, for he was also very good to Doctor Sperling, giving him slices of the meat which came up to me, and other good food. In his childhood he had been a playfellow of the doctor's children. He talked also occasionally a long time with the doctor, both on unlocking and locking his door, which did not please the servants.[90] The prison governor lay constantly in bed; he endeavoured as often as he could to come up again, but there was little prospect of it. So long as the keys were not taken from him, he was satisfied.

My maid Maren, Lars' daughter, had risen so high in favour at court, that she often sat in the women's apartment, and did various things. One day the woman said to me, 'That is a very faithful maiden whom you have! She speaks before them up there in a manner you would never believe.' I replied:

'I have permitted her to say all she knows. I have no fear of her calumniating me.' 'Have you not?' she said ironically. 'Why does she throw herself, then, on her bare knees, and curse herself if she should think of returning to you?' I said: 'She wished to remain with me (according to your own statement), but she was not allowed; so she need not curse herself.' 'Why then do you think,' said she, 'that she is so much in favour at court?' 'Do you mean,' I replied, 'that if anyone is in favour at court, it is because their lips are full of lies? I am assured my maid has calumniated no one, least of all me; I am not afraid.'

The woman was angry, and pouted in consequence for some time. Some weeks afterwards Maren, Lars' daughter, was set at liberty, and became waiting-maid to the Countess Friis: and Balcke brought me some linen which she still had belonging to me. The woman was not a little angry at this, especially as I said: 'So faithful I perceive is my maid to me, that she will not keep the linen, which she might easily have done, for I could not know whether it had not been taken from her with the rest.'

All my guards were very ill satisfied with Balcke, especially the woman, who was angry for several reasons. He slighted her, she said, for he had supplied a basin for the night-stool which was heavier than the former one (which leaked); but she was chiefly angry because he told her that she lived like a heathen, since she never went to the sacrament. For when I once received the holy communion, while Balcke was attending to me, he asked her if she would not wish to communicate also, to which she answered, 'I do not know German.' Balcke said, 'I will arrange that the clergyman shall come to you whose office it is to administer the Lord's Supper to the prisoners.' She replied that in this place she could not go with the proper devotion: if she came out, she would go gladly. Balcke admonished her severely, as a clergyman might have done. When the door was closed, she gave vent to puffing and blowing, and she always unfastened her jacket when she was angry.

I said nothing, but I thought the evil humour must have vent, or she will be choked; and this was the case, for she abused Balcke with the strongest language that occurred to her. She used unheard-of curses, which were terrible to listen to: among others, 'God damn him for ever, and then I need not curse him every day.' Also, 'May God make him evaporate like the dew before the sun!' I could not endure this cursing, and I said, 'Are you cursing this man because he held before you the word of God, and desires that you should be reconciled with God and repent your sins?' 'I do not curse him for that,' she said, 'but on account of the heavy basin which the accursed fellow has given me, and which I have to carry up the steep stairs;[91] the devil must have moved him to choose it! Does he want to make a priest of himself? Well, he is probably faultless, the saucy fellow!' and she began again with her curses.

I reproved her and said: 'If he now knew that you were cursing him in this way, do you not think he would bring it about that you must do penitence? It is now almost two years since you were at the Lord's table, and you can have the clergyman and you will not.' This softened her a little, and she said, 'How should he know it, unless you tell him?' I said, 'What passes here and is said here concerns no one but us two; it is not necessary that others should know.' With this all was well; she lay down to sleep, and her anger passed away; but the hate remained.

The prison governor continued to lie in great pain, and could neither live nor die. One day at noon, when Balcke unlocked (it was just twenty weeks since he had come to me), a man came in with him, very badly dressed, in a grey, torn, greasy coat, with few buttons that could be fastened, with an old hat to which was attached a drooping feather that had once been white but was now not recognisable from dirt. He wore linen stockings and a pair of worn-out shoes fastened with packthread.[92] Balcke went to the table outside and carved the joint; he then went to the door of the outer apartment, stood with his hat in his hand, made a low reverence, and said, 'Herewith I take my departure; this man is to be prison governor.' I enquired whether he would not come again to me. He replied, 'No, not after this time.' Upon this I thanked him for his courteous attendance, and wished him prosperity.[93]

Peder the coachman locked the door, and the new prison governor, whose name was Johan Jäger,[E37] never appeared before me the whole day, nor during the evening. I said to the woman in the morning, 'Ask Peder who the man is;' which she did, and returned to me with the answer that it was the man who had taken the Doctor prisoner; and that now he was to be prison governor, but that he had not yet received the keys. Not many days passed before he came with the Lord Steward to the old prison governor, and the keys were taken from the old man and given to him. The old man lived only to the day after this occurred. In both respects his curiosity was satisfied; he saw the man who was to be prison governor after him (to his grief), and the doctor who attended him obtained his Tyrelyre before the year was ended.

The new prison governor Jäger[E37b] did not salute me for several weeks, and never spoke to me. He rarely locked my doors, but he generally opened them himself. At length one day, when he had got new shoes on, he took his hat off when he had opened the door, and said 'Good morning.' I answered him, 'Many thanks.' The woman was very pleased while this lasted. She had her free talk with Peder the coachman (who still for a couple of months came to the tower as before) and with the prisoner Christian, who had great freedom, and obtained more and more freedom in this prison governor's time, especially as Rasmus the tower-warder was made gatekeeper, and a man of the name of Chresten was appointed in his place. Among other idle talk which she repeated to me, she said that this prison governor was forbidden to speak with me. I said, 'I am very glad, as he then can tell no lies about me.' I am of opinion that he did not venture to speak with me so long as Peder brought up the food to the tower, and was in waiting there; for when he had procured Peder's dismissal on account of stealing, he came in afterwards from time to time. The very first time he was intoxicated. He knew what Peder had said of Balcke, and he informed me of it.[94]

Before I mention anything of the prisoner Christian's designs against me, I will in a few words state the crime for which he was in prison. He had been a lacquey in the employ of Maans Armfelt. With some other lacqueys he had got into a quarrel with a man who had been a father to Christian, and who had brought him up from his youth and had taken the utmost care of him. The man was fatally wounded, and called out in the agonies of death: 'God punish thee, Christian! What a son you have been! It was your hand that struck me!' The other lacqueys ran away, but Christian was seized. His dagger was found bloody. He denied, and said it was not he who had stabbed the man. He was sentenced to death; but as the dead man's widow would not pay for the execution, Christian remained for the time in prison, and his master paid for his maintenance. He had been there three years already when I came to the prison, and three times he was removed; first from the Witch Cell to the Dark Church; and then here where I am imprisoned.[95] When I was brought here, he was placed where the Doctor is, and when the Doctor was brought in, Christian was allowed to go freely about the tower. He wound the clock for the tower-warder, locked and unlocked the cells below, and had often even the keys of the tower.

I remember once, when Rasmus the tower-warder was sitting at dinner with the prison governor in my outermost cell, and the prison governor wished to send Peder on a message, he said to Rasmus: 'Go and open! I want Peder to order something. 'Father,' said Rasmus, 'Christian has the key.' 'Indeed!' said the prison governor; 'that is pretty work!' And there it rested, for Rasmus said, 'I am perfectly sure that Christian will not go away.' Thus by degrees Christian's freedom and power increased after Peder the coachman left, and he waited on the prison governor at meals in my outermost room.

One day, when the woman had come down from above, where she had been emptying the utensils in my room, and the doors were locked, she said to me: 'This Christian who is here has been just speaking with me upstairs. He says he cannot describe the Doctor's miserable condition, how severe is his imprisonment, and what bad food he gets, since Balcke left. He has no longer any candle except during meal-time, and no light reaches him but through the hole in his door leading into the outer room. He begged me to tell you of it; his eyes were full of tears, such great pity had he for him.' I said: 'That is all that one can do, and it is the duty of a Christian to sympathise with the misfortune of one's neighbour. The poor man must have patience as well as I, and we must console ourselves with a good conscience. The harder he suffers the sooner comes the end; he is an old man.'

Two days afterwards she came again with some talk from Christian. The Doctor sent me his compliments, and he asked constantly if I was well; she said also, that Christian would give him anything I liked to send him. I regarded this as a snare, but I said that Christian could take a piece of roast meat when the prison governor was with me, and that he should look about for something into which wine could be poured, and then she could secretly give some from my glass, and beg Christian to give my compliments to the Doctor. This was accepted, and I had rest for a few days. Christian conformed entirely to the woman, caused a dispute between her and the tower-warder, and made it immediately right again; so that there was no lack of chatter. At last she said one day: 'That is an honest fellow, this Christian! He has told me how innocently he got into prison and was sentenced. He is afraid that you may think he eats and drinks all that you send to the Doctor. He swore with a solemn oath that he would be true to you, if you would write a word to the Doctor.[96] I hope you do not doubt my fidelity!' and she began to swear and to curse herself if she would deceive me. She said, he had taken a no less solemn oath, before she believed him. I said: 'I have nothing to write to him. I do not know what I have to write.' 'Oh!' said she, 'write only two words, so that the old man may see that he can trust him! If you wish for ink, Christian can give you some.' I replied: 'I have something to write with, if I choose to do so, and I can write without ink and paper.'

This she could not understand; so I took some pieces of sugared almonds, and made some letters on them with the large pin, placing on four almonds the words: *non ti fidar*! I divided the word *fidar*, and placed half on each almond. I had in this way rest for a day, and somewhat to beguile the time. Whether the Doctor could not see what was written on the almonds, or whether he wished to test Christian's fidelity, I know not, but Christian brought the woman a slip of paper from the Doctor to me, full of lamentations at our condition, and stating that my daughter Anna Cathrina, or else Cassetta, were the cause of his misfortune.

I wished to know more of this, so I wrote to him desiring information (we wrote to each other in Italian). He replied that one or the other had left his letter lying somewhere on the table, where it was found and despatched; for that a letter of his was the cause of his misfortune. I wrote back to him that it was not credible, but that he was suspected of having corresponded with my lord, and hence his letters had been seized. The more I tried to impress this upon him the more opinionated he became,[97] and he wrote afterwards saying that it was a scheme of Cassetta's to get him into the net, in order to bring me out of it. When he began to write in this way, I acquired a strange opinion of him, and fancied he was trying to draw something out of me which he could bring forward; and I reflected for some days whether I should answer. At last I answered him in this strain, that no one knew better than he that I was not aware of any treason; that the knowledge as to how his correspondence with my lord had become known was of no use to him; that I had no idea why he was sentenced, and that no sentence had been passed on me. Some weeks elapsed before the Doctor wrote. At last he communicated to me in a few words the sentence passed upon him, and we corresponded from time to time with each other.

The prison governor became gradually more accessible, came in at every meal-time, and related all sorts of jokes and buffooneries, which he had carried on in his youth: how he had been a drummer, and had made a Merry Andrew of himself for my brother-in-law Count Pentz, and how he had enacted a dog for the sake of favour and money, and had crawled under the table, frightening the guests and biting a dog for a ducat's reward. When he had been drinking (which was often the case) he juggled and played Punch, sometimes a fortune-teller, and the like.

When Chresten the tower-warder, and Christian the prisoner, heard the prison governor carrying on his jokes, they did the same, and made such a noise with the woman in the antechamber that we could not hear ourselves speak. She sat on Christian's lap, and behaved herself in a wanton manner. One day she was not very well, and made herself some warm beer and bread, placing it outside on the stove. The prison governor was sitting with me and talking, Chresten and Christian were joking with her outside, and Christian was to stir the warm beer and bread, and taste if it was hot enough. Chresten said to Christian, 'Drink it up if you are thirsty.' The words were no sooner said than the deed was done, and almost at the same moment the prison governor got up and went away. When the door was locked, the woman seemed to be almost fainting. I thought she was ill, and I was fearful that she might die suddenly, and that the guilt of her death might be laid on me, and I asked quickly, 'Are you ill?' She answered, 'I am bad enough,' confirming it with a terrible oath and beginning to unbutton her jacket. Then I saw that she was angry, and I knew well that she would give vent to a burst of execrations, which was the case.

She cursed and scolded those who had so treated her; a poor sick thing as she was, and she had not had anything to eat or drink all day. I said, 'Be quiet, and you shall have some warm beer.' She swore with a solemn oath, asking how it was to be got here? it was summer and there was no fire in the stove, and it was no use calling, as no one could hear. I said, 'If you will be silent, I will cause the pot to boil.' 'Yes,' and she swore with another fearful oath, 'I can indeed be silent, and will never speak of it.' So I made her take three pieces of brick, which were lying behind the night-stool, and place on these her pot of beer and bread (everything that she was to do was to be done in silence; she might not answer me with words but only with signs, when I asked her anything). She sat down besides the pot, stirring it with a spoon. I sat always on my bed during the day, and then the table was placed before me. I had a piece of chalk, and I wrote various things on the table, asking from time to time whether the pot boiled. She kept peeping in and shaking her head. When I had asked three times and she turned to me and saw that I was laughing, she behaved herself like a mad woman, throwing the spoon from her hand, turning over the stool, tearing open her jacket, and exclaiming, 'The devil may be jeered at like this!' I said, 'You are not worthy of anything better, as you believe that I can practise magic.' 'Oh (and she repeated a solemn oath) had I not believed that you could practise magic, I should never have consented to be locked up with you; do you know that?' I reflected for a moment what answer to give, but I said nothing, smiled, and let her rave on.

Afterwards she wept and bemoaned her condition. 'Now, now,' I said, 'be quiet! I will make the pot boil without witchcraft.' And as we had a tinder-box, I ordered her to strike a light, and to kindle three ends of candles, which she was to place under the pot. This made the pot boil, and she kissed her hand to me and was very merry. Once or twice afterwards I gave her leave to warm beer in this way: it could not always be done, for if the wind blew against the window (which was opened with a long pike) the smoke could not pass away. I said, 'Remember your oath and do not talk of what takes place here, or the lights will be taken from us; at any rate we shall lose some of them.' She asserted that she would not. I heard nothing of it at the time, but some years afterwards I found that she had said that I had taken up two half- loose stones from the floor (this was afterwards related in another manner by a clergyman, as will be mentioned afterwards). She had also said that I had climbed up and looked at the rope-dancers in the castle square, which was true. For as Chresten one day told the woman that rope-dancers would be exhibiting in the inner castle yard, and she informed me of it and enquired what they were, and I explained to her, she lamented that she could not get a sight of them. I said it could easily be done, if she would not talk about it afterwards. She swore, as usual, with an oath that she would not. So I took the bedclothes from the bed and placed the boards on the floor and set the bed upright in front of the window, and the night-stool on the top of it. In order to get upon the bedstead, the table was placed at the side, and a stool by the table in order to get upon the table, and a stool upon the table, in order to get upon the night-stool, and a stool on the night-stool, so that we could stand and look comfortably, though not both at once. I let her climb up first, and I stood and took care that the bed did not begin to give way; she was to keep watch when I was on the top. I knew, moreover, well that the dancers did not put forth their utmost skill at first.[98]

I could see the faces of the King and Queen: they were standing in the long hall, and I wondered afterwards that they never turned their eyes to the place where I stood. I did not let the woman perceive that I saw them. During this woman's time I once had a desire to see the people go to the castle-church and return from it. The bed was again placed upright, and I sat for a long time on the top, until everyone had come out of church. The woman did not venture to climb up; she said that she had been afraid enough the last time, and was glad when she had come down.

The first time I received the holy communion during this prison governor's time, two brass candlesticks which did not match were brought in, with tallow candles. This displeased the woman, though she said nothing to me. But when at length she was compelled to take the sacrament, after more than three years had elapsed since she had been at the Lord's table, she begged Chresten, the tower-warder, to go to her daughter (who was in the service of a carpenter in the town), and to get the loan of a pair of beautiful brass candlesticks and a couple of wax candles. If she could also procure for her a fine linen cloth, she was to do her best; she would pay for it.

Whether the woman had before thought of the candlesticks and candles which had been placed for me, or whether Chresten himself thought that it would not be proper to provide better for her, I know not, but shortly before the priest came, Chresten unlocked the outer door of my prison and said, 'Karen, hand me out the candlestick you have, and two candles.' Her behaviour is not to be described: she asked if he had not spoken with her daughter, and much of the same kind (I did not at the time know what she had desired of Chresten). He made no reply to her question, but asked for the candlestick and candles. For a long time she would not give them, but cursed and scolded. I was still lying down, and I asked her if I should be her maid, and should do it for her? whether she could withhold from him what he requested? So she handed them to him through the hole of the inner door, with so many execrations against him that it was terrible to listen to. He laughed aloud, and went away. This made her still more angry. I did my best to appease her, telling her that such conduct was a most improper preparation, and holding before her the sinfulness of her behaviour. She said she thought that the sin belonged to him who had given cause for it. I asked her, at last, in what the Lord's Supper consisted? whether it consisted in candlesticks and candles? I rebuked her for looking to externals and not to the essential; and I begged her to fall on her knees and pray heartily to God for forgiveness of her sins, that He might not impute her folly to her. She answered that she would do so, but she did not do it at once.

I imagine that the clergyman[99] was well informed by Chresten of all that concerned her, as he put to her so many questions: where she was born? whom she had served? and more of the same kind, and finally, whether she had her certificate of confession, and how long it was since she had received the Lord's Supper? After this he confessed her in a strange manner; at first as one who had deserved to do public penance for great sins, then as a criminal under sentence of death who was preparing for her end; at last consoling her, and performing his office. When all was over and she came in to me, I wished her joy. 'Joy, indeed' (she answered); 'there is not much good in it! This does me more harm than good! If I could only get out, I would indeed go straight to the sacrament; I reckon this as nothing!' I interrupted her quickly, and said: 'Reflect upon what you are saying! blaspheme not God—I will not hear that! You know well what God's Word says of those who receive Christ's body and blood unworthily and have trodden under foot his body?' 'Under foot?' said she. 'Yes, under foot!' I said, and I made a whole sermon upon it. She listened decently; but when I was silent, she said: 'He looked upon me as a malefactor, and as one under sentence of death. I have never murdered anyone (I thought, we know not what);[100] why should I die? God Almighty grant'——and with this she was silent. I preached to her again, and said that she had deserved eternal death on account of her sins, and especially because she had so long kept aloof from the Lord's table. 'This confession,' she said, 'I have to thank Chresten for; Balcke was also probably concerned in it.' And she began to curse them both. I threatened her with a second confession, if she did not restrain such words. I told her I could not justify myself before God to keep silence to it, and I said, 'If you speak in this way to Chresten, you may be sure he will inform against you.' This kept her somewhat in check, and she did not go out upon the stairs that noon.[101]

After that time she was not so merry by far with the man. She often complained to me that she was weak, and had strained herself lifting the new basin which Balcke had given her; she could not long hold out, she said, and she had asked the prison governor to let her go away, but that he had answered that she was to die in the tower. I said, 'The prison governor cannot yet rightly understand you; ask Chresten to speak for you.' This she did, but came back with the same answer. One day she said: 'I see well, dear lady, that you would be as gladly free of me as I should be to go. What have I for all my money? I cannot enjoy it, and I cannot be of service to you.' I said: 'Money can do much. Give some money to the prison-governor, and then he will speak for you. Request one of the charwomen to carry the basin instead of you, and this you could pay with very little.' She did the latter for some weeks; at length one day she said to me, 'I have had a silver cup made for the prison governor. (Her daughter came to her on the stairs as often as she desired, and she had permission to remain downstairs the whole afternoon, under pretext of speaking with her daughter. Whether she gave him presents for this, I know not, but I was well contented to be alone. She was, however, once afraid that I should tell the priest of it.) The fact was, the prison- governor did not dare to speak for her with the King. She asked my advice on the matter. I said, 'Remain in bed when the dinner is going on, and I will go out and speak with the prison-governor.' This was done. At first he raised some difficulties, and said, 'The Queen will say that there is some trick at the bottom of it.' I said they could visit and examine the woman when she came out; that we had not been such intimate friends; that I knew the woman had been sent to wait on me; when she could do so no longer, but lay in bed, I had no attendance from her, and still less was I inclined to wait on her; she did her work for money, and there were women enough who would accept the employment.

Three days afterwards, when the King came from Fridrichsborg, the prison-governor came in and said that the woman could go down in the evening; that he had another whom Chresten had recommended, and who was said to be a well-behaved woman (which she is).

Karen the daughter of Ole therefore went down, and Karen the daughter of Nels came up in her place. And I can truly say that it was one of the happiest days during my severe imprisonment; for I was freed of a faithless, godless, lying[102] and ill-behaved woman, and I received in her stead a Christian, true, and thoroughly good (perhaps too good) woman. When the first took her departure, she said, 'Farewell, lady! we are now both pleased.' I answered, 'That is perhaps one of the truest words you have ever spoken in your life.' She made no reply, but ran as fast as she could, so that no weakness nor illness were perceptible in her. She lived scarcely a year afterwards, suffering severe pain for six weeks in her bed, before she died; the nature of her malady I know not.

On the day after this Karen's arrival, she sat thoroughly depressed all the afternoon. I asked her what was the matter. She said, 'Oh! I have nothing to do, and I might not bring work with me! I weary to death.' I enquired what work she could do. 'Spinning,' she answered, 'is my work principally; I can also do plain needlework and can knit a little.' I had nothing to help her in this way; but I drew out some ends of silk, which I had kept from what I cut off, and which are too short to work with, and other tufts of silk from night- jackets and stockings; I had made a flax-comb of small pins,[103] fastened to a piece of wood; with this I combed the silk and made it available for darning caps; and I said to her, 'There is something for you to do; comb that for me!' She was so heartily pleased that it was quite a delight to me. I found from her account of this and that which had occurred in her life, that she had a good heart, and that she had often been deceived owing to her credulity. She had also known me in my prosperity; she had been in the service of a counsellor's lady who had been present at my wedding, and she could well remember the display of fireworks and other festivities; she wept as she spoke of it, and showed great sympathy with me. She was a peasant's daughter from Jutland, but had married the quarter-master of a regiment. By degrees I felt an affection for her, and begged her to speak to Christian and to enquire how the Doctor was; I told her that Christian could occasionally perform small services for us, and could buy one thing or another for us; for he had a lad, in fact sometimes two, who executed commissions for him, but that I had never trusted the other woman, so that he had never bought anything for me; besides, the other woman had not cared to spin; but that Christian should now procure us what we wanted in return for our candles. And as she did not care to drink wine (for at each meal the woman received at that time half-a-pint of French wine), I said: 'Give Chresten your wine as I give wine to Christian, then Chresten can let it stay with the cellar-clerk and can take it weekly, which will give him a profit on it, and then he will see nothing even if he remarks anything.'

This was done, and Christian got us two hand-distaffs. Mine was but small, but hers was a proper size. I spun a little and twisted it into thread, which is still in my possession. Christian procured her as much flax as she desired, and brought her up a whole wreath in his trousers. She spun a good deal on the hand-distaff, and I arranged my loom on a stool, which I placed on the table, fastening one beam with ribbon and cord which I had made myself, so that when the key was put into the staircase-door, I could in one pull loosen my loom and unfasten the other beam which was fastened to myself, and put all away before the inner door was opened. I made myself also a wooden skewer (I had before used a warp), so that I could weave alone; I had also obtained a real weaver's comb; so we were very industrious, each at her own work.

The prison governor was full of foolish jokes, and played tricks such as boys enjoy; he tried to jest with the woman, but she would not join him. Almost every day he was drunk at dinner-time when he came up. Afterwards he came rarely of an evening, but sent a servant instead, who would lie and sleep on the wall in the window. He wanted to jest with me also, and opened his mouth, telling me to throw something in and see if I could hit his mouth. I laughed and said, 'How foolish you are!' and begged him to come nearer, and I would see if I could hit him. 'No, no,' said he; 'I am not such a fool; I daresay you would box my ears.' One day he came up with a peculiar kind of squirt, round in form like a ball, and he placed a small tube in it, so small as scarcely to be seen; it was quite pretty. When pressed in any part, the water squirted out quite high and to a distance. He was saucy, and squirted me. When he saw that I was angry, he came to me with the squirt, ran away and sat down with his mouth as wide open as possible and begged me to squirt into it if I could. I would not begin playing with him, for I knew his coarseness well from his stories, and I gave him back the squirt. When Karen was bringing in the meat, the prison governor had the squirt between his legs, and was seated on a low stool, from which he could squirt into the woman's face; he was some distance from her, and the ball was not larger than a large plum. She knew nothing of the squirt (she is somewhat hasty in her words), and she exclaimed, 'May God send you a misfortune, Mr. governor! Are you insulting me?' The prison governor laughed like an insane man, so pleased was he at this.

By degrees he became less wild; he rarely came up sober, and he would lie on the woman's bed and sleep while I dined, so that Chresten and the woman had to help him off the bed when they had woke him. The keys of the prisons lay by his side, and the principal key close by (did he not take good care of his prisoners?).[104] He was not afraid that I should murder him. One evening he was intoxicated, and behaved as such; and began, after his fashion, to try and caress me, endeavouring to feel my knee and seized the edge of my petticoat. I thrust him away with my foot, and said nothing more than: 'When you are intoxicated, remain away from me, and do not come in, I tell you.' He said nothing, got up and went away; but he did not come in afterwards when he was tipsy, but remained outside in the anteroom, lying down in the window, where there was a broad stone bench against the wall; there he lay and slept for some time after my doors were locked, then the coachman and Chresten came and dragged him down. Occasionally he came in when he was not drunk, and he gave me at my request some old cards, which I sewed together and made into a box. Christian covered it with thin sticks of fir, which I afterwards stitched over, and I even secretly contrived to paint it. I have it in my possession. The prison governor saw it afterwards, but he never asked where the covering had come from.[105] In this box (if I may call it so) I keep all my work and implements, and it stands by day on my bed.

Christian's power increased. He waited not only outside at dinner, but he even locked my door in the face of the tower-warder. He came with the perfuming-pan into my room when the woman took away the night-stool; in fact, he subsequently became so audacious that he did everything he chose, and had full command over the prisoners below. Chresten availed himself also of the slack surveillance of the prison governor, and stayed sometimes the whole night out in the town, often coming in tipsy to supper. One evening Chresten was intoxicated, and had broken some panes of glass below with his hand, so that his fingers were bloody; he dashed my wine-cup on the ground, so that it cracked and was bent; and as the cup was quite bloody outside when he came in to me, and some blood seemed to have got into the wine, I spoke somewhat seriously with the prison governor about it. He said nothing but 'The man is mad,' took the cup and went himself down into the cellar, and had the cup washed and other wine put in it. How they afterwards made it up I know not. The indentations on the cup have been beaten out, but the crack on the edge is still there; this suits the cellar-clerk well, for now scarcely half a pint goes into the cup. Christian held his own manfully against the prison governor, when he had a quarrel with some of the prisoners below; and Chresten complained of this to the prison governor, who came in and wanted to place Christian in the Witch Cell; but he thrust the prison governor away, and said that he had nothing to do with him, and that he had not put him into the prison; and then harangued him in such a style that the Governor thanked God when he went away. Christian then called after him from the window, and said, 'I know secret tricks of yours, but you know none of mine.' (One I knew of, of which he was aware, and that not a small one. There was a corporal who had stabbed a soldier, and was sought for with the beating of drums: the prison governor concealed him for several weeks in the tower.) On the following morning Christian repented, and he feared that he might be locked up, and came to my door before it had been opened[106] (it often happened that the anteroom was unlocked before the food was brought up, and always in the winter mornings, when a fire was made in the stove outside), and he begged me to speak for him with the prison governor, which I did; so that things remained as they were, and Christian was as bold as before.

The woman and I lived in good harmony together. Occasionally there were small disputes between Christian and her, but at that time they were of no importance. I quieted his anger with wine and candles. This woman had a son, who died just after she had come to me, and a daughter who is still alive; at that time she was in the service of a tailor, but she is now married to a merchant. The daughter received permission occasionally to come and speak with her mother on the stairs. This annoyed Christian, as he thought that through her all sorts of things were obtained; and he threatened often that he would say what he thought, though he did not know it, and this frequently troubled the woman (she easily weeps and easily laughs). I could soon comfort her. We spent our time very well. I taught her to read, beginning with A B C, for she did not know a single letter. I kept to fixed hours for teaching her. She was at the time sixty years of age. And when she could spell a little,

[107] she turned the book one day over and over, and began to rub her eyes and exclaimed, 'Oh God, how strange it is! I do not know (and she swore by God) a single letter.' I was standing behind her, and could scarcely keep from laughing. She rubbed her eyes again, and (as she is rather hasty with her words) she pointed quickly to an O, and said, 'Is not that an O?' 'Yes,' I said, and I laughed when she turned to me. She then for the first time perceived that she was holding the book upside down; she threw herself on the bed and laughed till I thought she would burst.

One day when she was to read, and did not like to lay aside her distaff, it did not go smoothly, and she gave it up, and said, 'Am I not foolish to wish to learn to read in my old age? What good does it do me? I have spent much money on my son to have him taught to read, and see, is he not dead?' I knew how much she was able to do, and I let her go on speaking. She threw the book on her bed, sat down to her work, and said, 'What do I need to learn to read in a book? I can, thank God, read my morning and evening prayer.' (I thought to myself, 'badly enough.' She knew very little of her catechism.) I said (gently): 'That is true, Karen. It is not necessary for you to learn to read a book, as you can read very nicely by heart.' I had scarcely said this than she jumped up, took her book again, and began to spell. I neither advised her nor dissuaded her, but treated her like a good simple child.[108]

I fell ill during this year,[109] and as the prison governor no longer came in to me and sent the servant up of an evening, I begged the woman to tell him that I was ill, and that I wished a doctor to come to me. The woman told him this (for by this time he understood Danish, and the woman understood a little German), and when she said, 'I am afraid she will die,' he answered, 'Why the d——— let her die!' I had daily fevers, heat, but no shivering; and as an obstruction was the chief cause of my illness, I desired a remedy. The prison governor ridiculed the idea. When I heard this, I requested he would come to me, which he did. I spoke to him rather seriously; told him that it was not the King's will that he should take no more care of me than he did, that he had more care for his dog than for me (which was the case). Upon this his manner improved, and he enquired what I wished for, and I said what I desired, and obtained it. I had become rather excited at the conversation, so that I felt weak. The woman cried and said: 'I am afraid you will die, dear lady! and then the bad maids from the wash-house will wash your feet and hands.' (One of the maids below had sent very uncivil messages to me.) I replied that I should not say a word against that. 'What?' said she angrily, 'will you suffer that? No,' she added with an asseveration, 'I would not! I would not suffer it if I were in your place.' So I said, like that philosopher, 'Place the stick with the candlestick at my side, and with that I can keep them away from me when I am dead.'[110] This brought her to reason again, and she talked of the grave and of burial. I assured her that this did not trouble me at all; that when I was dead, it was all one to me; even if they threw my body in the sea, it would, together with my soul, appear before the throne of God at the last day, and might come off better perhaps than many who were lying in coffins mounted with silver and in splendid vaults. But that I would not say, as the prison governor did in his levity, that I should like to be buried on the hill of Valdby, in order to be able to look around me. I desired nothing else than a happy end. We spoke of the prison governor's coarseness; of various things which he did, on account of which it would go badly with him if the Queen knew it; of his godlessness, how that when he had been to the Lord's Supper, he said he had passed muster; and other things. There was no fear of God in him.

I requested to have the sacrament, and asked M. Buck to come to me at seven o'clock in the morning, for at about half-past eight o'clock the fever began. The priest did not come till half-past nine, when the fever heat had set in (for it began now somewhat later). When I had made my confession, he began to preach about murder and homicide; about David, who was guilty of Uriah's death, although he had not killed him with his own hand. He spoke of sin as behoved him, and of the punishment it brings with it. 'You,' he said, 'have killed General Fux, for you have bribed a servant to kill him.' I replied, 'That is not true! I have not done so!' 'Yes, truly,' he said; 'the servant is in Hamburg, and he says it himself.' I replied: 'If he has so said, he has lied, for my son gave Fux his death-blow with a stiletto. I did not know that Fux was in Bruges until I heard of his death. How could the servant, then, say that I had done it? It was not done by my order, but that I should not have rejoiced that God should have punished the villain I am free to confess.' To this he answered, 'I should have done so myself.' I said: 'God knows how Fux treated us in our imprisonment at Borringholm. That is now past, and I think of it no more.' 'There you are right,' he said, as he proceeded in his office.

When all was over, he spoke with the prison governor outside the door of my anteroom, just in front of the door of the Dark Church, and said that I made myself ill; that I was not ill; that my face was red from pure anger; that he had spoken the truth to me, and that I had been angry in consequence. Christian was standing inside the door of the Dark Church, for at this time there were no prisoners there, and he heard the conversation, and related it to me when I began to get up again and spoke with him at the door.

Some time afterwards Christian said to me, quite secretly, 'If you like, I will convey a message from you to your children in Skaane.' I enquired how this could be done. He said: 'Through my girl; she is thoroughly true; she shall go on purpose.' He knew that I had some ducats left, for Peder the coachman had confided it to him, as he himself told me. I accepted his offer and wrote to my children, and gave him a ducat for the girl's journey.[111] She executed the commission well, and came back with a letter from them and from my sister. [E40] The woman knew nothing of all this.

By degrees Christian began to be insolent in various ways. When he came with his boy's pouch, in which the woman was to give him food, he would throw it at her, and he was angry if meat was not kept for himself for the evening; and when he could not at once get the pouch back again, he would curse the day when he had come to my door and had spoken with me or had communicated anything to me. She was sad, but she said nothing to me. This lasted only for a day, and then he knocked again at the door and spoke as usual of what news he had heard. The woman was sitting on the bed, crossing herself fifteen times (he could not see her, nor could he see me). When he was gone, she related how fearfully he had been swearing, &c. I said: 'You must not regard this; in the time of the other Karen he has done as much.' His courage daily increased. The dishes were often brought up half-an-hour before the prison-governor came. In the meanwhile Christian cut the meat, and took himself the piece he preferred (formerly at every meal I had sent him out a piece of fish, or anything else he desired). The stupid prison governor allowed it to go on; he was glad, I imagine, that he was spared the trouble, and paid no attention to the fact that there was anything missing in the dish. I let it go on for a time, for it did not happen regularly every day. But when he wanted food for his boy, he would say nothing but 'Some food in my boy's pouch!' We often laughed over this afterwards, when he was away, but not at the time, for it grew worse from day to day. He could not endure that we should laugh and be merry; if he heard anything of the kind outside, he was angry. But if one spoke despondingly, he would procure what was in his power.[112] One day he listened, and heard that we were laughing; for the woman was just relating an amusing story of the mother of a schoolboy in Frederichsborg (she had lived there); how the mother of the boy did not know how to address the schoolmaster, and called him Herr Willas.[E41] He said, 'I am no Herr.' 'Then Master,' said the woman. 'I am no Master either,' he said; 'I am plain Willas.' Then the woman said: 'My good plain Willas! My son always licks the cream from my milk-pans when he comes home. Will you lick him in return, and that with a switch on his back?' While we were laughing at this, he came to the door and heard the words I was saying: 'I don't suppose that it really so happened; one must always add something to make a good story of it.' He imagined we were speaking of him, and that we were laughing at him. At meal-time he said to the woman, 'You were very merry to-day.' She said, 'Did you not know why? It is because I belong to the "Lætter"'[E42] (that was her family name). 'It would be a good thing,' he said, 'to put a stop to your laughter altogether; you have been laughing at me.' She protested that we had not, that his name had not been mentioned (which was the case); but he would not regard it. They fell into an altercation. She told me of the conversation, and for some days he did not come to the door, and I sent him nothing; for just at that time a poor old man was my neighbour, and I sent him a drink of wine. Christian came again to the door and knocked. He complained very softly of the woman; begged that I would reprove her for what she had said to him, as he had heard his name mentioned. I protested to him that at the time we were not even thinking of him, and that I could not scold her for the words we had spoken together. I wished to have repose within our closed door. 'Yes,' he answered; 'household peace is good, as the old woman said.' With this he went away.

Afterwards he caused us all sorts of annoyance, and was again pacified. Then he wished again that I should write to Skaane.[113] I said I was satisfied to know that some of my children were with my sister; where my sons were, and how it fared with them, I did not know: I left them in God's care. This did not satisfy him, and he spoke as if he thought I had no more money; but he did not at that time exactly say so. But one day, when he had one of his mad fits, he came to the door and had a can with wine (which I gave him at almost every meal) in his hand, and he said: 'Can you see me?' (for there was a cleft in the outermost door, but at such a distance one could not clearly see through). 'Here I am with my cup of wine, and I am going to drink your health for the last time.' I asked: 'Why for the last time?' 'Yes,' he swore, coming nearer to the door and saying: 'I will do no more service for you; so I know well that I shall get no more wine.' I said, 'I thank you for the services you have rendered me; I desire no more from you, but nevertheless you may still get your wine.' 'No!' he said; 'no more service! there is nothing more to be fetched.' 'That is true,' I answered. 'You do not know me,' said he; 'I am not what you think; it is easy to start with me, but it is not easy to get rid of me.' I laughed a little, and said: 'You are far better than you make yourself out to be. To-morrow you will be of another mind.'

He continued to describe himself as very wicked (it was, however, far from as bad as he really is). I could do nothing else but laugh at him. He drank from the can, and sat himself down on the stool outside. I called him and begged him to come to the door, as I wanted to speak with him. There he sat like a fool, saying to himself: 'Should I go to the door? No,' and he swore with a terrible oath, 'that I will not do! Oh yes, to the door! No, Christian, no!' laughing from time to time immoderately, and shouting out that the devil might take him and tear him in pieces the day on which he should go to my door or render me a service. I went away from the door and sat down horrified at the man's madness and audacity. Some days passed in silence, and he would accept no wine. No food was offered to him, for he continued, in the same way as before, to cut the meat before the prison governor came up. As the prison governor at this time occasionally again came in to me and talked with me, I requested him that Christian, as a prisoner, should not have the liberty of messing my food. This was, therefore, forbidden him in future.

Some days afterwards he threw the pouch to the woman on the stairs, and said: 'Give me some food for to-night in my lad's pouch.'[114] This was complied with with the utmost obedience, and a piece of meat was placed in the pouch. This somewhat appeased him, so that at noon he spoke with the woman, and even asked for a drink of wine; but he threatened the woman that he would put an end to the laughing. I did not fear the evil he could do to me, but this vexatious life was wearisome. I allowed no wine to be offered to him, unless he asked for some. He was in the habit every week of procuring me the newspapers[E43] for candles, and as he did not bring me the newspapers for the candles of the first week, I sent him no more. He continued to come every Saturday with the perfuming-pan, and to lock my door. When he came in with the fumigating stuff, he fixed his eyes upon the wall, and would not look at me. I spoke to him once and asked after the doctor, and he made no reply.

Thus it went on for some weeks; then he became appeased, and brought the woman the papers from the time that he had withheld them, all rolled up together and fastened with a thread. When the prison governor came in during the evening and sat and talked (he was slightly intoxicated), and Chresten had gone to the cellar, the woman gave him back the papers, thanking him in my name, and saying that the papers were of no interest to me; I had done without them for so many weeks, and could continue to do so. He was so angry that he tore the papers in two with his teeth, tore open his coat so that the buttons fell on the floor, threw some of the papers into the fire, howled, screamed, and gnashed with his teeth. I tried to find something over which I could laugh with the prison governor, and I spoke as loud as I could, in order to drown

Christian's voice.[115] The woman came in as pale as a corpse, and looked at me. I signed to her that she should go out again. Then Christian came close to my door and howled, throwing his slippers up into the air, and then against my door, repeating this frequently. When he heard Chresten coming up with the cups, he threw himself on the seat on which the prison governor was accustomed to lie, and again struck his slippers against the wall. Chresten gazed at him with astonishment, as he stood with the cups in his hand. He saw well that there was something amiss between the woman and Christian, and that the woman was afraid; he could not, however, guess the cause, nor could he find it out; he thought, moreover, that it had nothing to do with me, since I was laughing and talking with the prison governor. When the doors were closed, the lamentations found free vent. The woman said that he had threatened her; he would forbid her daughter coming on the stairs and carrying on her talk, and doing other things that she ought not. I begged her to be calm; told her he was now in one of his mad fits, but that it would pass away; that he would hesitate before he said anything of it, for that he would be afraid that what he had brought up to her would also come to light, and then he would himself get into misfortune for his trouble; that the prison governor had given her daughter leave to come to her, and to whom therefore should he complain? (I thought indeed in my own mind that if he adhered to his threat, he would probably find some one else to whom he could complain, as he had so much liberty; he could bring in and out what he chose, and could speak with whom he desired in the watchman's gallery.) She wept, was very much affected, and talked with but little sense, and said: 'If I have no peace for him, I will—yes, I will—.' She got no further, and could not get out what she would do. I smiled, and said at last: 'Christian is mad. I will put a stop to it to-morrow: let me deal with him! Sleep now quietly!'

She fell asleep afterwards, but I did not do so very quickly, thinking what might follow such wild fits. Next day towards noon I told her what she was to say to Christian; she was to behave as if she were dissatisfied, and begin to upbraid him and to say, 'The devil take you for all you have taught her! She has pulled off her slippers just as you do, and strikes me on the head with them. She is angry and no joke, and she took all the pretty stuff she had finished and threw it into the night-stool. "There," said she, "no one shall have any advantage of that."' At this he laughed like a fool, for it pleased him. 'Is she thoroughly angry?' he asked. 'Yes,' she replied; 'she is indeed.' At this he laughed aloud on the stairs, so that I heard it. For a fortnight he behaved tolerably well, now and then demanding wine and food; and he came moreover to the door and related, among other things, how he had heard that the prince (now our king) was going to be married. I had also heard it, though I did not say so, for the prison governor had told me of it, and besides I received the papers without him. And as I asked him no questions, he went away immediately, saying afterwards to the woman, 'She is angry and so am I. We will see who first will want the other.' He threatened the woman very much. She wished that I would give him fair words. I told her that he was not of that character that one could get on with him by always showing the friendly side.[116] As he by degrees became more insolent than could be tolerated, I said one day to the prison governor that I was surprised that he could allow a prisoner to unlock and lock my doors, and to do that which was really the office of the tower-warder; and I asked him whether it did not occur to him that under such circumstances I might manage to get out, if I chose to do so without the King's will? Christian was a prisoner, under sentence of death; he had already offered to get me out of the tower. The prison governor sat and stared like one who does not rightly understand, and he made no reply but 'Yes, yes!' but he acted in conformity with my warning, so that either he himself locked and unlocked, or Chresten did so. (I have seen Christian snatching the keys out of Chresten's hand and locking my door, and this at the time when he began to make himself so angry.)

If Christian had not been furious before, he became so now, especially at the time that Chresten came in with the perfuming-pan when the woman was above. He would then stand straight before me in the anteroom, looking at me like a ghost and gnashing his teeth; and when he saw that I took the rest of the fumigating stuff from Chresten's hand (which he had always himself given me in paper), he burst into a defiant laugh. When the doors were unlocked in the evening, and Christian began talking with the woman, he said: 'Karen, tell her ladyship that I will make out a devilish story with you both. I have with my own eyes seen Chresten giving her a letter. Ay, that was why she did not let me go in with the perfuming-pan, because I would not undertake her message to Skaane. Ay, does she get the newspapers also from him? Yes, tell her, great as are the services I have rendered her, I will now prepare a great misfortune for her.' God knows what a night I had! Not because I feared his threat, for I did not in the least regard his words; he himself would have suffered the most by far. But the woman was so sad that she did nothing but lament and moan, chiefly about her daughter, on account of the disgrace it would be to her if they put her mother into the Dark Church, nay even took her life. Then she remembered that her daughter had spoken with her on the stairs, and she cried out again: 'Oh my daughter! my daughter! She will get into the house of correction!' For some time I said nothing more than 'Calm yourself; it will not be as bad as you think,' as I perceived that she was not capable of listening to reason, for she at once exclaimed 'Ach! ach!' as often as I tried to speak, sitting up in bed and holding her head between her two hands and crying till she was almost deluged. I thought, 'When there are no more tears to come, she will probably stop.'

I said at length, when she was a little appeased: 'The misfortune with which the man threatens us cannot be averted by tears. Calm yourself and lie down to sleep. I will do the same, and I will pray God to impart to me His wise counsel for the morrow.' This quieted her a little; but when I thought she was sleeping, she burst forth again with all the things that she feared; she had brought in to me slips of paper, knife and scissors, and other things furnished by him contrary to order. I answered only from time to time: 'Go to sleep, go to sleep! I will talk with you to-morrow!' It was of no avail. The clock struck two, when she was still wanting to talk, and saying, 'It will go badly with the poor old man down below!'[117] I made as if I were asleep, but the whole night, till five o'clock and longer, no sleep came to my eyes.

When the door was unlocked at noon, I had already intimated to her what she was to say to Christian, and had given her to understand that he thought to receive money from her and candles from me by his threats, and that he wanted to force us to obey his pleasure; but that he had others to deal with than he imagined. She was only to behave as if she did not care for his talk, and was to say nothing but 'Good day,' unless he spoke to her; and if he enquired what I had said, she was to act as if she did not remember that she was to tell me anything. If he repeated his message, she was to say: 'I am not going to say anything to her about that. Are you still as foolish as you were last night? Do what you choose!' and then go away. This conversation took place, and he threatened her worse than before. The woman remained steadfast, but she was thoroughly cast down when our doors were locked; still, as she has a light heart, she often laughed with the tears in her eyes. I knew well that Christian would try to recover favour again by communicating me all kind of news in writing, but I had forbidden the woman to take his slips of paper, so that he got very angry. I begged her to tell him that he had better restrain himself if he could; that if he indulged his anger, it would be worse for him. At this he laughed ironically, and said, 'Tell her, it will be worse for her. Whatever I have done for her, she has enticed me to by giving me wine: tell her so. I will myself confess everything; and if I come to the rack and wheel, Chresten shall get into trouble. He brought her letters from her children.' (The rogue well knew that I had not allowed the woman to be cognisant neither of the fact that he had conveyed for me a message to Skaane to my children, nor of the wax in which the tower keys were impressed; this was why he spoke so freely to her.) When our doors were locked, this formed the subject of our conversation. I laughed at it, and asked the woman what disgrace could be so great as to be put on the wheel; I regarded it as thoughtless talk, for such it was, and I begged her to tell him that he need not trouble himself to give himself up, as I would relieve him of the trouble, and (if he chose) tell the prison governor everything on the following day that he had done for me; he had perhaps forgotten something, but that I could well remember it all.

When the woman told him this, he made no answer, but ran down, kept quiet for some days, and scarcely spoke to the woman. One Saturday, when the woman had gone upstairs with the night-stool, he went up to her and tried to persuade her to accept a slip of paper for me, but she protested that she dare not. 'Then tell her,' he said, 'that she is to give me back the scissors and the knife which I have given her. I will have them, and she shall see what I can do. You shall both together get into trouble!' She came down as white as a corpse, so that I thought she had strained herself. She related the conversation and his request, and begged me much to give him back the things, and that then he would be quiet. I said: 'What is the matter with you? are you in your senses? Does he not say that we shall get into trouble if he gets the scissors and knife back again? Now is not the time to give them to him. Do you not understand that he is afraid I shall let the things be seen? My work, he thinks, is gone, and the papers are no longer here, so that there is nothing with which he can be threatened except these things. You must not speak with him this evening. If he says anything, do not answer him.' In the evening he crept in, and said in the anteroom to her, 'Bring me the scissors and the knife!' She made no answer. On the following morning, towards noon, I begged her to tell him that I had nothing of his; that I had paid for both the scissors and knife, and that more than double their value. He was angry at the message, and gnashed with his teeth. She went away from him, and avoided as much as possible speaking with him alone. When he saw that the woman would not take a slip of paper from him, he availed himself of a moment when the prison governor was not there, and threw in a slip of paper to me on the floor. A strange circumstance was near occurring this time: for just as he was throwing in the paper, the prison governor's large shaggy dog passed in, and the paper fell on the dog's back, but it fell off again in the corner, where the dog was snuffling.

Upon the paper stood the words: 'Give me the knife and scissors back, or I will bring upon you as much misfortune as I have before rendered you good service, and I will pay for the knife and scissors if I have to sell my trousers for it. Give them to me at once!' For some days he went about like a lunatic, since I did not answer him, nor did I send him a message through the woman; so that Chresten asked the woman what she had done to Christian, as he went about below gnashing his teeth and howling like a madman. She replied that those below must best know what was the matter with him; that he must see he was spoken with in a very friendly manner here. At noon on Good Friday, 1667,[118] he was very angry, swore and cursed himself if he did not give himself up, repeating all that he had said before, and adding that I had enticed him with wine and meat, and had deceived him with candles and good words. That he cared but little what happened to him; he would gladly die by the hand of the executioner; but that I, and she, and Chresten, should not escape without hurt.

The afternoon was not very cheerful to us. The woman was depressed. I begged her to be calm, told her there was no danger in such madness, though it was very annoying, and harder to bear than my captivity; but that still I would be a match for the rogue. She took her book and read, and I sat down and wrote a hymn upon Christ's sufferings, to the tune 'As the hart panteth after the water-springs.'[119]

Christian had before been in the habit of bringing me coloured eggs on Easter-Eve; at this time he was not so disposed. When the door was locked, I said to Chresten, 'Do not forget the soft-boiled eggs to-morrow.' When the dinner was brought up on Easter-Day, and the eggs did not come at once (they were a side dish), Christian looked at me, and made a long nose at me three or four times. (I was accustomed to go up and down in front of the door of my room when it was unlocked.) I remained standing, and looked at him, and shrugged my shoulders a little. Soon after these grimaces, Chresten came with a dish full of soft-boiled eggs. Christian cast down his eyes at first, then he raised them to me, expecting, perhaps, that I should make a long nose at him in return; but I intended nothing less. When the woman went to the stairs, he said, 'There were no coloured eggs there.' She repeated this to me at once, so that I begged her to say that I ate the soft-boiled eggs and kept the coloured ones, as he might see (and I sent him one of the last year's, on which I had drawn some flowers; he had given it to me himself for some candles). He accepted it, but wrote me a note in return, which was very extraordinary. It was intended to be a highflown composition about the egg and the hen. He tried to be witty, but it had no point. I cannot now quite remember it, except that he wrote that I had sent him a rotten egg; that his egg would be fresh, while mine would be rotten.[120] He threw the slip of paper into my room. I made no answer to it. Some days passed again, and he said nothing angry; then he recommenced. I think he was vexed to see Chresten often receive my wine back again in the cup. At times I presented it to the prison governor. Moreover, he received no food, either for himself or his boy. One day he said to the woman, 'What do you think the prison governor would say if he knew that you give the prisoners some of his food to eat?' (The food which came from my table was taken down to the prison governor.) 'Tell her that!' The woman asked whether she was to say so to me, as a message from him. 'As whose message otherwise?' he answered. I sent him word that I could take as much as I pleased of the food brought me: that it was not measured out and weighed for me, and that those who had a right to it could do what they liked with what I did not require, as it belonged to no one. On this point he could not excite our fear. Then he came back again one day to the old subject, that he would have the scissors and the knife, and threatening to give himself up; and as it was almost approaching the time when I received the Lord's Supper, I said to the woman: 'Tell him once for all, if he cannot restrain himself I will inform against him as soon as the priest comes, and the first Karen shall be made to give evidence; she shall, indeed, be brought forward, for she had no rest on his account until I entered into his proposals. Whether voluntarily or under compulsion, she shall say the truth, and then we shall see who gets into trouble.' He might do, I sent word, whatever he liked, but I would be let alone; he might spare me his notes, or I would produce them. When the woman told him this, he thought a little, and then asked, 'Does she say so?' 'Yes,' said the woman, 'she did. She said still further: "What does he imagine? Does he think that I, as a prisoner who can go nowhere, will suffer for having accepted the services of a prisoner who enjoys a liberty which does not belong to him?"' He stood and let his head hang down, and made no answer at all. This settled the fellow, and from that time I have not heard one unsuitable word from him. He spoke kindly and pleasantly with the woman on the stairs, related what news he had heard, and was very officious; and when she once asked him for his cup to give him some wine, he said sadly, 'I have not deserved any wine.' The woman said he could nevertheless have some wine, and that I desired no more service from him. So he received wine from time to time, but nothing to eat.[121] On the day that I received the Lord's Supper, he came to the door and knocked softly. I went to the door. He saluted me and wished me joy in a very nice manner, and said that he knew I had forgiven those who had done aught against me. I answered in the affirmative, and gave no further matter for questions; nor did he, but spoke of other trivialities, and then went away. Afterwards he came daily to the door, and told me what news he had heard; he also received wine and meat again. He told me, among other things, that many were of opinion that all the prisoners would be set at liberty at the wedding of the prince (our present king) which was then talked of; that the bride was to arrive within a month (it was the end of April when this conversation took place), and that the wedding was to be at the palace.

The arrival of the bride was delayed till the beginning of June, and then the wedding was celebrated in the palace at Nykjöbing in Falster. Many were of opinion that it took place there in order that the bride might not intercede for me and the doctor.[122] When the bride was to be brought to Copenhagen, I said to Christian: 'Now is the time for you to gain your liberty. Let your girl wait and fall on one knee before the carriage of the bride and hold out a supplication, and then I am sure you will gain your liberty.' He asked how the girl should come to be supplicating for him. I said, 'As your bride—' 'No (and he swore with a terrible oath), she is not that! She imagines it, perhaps, but (he swore again) I will not have her.' 'Then leave her in the idea,' I said, 'and let her make her supplication as for her bridegroom.' 'Yes,' he said, in a crestfallen tone, 'she may do that.' It was done, as I had advised, and Christian was set at liberty on June 11, 1667. He did not bid me good-bye, and did not even send me a message through the tower-warder or the boy. His gratitude to the girl was that he smashed her window that very evening, and made such a drunken noise in the street, that he was locked up in the Town- hall cellar.[123] He came out, however, on the following day. His lad Paaske took leave of his master. When he asked him whether he should say anything from him to us, he answered, 'Tell them that I send them to the devil.' Paaske, who brought this message, said he had answered Christian, 'Half of that is intended for me' (for Christian had already suspected that Paaske had rendered services to the woman). We had a hearty laugh over this message; for I said that if Paaske was to have half of it, I should get nothing. We were not a little glad that we were quit of this godless man.

We lived on in repose throughout the year 1668. I wrote and was furnished with various handiwork, so that Chresten bought nothing for me but a couple of books, and these I paid doubly and more than doubly with candles. Karen remained with me the first time more than three years; and as her daughter was then going to be married, and she wished to be at the wedding, she spoke to me as to how it could be arranged, for she would gladly have a promise of returning to me when the woman whom I was to have in her stead went away. I did not know whether this could be arranged; but I felt confident that I could effect her exit without her feigning herself ill. The prison governor had already then as clerk Peder Jensen Tötzlöff,[E44] who now and then performed his duties. To this man I made the proposal, mentioning at the same time with compassion the ill health of the woman. I talked afterwards with the prison governor himself about it, and he was quite satisfied; for he not only liked this Karen very much, but he had moreover a woman in the house whom he wished to place with me instead.

Karen, Nils' daughter, left me one evening in 1669, and a German named Cathrina ——[E45] came in her place. Karen took her departure with many tears. She had wept almost the whole day, and I promised to do my utmost that she should come to me when the other went away. Cathrina had been among soldiers from her youth up; she had married a lieutenant at the time the prison governor was a drummer, and had stood godmother to one of his sons. She had fallen into poverty after her husband's death, and had sat and spun with the wife of the prison governor for her food. She was greatly given to drinking, and her hands trembled so that she could not hold the cup, but was obliged to support it against her person, and the soup-plate also. The prison governor told me before she came up that her hands occasionally trembled a little, but not always—that she had been ill a short time before, and that it would probably pass off. When I asked herself how it came on, she said she had had it for many years. I said, 'You are not a woman fit to wait upon me; for if I should be ill, as I was a year or somewhat less ago, you could not properly attend to me.' She fell at once down on her knees, wept bitterly, and prayed for God's sake that she might remain; that she was a poor widow, and that she had promised the prison governor half the money she was to earn; she would pray heartily to God that I might not be ill, and that she would be true to me, aye, even die for me.

It seemed to me that this last was too much of an exaggeration for me to believe it (she kept her word, however, and did what I ordered her, and I was not ill during her time). She did not care to work. She generally laid down when she had eaten, and drew the coverlid over her eyes, saying 'Now I can see nothing.' When she perceived that I liked her to talk, she related whole comedies in her way, often acting them, and representing various personages. If she began to tell a story, and I said in the middle of her narrative, 'This will have a sorrowful ending,' she would say, 'No, it ends pleasantly,' and she would give her story a good ending. She would do the reverse, if I said the contrary. She would dance also before me, and that for four persons, speaking as she did so for each whom she was representing, and pinching together her mouth and fingers. She called comedians 'Medicoants.' Various things occurred during her time, which prevented me from looking at her and listening to her as much as she liked.[124]

It happened that Walter,[E46] who in consequence of Dina's affair had been exiled from Denmark, came over from Sweden and remained incognito at Copenhagen. He was arrested and placed in the tower here, below on the ground floor. He was suspected of being engaged in some plot. At the same time a French cook and a Swedish baker were imprisoned with him, who were accused of having intended to poison the King and Queen. The Swede was placed in the Witch Cell, immediately after Walter's arrest. Some days elapsed before I was allowed to know of Walter's arrival, but I knew of it nevertheless. One day at noon, when Walter and the Frenchman were talking aloud (for they were always disputing with each other), I asked the prison governor who were his guests down below, who were talking French. He answered that he had some of various nations, and related who they were, but why they were imprisoned he knew not, especially in Walter's case.

The two before-mentioned quarrelled together, so that Walter was placed in the Witch Cell with the Swede, and the Frenchman was conveyed to the Dark Church, where he was ill, and never even came to the peep-hole in the door, but lay just within. I dared not send him anything, on account of the accusation against him. Walter was imprisoned for a long time, and the Frenchman was liberated. When M. Bock came to me, to give me Christ's body and blood, I told him before receiving the Lord's Supper of Walter's affair, which had been proved, but I mentioned to him that at the time I had been requested to leave Denmark through Uldrich Christian Gyldenlöve. Gyldenlöve had sworn to me that the king was at the time not thoroughly convinced of the matter, and I had complained that his Majesty had not taken pains to convince himself; and I requested the priest to ask the Stadtholder to manage that Walter should now be examined in Dina's affair, and that he and I should be confronted together in the presence of some ministers; that this could be done without any great noise, for the gentlemen could come through the secret passage into the tower. The priest promised to arrange this;[125] he did so, and on the third day after Walter was placed in the Dark Church, so that I expected for a long time every day that we should be examined, but it was prevented by the person whose interest it was to prevent it.[E47]

Walter remained imprisoned,[126] and quarrelled almost daily with Chresten, calling him a thief and a robber. (Chresten had found some ducats which Walter had concealed under a stool; the foolish Walter allowed the Swede to see that he hid ducats and an ink-bottle between the girths under the stool, and he afterwards struck the Swede, who betrayed him.) Chresten slyly allowed Walter to take a little exercise in the hall of the tower, and in the meanwhile he searched the stool. It may well be imagined that at the everlasting scolding Chresten was annoyed, and he did not procure Walter particularly good food from the kitchen; so that sometimes he could not eat either of the two dishes ordered for him; and when Walter said one day, 'If you would give me only one dish of which I could eat, it would be quite enough,' Chresten arranged it so that Walter only received one dish, and often could not eat of that. (This was to Chresten's own damage, for he was entitled to the food that was left; but he was ready to forego this, so long as he could annoy the others.)

Once Chresten came to him with a dish of rice-porridge, and began at once to quarrel with him, so that the other became angry (just as children do), and would eat nothing. Chresten carried the porridge away again directly, and laughed heartily. I said to Chresten, in the prison governor's presence, 'Though God has long delayed to punish Walter, his punishment is all the heavier now, for he could scarcely have fallen into more unmerciful hands than yours.' He laughed heartily at this, and the prison governor did the same. And as there is a hole passing from the Dark Church into the outer room, those who are inside there can call upstairs, so that one can plainly hear what is said. So Walter one day called to the prison governor, and begged him to give him a piece of roast meat; the prison governor called to him, 'Yes, we will roast a rat for you!' I sent him a piece of roast meat through Chresten; when he took it, and heard that I had sent it to him, he wept.

Thus the time passed, I had always work to do, and I wrote also a good deal. [127] The priest was tired of administering the Lord's Supper to me, and he let me wait thirteen and fourteen days; when he did come, he performed his office *par manière d'acquit.* I said nothing about it, but the woman, who is a German, also received the Lord's Supper from him; she made much of it, especially once (the last time he confessed her); for then I waited four days for him before it suited him to come, and at last he came. It was Wednesday, about nine o'clock. He never greeted us, nor did he wish me joy to the act I intended to perform. This time he said, as he shook hands, 'I have not much time to wait, I have a child to baptise.' I knew well that this could not be true, but I answered 'In God's name!' When he was to receive the woman's confession, he would not sit down, but said 'Now go on, I have no time,' and scarcely gave her time to confess, absolved her quickly, and read the consecrating service at posthaste speed. When he was gone, the woman was very impatient, and said that she had received the holy communion in the field from a military chaplain, with the whole company (since they were ready to attack the enemy on the following day), but that the priest had not raced through God's word as this one had done; she had gained nothing from it.

I comforted her as well as I could, read and sang to her, told her she should repent and be sorry for her sins, and labour to amend her ways, and not be distracted by the want of devotion in the priest; she could appropriate to herself Christ's sufferings and merits for the forgiveness of her sins, for the priest had given her his body and blood in the bread and wine. 'Yes,' she answered, 'I shall, with God's will, be a better Christian.' I said 'Will you keep what you have promised me?' Her vow was, not to drink herself tipsy, as she had once done. I will not omit to mention this. She received, as I have before said, half a pint of French wine at each meal, and I half a measure of Rhine wine. She could drink both portions without being quite intoxicated, for at her meal she drank the French wine and lay down; and when she got up in the afternoon she drank my wine.[128] In the evening she kept my wine for breakfast, but once she had in her cup both my wine and her own, so that at noon she had two half-pints of wine; she sat there and drank it so quietly, and I paid no attention to her, being at the moment engaged in a speculation about a pattern which I wanted to knit; at length I looked at her because it was so long before she laid down; then she turned over all the vessels, one after another, and there was nothing in them. I accosted her and said, 'How is it?

have you drank all the wine?' She could scarcely answer. She tried to stand up, and could not. 'To bed, you drunken sow,' said I. She tried to move, but could not; she was sick, and crept along by the wall to fetch a broom. When she had the broom, she could do nothing with it. I told her to crawl into bed and lie down; she crawled along and fell with her face on the bed, while her feet were on the ground. There she was sick again, and remained so lying, and slept. It is easy to imagine how I felt.

She slept in this way for a couple of hours, but still did not quite sleep off her intoxication; for when she wanted afterwards to clean herself and the room, she remained for a long time sitting on a low stool, the broom between her knees and her hair about her ears. She took off her bodice to wash it, and so she sat with her bosom uncovered, an ugly sight; she kept bemoaning herself, praying to God to help her, as she was nigh unto death. I was angry, but I could scarcely help laughing at this sad picture. When the moaning and lamenting were over, I said angrily, 'Yes, may God help you, you drunkard; to the guards' station you ought to go; I will not have such a drunkard about me; go and sleep it out, and don't let me hear you talk of God when you are not sober, for then God is far from you and the d——l is near!' (I laughed afterwards at myself.) She laid down again, and about four o'clock she was quite sober, made herself perfectly clean, and sat quietly weeping. Then she threw herself with great excitement at my feet, clung to them, howled and clamoured, and begged for God's sake that I would forgive her this once, and that it should never happen again; said how she had kept the wine &c.; that if I would only keep her half a year, she would have enough to purchase her admission into the hospital at Lübeck.

I thought I would take good care that she did not get so much again at once, and also that perhaps if I had another in her place she might be worse in other things. Karen could not have come at this time, for her daughter was expecting her confinement, and I knew that she would then not be quiet. So I promised her to keep her for the time she mentioned. She kept her word moreover, and I so arranged it six weeks later that she received no more wine, and from this time the woman received no wine; my wine alone could not hurt her. She was quite intimate with Walter. She had known him formerly, and Chresten was of opinion that he had given her all his money before he was ill; for he said that Walter had no money any longer. What there was in it I know not. Honest she was not, for she stole from me first a brass knitting- pin, which I used at that time; it was formed like a bodkin, and the woman never imagined but that it was gold. As my room is not large, it could soon be searched, but I looked for three days and could not find the pin. I was well aware that she had it, for it is not so small as not to be seen, so I said afterwards, 'This brass pin is of no great importance; I can get another for two pence.' The next day she showed me the pin, in a large crevice on the floor between the stones. But when she afterwards, shortly before she left, found one of my gold earrings which I had lost, and which undoubtedly had been left on the pillow, for it was a snake ring, this was never returned, say what I would about it. She made a show of looking for it in the dirt outside; she knew I dared not say that I had missed it.

The prison governor at this time came up but rarely; Peder Jensen waited on me.[129] His Majesty was ill for a short time, and died suddenly on February 9, 1670. And as on the same day at twelve o'clock the palace bell tolled, I was well aware what this indicated, though the woman was not. We conversed on the subject, who it might be. She could perceive that I was sad, and she said: 'That might be for the King, for the last time I saw him on the stairs, getting out of the carriage, he could only move with difficulty, and I said to myself that it would soon be over with him. If he is dead, you will have your liberty, that is certain.' I was silent, and thought otherwise, which was the case. About half-past four o'clock the fire was generally lighted in the outside stove, and this was done by a lad whom Chresten at that time employed. I called him to the door and asked him why the bell had tolled for a whole hour at noon. He answered, 'I may not say; I am forbidden.' I said that I would not betray him. He then told me that the King had died in the morning. I gave free vent to my tears, which I had restrained, at which the woman was astonished, and talked for a long time.

I received all that she said in silence, for I never trusted her. I begged her to ask Chresten, when he unlocked the door, what the tolling intimated. She did so, but Chresten answered that he did not know. The prison governor came up the same evening, but he did not speak with me. He came up also the next day at noon. I requested to speak with him, and enquired why the bell had sounded. He answered ironically, 'What is that to you? Does it not ring every day?' I replied somewhat angrily: 'What it is to me God knows! This I know, that the castle bell is not tolled for your equals!' He took off his hat and made me a bow, and said, 'Your ladyship desires nothing else?' I answered, 'St. Martin comes for you too.'[E49] 'St. Martin?' he said, and laughed, and went away and went out to Walter, standing for a long time whispering with him in front of the hole; I could see him, as he well knew.[130] He was undoubtedly telling him of the King's death, and giving him hope that he would be liberated from prison. God designed it otherwise. Walter was ill, and lay for a long time in great misery. He behaved very badly to Chresten; took the dirt from the floor and threw it into the food; spat into the beer, and allowed Chresten to see him do so when he carried the can away. Every day Chresten received the titles of thief and rogue, so that it may easily be imagined how Chresten tormented him. When I sent him some meat, either stewed or roasted, Chresten came back with it and said he would not have it. I begged Chresten to leave it with him, and he would probably eat it later. This he did once, and then Chresten showed me how full it was of dirt and filth.[131]

When Chresten had to turn Walter in bed, the latter screamed so pitifully that I felt sympathy with him, and begged Chresten not to be so unmerciful to him. He laughed and said, 'He is a rogue.' I said, 'Then he is in his master's hands.' This pleased Chresten well. Walter suffered much pain; at length God released him. His body was left in the prison until his brother came, who ordered it to be buried in the German Church. When I heard that Karen could come to me again, and the time was over which I had promised the other to keep her, Cathrina went down and Karen returned to me. This was easily effected, for the prison governor was not well pleased with Cathrina; she gave him none of her money, as she had promised, but only empty words in its place, such as that he was not in earnest, and that he surely did not wish to have anything from her, &c.[132] The prison governor began immediately to pay me less respect, when he perceived that my liberation was not expected.

When the time came at which I was accustomed to receive the holy communion, I begged the prison governor that he should manage that I should have the court preacher, D. Hans Læt, as the former court preacher, D. Mathias Foss, had come to me on the first occasion in my prison. The prison governor stated my desire, and his Majesty assented. D. Hans Læt was already in the tower, down below, but he was called back because the Queen Dowager (who was still in the palace) would not allow it; and the prison governor sent me word, through Peder Jensen, that the King had said I was to be content with the clergyman to whom I was accustomed, so that the necessary preparation for the Lord's Supper was postponed till the following day, when Mag. Buck came to me and greeted me in an unusual manner, congratulating me in a long oration on my intention, saluting me 'your Grace.' When he was seated, he said, 'I should have been glad if D. Hans Læt had come in my place.' I replied, 'I had wished it also.' 'Yes,' he said, 'I know well why you wished it so. You wish to know things, and that is forbidden me. You have already caused one man to lose his employ.' I asked him whether I had ever desired to know anything from him? 'No,' he replied, 'you know well that you would learn nothing from me; for that reason you have asked me nothing.' 'Does the Herr Mag, then,' I said, 'mean that I desired D. Hans Læt in order to hear news of him?' He hesitated a little, and then said, 'You wanted to have D. Hans Læt in order that he might speak for you with the King.' I said, 'There may perhaps be something in that.' Upon this he began to swear all kinds of oaths (such as I have never heard before),[133] that he had spoken for me. (I thought: 'I have no doubt you have spoken of me, but not in my favour.') He had given me a book which I still have; it is 'St.

Augustini Manuali;' the Statholder Gabel had bought it, as he said more than once, protesting by God that it had cost the Herr Statholder a rix-dollar. (I thought of the 5,000 rix-dollars which Gabel received, that we might be liberated from our confinement at Borringholm, but I said nothing; perhaps for this reason he repeated the statement so often.) I asked him whom I had caused to lose his employ. He answered, 'Hans Balcke.[134] He told you that Treasurer Gabel was Statholder, and he ought not to have done so.' I said, 'I do not believe that Balcke knew that he ought not to say it, for he did not tell it to me as a secret. One might say just as well that H. Magister had caused Balcke to lose his place.' He was very angry at this, and various disputes arose on the subject. He began again just as before, that I wanted to have D. Læt, he knew why. I said, 'I did not insist specially on having D. Læt; but if not him, the chaplain of the castle, or another.' He asked, 'Why another?' I replied, 'Because it is not always convenient to the Herr Magister. I have been obliged to wait for him ten, twelve, and even fourteen days, and the last time he administered his office in great haste, so that it is not convenient for him to come when I require him.' He sat turning over my words, not knowing what to answer, and at last he said; 'You think it will go better with you now because King Frederick is dead. No, you deceive yourself! It will go worse with you, it will go worse with you!' And as he was growing angry, I became more composed and I asked gently why so, and from what could he infer it? He answered, 'I infer it from the fact that you have not been able to get your will in desiring another clergyman and confessor; so I assure you things will not be better with you. If King Frederick is dead, King Christian is alive.' I said: 'That is a bad foundation; your words of threatening have no basis. If I have not this time been able to obtain another confessor, it does not follow that I shall not have another at another time. And what have I done, that things should go worse with me?' He was more and more angry, and exclaimed aloud several times, 'Worse, yes, it will be worse!' Then I also answered angrily, 'Well, then let it come.'

Upon this he was quite silent, and I said: 'You have given me a good preparation; now, in God's name!' Then I made my confession, and he administered his office and went away without any other farewell than giving me his hand. I learned afterwards that before M. Buck came to me he went to the prison governor, who was in bed, and begged him to tell Knud, who was at that time page of the chamber,[E50] what a sacramental woman I was; how I had dug a hole in the floor in order to speak with the doctor (which was an impossibility), and how I had practised climbing up and looking out on the square. He begged him several times to tell this to the page of the chamber: 'That is a sacramental woman!'[135]

In the end of April in the same year my door was opened one afternoon, and the prison governor came in with some ladies, who kept somewhat aside until he had said, 'Here are some of the maids of honour, who are permitted to speak to you.' There came in first a young lady whom I did not know. Next appeared the Lady Augusta of Glücksburg, whom I recognised at once, as she was but little altered. Next followed the Electoral Princess of Saxony, whom I at once recognised from her likeness to her royal father, and last of all our gracious Queen, whom I chiefly looked at, and found the lineaments of her countenance just as Peder Jensen had described them. I saw also a large diamond on her bracelet, and one on her finger, where her glove was cut. Her Majesty supported herself against the folding table as soon as she had greeted me. Lady Augusta ran up and down into every corner, and the Electoral Princess remained at the door. Lady Augusta said: 'Fye, what a disgusting room this is! I could not live a day in it. I wonder that you have been able to endure it so long.' I answered, 'The room is such as pleases God and his Majesty, and so long as God will I shall be able to endure it.' She began a conversation with the prison governor, who was half tipsy, and spoke with him about Balcke's marriage, whose wedding with his third wife was taking place on that very day; she spoke against marrying so often, and the prison governor replied with various silly speeches. She asked me if I was plagued with fleas. I replied that I could furnish her with a regiment of fleas, if she would have them. She replied hastily with an oath, and swore that she did not want them.

Her question made me somewhat ironical, and I was annoyed at the delight she exhibited at my miserable condition; so when she asked me whether I had body or wall lice, I answered her with a question, and enquired whether my brother-in-law Hanibal Sehested was still alive? This question made her somewhat draw in, for she perceived that I knew her. She made no answer. The Electoral Princess, who probably had heard of my brother-in-law's intrigues with Lady Augusta,[E51] went quickly up to the table (the book lay on it, in which Karen used to read, and which she had brought in with her), took the book, opened it and asked whether it was mine. I replied that it belonged to the woman whom I had taught to read, and as I gave the Electoral Princess her fitting title of Serene Highness, Lady Augusta said: 'You err! You are mistaken; she is not the person whom you think.' I answered, 'I am not mistaken.' After this she said no more, but gave me her hand without a word. The gracious Queen looked sadly on, but said nothing. When her Majesty gave me her hand, I kissed it and held it fast, and begged her Majesty to intercede for me, at any rate for some alleviation of my captivity. Her Majesty replied not with words, but with a flood of tears. The virtuous Electoral Princess cried also; she wept very sorrowfully. And when they had reached the anteroom and my door was closed, both the Queen and the

Electoral Princess said, 'It is a sin to treat her thus!' They shuddered; and each said, 'Would to God that it rested with me! she should not stay there.' Lady Augusta urged them to go away, and mentioned it afterwards to the Queen Dowager, who said that I had myself to thank for it; I had deserved to be worse treated than this.

When the King's funeral was over, and the Queen Dowager had left the castle, I requested the prison governor that he should execute my message and solicit another clergyman for me, either the chaplain of the castle or the arsenal chaplain, or the one who usually attended to the prisoners; for if I could get no other than M. Buck, they must take the sin on their own heads, for that I would not again confess to him. A short time elapsed, but at length the chaplain of the castle, at that time M. Rodolff Moth, was assigned me. God, who has ever stood by me in all my adversity, and who in my sorrow and distress has sent me unexpected consolation, gave me peculiar comfort in this man. He consoled me with the Word of God; he was a learned and conversable man, and he interceded for me with his Majesty. The first favour which he obtained for me was, that I was granted another apartment on July 16, 1671, and Bishop D. Jesper's postil.

He afterwards by degrees obtained still greater favours for me. I received 200 rix-dollars as a gift, to purchase such clothes for myself as I desired, and anything I might wish for to beguile the time.[136]

In this year her Majesty the Queen became pregnant, and her Majesty's mother, the Landgravine of Hesse, came to be with her in her confinement. On September 6 her Serene Highness visited me in my prison, at first wishing to remain incognito. She had with her a Princess of Curland, who was betrothed to the son of the Landgravine; her lady in waiting, a Wallenstein by birth; and the wife of her master of the household. The Landgravine greeted me with a kiss, and the others followed her example. I did not at that time recognise the wife of the master of the household, but she had known me formerly in my prosperity at the Hague, when she had been in the service of the Countess Leuenstein, and the tears stood in her eyes.

The Landgravine lamented my hard fate and my unhappy circumstances. I thanked her Serene Highness for the gracious sympathy she felt with me, and said that she might help much in alleviating my fetters, if not in liberating me from them entirely. The Landgravine smiled and said, 'I see well you take me for another than I am.' I said, 'Your Serene Highness's deportment and appearance will not allow you to conceal your rank, were you even in peasant's attire.' This pleased her; she laughed and jested, and said she had not thought of that. The lady in waiting agreed with me, and said that I had spoken very justly in saying that I had recognised her by her royal appearance. Upon this the Landgravine said, 'You do not know her?' pointing to the Princess of Curland. She then said who she was, and afterwards who her lady in waiting was, and also the wife of the master of the household, who was as I have before mentioned. She spoke of the pity which this lady felt for me, and added 'Et moy pas moins.' I thanked her 'Altesse très-humblement et la prioit en cette occasion de faire voir sa généreuse conduite.' Her Serene Highness looked at the prison governor as though she would say that we might speak French too long; she took off her glove and gave me her hand, pressing mine and saying, 'Croyez-moy, je fairez mon possible.' I kissed her Serene Highness's hand, and she then took leave of me with a kiss.

The virtuous Landgravine kept her word, but could effect nothing. When her Majesty the Queen was in the perils of childbirth, she went to the King and obtained from him a solemn promise that if the Queen gave birth to a son I should receive my liberty. On October 11, in the night between one and two o'clock, God delivered her Majesty in safety of our Crown Prince. When all present were duly rejoicing at the Prince's birth, the Landgravine said, 'Oh! will not the captive rejoice!' The Queen Dowager enquired 'Why?' The Landgravine related the King's promise. The Queen Dowager was so angry that she was ill. She loosened her jacket, and said she would return home; that she would not wait till the child was baptised. Her coach appeared in the palace square. The King at length persuaded her to remain till the baptism was over, but he was obliged to promise with an oath that I should not be liberated. This vexed the virtuous Landgravine not a little, that the Queen should have induced her son to break his promise; and she persisted in saying that a king ought to keep his vow. The Queen Dowager answered, 'My son has before made a vow, and this he has broken by his promise to your Serene Highness.' The Landgravine said at last: 'If I cannot bring about the freedom of the prisoner, at least let her, at my request, be removed to a better place, with somewhat more liberty. It is not to the King's reputation that she is imprisoned there. She is, after all, a king's daughter, and I know that much injustice is done to her.' The Queen Dowager was annoyed at these words, and said, 'Now, she shall not come out; she shall remain where she is!' The Landgravine answered, 'If God will, she will assuredly come out, even though your Majesty may will it not;' so saying, she rose and went out.

On October 18 the lady in waiting, Wallenstein, sent for Peder Jensen Tötzlöff, and delivered to him by command a book entitled, D. Heinrich Müller's 'Geistliche Erquickstunden,'[E53] which he gave me with a gracious message from the Landgravine. On the same day I sent her Serene Highness, through Tötzlöff, my dutiful thanks, and Tötzlöff took the book back to the lady in waiting, with the request that she would endeavour to prevail on her Highness to show me the great favour of placing her name and motto in the book, in remembrance of her Highness's generosity and kindness. I lamented my condition in this also, that from such a place I could not spread abroad her Serene Highness's praise and estimable benefits, and make the world acquainted with them; but that I would do what I could, and I would include her Serene Highness and all her family in my prayers for their welfare both of soul and body. (This I have done, and will do, so long as God spares my life.)

On October 23 I received the book back through Tötzlöff, and I found within it the following lines, written by the Landgravine's own hand:

1671.

> Ce qui n'est pas en ta puissance
> Ne doit point troubler ton repos;
> Tu balances mal à propos
> Entre la crainte et l'espérance.
> Laisse faire ton Dieu et ton roy,
> Et suporte avec passience ce qu'il résoud pour toy.

Je prie Dieu de vous faire cette grâce, et que je vous puisse tesmoigner combien je suis,

Madame, vostre très-affectionée à vous servir,

The book is still in my possession, and I sent word through Tötzlöff to the lady in waiting to request her to convey my most humble thanks to her Highness; and afterwards, when the Landgravine was about to start on her journey, to commend me to her Serene Highness's favour.

In the same year, 1671, Karen, Nils' daughter, left me on account of ill health. For one night a woman was with me named Margrete, who was a serf from Holstein. She had run away from her master. She was a very awkward peasant woman, so towards evening on the following day she was sent away, and in her place there came a woman named Inger, a person of loose character. This woman gave herself out as the widow of a non-commissioned officer, and that she had long been in service at Hamburg, and nursed lying-in women. It happened with her, as is often the case, that one seeks to obtain a thing, and that to one's own vexation. Chresten had spoken for this woman with the prison governor, and had praised her before me, but the prison governor took upon another recommendation the before-mentioned Margrete. So long as there was hope that the Landgravine might obtain my freedom, this woman was very amenable, but afterwards she began by degrees to show what was in her, and that it was not for nothing that she resembled Dina.

She caused me annoyance of various kinds, which I received with patience, thinking within myself that it was another trial imposed by God upon me, and Dina's intrigues often came into my mind, and I thought, 'Suppose she should devise some Dina plot?' (She is capable of it, if she had only an instigator, as Dina had.) Among other annoyances, which may not be reckoned among the least, was this: I was one day not very well, having slept but little or not at all during the night, and I had lain down to sleep on the bed in the day; and she would give me no rest, but came softly past me in her socks, and in order to wake me teased a dog which I had,[137] so that he growled. I asked her why she grudged my sleeping? She answered, 'I did not know that you were asleep.' 'Why, then,' I said, 'did you go by in your stockings?' She replied, 'If you saw that, then you were not asleep,' and she laughed heartily by herself. (She sat always in front of my table with her back turned to me; whether it was because she had lost one eye that she sat in that position to the light, I know not.)

I did not care for any conversation with her, so I lay still; and when she thought I was asleep, she got up again and teased the dog. I said, 'You tax my patience sorely; but if once my passion rises, you will certainly get something which will astonish you, you base accursed thing!' 'Base accursed thing,' she repeated to herself with a slight laugh. I prayed to God that he would restrain me, so that I might not lay violent hands on this base creature. And as I had the other apartment (as I have before mentioned),[138] I went out and walked up and down between four and five o'clock. She washed and splashed outside, and spilled the water exactly where I was walking. I told her several times to leave her splashing, as she spilled the water in all directions on the floor, so that I made my clothes dirty, and often there was not a drop of water for my dog to drink, and the tower-warder had to fetch her water from the kitchen spring. This was of no avail. One day it occurred to her, just as the bell had sounded four, to go out and pour all the water on the floor, and then come back again. When I went to the door, I perceived what she had done. Without saying a word, I struck her first on one cheek and then on the other, so that the blood ran from her nose and mouth, and she fell against her bench, and knocked the skin from her shin-bone. She began to be abusive, and said she had never in her life had such a box on her ears. I said immediately, 'Hold your tongue, or you will have another like it! I am now only a little angry, but if you make me really angry I shall strike you harder.' She was silent for the time, but she caused me all the small annoyance she could.

I received it all with gentleness, fearing that I might lay violent hands on her. She scarcely knew what to devise to cause me vexation; she had a silver thimble on which a strange name was engraved; she had found it, she said, in a dust-heap in the street. I once asked her where she had found some handkerchiefs which she had of fine Dutch linen, with lace on them, which likewise were marked with another name; they were embroidered with blue silk, and there was a different name on each. She had bought them, she said, at an auction at Hamburg.[139] I thought that the damage she had received on one of her eyes might very likely have arisen from her having 'found' something of that kind,[E54] and as I soon after asked her by what accident she had injured her eye, she undoubtedly understood my question well, for she was angry and rather quiet, and said, 'What injury? There is nothing the matter with my eye; I can, thank God, see with both.' I let the matter rest there. Soon after this conversation she came down one day from upstairs, feeling in her pocket, though she said nothing until the afternoon, when the doors were locked, and then she looked through all her rubbish, saying 'If I only knew where it could be?' I asked what she was looking for. 'My thimble,' she said. 'You will find it,' I said; 'only look thoroughly!' And as she had begun to look for it in her pockets before she had required it, I thought she might have drawn it out of her pocket with some paper which she used, and which she had bought. I said this, but it could not be so.

On the following day, towards noon, she again behaved as if she were looking for it upstairs; and when the door was closed she began to give loose to her tongue, and to make a long story about the thimble, where it could possibly be. 'There was no one here, and no one came in except us two;' and she gave me to understand that I had taken it; she took her large box which she had, and rummaged out everything that was in it, and said, 'Now you can see that I have not got it.' I said that I did not care about it, whether she had it or no, but that I saw that she accused me of stealing. She adhered to it, and said, 'Who else could have taken it? There is no one else here, and I have let you see all that is mine, and it is not there.' Then for the first time I saw that she wished that I should let her see in the same manner what I had in my cardbox, for she had never seen anything of the work which I had done before her time. I said, 'I do not care at all what you do with your thimble, and I respect myself too much to quarrel with you or to mind your coarse and shameless accusation. I have, thank God, enough in my imprisonment to buy what I require, &c. But as you perhaps have stolen it, you now imagine that it has been stolen again from you, if it be true that you have lost it.' To this she made no answer, so that I believe she had it herself, and only wanted by this invention to gain a sight of my things. As it was the Christmas month and very cold, and Chresten was lighting a fire in the stove before the evening meal, I said to him in her presence, 'Chresten, you are fortunate if you are not, like me, accused of stealing, for you might have found her thimble upstairs without having had it proclaimed from the pulpit; it was before found by Inger, and not announced publicly.'

This was like a spark to tinder, and she went to work like a frantic being, using her shameless language. She had not stolen it, but it had been stolen from her; and she cursed and swore. Chresten ordered her to be silent. He desired her to remember who I was, and that she was in my service. She answered, 'I will not be silent, not if I were standing before the King's bailiff!' The more gently I spoke, the more angry was she; at length I said, 'Will you agree with me in one wish?—that the person who last had the thimble in her possession may see no better with her left eye than she sees with her right.' She answered with an oath that she could see with both eyes. I said, 'Well, then, pray God with me that she may be blind in both eyes who last had it.' She growled a little to herself and ran into the inner room, and said no more of her thimble, nor did I. God knows that I was heartily weary of this intercourse.

I prayed God for patience, and thought 'This is only a trial of patience. God spares me from other sorrow which I might have in its stead.' I could not avail myself of the occasion of her accusing me of theft to get rid of her, but I saw another opportunity not far off. The prison governor came one day to me with some thread which was offered for sale, rather coarse, but fit for making stockings and night-waistcoats. I bought two pounds of it, and he retained a pound, saying, 'I suppose the woman can make me a pair of stockings with it?' I answered in the affirmative (for she could do nothing else but knit). When he was gone, she said, 'There will be a pair of stockings for me here also, for I shall get no other pay.' I said, 'That is surely enough.' The stockings for the prison governor were finished. She sat one day half asleep, and made a false row round the stocking below the foot. I wanted her to undo it. 'No,' said she, 'it can remain as it is; he won't know but that it is the fashion in Hamburg.'[140]

When his stockings were finished, she began a pair for herself of the same thread, and sat and exulted that it was the prison governor's thread. This, it seemed to me, furnished me with an opportunity of getting rid of her. And as the prison governor rarely came up, and she sent him down the stockings by Tötzlöff, I begged Tötzlöff to contrive that the prison governor should come up to me, and that he should seat himself on the woman's bed and arrange her pillow as if he wanted to lean against it (underneath it lay her wool). This was done. The prison governor came up, took the knitting in his hand, and said to Inger, 'Is this another pair of stockings for me?' 'No, Mr. Prison governor,' she answered, 'they are for me. You have got yours. I have already sent you them.' 'But,' said he, 'this is of my thread; it looks like my thread.' She protested that it was not his thread. As he went down to fetch his stockings and the scales, she said to me, 'That is not his thread; it is mine now,' and laughed heartily. I thought, 'Something more may come of this.'

The prison governor came with the scales and his stockings, compared one thread with the other, and the stockings weighed scarcely half a pound. He asked her whether she had acted rightly? She continued to assert that it was her thread; that she had bought it in Hamburg, and had brought it here. The prison governor grew angry, and said that she lied, and called her a bitch. She swore on the other hand that it was not his thread; that she would swear it by the Sacrament. The prison governor went away; such an oath horrified him. I was perfectly silent during this quarrel. When the prison governor had gone, I said to the woman, 'God forbid! how could you say such words? Do you venture to swear a falsehood by the Sacrament, and to say it in my presence, when I know that it is the prison governor's thread? What a godless creature you are!' She answered, with a half ridiculous expression of face, 'I said I would take the Sacrament upon it, but I am not going to do so.' 'Oh Dina!' I thought, 'you are not like her for nothing; God guard me from you!' And I said, 'Do you think that such light words are not a sin, and that God will not punish you for them?' She assumed an air of authority, and said, 'Is the thread of any consequence? I can pay for it; I have not stolen it from him; he gave it to me himself. I have only done what the tailors do; they do not steal; it is given to them. He did not weigh out the thread for me.' I answered her no more than 'You have taken it from him; I shall trouble myself no more about it;' but I begged Tötzlöff to do all he could that I should be rid of her, and have another in her place of a good character.

Tötzlöff heard that Karen had a desire to return to me; he told me so. The prison governor was satisfied with the arrangement. It was kept concealed from Inger till all was so settled that Karen could come up one evening at supper-time. When the prison governor had unlocked the door, and had established himself in the inner room, and the woman had come out, he said: 'Now, Inger, pack your bundle! You are to go.' 'Yes, Mr. Prison governor,' she answered, and laughed, and brought the food to me, and told me what the prison governor had said, saying at the same time, 'That is his joke.' 'I heard well,' I answered, 'what he said; it is not his joke, it is his real earnestness.' She did not believe it; at any rate she acted as if she did not, and smiled, saying, 'He cannot be in earnest;' and she went out and asked the prison governor whether he was in earnest. He said, 'Go! go! there is no time for gossip!' She came into me again, and asked if I wished to be rid of her. I answered, 'Yes.' 'Why so?' she asked. I answered: 'It would take me too long to explain; the other woman who is to remain here is below.' 'At any rate,' said she, 'let me stay here over the night.' ('Ah, Dina!' I thought.) 'Not a quarter of an hour!' I answered; 'go and pack your things! That is soon done!' She did so, said no word of farewell, and went out of the door.

Thus Karen came to me for the third time, but she did not remain an entire year, on account of illness.[141]

In the year 1673 M. Moth became vice-bishop in Fyn. I lost much in him, and in his place came H. Emmeke Norbye, who became court preacher, and who had formerly been a comrade of Griffenfeldt; but Griffenfeldt did not acknowledge him subsequently, so that he could achieve nothing for me with Griffenfeldt.[E55] He one day brought me as answer (when I sent him word among other things that his Majesty would be gracious if only some one would speak for me), 'It would be as if a pistol had been placed at the King's heart, and he were to forgive it.'

In the same year my sister Elisabeth Augusta sent me a message through Tötzlöff and enquired whether I had a fancy for any fruit, as she would send me some. I was surprised at the message, which came to me from my sister in the tenth year of my captivity, and I said, 'Better late than never!' I sent her no answer.

One funny thing I will yet mention, which occurred in the time of Karen, Nils' daughter. Chresten, who had to make a fire in the stove an hour before supper (since it had no flue), so that the smoke could pass out at the staircase door before I supped, did not come one evening before six o'clock, and was then quite tipsy. And as I was sitting at the time near the stove in the outer apartment on a log of wood, which had been hewed as a seat, I said it was late to make the fire, as he must now go into the kitchen. He paid no attention to my gentle remark, until I threatened him with hard words, and ordered him to take the wood out. He was angry, and would not use the tongs to take the wood out, nor would he permit Karen to take them out with the tongs; but he tore them out with his hands, and said, 'Nothing can burn me.' And as some little time elapsed before the wood was extinguished, he began to fear that it would give little satisfaction if he so long delayed fetching the meal. He seated himself flat on the ground and was rather dejected; presently he burst out and said, 'Oh God, you who have had house and lands, where are you now sitting?' I said, 'On a log of wood!' He answered, 'I do not mean your ladyship!' I asked, 'Whom does your worship mean, then?' He replied, 'I mean Karen.' I laughed, and said no more.

To enumerate all the contemptuous conduct I endured would be too lengthy, and not worth the trouble. One thing I will yet mention of the tower-warder Chresten, who caused me great annoyance at the end of this tenth year of my imprisonment. Among other annoyances he once struck my dog, so that it cried. I did not see it, but I heard it, and the woman told me it was he who had struck the dog. I was greatly displeased at it. He laughed at this, and said, 'It is only a dog.' I gave him to understand that he struck the dog because he did not venture to strike me. He laughed heartily at the idea, and I said, 'I do not care for your anger so long as the prison governor is my friend' (this conversation took place while I was at a meal, and the prison governor was sitting with me, and Chresten was standing at the door of my apartment, stretching out his arms.) I said, 'The prison governor and you will both get into heavy trouble, if I choose. Do you hear that, good people?' (I knew of too many things, which they wished to hide, in more than one respect.) The prison governor sat like one deaf and dumb, and remained seated, but Chresten turned away somewhat ashamed, without saying another word. He had afterwards some fear of me, when he was not too intoxicated; for at such times he cared not what he said, as regards high or low. He was afterwards insolent to the woman, and said he would strike the dog, and that I should see him do so. This, however, he did not do.

Chresten's fool-hardiness increased, so that Peder Tötzlöff informed the prison governor of his bad behaviour, and of my complaints of the wild doings of the prisoners, who made such a noise by night that I could not sleep for it, for Chresten spent the night at his home, and allowed the prisoners to do as they chose. Upon this information, the prison governor placed a padlock upon the tower door at night, so that Chresten could not get out until the door was unlocked in the morning. This annoyed him, and he demanded his discharge, which he received on April 24, 1674; and in his place there came a man named Gert, who had been in the service of the prison governor as a coachman.

In this year, the ——— May, I wrote a spiritual 'Song in Remembrance of God's Goodness,' after the melody 'Nun ruhen alle Wälder.'

I.

My heart! True courage find!
God's goodness bear in mind,
And how He, ever nigh,
Helps me my load to bear,
Nor utterly despair
Tho' in such heavy bonds I lie.

II.

Ne'er from my thoughts shall stray
How once I lingering lay
In the dark dungeon cell;
My cares and bitter fears,
And ridicule and tears,
And God the Lord upheld me well.

III.

Think on my misery
And sad captivity
Thro' many a dreary year!
Yet nought my heart distresses;
The Lord He proves and blesses,
And He protects me even here!

IV.

Come heart and soul elate!
And let me now relate
The wonders of God's skill!
He was my preservation
In danger and temptation,
And kept me from impending ill.

V.

The end seemed drawing near,
I wrung my hands with fear,
Yet has He helped me e'er;
My refuge and my guide,
On Him I have relied,
And He has ever known my care.

VI.

Thanks to Thee, fount of good!
Thou canst no evil brood,
Thy blows are fatherly;
When cruel power oppressed me,
Thy hand has ever blessed me,
And Thou has sheltered me!

VII.

Before Thee, Lord, I lie;
Give me my liberty

Before my course is run;
Thy Gracious Hands extend
And let my suffering end!
Yet not my will, but Thine, be done.

In this year, on July 25, his royal Majesty was gracious enough to have a large window made again in my inner apartment; it had been walled up when I had been brought into this chamber. A stove was also placed there, the flue of which passed out into the square. The prison governor was not well satisfied at this, especially as he was obliged to be present during the work; this did not suit his laziness. My doors were open during the time; it was twelve days before the work was finished. He grumbled, and did not wish that the window should be made as low as it had been before I was imprisoned here; I persuaded the mason's journeyman to cut down the wall as low as it had before been, which the prison governor perceived from the palace square, and he came running up and scolded, and was thoroughly angry. But it was not to be changed, for the window-frame was already made. I asked him what it mattered to him if the window was a stone lower; it did not go lower than the iron grating, and it had formerly been so. He would have his will, so that the mason walled it up a stone higher while the prison governor was there, and removed it again afterwards, for the window-frame, which was ready, would not otherwise have fitted.

In the same year Karen, Nils' daughter, left me for the third and last time, and in her stead came a woman named Barbra, the widow of a bookbinder. She is a woman of a melancholy turn. Her conscience is aroused sometimes, so that she often enumerates her own misdeeds (but not so great as they have been, and as I have found out by enquiry). She had two children, and it seems from her own account that she was to some extent guilty of their death, for she says: 'Who can have any care for a child when one does not love its father?' She left her husband two years before he died, and repaired to Hamburg, supporting herself by spinning; she had before been in the service of a princess as a spinning-maid. Her father is alive, and was bookbinder to the King's Majesty; he has just now had a stroke of paralysis, and is lying very ill. She has no sympathy with her father, and wishes him dead (which would perhaps be the best thing for him); but it vexes me that she behaves so badly to her sister, who is the wife of a tailor, and I often tell her that in this she is committing a double sin; for the needy sister comes from time to time for something to eat. If she does not come exactly on the evening which she has agreed upon, she gets nothing, and the food is thrown away upstairs. When at some length I place her sin before her, she says, 'That meat is bad.' I ask her why she let it get bad, and did not give it in time to her sister. To this she answers that her sister is not worthy of it. I predict evil things which will happen to her in future, as they have done to others whom I enumerate to her. At this she throws back her head and is silent.

At this time her Majesty the Queen sent me some silkworms to beguile the time. When they had finished spinning, I sent them back to her Majesty in a box which I had covered with carnation-coloured satin, upon which I had embroidered a pattern with gold thread. Inside, the box was lined with white taffeta. In the lid I embroidered with black silk a humble request that her Majesty would loose my bonds, and would fetter me anew with the hand of favour. Her Majesty the virtuous Queen would have granted my request had it rested with her.

The prison governor became gradually more sensible and accommodating, drank less wine, and made no jokes. I had peace within my doors. The woman sat during the day outside in the other apartment, and lay there also in the night, so that I began not to fret so much over my hard fate. I passed the year with reading, writing, and composing.

For some time past, immediately after I had received the yearly pension, I had bought for myself not only historical works in various languages, but I had gathered and translated from them all the famous female personages, who were celebrated as true, chaste, sensible, valorous, virtuous, God-fearing, learned, and steadfast; and in anno 1675, on January 9, I amused myself with making some rhymes to M. Thomas Kingo, under the title, 'To the much- famed Poet M. Thomas Kingo, a Request from a Danish Woman in the name of all Danish Women.' The request was this, that he would exhibit in befitting honour the virtuous and praiseworthy Danish women. There are, indeed, virtuous women belonging to other nations, but I requested only his praise of the Danish. This never reached Kingo; but if my good friend to whom I entrust these papers still lives, it will fall probably into your hands, my beloved children.

In the same year, on May 11, I wrote in rhyme a controversial conversation between Sense and Reason; entitled, 'Controversial Thoughts by the Captive Widow, or the Dispute between Sense and Reason.'

Nothing else occurred this year within the doors of my prison which is worth recording, except one event—namely, when the outermost door of the anteroom was unlocked in the morning for the sake of sweeping away the dirt and bringing in fresh water, and the tower-warder occasionally let it stand open till meal-time and then closed it again, it happened that a fire broke out in the town and the bells were tolled. I and the woman ran up to the top of the tower to see where it was burning.

When I was on the stairs which led up to the clock-work, the prison governor came, and with him was a servant from the silver-chamber. He first perceived my dog, then he saw somewhat of the woman, and thought probably that I was there also; he was so wise as not to come up the stairs, but remained below at the lowest holes, from whence one can look out over the town, and left me time enough to get down again and shut my door. Gert was sorry, and came afterwards to the door and told me of his distress. I consoled him, and said there was nothing to fear. Before the prison governor opened the door at noon, he struck Gert with his stick, so that he cried, and the prison governor said with an oath, 'Thou shalt leave.' When the prison governor came in, I was the first to speak, and I said: 'It is not right in you to beat the poor devil; he could not help it. The executioner came up as he was going to lock my door, and that made him forget to do so.' He threatened Gert severely, and said, 'I should not have minded it so much had not that other servant been with me.'

The words at once occurred to me which he had said to me a long time before, namely that no woman could be silent, but that all men could be silent (when he had asserted this, I had thought, if this be so, then my adversaries might believe that I, had I known of anything which they had in view, should not have been able to keep silence). So I now answered him thus: 'Well, and what does that signify? It was a man; they can all keep silence; there is no harm done.' He could not help laughing, and said, 'Well, you are good enough.' I then talked to him, and assured him that I had no desire to leave the tower without the King's will, even though day and night all the tower doors were left open, and I also said that I could have got out long ago, if that had been my design. Gert continued in his service, and the prison governor never told Gert to shut me in in the morning.[142]

At this time I had bought myself a clavicordium, and as Barbra could sing well, I played psalms and she sang, so that the time was not long to us. She taught me to bind books, so far as I needed.[E56]

My father confessor, H. Emmeke, became a preacher at Kiöge anno 1676. In the same year my pension was increased, and I received yearly 250 rix- dollars. It stands in the order that the 200 rix-dollars were to be used for the purchase of clothes and the remaining fifty to buy anything which might beguile the time.[E57] God bless and keep his gracious Majesty, and grant that he may live to enjoy many happy years.

Brant was at this time treasurer.

On December 17 in this same year Barbra left me, and married a bookbinder's apprentice; but she repented it afterwards. And as her husband died a year and a half after her marriage, and that suddenly, suspicion fell upon Barbra. She afterwards went to her brother's house and fell ill. Her conscience was awakened, and she sent for Tötzlöff and told almost in plain terms that she had poisoned her husband, and begged him to tell me so. I was not much astonished at it, for according to her own account she had before killed her own children; but I told Peder Tötzlöff that he was not to speak of it; if God willed that it should be made known, it would be so notwithstanding; the brother and the maid in the house knew it; he was not to go there again, even if she sent a message to him. She became quite insane, and lay in a miserable condition. The brother subsequently had her removed to the plague-house.

In Barbra's place there came to me a woman named Sitzel, daughter of a certain Klemming; Maren Blocks had brought about her employment, as Sitzel owed her money. She is a dissolute woman, and Maren gave her out as a spinster; she had a white cap on her head when she came up. Sitzel's debt to Maren had arisen in this way: that Maren—since Sitzel could make buttons, and the button-makers had quarrelled with her—obtained for her a royal licence in order to free her from the opposition of the button-makers, under the pretext that she was sickly. When the door was locked in the evening, I requested to see the royal licence which Maren had obtained for her. And when I saw that she was styled in it the sickly woman, I asked her what her infirmity was. She replied that she had no infirmity. 'Why, then,' I asked, 'have you given yourself out as sickly?' She answered, 'That was Maren Block's doing, in order to get for me the royal licence.' 'In the licence,' I said, 'you are spoken of as a married woman, and not as a spinster; have you, then, been seduced?' She hung her head and said softly, 'Yes.'

I was not satisfied. I said, 'Maren Block has obtained the royal licence for you by lies, and has brought you to me by lies; what, then, can I expect from your service?' She begged my pardon, promised to serve me well, and never to act contrary to my wishes. She is a dangerous person; there is nothing good in her; bold and shameless, she is not even afraid of fighting a man. She struck two button-makers one day, who wanted to take away her work, till they were obliged to run away. With me she had no opportunity of thus displaying her evil passions, but still they were perceptible in various ways. One day I warded off a scuffle between her and Maren Blocks; for when Maren Blocks had got back the money which she had expended on the royal licence for Sitzel, she wanted to remove her from me, and to bring another into her place; but I sent word to Maren Blocks that she must not imagine she could send me another whom I must take. It was enough that she had done this time.[143]

In the place of H. Emmeke Norbye, H. Johan Adolf Borneman became palace-preacher; a very learned and sensible man, who now became my father confessor, and performed the duties of his office for the first time on April 10, 1677.

On October 9, in the same year, my father confessor was Magister Hendrich Borneman, dean of the church of Our Lady (a learned and excellent man), his brother H. Johan Adolf Borneman having accompanied the King's Majesty on a journey.

I have, thank God, spent this year in repose: reading, writing, and composing various things.

Anno 1678 it was brought about for me that my father-confessor, H. Johan Adolf Borneman, should come to me every six weeks and preach a short sermon.

In this year, on Easter-Day, Agneta Sophia Budde was brought to the tower. Her prison was above my innermost apartment. She was accused of having designed to poison the Countess Skeel; and as she was a young person, and had a waiting-woman in her attendance who was also young, they clamoured to such an extent all day that I had no peace for them. I said nothing, however, about it, thinking she would probably be quiet when she knew that her life was at stake. But no! she was merry to the day on which she was executed!
[144]

In the same year, on the morning of July 9, the tower-warder Gert was killed by a thief who was under sentence of death, and to whom he had allowed too great liberty. I will mention this incident somewhat more in detail, as I had advised Gert not to give this prisoner so much liberty; but to his own misfortune he paid no attention to my advice. This thief had broken by night into the house of a clergyman, and had stolen a boiling-copper, which he had carried on his head to Copenhagen; he was seized with it at the gate in the morning, and was placed here in the tower. He was condemned to be hanged (he had committed various other thefts). The priest allowed the execution to be delayed; he did not wish to have him hanged. Then it was said he was to go to the Holm; but he remained long in prison. At first, and until the time that his going to the Holm was talked of, he was my neighbour in the Dark Church; he behaved quite as a God-fearing man, read (apparently) with devotion, and prayed to God for forgiveness of his sins with most profound sighs. The rogue knew that I could hear him, and I sent him occasionally something to eat. Gert took pity on him, and allowed him to go by day about the basement story of the tower, and shut him up at night again.

Afterwards he allowed him also at night to remain below. And as I had seen the thief once or twice when my door stood open, and he went past, it seemed to me that he had a murderous countenance; and for this reason, when I heard that the thief was not placed of an evening in the Dark Church, I said to Gert that he ventured too far, in letting him remain below at night; that there was roguery lurking in him; that he would certainly some day escape, and then, on his account, Gert would get into trouble. Gert was not of opinion that the thief wished to run away; he had no longer any fear of being hanged; he had been so delighted that he was to go to the Holm, there was no danger in it. I thought 'That is a delight which does not reach further than the lips,' and I begged him that he would lock him up at night. No; Gert feared nothing; he even went farther, and allowed the thief to go up the tower instead of himself, and attend to the clock-work.

Three days before the murder took place, I spoke with Gert, when he unlocked my door in the morning, of the danger to which he exposed himself by the liberty he allowed the thief, but Gert did not fear it. Meanwhile my dog placed himself exactly in front of Gert, and howled in his face. When we were at dinner, the dog ran down and howled three times at the tower-warder's door. Never before had I heard the dog howl.

On July 19 (as I have said), when Gert's unfortunate morning had arrived, the thief came down from the clock-work, and said that he could not manage it alone, as the cords were entangled. The rogue had an iron rod ready above, in order to effect his project. Gert went upstairs, but was carried down. The thief ran down after Gert was dead, opened his box, took out the money, and went out of the tower.

It was a Friday, and the bells were to be rung for service. Those whose duty it was to ring them knocked at the tower door, but no one opened. Tötzlöff came with the principal key and opened, and spoke to me and wondered that Gert was not there at that time of the day. I said: 'All is not right; this morning between four and five I was rather unwell, and I heard three people going upstairs and after a time two coming down again.' Tötzlöff locked my door and went down. Just then one of the ringers came down, and informed them that Gert was lying upstairs dead. When the dead man was examined, he had more than one wound, but all at the back of the head. He was a very bold man, courageous, and strong; one man could not be supposed to have done this to him.

The thief was seized the same evening, and confessed how it had happened: that, namely, a prisoner who was confined in the Witch Cell, a licentiate of the name of Moritius, had persuaded him to it. This same Moritius had great enmity against Gert. It is true that Gert took too much from him weekly for his food. But it is also true that this Moritius was a very godless fellow; the priest who confesses him gives him no good character. I believe, indeed, that Moritius was an accessory, but I believe also that another prisoner, who was confined in the basement of the tower, had a hand in the game. For who should have locked the tower-door again after the imprisoned thief, had not one of these done so? For when the key was looked for, it was found hidden above in the tower; this could not have been done by the thief after he was out of the tower. The thief, moreover, could not have unlocked Gert's box and taken his money without the knowledge of Moritius. The other prisoner must also have been aware of it. It seems to me that it was hushed up, in order that no more should die for this murder; for the matter was not only not investigated as was befitting, but the thief was confined down below in the tower. He was bound with iron fetters, but Moritius could speak with him everyday: and for this reason the thief departed from his earlier statement, and said that he alone had committed the murder. He was executed on August 8, and Moritius was taken to Borringholm, and kept as a prisoner there.[E55b]

In Gert's place a tower-warder of the name of Johan, a Norwegian, was appointed—a very simple man. The servants about court often made a fool of him. The imprisoned young woman and her attendant did so the first time after his arrival that the attendant had to perform some menial offices upstairs. The place to which she had to go was not far from the door of their prison. The tower-warder went down in the meanwhile, and left the door open. They ran about and played. When they heard him coming up the stairs, they hid themselves. He found the prison empty, and was grieved and lamented. The young woman giggled like a child, and thus he found her behind a door. Johan was glad, and told me the story afterwards. I asked why he had not remained with them. 'What,' he answered, 'was I to remain at their dirty work?' There was nothing to say in reply to such foolish talk.

I had repose within my doors, and amused myself with reading, writing and various handiwork, and began to make and embroider my shroud, for which I had bought calico, white taffeta, and thread.

On April 7 a young lad escaped from the tower, who had been confined on the lower story with iron fetters round his legs. This prisoner found opportunity to loosen his fetters, and knew, moreover, that the booby Johan was wont to keep the tower key under his pillow. He kept an iron pin in readiness to unlock the door of the room when the tower-warder was asleep; he opened it gently, took the key, locked in the booby again, and quitted the tower. The simple man was placed in confinement, but after the expiration of six weeks he was set at liberty.

In his place there came a man named Olle Mathison, who was from Skaane; he had his wife with him in the tower. Towards the end of this year, on December 25, I became ill of a fever, and D. Mynchen received orders to visit me and to take me under his care—an order which he executed with great attention. He is a very sensible man, mild and judicious in his treatment. Ten days after I recovered my usual health.

In the beginning of the year 1680 Sitzel, Klemming's daughter, was persuaded by Maren Blocks to betroth herself to one of the King's body- guard. She left me on November 26. In her place I had a woman named Margrete. When I first saw her, she appeared to me somewhat suspicious, and it seemed to me that she was with child; however, I made no remark till the last day of the month of January. Then I put a question to her from which she could perceive my opinion. She answered me with lies, but I interrupted her at once; and she made use of a special trick, which it is not fit to mention here, in order to prove her false assertion; but her trick could not stand with me, and she was subsequently obliged to confess it. I asked her as to the father of the child (I imagined that it was the King's groom of the chamber, who had been placed in arrest in the prison governor's room, but I did not say so). She did not answer my question at the time, but said she was not so far advanced; that her size was owing rather to stoutness than to the child, as it was at a very early stage.

This woman, before she came to me, had been in the service of the prison governor's wife, and the prison governor had told me she was married. So it happened that I one day asked her of her life and doings; upon which she told me of her past history, where she had served, and that she had had two bastards, each by a different father; and pointing to herself, she added: 'A father shall also acknowledge this one, and that a brave father! You know him well!' I said, 'I have seen the King's groom of the chamber in the square, but I do not know him.' She laughed and answered (in her mother-tongue), 'No, by God, that is not he; it is the good prison governor.' I truly did not believe it. She protested it, and related some minute details to me.

I thought I had better get rid of her betimes, and I requested to speak with the prison governor's wife, who at once came to me. I told her my suspicion with regard to the woman, and on what I based my suspicion; but I made no remark as to what the woman had confessed and said to me. I begged the prison governor's wife to remove the woman from me as civilly as she could. She was surprised at my words, and doubted if there was truth in them. I said, 'Whether it be so or not, remove her; the sooner the better.' She promised that it should be done, but it was not. Margrete seemed not to care that it was known that she was with child; she told the tower-warder of it, and asked him one day, 'Ole, how was it with your wife when she had twins?' Ole answered: 'I know nothing about it. Ask Anne!' Margrete said that from certain symptoms she fancied she might have twins.

One day, when she was going to sew a cloth on the arms of my arm-chair, she said, 'That angel of God is now moving!' And as the wife of the prison governor did not adhere to her word, and Margrete's sister often came to the tower, I feared that the sister might secretly convey her something to remove the child (which was no doubt subsequently the case), so I said one day to Margrete: 'You say that the prison governor is your child's father, but you do not venture to say so to himself.' 'Yes!' she said with an oath, 'as if I would not venture! Do you imagine that I will not have something from him for the support of my child?' 'Then I will send for him,' I said, 'on purpose to hear what he will say.' (It was at that time a rare occurrence for the prison governor to come to me.) She begged me to do so; he could not deny, she said, that he was the father of her child. The prison governor came at my request. I began my speech in the woman's presence, and said that Margrete, according to her own statement, was with child; who the father was, he could enquire if he chose. He asked her whether she was with child? She answered, 'Yes, and you are the father of it.' 'O!' he said, and laughed, 'what nonsense!' She adhered to what she had said, protested that no other was the child's father, and related the circumstances of how it had occurred. The prison governor said, 'The woman is mad!' She gave free vent to her tongue, so that I ordered her to go out; then I spoke with the prison governor alone, and begged him speedily to look about for another woman for me, before it came to extremities with her. I supposed he would find means to stop her tongue. I told him the truth in a few words—that he had brought his paramour to wait on me. He answered, 'She lies, the malicious woman! I have ordered Tötzlöff already to look about for another. My wife has told me what you said to her the other day.' After this conversation the prison governor went away. Peder Tötzlöff told me that an English woman had desired to be with me, but could not come before Easter.

Four days afterwards Margrete began to complain that she felt ill, and said to me in the forenoon, 'I think it will probably go badly with me; I feel so ill.' I thought at once of what I had feared, namely of what the constant visits of her sister indicated, and I sent immediately to Peder Tötzlöff, and when he came to me I told him of my suspicion respecting Margrete, and begged him to do his utmost to procure me the English woman that very day. Meanwhile Margrete went up stairs, and remained there about an hour and a quarter, and came down looking like a corpse, and said, 'Now it will be all right with me.' What I thought I would not say (for I knew that if I had enquired the cause of her bad appearance she would have at once acknowledged it all, and I did not want to know it), so I said, 'If you keep yourself quiet, all will be well. Another woman is coming this evening.' This did not please her; she thought she could now well remain. I paid no regard to this nor to anything else she said, but adhered to it—that another woman was coming. This was arranged, and in the evening of March 15 Margrete left, and in her place came an English woman, named Jonatha, who had been married to a Dane named Jens Pedersen Holme.

When Margrete was gone, I was blamed by the wife of the prison governor, who said that I had persuaded Margrete to affirm that her husband was the father of Margrete's child.

Although it did not concern me, I will nevertheless mention the deceitful manner in which the good people subsequently brought about this Margrete's marriage. They informed a bookbinder's apprentice that she had been married, and they showed both him and the priest, who was to give them the nuptial benediction, her sister's marriage certificate.[145]

In the same year, on the morning of Christmas Day, God loosened D. Otto Sperling's heavy bonds, after he had been imprisoned in the Blue Tower seventeen years, eight months, twenty-four days, at the age of eighty years minus six days. He had long been ill, but never confined to his bed. Doctor München twice visited him with his medicaments. He would not allow the tower-warder at any time to make his bed, and was quite angry if Ole offered to do so, and implied that the doctor was weak. He allowed no one either to be present when he laid down. How he came on the floor on Christmas night is not known; he lay there, knocking on the ground. The tower-warder could not hear his knocking, for he slept far from the doctor's room; but a prisoner who slept on the ground floor heard it, and knocked at the tower-warder's door and told him that the doctor had been knocking for some time. When Ole came in, he found the doctor lying on the floor, half dressed, with a clean shirt on. He was still alive, groaned a good deal, but did not speak. Ole called a prisoner to help him, and they lifted him on the bed and locked the door again. In the morning he was found dead, as I have said.

A.D. 1682, in the month of April, I was sick and confined to my bed from a peculiar malady which had long troubled me—a stony matter had coagulated and had settled low down in my intestines. Doctor München used all available means to counteract this weakness; but he could not believe that it was of the nature I thought and informed him; for I was perfectly aware it was a stone which had settled in the duct of the intestines. He was of opinion, if it were so, that the medicaments which he used would remove it.[146] At this time the doctor was obliged to travel with his Majesty to Holstein. I used the remedies according to Doctor München's directions, but things remained just as before. It was not till the following morning that the remedies produced their effect; and then, besides other matter, a large stone was evacuated, and I struck a piece out of it with a hammer in order to see what it was inside; I found it to be composed of a substance like rays, having the appearance of being gilded in some places and in others silvered. It is almost half a finger in length and full three fingers thick, and it is still in my possession. When Doctor München returned, I sent him word how it was with me. He was at the time with the governess of the royal children, F. Sitzele Grubbe. Doctor München desired

Tötzlöff to request me to let him see the stone. I sent him word that if he would come to me, he should see it. I would not send it to him, for I well knew that I should never get it again.

A.D. 1682, June 11, I wrote the following spiritual song.

It can be sung to the melody, 'Siunge wii af Hiærtens-Grund.'[E59]

I.

What is this our mortal life
Otherwise than daily strife?
What is all our labour here,
The servitude and yoke we bear?
Are they aught but vanity?
Art and learning what are ye?
Like a vapour all we see.

II.

Why, then, is thy anxious breast
Filled with trouble? Be at rest!
Why, then, dost thou boldly fight
The phantoms vain that mock thy sight?
Is there any, small or grand,
Who can payment duly hand
At the creditor's demand?

III.

Naked to the world I came,
And I leave it just the same;
The Lord has given and He takes;
It is well whate'er He makes.
To the Lord all praises be;
I will trust Him heartily!
And my near deliverance see.

IV.

One thing would I ask of Thee.
That Thy House I once may see,
And once more with song and praise
May my pious offering raise,
And magnify Thy grace received,
And all that Jesus has achieved
For us who have in Him believed.

V.

If Thou sayest unto me,
'I have no desire in thee,
There is no place for thee above;'
Oh Jesus! look Thou down in love!

Can I not justly to Thee say
'Let me but see Thy wounds, I pray:'
God's mercy cannot pass away.

On June 27, the Queen sent me some silk and silver, with the request that I would embroider her a flower, which was traced on parchment; she sent also another flower which was embroidered, that I might see how the work should be done, which is called the golden work. I had never before embroidered such work, for it affects the eyes quickly; but I undertook it, and said I would do it as well as I could. On July 9, I sent the flower which I had embroidered to the governess of the royal children, F. Sitzele Grubbe, with the request that she would present it most humbly to her Majesty the Queen. The Queen was much pleased with the flower, and told her that it excelled the others which certain countesses had embroidered for her.

I afterwards embroidered nine flowers in silver and silk in this golden work, and sent them to the Queen's mistress of the robes, with the request that she would present them most humbly to her Majesty the Queen. The mistress of the robes assured me of the Queen's favour, and told me that her Majesty was going to give me two silver flagons, but I have not heard of them yet. In the same year I embroidered a table-cover with floss silk, in a new design devised by myself, and I trimmed it with taffeta and silver fringe; this also I begged Lady Grubbe, the governess of the King's children, to present most humbly to her Majesty, and it was graciously received. On November 29, I completed the work which I had made for my death-gear. It was embroidered with thread. On one end of the pillow I worked the following lines:

Full of anxiety and care, in many a silent night,
This shroud have I been weaving with sorrowful delight!

On the other end I embroidered the following: (N.B. The pillow was stuffed with my hair).

When some day on this hair my weary head will lie,
My body will be free and my soul to God will fly.

On the cloth for the head I embroidered:

I know full well, my Jesus, Thou dost live,
And my frail body from the dust wilt give,
And it with marvellous beauty will array
To stand before Thy throne on the great day.
Fulfilled with heavenly joy I then shall be,
And Thee, great God, in all Thy splendour see.
Nor unknown wilt Thou to mine eyes appear!
Help Jesus, bridegroom, be Thou ever near!

Her Majesty the Queen was always gracious to me, and sent me again a number of silkworms that I might amuse myself with feeding them for her, and I was to return what they spun. The virtuous Queen also sent me sometimes oranges, lemons, and some of the large almanacs, and this she did through a dwarf, who is a thoroughly quick lad. His mother and father had been in the service of my deceased sister Sophia Elizabeth and my brother-in- law Count Pentz.

The governess of the royal children, F. Sitzel Grubbe, was very courteous and good to me, and sent me several times lemons, oranges, mulberries, and other fruits, according to the season of the year.

A young lady, by birth a Donep, also twice sent me fruit.

The maids of honour once sent me some entangled silk from silkworms, which they wanted to spin, and did not rightly know how to manage it; they requested me to arrange it for them. I had other occupation on hand which I was unwilling to lay aside (for I was busy collecting my heroines), but nevertheless I acceded to their wish.[E60] My captivity of nearly twenty years could not touch the heart of the Queen Dowager (though with a good conscience I can testify before God that I never gave her cause for such inclemency). My most gracious hereditary King was gracious enough several times in former years to intercede for me with his royal mother, through the high ministers of the State. Her answer at that time was very hard; she would entitle them 'traitors,' and, 'as good as I was,' and would point them to the door. All the favours which the King's majesty showed me—the outer apartment, the large window, the money to dispose of for myself—annoyed the Queen Dowager extremely; and she made the King's majesty feel her displeasure in the most painful manner. And as she had also learned (she had plenty of informers) that I possessed a clavicordium, this annoyed her especially, and she spoke very angrily with the King about it; on which account the prison governor came to me one day and said that the King had asked him how he had happened to procure me a clavicordium. 'I stood abashed,' said the prison governor, 'and knew not what to say.' I thought to myself, 'You know but little of what is happening in the tower.' I did not see him more than three times a year. I asked who had told the King of the clavicordium. He answered: 'The old Queen; she has her spies everywhere, and she has spoken so hardly to the King that it is a shame because he gives you so much liberty;' so saying, he seized the clavicordium just as if he were going to take it away, and said, 'You must not have it!' I said, 'Let it alone! I have permission from his Majesty, my gracious Sovereign, to buy what I desire for my pastime with the money he graciously assigns me. The clavicordium is in no one's way, and cannot harm the Queen Dowager.' He pulled at it nevertheless, and wanted to take it down; it stood on a closet which I had bought. I said, with rather a loud voice, 'You must let it remain until you return me the money I gave you for it; then you may do with it what you like.' He said, 'I will tell the King that.' I begged him to do so. There was nothing afterwards said about it,[147] and I still have the clavicordium, though I play on it rarely. I write, and hasten to finish my heroines, so that I may have them ready, and that no sickness nor death may prevent my completing them, nor the friend to whom I confide them may leave me, and so they would never fall into your hands, my dearest children.

On September 24, M. Johan Adolf, my father confessor, was promoted; he became dean of the church of Our Lady. He bade me a very touching farewell, having administered the duties of his office to me for nearly six years, and been my consolation. God knows how unwillingly I parted with him.

At the beginning of this year H. Peder Collerus was my father confessor; he was at the time palace-preacher. He also visited me with his consolatory discourse every six weeks. He is a learned man, but not like Hornemann.

On April 3, an old sickly dog was sent to me in the Queen's name. I fancy the ladies of the court sent it, to be quit of the trouble. A marten had bit its jaw in two, so that the tongue hung out on one side. All the teeth were gone, and a thin film covered one eye. It heard but little, and limped on one side. The worst, however, was, that one could easily see that it tried to exhibit its affection beyond its power. They told me that her Majesty the Queen had been very fond of the dog. It was a small 'King Charles;' its name was 'Cavaillier.' The Queen expressed her opinion that it would not long trouble me. I hoped so also.[E66b]

On August 12 of this year I finished the work I had undertaken, and since my prefatory remarks treated of celebrated women of every kind, both of valiant rulers and sensible sovereigns, of true, chaste, God-fearing, virtuous, unhappy, learned, and steadfast women, it seemed to me that all of these could not be reckoned as heroines; so I took some of them out and divided them into three parts, under the title, 'The Heroines' Praise.' The first part is to the honour of valiant heroines. The second part speaks of true and chaste heroines. The third part of steadfast heroines. Each part has its appendix. I hope to God that this my prison work may come into your hands, my dearest children. Hereafter I intend, so God will, to collect the others: namely, the sensible, learned, god-fearing, and virtuous women; exhibiting each to view in the circumstances of her life.[E61]

I will mention from her own statement somewhat of Jonatha, who now attended on me. I will pass over the long story of how she left her mother; the fact is, that against her mother's will she married a Danish merchant, named Jens Pedersen Holme. But her life and doings (according to her own statement) are so strange, that it may be worth while to record somewhat of them. After they were married, she says, it vexed her, and was always in her mind that she had made her mother angry, and had done very wrong. Her mother had sent her also a hard letter, which distressed her much; and she behaved refractorily towards her husband, and in many ways like a spoilt unreasonable child, sometimes even like one who had lost her reason and was desperate.

It seems also that her husband treated her as if her mind was affected, for he had her looked after like a child, and treated her as such. She told him once that she was intending to drown herself in the Peblingesö,[E62] and at another time that she would strike him dead. The husband feared neither of these threats; still he had her watched when she went out, to see which way she took. Once she had firmly resolved to drown herself in the Peblingesö, for this place pleased her; she was even on her way there, but was brought back. She struck her husband, too, once after her fashion. He had come home one day half intoxicated, and had laid down on a bed, so that his legs rested on the floor. She says she intended at the time to strike him dead; she took a stick and tried to see if he were asleep, talking loudly to herself and scolding, and touching him softly on the shinbone with the stick. He behaved as if he were asleep. Then she struck him a little harder. Upon this he seized the stick and took it away from her, and asked what she had in her mind. She answered, 'To kill you.' 'He was grieved at my madness,' she said, 'and threw himself on his knees, praying God to govern me with His good spirit and give me reason.' The worst is that it once came into her mind not to sleep with her husband, and she laid down on a bench in the room. For a long time he gave her fair words, but these availed nothing. At last he said, 'Undress yourself and come and lie down, or I shall come to you.' She paid no attention to this; so he got up, undressed her completely, slapped her with his hand, and threw her into bed. She protested that for some days she was too bruised to sit; this proved availing, and she behaved in future more reasonably.

Little at peace as she was with her husband when she had him with her, she was greatly grieved when he left her to go to the West Indies. He sent by return vessels all sorts of goods to sell, and she thus maintained herself comfortably.

It happened at last that the man died in the West Indies, and a person who brought her the news stated that he had been poisoned by the governor of the place named ———, at an entertainment, and this because he was on the point of returning home, and the governor was afraid that Holme might mention his evil conduct. These tidings unsettled her mind so, that she ran at night, in her mere night-dress, along the street, and squabbled with the watchmen. She went to the admiral at the Holm, and demanded justice upon the absent culprit, and accused him, though she could prove nothing.

Thus matters went on for a time, until at last she gained repose, and God ordained it that she came to me. My intercourse with her is as with a frail glass vessel, for she is weak in many respects. She often doubts of her salvation, and enumerates all her sins. She laments especially having so deeply offended her mother, and thus having drawn down a curse upon her. When this fear comes upon her, I console her with God's word, and enter fully into the matter, showing her, from Holy Scripture, on what a repentant sinner must rely for the mercy of God. Occasionally she is troubled as to the interpretation of Holy Scripture, as all passages do not seem to her to agree, but to contradict each other. In this I help her so far as my understanding goes, so that sometimes she heartily thanks God that she is come to me, where she finds rest and consolation.

After she had been with me for a year or two, she learned that the governor, whom she suspected, had come to Copenhagen. She said to me, 'I hear the rogue is come here; I request my dismissal.' I asked her why. 'Because,' she replied, 'I will kill him.' I could scarcely keep from laughing; but I said, 'Jesus forbid! If you have any such design, I shall not let you go.' And as she is a person whose like I have never known before—for she could chide with hard words, and yet at the same time she was modest and well-behaved—I tried to make her tell me and show me how she designed to take the governor's life. (She is a small woman, delicately formed.) Then she acted as if her enemy were seated on a stool, and she had a large knife under her apron. When he said to her, 'Woman, what do you want?' she would plunge the knife into him, and exclaim, 'Rogue, thou hast deserved this.' She would not move from the place, she would gladly die, if she could only take his life. I said, 'Still it is such a disgrace to die by the hand of the executioner.' 'Oh, no!' she replied, 'it is not a disgrace to die for an honourable deed;' and she had an idea that any one thus dying by the hand of the executioner passed away in a more Christian manner than such as died on a bed of sickness; and that it was no sin to kill a man who, like a rogue, had murdered another. I asked her if she did not think that he sinned who killed another. 'No,' she replied, 'not when he has brought it upon himself.' I said, 'No one may be his own judge, either by the law of God or man; and what does the fifth commandment teach us?'[E63] She answered as before, that she would gladly die if she could only take the rogue's life. (I must add that she said she could not do it on my account, for I would not let her out.) She made a sin of that which is no sin, and that which is sin she will not regard as such. She says it is a sin to kill a dog, a cat, or a bird; the innocent animals do no harm; in fact, it is a still greater sin to let the poor beasts hunger. I asked her once whether it was a sin to eat meat. 'No,' she answered; 'it is only a sin to him who has killed the animal.' She protested that if she were obliged to marry, and had to choose between a butcher and an executioner, she would prefer the latter. She told me of various quarrels she had had with those who had either killed animals or allowed them to hunger.

One story I will not leave unmentioned, as it is very pretty. She sold, she said, one day some pigs to a butcher. When the butcher's boy was about to bind the pigs' feet and carry them off hanging from a pole, she was sorry for the poor pigs, and said, 'What, will you take their life? No, I will not suffer that!' and she threw him back his money. I asked her if she did not know that pigs were killed, and for what reason she thought the butcher had bought them. 'Yes,' she replied, 'I knew that well. Had he let them go on their own legs, I should have cared nothing about it; but to bind the poor beasts in this way, and to hear them cry, I could not endure that.' It would take too long to enumerate all the extravagant whims which she related of herself. But with all this she is not foolish, and I well believe she is true to any one she loves. She served me very well, and with great care.

The above-mentioned governor[E64] was killed by some prisoners on board the vessel, when he was returning to the West Indies. By a strange chance the vessel with the murderers came to Copenhagen. (They were sentenced to death for their crime.) Jonatha declared that the governor had had only too good a death, and that it was a sin that any one should lose his life on account of it. I practise speaking the English language with Jonatha. She has forgotten somewhat of her mother tongue, since she has not spoken it for many years; and as she always reads the English Bible, and does not at once understand all the words, I help her; for I not only can perceive the sense from the preceding and following words, but also because some words resemble the French, though with another accent. And we often talk together about the interpretation of Holy Scripture. She calls herself a Calvinist, but she does not hold the opinions of Calvinists. I never dispute with her over her opinions. She goes to the Lord's Supper in the Queen's church[E65]. Once, when she came back to me from there, she said she had had a conversation upon religion with a woman, who had told her to her face that she was no Calvinist. I asked her of what religion the woman imagined that she was. She replied: 'God knows that. I begged her to mind her own business, and said, that I was a Christian; I thought of your grace's words (but I did not say them), that all those who believe on Christ and live a Christian life, are Christians, whatever name they may give to their faith.'

In this year 1684 I saw the Queen Dowager fall from the chair in which she was drawn up to the royal apartment. The chair ran down the pulleys too quickly, so that she fell on her face and knocked her knee. During this year her weakness daily increased, but she thought herself stronger than she was. She appeared at table always much dressed, and between the meals she remained in her apartments.

I kept myself patient, and wrote the following:—

Contemplation on Memory and Courage, recorded to the honour of God by the suffering Christian woman in the sixty-third year of her life, and the almost completed twenty-first year of her captivity.

> The vanished hours can ne'er come back again,
> Still may the old their youthful joys retain;
> The past may yet within our memory live,
> And courage vigour to the old may give.
> Yet why should I thus sport with Memory's truth,
> And harrow up the fairer soil of youth?
> No fruit it brings, fallow and bare it lies,
> And the dry furrow only pain supplies!
> In my first youth, in honourable days
> Upon such things small question did I raise.
> Then years advanced with trouble in their train,
> And spite of show my life was fraught with pain.
> The holy marriage bond—my rank and fame,
> Increased my foes and made my ill their aim.
> Go! honour, riches, vanish from my mind!
> Ye all forsook me and left nought behind.
> 'Twas ye have brought me here thro' years to lie;
> Thus can man's envy human joy deny!
> My God alone, He ne'er forsook me here,
> My cross He lightened, and was ever near;
> And when my heart was yielding to despair,
> He spoke of peace and whispered He was there.
> He gave me power and ever near me stood,
> And all could see how truly God was good.
>
> What Courage can achieve I next will heed;
> He who is blessed with it, is blest indeed.
> To the tired frame fresh power can Courage give,
> Raising the weary mind anew to live;
> I mean that Courage Reason may instil

Not the foolhardiness that leads to ill.
Far oftener is it that the youth will lie
Helpless, when Fortune's favours from him fly,
Than that the old man should inactive stay,
Who knows full well how Fortune loves to play.
Fresh Courage seizes him; from such a shield
Rebound the arms malicious foes may wield.
Courage imparts repose, and trifles here,
Beneath its influence, as nought appear;
But a vain loan, which we can only hold
Until the lender comes, and life is told.
Courage pervades the frame and vigour gives,
And a fresh energy each part receives;
With appetite and health and cheerful mind,
And calm repose in hours of sleep we find,
So that no visions in ill dreams appear,
And spectre forms filling the heart with fear.
Courage gives honied sweetness to our food
And prison fare, and makes e'en death seem good.
'Tis well! my mind is fresh, my limbs are sound,
And no misfortune weighs me to the ground.
Reason and judgment come from God alone,
And the five senses unimpaired I own.
The mighty God in me His power displays,
Therefore join with me in a voice of praise
And laud His name: For Thou it is, oh God,
Who in my fear and anguish nigh me stood.
Almighty One, my thanks be ever thine!
Let me ne'er waver nor my trust resign.
Take not the courage which my hope supplies,
Till my soul enters into Paradise.

Written on February 28, 1684, that is the thirty-sixth anniversary since the illustrious King Christian the Fourth bade good-night to this world, and I to the prosperity of my life.

I have now reached the sixty-third year of my age, and the twentieth year, sixth month, and fifteenth day of my imprisonment. I have therefore spent the third part of my life in captivity. God be praised that so much time is past. I hope the remaining days may not be many.

Anno 1685, January 14, I amused myself with making some verses in which truth was veiled under the cloak of jest, entitled: 'A Dog, named Cavaillier, relates his Fate.'

The rhymes, I suppose, will come into your hands, my dearest children.[E66]

On February 20, the Queen Dowager Sophia Amalia died. She did not think that death would overtake her so quickly; but when the doctor warned her that her death would not be long delayed, she requested to speak with her son. But death would not wait for the arrival of his Majesty, so that the Queen Dowager might say a word to him. She was still alive; she was sitting on a chair, but she was speechless, and soon afterwards, in the same position, she gave up her spirit.

After the death of this Queen I was much on the lips of the people. Some thought that I should obtain my liberty; others believed that I should probably be brought from the tower to some other place, but should not be set free.

Jonatha, who had learned from Ole the tower-warder, some days before the death of the Queen, that prayers were being offered up in the church for the Queen (it had, however, been going on for six weeks, that this prayer had been read from the pulpit), was, equally with Ole the tower-warder, quite depressed. Ole, who had consoled himself and her hitherto with the tidings from the Queen's lacqueys, that the Queen went to table and was otherwise well, though she occasionally suffered from a cough, now thought that there was danger, that death might result, and that I, if the Queen died, might perhaps leave the prison. They did their best to conceal their sorrow, but without success. They occasionally shed secretly a few tears. I behaved as if I did not remark it, and as no one said anything to me about it, I gave no opportunity for speaking on the subject. A long time previously I had said to Jonatha (as I had done before to the other women) that I did not think I should die in the tower. She remembered this and mentioned it. I said: 'All is in God's hand. He knows best what is needful for me, both as regards soul and body; to Him I commend myself.' Thus Jonatha and Ole lived on between hope and fear.

On March 15, the reigning Queen kept her Easter. Jonatha came quite delighted from her Majesty's church, saying that a noble personage had told her that I need not think of getting out of the prison, although the Queen was dead; she knew better and she insisted upon it. However often I asked as to who the personage was, she would not tell me her name. I laughed at her, and said, 'Whoever the personage may be, she knows just as much about it as you and I do.' Jonatha adhered to her opinion that the person knew it well. 'What do you mean?' I said; 'the King himself does not know. How should others know?' 'Not the King! not the King!' she said quite softly. 'No, not the King!' I answered. 'He does not know till God puts it into his heart, and as good as says to him, "Now thou shalt let the prisoner free!"' She came somewhat more to herself, but said nothing. And as she and Ole heard no more rumours concerning me, they were quite comforted.

On March 26, the funeral of the Queen Dowager took place, and her body was conveyed to Roskild.

On April 21, I supplicated the King's Majesty in the following manner. I possessed a portrait engraving of the illustrious King Christian the Fourth, rather small and oval in form. This I illuminated with colours, and had a carved frame made for it, which I gilded myself. On the piece at the back I wrote the following words:—

> My grandson, and great namesake,
> Equal to me in power and state;
> Vouchsafe my child a hearing,
> And be like me in mercy great!

Besides this, I wrote to his Excellency Gyldenlöve, requesting him humbly to present the Supplique to the King's majesty, and to interest himself on my behalf, and assist me to gain my liberty. His Excellency was somewhat inconvenienced at the time by his old weakness, so that he could not himself speak for me; but he begged a good friend to present the engraving with all due respect, and this was done on April 24.[E67]

Of all this Jonatha knew nothing. Peder Jensen Tötzlöff was my messenger. He has been a comfort to me in my imprisonment, and has rendered me various services, so that I am greatly bound to him. And I beg you, my dearest children, to requite him in all possible ways for the services he has rendered me.

On May 2, it became generally talked of that I should assuredly be set at liberty, and some asked the tower-warder whether I had come out the evening before, and at what time; so that Ole began to fear, and could not bear himself as bravely as he tried to do. He said to me in a sad tone: 'My good lady! You will certainly be set at liberty. There are some who think you are already free.' I said, 'God will bring it to pass.' 'Yes,' said he, 'but how will it fare with me then?' I answered, 'You will remain tower-warder, as you now are.' 'Yes,' said he, 'but with what pleasure?' and he turned, unable to restrain his tears, and went away. Jonatha concluded that my deliverance was drawing near, and endeavoured to conceal her sorrow. She said, 'Ole is greatly cast down, but I am not.' (And the tears were standing in her eyes.) 'It is said for certain that the King is going away the day after to-morrow. If you are set at liberty, it will be this very day.' I said, 'God knows.' Jonatha expressed her opinion that I was nevertheless full of hope. I said I had been hopeful ever since the first day of my imprisonment; that God would at last have mercy on me, and regard my innocence. I had prayed to God always for patience to await the time of His succour; and God had graciously bestowed it on me. If the moment of succour had now arrived, I should pray to God for grace to acknowledge rightly His great benefits. Jonatha asked if I were not sure to be set free before the King started for Norway; that it was said for certain that the King would set out early on the following morning. I said: 'There is no certainty as to future things. Circumstances may occur to impede the King's journey, and it may also happen that my liberty may be prevented, even though at this hour it may perhaps be resolved upon. Still I know that my hope will not be confounded. But you do not conceal your regret, and I cannot blame you for it. You have cause for regret, for with my freedom you lose your yearly income and your maintenance.[148] Remember how often I have told you not to throw away your money so carelessly on your son. Youcannot know what may happen to you in your old age. If I die, you will be plunged into poverty; for as soon as you receive your money, you expend it on the apprenticeship of your son, who returns you no thanks for it.[149] You have yourself told me of his bad disposition, and how wrongly he has answered you when you have tried to give him good advice. Latterly he has not ventured to do so, since I read him a lecture, and threatened that I would help to send him to the House of Correction. I fear he will be a bad son to you.' Upon this she gave free vent to her tears, and begged that if I obtained my liberty I would not abandon her. This I promised, so far as lay in my power; for I could not know what my circumstances might be.

In this way some days elapsed, and Jonatha and Ole knew not what the issue might be.

On May 19, at six o'clock in the morning, Ole knocked softly at my outer door. Jonatha went to it. Ole said softly, 'The King is already gone; he left at about four o'clock.' I know not if his hope was great; at any rate it did not last long. Jonatha told me Ole's news. I wished the King's Majesty a prosperous journey (I knew already what order he had given), and it seemed to me from her countenance she was to some extent contented. At about eight o'clock Tötzlöff came up to me and informed me that the Lord Chancellor Count Allefeldt had sent the prison governor a royal order that I was to be released from my imprisonment, and that I could leave when I pleased. (This order was signed by the King's Majesty the day before his Majesty started.)

His Excellency had accompanied the King. Tötzlöff asked whether I wished him to lock the doors, as I was now free. I replied, 'So long as I remain within the doors of my prison, I am not free. I will moreover leave properly. Lock the door and enquire what my sister's daughter, Lady Anna Catharina Lindenow, says, whether his Excellency[E68] sent any message to her (as he promised) before he left. When Tötzlöff was gone, I said to Jonatha, 'Now, in Jesus' name, this very evening I shall leave. Gather your things together, and pack them up, and I will do the same with mine; they shall remain here till I can have them fetched.' She was somewhat startled, but not cast down. She thanked God with me, and when the doors were unlocked at noon and I dined, she laughed at Ole, who was greatly depressed. I told her that Ole might well sigh, for that he would now have to eat his cabbage without bacon.

Tötzlöff brought me word from my sister's daughter that his Excellency had sent to her to say that she was free to accompany me from the tower, if she chose. It was therefore settled that she was to come for me late the same evening.

The prison governor was in a great hurry to get rid of me, and sent the tower-warder to me towards evening, to enquire whether I would not go. I sent word that it was still too light (there would probably be some curious people who had a desire to see me).

Through a good friend I made enquiry of her Majesty the Queen, whether I might be allowed the favour of offering my humble submission to her Majesty (I could go into the Queen's apartment through the secret passage, so that no one could see me). Her Majesty sent me word in reply that she might not speak with me.

At about ten o'clock in the evening, the prison governor opened the door for my sister's daughter. (I had not seen him for two years.) He said, 'Well, shall we part now?' I answered, 'Yes, the time is now come.' Then he gave me his hand, and said 'Ade!' (Adieu). I answered in the same manner, and my niece laughed heartily.

Soon after the prison governor had gone, I and my sister's daughter left the tower. Her Majesty the Queen thought to see me as I came out, and was standing on her balcony, but it was rather dark; moreover I had a black veil over my face. The palace-square, as far as the bridge and further, was full of people, so that we could scarcely press through to the coach.

The time of my imprisonment was twenty-one years, nine months, and eleven days.

King Frederick III. ordered my imprisonment on August 8, A.D. 1663; King Christian V. gave me my liberty on May 18, 1685. God bless my most gracious King with all royal blessing, and give his Majesty health and add many years to his life.

This is finished in my prison.

On May 19, at ten o'clock in the evening, I left my prison. To God be honour and praise. He graciously vouchsafed that I should recognise His divine benefits, and never forget to record them with gratitude.

Dear children! This is the greatest part of the events worth mentioning which occurred to me within the doors of my prison. I live now in the hope that it may please God and the King's Majesty that I may myself show you this record. God in His mercy grant it.

1685. Written at Husum[E69] June 2, where I am awaiting the return of the King's Majesty from Norway:

A.D. 1683. New Year's Day. To Myself.

> Men say that Fortune is a rare and precious thing,
> And they would fain that Power should homage to her bring.
> Yet Power herself is blind and ofttimes falleth low,
> Rarely to rise again, wherefore may Heaven know.
> To-day with humorous wiles she holds her sovereign sway,
> And could one only trust her, there might be goodly prey.
> Yet is she like to Fortune, changeful the course she flies,
> And both, oh earthly pilgrim, are but vain fraud and lies.
> The former is but frail, the other strives with care,
> And both alas! are subject to many a plot and snare.
> Thou hast laid hold on Fortune with an exultant mind,
> Affixed perhaps to-morrow the fatal *mis* we find;
> Then does thy courage fail, this prefix saddens thee,
> Wert thou thyself Goliath or twice as brave as he.
> And thou who art so small—already grey with care—
> Thou know'st not whether evil this year thy lot may share.
> For Fortune frolics ever, now under, now above,
> Emerging here and there her varied powers to prove.
> All that is earthly comes and vanishes again,
> Therefore I cling to that which will for aye remain.

On March 14, 1683, I wrote the following:—

> True is the sentence we are sometimes told:
> A friend is worth far more than bags of gold.
> Yet would I gladly ask, where do we find
> A friend so virtuous that he is well inclined
> To help another in his need and gloom
> Without a thought of recompense to come?
> Naught is there new in this, for selfish care
> To every child of Eve has proved a snare.
> Each generation hears the last complain,

And each repeats the same sad tale again;—
That the oppressed by the wayside may lie,
When naught is gained but God's approving eye.

See, at Bethesda's pool, how once there came
The halting impotent, some help to claim
Among those thousands. Each of pity free,
Had no hand for him in his misery
To bring him to the angel-troubled stream.
Near his last breath did the poor sufferer seem,
Weary and penniless; when One alone
Who without money works His wise own
Will, turned where the helpless suppliant lay,
And gently bade him rise and go his way.

Children of grief, rejoice, do not despair;
This Helper still is here and still will care
What He in mercy wills. He soothes our pain,
And He will help, asking for naught again.
And in due time He will with gracious hand
Unloose thy prison bars and iron band.

A.D. 1684. The first day. To Peder Jensen Tötzlöff.

Welcome, thou New Year's day, altho' thou dost belong
To those by Brahe reckoned the evil days among,
Declaring that whatever may on this day begin
Can never prosper rightly, nor true success can win.
Now I will only ask if from to-day I strive
The evil to avoid and henceforth good to live,
Will this not bring success? Why should a purpose fail,
Altho' on this day made? why should it not prevail?
Oh Brahe, I believe, when we aright begin,
To-day or when it be, and God's good favour win,
The issue must be well, and all that matters here
Is to commend our ways to our Redeemer dear.

Begin with Jesus Christ this as all other days.
Pray that thy plans may meet with the Almighty's praise,
So may'st thou happy be, and naught that man can do
Can hinder thy designs, unless God wills it so!
May a rich meed of blessing be on thy head bestow'd,
And the Lord Jesus Christ protect thee on thy road
With arms of grace. Such is my wish for thee,
Based on the love of God; sure, that He answers me.

LONDON: PRINTED BY
SPOTTISWOODE AND CO., NEW-STREET SQUARE
AND PARLIAMENT STREET

FOOTNOTES

[1] *Le Comte d'Ulfeld, Grand Maistre de Danemarc. Nouvelle historique*, i.-ii. Paris, 1678. 8vo. An English translation, with a supplement, appeared 1695: *The Life of Count Ulfeldt, Great Master of Denmark, and of the Countess Eleonora his Wife.* Done out of French. With a supplement. London. 1695. 8vo.

Another novel by the same author, called *Casimir King of Poland*, is perhaps better known in this country, through a translation by F. Spence in vol. ii. of *Modern Novels*, 1692.

[2] It is by a slip of memory that Mr. Birket Smith, in his first Danish edition of Leonora Christina's memoir of her life in prison, describes this work under the name of *De feminis eruditis*.

[3] La Valette's account of his participation in the Thirty Years' War is entirely fictitious, as almost all that he tells of Ulfeldt's travels, &c.

[4] See *Caroli Ogerii Ephemerides sive, Iter Danicum, Svecicum, Polonicum, &c.* Paris, 1656. 8vo. p. 36, 37, 40, by D'Avaux's secretary, Ogier.

[5] La Valette's account of a lawsuit instituted by the King against Kirstine Munk, in which she was defended by Ulfeldt—of Ulfeldt's duel with Hannibal Sehested, afterwards his brother-in-law, &c.—is entirely fictitious. No such things took place.

[6] This autobiographical sketch is written in the form of a letter to Dr. Otto Sperling the younger, the son of Corfits Ulfeldt's old friend, who was for some years Leonora's fellow-prisoner in the Blue Tower.

[7] It is curious that Leonora seems for a long time to have been under a mistake as to the date of her birthday. The right date is July 18, new style.

[8] On the South Coast of Norway.

[9] Count Christian Pentz, to whom Sophia was married in 1634.

[10] Hannibal Sehestedt afterwards married Leonora's younger sister Christiana; he became a powerful antagonist of Ulfeldt, and is mentioned often in the following Memoir.

[11] Frantz Albrecht, Duke of Saxe-Lauenburg, the same who in the Thirty Years' War alternately served the Protestants and the Imperialists. In the battle of Lützen he was near Gustav Adolf when he fell, and he was regarded by many as the one who treacherously fired the fatal shot.

[12] That is, the King's eldest son Christian, who was elected his successor, but died before him.

[13] In the margin the following addition is inserted: 'She had at that time an unusual memory. She could at one and the same time recite one psalm by heart, write another, and attend to the conversation. She had tried this more than once, but I think that she has thereby spoilt her memory, which is not now so good.'

[14] Namely, Magdalena Sybilla of Saxony, then newly married (October 5, 1634) to Prince Christian, the eldest son and elected successor of Christian IV. M. Sophia's wedding to Chr. Pentz was celebrated on the 10th of the same month.

[15] V.R. probably stands for Viceroy, by which term Leonora no doubt indicates the post of Governor of Copenhagen.

[16] The old friend is Dr. Otto Sperling, sen., a physician in extensive practice at Copenhagen, and intimate friend of Ulfeldt. Mr. Biel… signifies most probably a certain Christian Bielke, whose portrait still exists at Rosenborg Castle, in Copenhagen, with an inscription that he was killed in a duel by Bartram Rantzau on Easter eve 1642. If this date is true, Bielke cannot have accompanied Leonora's brother Count Valdemar on his journey to Russia, as this journey only took place in 1643. Count Valdemar was to marry a Russian princess, but it was broken off on his refusing to join the Greek

church.

[17] Dr. Otto Sperling, senior.

[18] Prince Ruprecht, Duke of Cumberland, nephew of Charles I.

[19] Namely, the process against Dina. *See* Introduction.

[20] Ulfeldt had not really the permission of the King to leave the country in the way he did. These words must therefore be understood to mean that the favourable termination of the trial concerning Dina's accusations had liberated Ulfeldt from the special obligation to remain in Copenhagen, which his position in reference to that case imposed upon him.

[21] That is, Ebbe Ulfeldt,—a relative of Corfitz who left Denmark in 1651 and afterwards lived in Sweden.

[22] This date is erroneous; the journey took place in November and December 1656.

[23] U.C. Gyldenlöve, illegitimate son of Christian IV. and half-brother of Leonora.

[24] Probably Povl Tscherning, a well-known man of the time, who held the office of Auditor-General.

[25] In order to understand how she could wait for ten days at Apenrade, it must be borne in mind that the duchy of Slesvig was at that time divided into several parts, of which some belonged to the King, others to the Duke of Gottorp. Haderslev and Flensborg belonged to the King, but Apenrade to the Duke; in this town, therefore, she was safe from the pursuit of the Danish authorities.

[26] The governor of Flensborg at that time was Detlef v. Ahlefeld, the same who in 1663 was sent to Königsberg to receive information from the court of Brandenburg on the last intrigues of Ulfeldt.

[27] The clerk Holst was shortly after, when the Swedes occupied Flensborg, put to a heavy ransom by Ulfeldt, in punishment of his conduct to Leonora. Documents which still exist show that he applied to the Danish Government for compensation, but apparently in vain.

[28] Count Jakob Casimir de la Gardie, a Swedish nobleman. Count Wrangel was the Swedish General.

[29] The funeral took place with great pomp in the church of St. Knud, at Odense, on June 23, 1658, together with that of Sophia Elizabeth, Leonora's sister, who is mentioned in the beginning of the Autobiography.

[30] The young lady was Birgitte Rantzau, who was engaged to Korfits Trolle, a Danish nobleman, who had been very active in preparing the intended rising of the citizens of Malmöe against the Swedes. Ulfeldt was accused of having favoured and assisted this design (*see* the Introduction), and he had brought Trolle's bride over to Copenhagen, or accompanied them thither.

[31] Wolf and Kield were servants of Ulfeldt.

[32] The person alluded to is a Bartholomæus Mikkelsen, who was executed as ringleader of the conspiracy.

[33] Bornholm. (*See* the Introduction.)

[34] She refers no doubt to a servant who accompanied them of the name of Pflügge.

[35] The original of this letter to the King exists still.

[36] It will be remembered from the Introduction that Fuchs was killed two years after by one of Leonora's sons at Bruges.

[37] This account of what happened during their imprisonment at Hammershuus, written by Leonora herself, is also mentioned in her Record of her prison-life in the Blue Tower. But no copy of it has yet come to light. Uhlfeldt's so-called apology contains much information on this subject.

[38] Fuchs' own report on this subject still exists, and in it he estimates the iron employed at three tons.

[39] The precise date was June 15, 1661, but the order for their separation is dated already on the 4th of April.

[40] Leonora alludes to the wife of the then Duke of York, afterwards James II., who was the daughter of Lord Edward Clarendon.

[41] The apology of Uhlfeldt contains an account of this whole transaction. He states that when he asked his wife through the window whether they ought to sign and live rather than die in prison, which would otherwise be their lot, Leonora answered with the following Latin verse:

> Rebus in adversis facile est contemnere mortem,
> Fortius ille facit, qui miser esse potest.
> Accidit in puncto, quod non speratur in anno.

[42] Ellensborg was the ancient seat of the Ulfeldt family, which had been sold to Ellen Marsvin, Leonora's grandmother, and Leonora inherited it from her mother. It is now called Holckenhavn, and the seat of Count Holck.

[43] Namely Casetta, a Spanish nobleman, who afterwards married their daughter Anna Katherine, but both he and their children died soon. (*See* the Introduction.)

[44] Charles the Second's Grandmother, Anna, the Queen of James I. was sister of Leonora Christina's father, Christian IV.

[45] Sir Henry Bennet, afterwards Lord Arlington.

[46] A certain Mr. Mowbray.

[47] Elsewhere she writes the name Broughton.

[48] Sir George Askew.

[49] Compare with this account the following extracts in the *Calendar of State Papers*, domestic series, 1663, 1664, pp. 196, 197, 200:—

1663—*July 8.*—Warrant to Captain Strode, governor of Dover Castle, to detain Elionora Christiana, Countess of Uhlfeldt, with her husband, if he be found with her, and their servants; to keep her close prisoner, and secure all her papers, according to instructions to be given by Thos. Parnell.

July 8.—Warrant to Thos. Parnell to observe the movements of the said Countess of Uhlfeldt; to seize her should she attempt to embark at Gravesend with her papers, and to detain her close prisoner.

(*July*).—Instructions (by Sec. Bennet) to Thos. Parnell, to go to Dover Castle to deliver instructions, and assist in their execution, relative to a certain lady (the Countess of Uhlfeldt), who is not to be permitted to depart, whether she have a pass or not; but to be invited, or if needful compelled, to lodge at the castle, where the best accommodation is to be provided for her. It is suspected that her husband lies concealed in the kingdom, and will also try to pass with his lady, but he also is to be detained, and her servants also.

July 11.—Thos. Parnell to Williamson. 'Found the Countess (of Uhlfeldt) at Dover, and by the aid of the Lieut.-Governor sent the searcher to her inn, to demand her pass. She said she had none, not knowing it would be wanted. She submitted patiently to be taken to the castle, and lodged there till a message was sent to town. The Regent's gentleman, the bearer will give an account of all things.'

[50] Several letters written by Leonora during her imprisonment at Dover to Charles II., Sir Henry Bennet, &c., are printed in a Danish periodical, *Danske Samlinger*, vol. vi.

[51] Reckoning the patacoon to 4s. 8d., this claim would be nearly 5,000*l*.

[52] Leonora did not know that the governor of the castle was in the plot.

[53] Additional light is thrown on the arrest of Leonora Christina at Dover by the following extracts in the *Calendar of State Papers*, p. 224, 225:—

August 1, Whitehall.—(Sec. Bennet) to Capt. Strode. The King is satisfied with his account of the lady's escape and his own behaviour; continue the same mask, of publishing His Majesty's displeasure against all who contributed to it, especially his lieutenant, and this more particularly in presence of M. Cassett, lest he may suspect connivance. Cassett is to continue prisoner some time. The Danish Resident is satisfied with the discretion used, but says his point would not have been secured had the lady gone to sea without interruption.

August 1?—Account (proposed to be sent to the Gazette?) relative to Count Uhlfeldt—recording his submission in 1661, the present sentence against him, his further relapse into crime after a solemn recantation, also signed by his wife who was his accomplice, though her blood saved her from sharing his sentence, but who has now betrayed herself into the hands of the King of Denmark. She was in England when the conspiracy against the King of Denmark's life was detected. The King of England had her movements watched, when she suddenly went off without a pass, for want of which she was stayed by the Governor of Dover Castle, who accommodated her in the castle. The Resident of Denmark posted to Dover, and secured the master of a ship then in the road, with whom he expected her to tamper, which she did, escaped through the castle window, and entering a shallop to go on board, was seized and conveyed to Denmark. With note (by Lord Chancellor Clarendon) that he is not satisfied with this account, but will prepare a better for another week.

[54] In the margin is added: 'As I now hope that what I write may come into your hands, my captivity during the last three years also having been much lightened.'

[55] A pen has afterwards been drawn through this paragraph, but the observations occur in the manuscript.

[56] The conclusion of the Preface, from the words 'Meanwhile let the will of God,' etc. has afterwards been erased, when the manuscript was continued beyond the date assigned in the Preface; and the following paragraphs, 'I bear also in mind,' etc. were intended to form a new conclusion, but do not seem to have been properly worked in.

[57] Afterwards altered to anno 1685, the 19th of May.

[58] In the margin is added: 'I had a ring on with a table-diamond worth 200 rix-dollars. I bit this out, threw the gold in the sea, and kept the stone in my mouth. It could not be observed by my speech that there was anything in my mouth.'

[59] That is the Aulefeldt mentioned in the Preface under the name of Anfeldt.

[60] In the margin is added: 'The sorrow manifested by many would far rather have depressed me; for several people, both men and women, shed tears, even those whom I did not know.'

[61] This paragraph was afterwards struck out, the contents being transferred to the Preface.

[62] This passage was afterwards altered thus: 'God blinded their eyes so that they did not perceive my earrings, in each of which there is a large rose diamond, and from which I have now removed the stones. The gold, which is in form of a serpent, is still in my ears. They also did not perceive that something was fastened round my knee.'

[63] That is, give information.

[64] In the margin the following explanatory note is added: 'When his Majesty (Christian IV.) was dead, there was no prince elected, so that the States were free to choose the king whom they desired, wherefore the Duke of Holstein, Duke Frederick, promised my deceased lord that if he would contrive that he should be elected king, the land of Fyen should belong to him and a double alliance between his children and ours should be concluded. But my lord rejected this proposal and would not assist in dispossessing the son of Christian IV. of the kingdom. The prince had obtained several votes, but my lord contested them.'

[65] It had happened as I thought. There were some in the council who refused to sign, some because they had not been present at the time of the procedure, and others because they had not seen on what the sentence was founded; but they were nevertheless compelled to sign with the others, on the peril of the king's displeasure. [Marginal note.]

[66] In the margin is added, 'and asked whether I was permitted to appeal against this sentence. All were silent.'

[67] In the margin: 'The feather-bed had an old cover, and was fresh filled when I was lying in the roads; the needle, in the hurry, had therefore been left in.'

[68] In the margin: 'I myself heard this conversation.'

[69] When I took my meals, the woman had opportunity of talking with the three men. The coachman helped the tower-warder Rasmus to bring up the food. [Marginal note.]

[70] I could not see when she spoke with any one, for she did so on the stairs. [Marginal note.]

[71] In the margin is added: 'There was none.'

[72] Did not this accord well with the statement that my lord had offered the kingdom of Denmark to two potentates? [Marginal note.]

[73] In the margin is noted: 'I had never seen La Rosche nor his companion till I did so at Dover.'

[74] In the margin is added: 'The prison governor told the woman about the magnificence of the festivity and Peder also told her of it, so that it seemed to her that I could know somewhat from customs of former times.'

[75] The Queen wished that this wooden statue should be brought into my outer chamber, and so placed in front of the door that it would tumble into me when my inner door was opened; but the King would not permit it. [Addition in the margin.]

[76] In the margin is this note: 'Once when I asked the prison governor for some scissors to cut my nails, he answered, and that loudly, "What! what! her nails shall grow like eagles' claws, and her hair like eagles' feathers!" I know well what I thought—if I had only claws and wings!'

[77] I removed my nails with the needle, scratching them till they came away. I let the nail of the little finger of my right hand grow, in order to see how long it would become; but I knocked it off unawares, and I still have it. [Marginal note.]

[78] The prison cell is outside that in which the doctor is immured. It is quite dark where he is. [Note in the margin.]

[79] In the margin is added: 'When the prison governor was singing to himself on those first days, he said, "You must sing, my bird; where is your velvet robe?" laughing at the same time most heartily. I inferred from that song who it was.'

[80] In the margin is added: 'In order to grieve the Doctor and to frighten him, the prison governor unlocked his cell early on the morning after sentence had been passed, and behaved as if the priest were coming to him.'

[81] That is, give information.

[82] In the margin is added: 'Peder had some time before thrown into me eight ducats in a paper, saying, as he closed the door, "Your maid!" And as the woman knew it, I gave her one of them and Peder one. I know not whether my maid had given him more; she had many more concealed on her person.'

[83] In the margin is added: 'As my linen was washed in the servants' hall, it once happened that a maid there must unawares have forgotten a whole skein of thread in a clean chemise, at which I said to the woman: "You see how the ravens bring me thread!" She was angry and abused me; I laughed, and answered her jestingly.'

[84] In the margin is added: 'I wrote different things from the Bible on the paper in which the sugar was given me. My ink-bottle was made of the piece of pewter lid which the woman had found, the ink was made from the smoke of the candle collected on a spoon, and the pen from a fowl's feather cut by the piece of glass. I have this still in my possession.'

[85] In the margin is added: 'The prison governor told me afterwards that the clay things were placed in the King's art-cabinet, besides a rib of mutton, which I used as a knife, which he also gave to the King; hoping (he said) in this way to obtain a knife for me.'

[86] In the margin is added: 'The day that the prison governor had taken away the clay things the woman was very angry with me, because I gave him a small jug which I had made; she said it was made in ridicule of her, the old slut with the jug! I ought to have given him the cat which I had also made. I said, "I can still do so."'

[87] In the margin is added: 'At first when the prison governor's fear was so great, he did not venture to be alone in the outer room. Peder and the tower warder were not allowed both to leave him at the same time. I did not know the reason for this.'

[88] In the margin is added: 'Some time after this dispute I had a quarrel with her about some beer, which she was in the habit of emptying on the floor, saying, "This shall go to the subterraneous folk." I had forbidden her to do so, but she did it again, so I took her by the head and pushed it back with my

hand. She was frightened, for this feels just as if one's head was falling off. I said, "That is a foretaste."'

[89] In the margin is added: 'I made the snuffers serve as scissors. When Balcke came to me and brought me at my desire material for drawers, and requested to know the size, I said I could make them myself. He laughed, and said, "Who will cut them out?" I replied I could do it myself with the snuffers. He begged to see me do it, and looked on with no little astonishment.'

[90] In the margin is added: 'While Balcke filled the place of prison governor, he drank my wine at every meal, which had formerly fallen to the tower warder, the coachman, or the prisoner Christian, when the old prison governor had not wished for it, so that this also contributed to Balcke's dismissal.'

[91] In the margin: 'It is indeed a bad flight of stairs to the place where the basin was emptied.'

[92] In the margin is added: 'Gabel had said (I was afterwards informed) that I was frightened at the appearance of the man, and thought it was the executioner. I did not regard him as such, but as a poor cavalier, and I imagined he was to undertake the duties which Peder the coachman performed.'

[93] In the margin: 'Balcke has waited upon me for twenty weeks, and he was accused of having told me what happened outside. In proof of this it was alleged that he had told me that Gabel had been made Statholder, to whom I afterwards gave this title in M. Buck's hearing. Balcke one day could not restrain himself from laughing, for while he was standing and talking with me, the woman and the man were standing on the stairs outside, chuckling and laughing; and he said, "Outside there is the chatter market. Why does not Peder so arrange it that it is forbidden? You can get to know all that goes on in the world without me."'

[94] In the margin is added: 'While Balcke waited on me, a folding table was brought in for the bread and glasses, and also for the woman's food, which she did not take till the doors had been locked. There was nothing there before but the night-stool to place the dishes on: that was the woman's table.'

[95] In the margin is added: 'At that time there was a large double window with iron grating, which was walled up when I was brought here; and Christian told me afterwards how the maids in the store-room had supplied him with many a can of beer, which he had drawn up by a cord.'

[96] In the margin is this note: 'Christian had at that time given me some pieces of flint which are so sharp that I can cut fine linen with them by the thread. The pieces are still in my possession, and with this implement I executed various things.'

[97] In the margin is added: 'Such is his character.'

[98] In the margin is added: 'These rope-dancers did things that I had never seen before. One had a basket attached to each leg, and in each basket was a boy of five years of age, and a woman fell upon the rope and jumped up again. But during the time of the other woman, I saw a man suspended by his chin and springing back upon the rope.'

[99] In the margin is added: 'This was the priest who attended to the prisoners, and as he confessed her in the anteroom, I heard every word said by him, but not her replies.'

[100] In the margin is added: 'Her child.'

[101] In the margin is added: 'She was in every respect a malicious woman, and grudged a little meat to any prisoner. A poor sacristan was my neighbour in the Dark Church, and I gave her a piece of meat for him. She would not take it to him, which she could easily have done without anyone seeing. When I saw the meat afterwards, I found fault with her. Then she said, "Why should I give it to him? He has never given me anything. I get nothing for it." I said, "You give nothing of your own away." This sacristan was imprisoned because he had taken back his own horse, the man to whom he had sold it not having paid him. He sang all day long, and on Sunday he went through the service like a clergyman, with the responses, &c.'

[102] In the margin is added: 'She had begged Chresten, for more than half a year before she left, to tell the prison-governor that her life hung on a thread; that I had a ball of clay in my handkerchief, and that I had threatened to break her head to pieces with it (I had said one day that a person with a ball of that kind could kill another). She invented several similar lies, as I subsequently heard.'

[103] In the margin is added: 'The pins I had obtained some time ago from the first woman. She had procured them with some needles, and, thinking to hide them from me, she carried them in her bosom in

a paper and forgot them. In the evening when she dropped her petticoat to go to bed, the paper fell on the floor. I knew from the sound what it was. One Saturday, when she went upstairs with the night-stool, I took the pins out of her box, and she never ventured to ask for them; she saw me using them afterwards, and said nothing about them.'

[104] In the margin is noted: 'I said one day to the woman, "Were it not for the Queen, who would make the King angry with me, I would retaliate upon the prison governor for having decoyed Doctor Sperling. I would take the keys when he was sleeping, and wait for Chresten to come with the cups, and then I would go up the King's stairs and take the keys to the King, just as the lacquey did with the old prison-governor. But I should gain nothing from this King, and perhaps should be still more strictly confined."'

[105] In the margin is noted: 'At first, when this Karen did not know the prison governor, she did not venture so boldly to the prisoners in the Dark Church to give them anything, for she said, "The prison governor stares at me so." I said, "It is with him as with little children; they look staring at a thing, and do not know what it is." It is the case with him, he does not trouble himself about anything.'

[106] In the margin is added: 'The hinges of my outer door are so far from the wall that they are open more than a hand's breadth, so that I have got in large things between them; and above they are still more open, and when I put my arm through the peep-hole of the inner door and stretch it out, I can reach to the top of the outer one, though the woman cannot.'

[107] In the margin: 'She has a curious manner of spelling. She cannot spell a word of three syllables; for when she has to add the two syllables to the third, she has forgotten the first. If I urge her, however, she can read the word correctly when she has spelt the first syllable. She spells words of two syllables and reads those of four.'

[108] In the margin: 'Once she asked me whether she could not get a book in which there was neither q nor x, for she could not remember these letters. I answered, "Yes, if you will yourself have such a book printed."'

[109] In the margin of the MS. is added: 'When this Karen came to me she left me no peace till I allowed her to clean the floor; for I feared that which happened, namely that the smell would cause sickness. In one place there was an accumulation of dirt a couple of feet thick. When she had loosened it, it had to remain till the door was opened. I went to bed, threw the bed-clothes over my head, and held my nose.'[E38]

[110] In the margin is added: 'On the stick there was a tin candlestick, which was occasionally placed at the side of my bed. I used it for fixing my knitting.'[E39]

[111] In the margin: 'The girl was a prostitute to whom he had promised marriage, and the tower-warder —both the former one and Chresten—let her in to Christian, went out himself, and left them alone.'

[112] In the margin: 'In the time of his good humour he had procured me, for money and candles, all that I desired, so that I had both knife and scissors, besides silk, thread, and various things to beguile the time. This vexed him afterwards.'

[113] In the margin: 'Immediately after the girl had been in Skaane, he gave her a box full of pieces of wax, on which were the impressions of all the tower keys; and amongst them was written, "My girl will have these made in Skaane." I had this from the woman, who was just then carrying up the night-stool, and on the following Saturday I gave the box back with many thanks, saying I did not care to escape from the tower in this way. This did not please him, as I well saw.'

[114] In the margin is added: 'At this time there was a peasant imprisoned in the Dark Church for having answered the bailiff of the manor with bad language. I sent him food. He was a great rogue. I know not whether he were incited by others, but he told Karen that if I would write to my children, he would take care of the letter. I sent him word that I thanked him; I had nothing to say to them and nothing to write with. The rogue answered, "Ah so! Ah so!"'

[115] In the margin: 'It was wonderful that the governor did not hear the noise which Christian made. He was telling me, I remember, at the time, how he had frightened one of the court servants with a mouse in a box.'

[116] In the margin is added: 'He enticed the prison governor to throw a kitten that I had down from the top of the tower, and he laughed at me ironically as he told the woman of his manly act, and said, "The

cat was mangy! the cat was mangy!" I would not let him see that it annoyed me.'

[117] In the margin is added: '1666. While Karen, Nils' daughter, waited on me, a Nuremberger was my neighbour in the Dark Church; he was accused of having coined base money. She carried food to him every day. He sang and read day and night, and sang very well. He sang the psalm 'Incline thine ear unto me, O Lord,' slowly at my desire. I copied it, and afterwards translated it into Danish. And as he often prayed aloud at night and confessed his sins, praying God for forgiveness and exclaiming again and again, 'Thou must help me, God! Yes, God, thou must help me, or thou art no God. Thou must be gracious;' thus hindering me from sleep, I sent him word through Karen to pray more softly, which he did. He was taken to the Holm for some weeks, and was then set at liberty.

[118] In the MS. this date '1667' is in the *margin*, not in the text.

[119] In the margin is added: 'This very hymn was afterwards the cause of Christian's being again well-behaved, as he subsequently himself told me, for he heard me one day singing it, and he said that his heart was touched, and that tears filled his eyes. I had at that time no other writing-materials than I have before mentioned.'

[120] What he meant by it I know not; perhaps he meant that I should die in misery, and that he should live in freedom. That anticipation has been just reversed, for his godless life in his liberty threw him subsequently into despair, so that he shot himself. Whether God will give me freedom in this world is known to Him alone.

[121] In the margin is added: 'He could not prevent his boy Paaske from having a piece of meat placed for him in front of the door.'

[122] In the margin is added: 'The bride had supplicated for me at Nykjöbing, but had not gained her object. This was thought to be dangerous both for the land and people.'

[123] In the margin is added: 'It was a Sunday; this was the honour he showed to God. He went into the wine-house instead of into God's house. He came out about twelve o'clock.'

[124] In the margin is added: 'A few months after she had come to me, she had an attack of ague. She wept, and was afraid. I was well satisfied with her, and thought I would see what faith could do, so I wrote something on a slip of paper and hung it round her neck. The fever left her, and she protested that all her bodily pains passed all at once into her legs when I hung the paper round her neck. Her legs immediately became much swollen.'

[125] In the margin is added: 'When the priest left me, he spoke with Walter in front of the grated hole, told him of my desire, and its probable result. Walter laughed ironically, and said, "My hair will not stand on end for fear of that matter being mooted again. The Queen knows that full well. Say that too!" While Walter was in the Witch Cell hole, he had written to the Queen, but the King received the paper.'

[126] In the margin is noted: 'I looked through a hole in my outermost door at the time that Walter was brought up in the Dark Church. He wept aloud. I afterwards saw him once in front of the hole of the door of his cell. He was very dirty, and had a large beard full of dirt, very clotted.'

[127] In the margin is added: 'From books which had been secretly lent me, and I did so with the pen and ink I have before mentioned, on any pieces of paper which I happened to procure.'

[128] In the margin is noted: 'Chresten was not well satisfied with the woman, for in her time he never received a draught of wine, so that he once stole the wine from her can and substituted something impure in its place; at this she made a great noise, begged me for God's sake to give her leave to strike Chresten with the can. She did not gain permission to do so; she told Chresten afterwards that she had not dared to do it, for my sake. She had a great scar on one cheek, which a soldier had once given her for a similar act.'

[129] In the margin is added: 'At this time I had six prisoners for my neighbours. Three were peasants from Femeren, who were accused of having exported some sheep; the other three were Danish. They were divided in two parties, and as the Danes were next the door, I gave them some food; they had moreover been imprisoned some time before the others. When the Danes, according to their custom, sang the morning and evening psalms, the Germans growled forth with all their might another song in order to drown their voices; they generally sang the song of Dorothea.' [E48]

[130] In the margin is added: 'As I was to receive clothes, I asked for mourning clothes. Then the prison governor asked me for whom I wished to mourn, and this in a most ironical manner. I answered: "It is not for your aunt; it is not for me to mourn for her, although your aunt has been dead long. I think you have as good reason for wearing mourning as I." He said he would report it. I did not receive them at once.'

[131] In the margin is added: 'Chresten showed me once some bread, from which Walter had taken the crumb, and had filled it full of straw and dirt, in fact, of the very worst kind.'

[132] In the margin is added; 'The prison governor also severely reprimanded the woman because she had told me that the King was dead; that it would not go as well with me as I thought. She gave him word for word.'

[133] In the margin is added: 'Among his terrible curses was one that his tongue might be paralysed if he had not spoken for me. The following year God struck him with paralysis of the tongue; he had a stroke from anger, and lived eight days afterwards; he was in his senses, but he was not able to speak, and he died; but he lived to see the day when another clergyman administered the holy communion to me.'

[134] In the margin is added: 'I saw now that this was the cause of Balcke's dismissal.'

[135] In the margin is added: 'Chresten, who was ill satisfied both with Karen and with me, gave us a different title one day, when he was saying something to one of the house-servants, upon which the latter asked him who had said it? Chresten answered, 'She who is kept up there for her.' When I was told of this, I laughed and said, 'That is quite right, we are two "shes."'

[136] In the margin is noted: 'Some of my money I expended on books, and it is remarkable that I obtained from M. Buck's books (which were sold by auction) among others the great Martilegium, in folio, which he would not lend me. I excerpted and translated various matters from Spanish, Italian, French, and German authors. I especially wrote out and translated into Danish the female personages of different rank and origin, who were mentioned with praise by the authors as valiant, true, chaste and sensible, patient, steadfast and scholarly.' [E52]

[137] In the margin is added: 'This dog was of an Icelandic breed, not pretty, but very faithful and sagacious. He slept every afternoon on the stool, and when she had fallen asleep, she let her hands hang down. Then the dog would get up and run softly and bite her finger till the blood came. If she threw down her slippers, he would take one and sit upon it. She never got it back again without a bloody finger.'

[138] In the margin is this note: 'In the year 1672, on the 4th May, one of the house-servants was arrested for stealing. Adam Knudt, at that time gentleman of the chamber, himself saw him take several ducats early one morning from the King's trousers, which were hanging against the walls. He was at first for some hours my neighbour in the Dark Church. He was then placed in the Witch Cell, and as he was to be tortured, he received secret warning of it (which was forbidden), so that when the executioner came he was found to have hung himself. That is to say, he was said to have hung himself, though to all appearance this was not possible; he was found with a cloth round his neck, which was a swaddling-cloth belonging to one of Chresten, the tower-warder's, children. Chresten became my neighbour, and was ostensibly brought to justice, but he was acquitted and reinstated in his office.

[139] In the margin is added: 'She was so proud of her knowledge of German that when she sang a morning hymn (which, however rarely happened) she interspersed it with German words. I once asked her if she knew what her mother's cat was called in Danish, and I said something at which she was angry.

[140] In the margin is added: 'There was no similar row on the other stocking. The prison governor never mentioned it.'

[141] In the margin is noted: 'I must remember one thing about Karen, Nils' daughter. When anything gave her satisfaction, she would take up her book directly and read. I asked her whether she understood what she read. "Yes, of course," she answered, "as truly as God will bless you! When a word comes that I don't understand, I pass it over." I smiled a little in my own mind, but said nothing.'

[142] In the margin is noted: 'At my desire the prison governor gave me a rat whose tail he had cut off;

this I placed in a parrot's cage, and gave it food, so that it grew very tame. The woman grudged me this amusement; and as the cage hung in the outer apartment, and had a wire grating underneath, so that the dirt might fall out, she burned the rat with a candle from below. It was easy to perceive it, but she denied it.'

[143] In the margin stood originally the following note, which has afterwards been struck out: 'In this year, 1676, the prison governor married for the third time; he married a woman who herself had had two husbands. Anno 1677, Aug. 9, died my sister Elisabeth Augusta.'

[144] On a piece of paper which is fastened to the MS. by a pin is the following note referring to the same matter: 'On March 4, in the same year 1678, a woman named Lucia, who had been in the service of Lady Rigitze Grubbe, became my neighbour. She was accused by Agneta Sophia Budde, as the person who at the instigation of her mistress had persuaded her to poison Countess F. Birrete Skeel, and that Lucia had brought her the poison. There was evidence as to the person from whom Lucia had bought the poison. This woman was a steady faithful servant. She received everything that was imposed upon her with the greatest patience, and held out courageously in the Dark Cell. She had two men as companions, both of whom cried, moaned and wept. From the Countess Skeel (who had to supply her with food) meat was sent her which was full of maggots and mouldy bread. I took pity on her (not for the sake of her mistress, for she had rendered me little good service, and had rewarded me evil for the benefits of former times, but out of sympathy). And I sent her meat and drink and money that she might soften Gert, who was too hard to her. She was tortured, but would not confess any thing of what she was accused, and always defended her mistress. She remained a long time in prison.[E58]

[145] In the margin is added: 'Ole the tower-warder was cudgelled on his back by the prison governor when Margrete was gone, and he was charged with having said what Margrete had informed him respecting her size.'

[146] In the margin is added: 'Other natural matter was evacuated, but the stone stuck fast in the duct, and seemed to be round, for I could not gain hold of it with an instrument I had procured for the purpose.'

[147] In the margin is added: 'The prison governor told me afterwards that the King laughed when he had told his Majesty my answer about the clavicordium, and had said, "Yes, yes."'

[148] In the margin is added: 'The woman who attended on me received eight rix-dollars monthly.'

[149] In the margin: 'She had him learn wood-carving.'

ENDNOTES

[E1] This journey really took place in November and December, 1656.

[E2] This man was a German by birth, but settled in Denmark, where he was nobilitated under the name of Lövenklau. His bad conduct obliged him to leave the country, and he went to Sweden, where he had lived before he came to Denmark, and where Ulfeldt, then in Sweden, procured him an appointment as a colonel in the army. This kindness he repaid by informing the Danish Government against Ulfeldt in 1654, in consequence of which he was not only allowed to return to Denmark, but even obtained a lucrative office in Norway. Here he quarrelled with the viceroy, Niels Trolle, and tried to serve him as he had served Ulfeldt; but he failed to establish his accusations against Trolle, and was condemned into the forfeiture of his office and of his patent of nobility. He then left Denmark at least for a season, and how he came to apply to Leonora Christina for assistance is not known, as she has omitted to mention it in the Memoir itself, though she evidently intended to do so.

[E3] This Count Rantzow was the same who had negotiated the compromise with Ulfeldt and Leonora at Bornholm in 1661, and in fact brought it about. It was currently reported in Copenhagen at the time that he had received a large sum of money from Ulfeldt on that occasion, and he afterwards showed his friendly disposition towards him by promising him to intercede with the King for Christian Ulfeldt when the latter had killed Fuchs. Leonora, however, speaks of him as an enemy probably because he presided in the High Court of Appeal which condemned Ulfeldt as a traitor. But the facts of the case left him scarcely any other alternative than that of judging as he did, nor would it have been surprising if Ulfeldt's last conduct had altered Rantzow's feelings towards him. Rantzow also presided in the commission which examined Leonora in the Blue Tower.

[E4] Abel Catharina is mentioned in the Memoir itself as the person who searched Leonora when she first entered her prison, and did so in a very unbecoming manner; she acted, however, under the orders of the Mistress of the Robes, M. v. Haxthausen. Abel Catharina is otherwise chiefly known as the founder of a charity for old women in Copenhagen, which still bears her name.

[E5] This name is mis-spelt for Ahlefeldt. This officer received Leonora on her arrival at Copenhagen, as she relates herself. He had distinguished himself in the siege of Copenhagen in 1659, and died as a Lieutenant-General.

[E6] Christoffer Gabel is mentioned several times in the Autobiography. He was an influential man at the time, in great favour at court, and he had a great part in effecting the release of Ulfeldt from the prison at Bornholm, for which he, according to Leonora's statement, received 5,000 dollars from Ulfeldt. Both he and Reedtz were members of the court which condemned Ulfeldt.

[E7] The passage alluded to occurs in Epictet's Encheiridion, chap. 43 (in some editions chap. 65), where he says: 'Every matter has two handles, one by which it may be carried (or endured), the other by which it cannot be carried (or endured). If thy brother has done thee injury, do not lay hold of this matter from the fact that he has done thee an injury, for this is the handle by which it cannot be carried (or endured); but rather from this side: that he is thy brother, educated with thee; and thou wilt lay hold of the matter from that side from which it may be managed.' It is easily seen how Leonora makes use of the double meaning of the Greek word [Greek: phorêtos], which is equally well used of an object which can be carried in the literal physical sense, and of a matter which can be endured or borne with.

[E8] Birgitte Speckhans was the wife of Frants v. Speckhans, master of ceremonies, afterwards Privy Councillor, &c. She had formerly been in the service of Leonora Christina, who was then at the height of her position, and ever afterwards proved herself a friend of her and Ulfeldt. It was in her house that they stayed after escaping from Malmöe, and she kept some of their movable goods for them during their imprisonment at Hammershuus.

[E9] Birgitte Ulfeldt was a younger sister of Corfitz, who, in a letter to Sperling, declares her to be his and Leonora's bitterest enemy. What is known of her life is certainly not to her advantage.

[E10] This is the famous Jos. Borro or Burrhus, physician and alchymist. He is often mentioned in books of the seventeenth century, on account of his wonderful cures and alleged knowledge of the art of making gold. In 1667 he came to Denmark, where King Fredrik III. spent considerable sums on the establishment of large laboratories for him, in a building which is still known as 'The Gold-house.'

[E11] D'Aranda was one of the most influential families in Bruges. One of them, by name Bernard, was some time in the Danish army, afterwards secretary to Corfitz Ulfeldt, and employed by him in diplomatic missions. He died in 1658, but when Ulfeldt came to Bruges in 1662 he lived for some time with one of Bernard's brothers.

[E12]
[E12b] H. Bielke was Admiral of the realm; his wife was an Ulfeldt, and it was he who procured Corfitz Ulfeldt his leave of absence in 1662, of which he made such regretable use. He, too, was one of the judges that convicted him. Oluf Brokkenhuus was Corfitz Ulfeldt's brother-in-law; Elizabeth Parsbjerg was the widow of his elder brother Lauridts Ulfeldt. Marie Ulfeldt was sister of Corfitz.

[E13] Charles de Goutant, Duc de Biron, a celebrated French General, some time favourite of Henry IV. King of France, was found guilty of conspiring against his master with the courts of Spain and Savoy. Henry IV. forgave him, but he recommenced his intrigues. It is supposed that the King would have forgiven him a second time if he had confessed his crime; but he refused to do so, and was beheaded in 1602.

[E14] This lady is known under the name of Haxthausen; and Schaffshausen is probably a mistake on Leonora's part, although of course she may have been married to an officer of this name before she married N. v. Haxthausen. She was a German by birth.

[E15] Elizabeth Augusta, a younger sister of Leonora, married Hans Lindenow, a Danish nobleman, who died in the siege of Copenhagen, 1659.

[E16] That Leonora here speaks of her husband as her 'late lord,' is due only to the fact that the Memoir was not written till after his death; at the time of these events he was still alive.

[E17] When the sentence on Ulfeldt had become publicly known, the most absurd rumours circulated in Copenhagen, and found their way to foreign newspapers. For instance *the kingdom's* Intelligencer, No. 33, Aug. 10-17, 1663, says, in a correspondence from Hamburg: 'They say the traitors intended to set Copenhagen on fire in divers places, and also the fleet, to destroy the King and family, to blow up the King's palace, and deliver the crown over to another.' The Government itself, on hearing of Ulfeldt's plots, made great military preparations.

[E18] The sentence on Ulfeldt was given on July 24, but probably not published till a few days later.

[E19] A line has been drawn in the MS. through the two last paragraphs, and their contents transferred to the continuation of the Preface.

[E20] Leonora refers to the betrothal of Prince Johan George of Saxony and Anna Sophia, the eldest daughter of Fredrik III., of which an account occurs in the sequel.

[E21] A copy of the fragments which had been recovered of this letter is still in existence.

[E22] Ulfeldt received this present probably in 1647, when in France as ambassador, on which occasion Queen Anna is known to have presented to Leonora a gold watch set with diamonds of great value.

[E23] The lady alluded to is Helvig Margaretha Elizabeth Rantzow, widow of the famous General Josias Rantzow, who died as a maréchal of France. She had become a Romanist, and took the veil after her husband's death. Subsequently she founded the new order of the Annunciata. In 1666 the first convent of this order, of which she was abbess, removed to Hildesheim, where she died in 1706.

[E24] Margrete Rantzow was the sister of that Birgitte Rantzow to whom there is an allusion in the Autobiography of Leonora, where she relates the examination to which she was subjected at Malmöe. Margrete's husband was Ove Thott, a nobleman in Skaane, who had taken an important part in the preparations for a rising against the Swedes, in which Corfitz Ulfeldt was implicated.

[E25] The book in question is probably Philip Sidney's work, 'The Countess of Pembroke's Arcadia,' a famous book of its time, which Leonora, who does not seem to have known it, has understood to be a book by the Countess of Pembroke. It is true, however, that Philip's sister, Mary Sidney, Countess of

Pembroke, had translated a French play, Antonius (1592, and again 1595).

[E26] La Roche Tudesquin had some time been in the Danish army, but had returned to France when Hannibal Sehested, while in Paris as Ambassador from the King of Denmark, received information from a certain Demoiselle Langlois that La Roche was implicated in a conspiracy for surrendering the principal Danish fortresses to a foreign prince. He and a friend of his, Jaques Beranger, were arrested in Brussels in September 1663, but not, as Leonora says, immediately brought to Copenhagen. The Spanish Government did not consent to their extradition till the following year, and they were not placed in the Blue Tower till June 1664. La Roche seems to have been guilty of peculation while in the Danish service, but the accusation of treason seems to have been unfounded.

[E27] In the MS. a pen is drawn through this paragraph, of which the contents were to form part of the Preface. The date of Count Rantzow is moreover not correctly given; he died on November 8, five days before the execution of Ulfeldt's effigy.

[E28] The execution took place on November 13. The King's order concerning it to the prison governor, Jochum Waltpurger, exists still. It is to this effect: 'V. G. T., Know that you have to command the executioner in our name, that to-day, November 13, he is to take the effigy of Corfitz, formerly called Count of Ulfeldt, from the Blue Tower where it is now, and bring it on a car to the ordinary place in the square in front of the castle; and when he has come to the place of justice, strike off the right hand and the head, whereafter he is to divide the body into four parts on the spot, and carry them away with him, whilst the head is to be placed on a spike on the Blue Tower for remembrance and execration.' The order was afterwards altered in this particular, that the head was to be placed on the town hall, and the four parts of the body one at each of the gates of the city. The executioner was subsequently ordered to efface the arms of Corfitz and his wife wherever they occurred in the town; for instance, on their pews in the churches. Leonora states in her Autobiography that the prison governor some time after told her that the Queen had desired that the effigy should be placed in the antechamber of Leonora's prison, and that she should be ordered to see it there; but that the king refused his consent.

[E29] The date of Ulfeldt's death is variously given as the 20th or the 27th of February, 1664. The latter date is given in a letter from his son Christian to Sperling, and elsewhere, (for instance, in a short Latin Biography of Ulfeldt called 'Machinationes Cornificii Ulefeldii,' published soon after); but the better evidence points to the earlier date. Christian Ulfeldt was not, it seems, at Basle at the time, and may have made a mistake as to the date, though he indicates the right day of the week (a Saturday), or he may have had reason for purposely making a misleading statement. In Copenhagen the report of his death was long suspected to be a mere trick.

[E30] Ulfeldt and Leonora had twelve children in all, of which seven were alive when Corfitz died; and it so happened as, explained before, that the youngest, Leo, was the only one who continued the name. It is from him that Count Waldstein, the owner of the MS., is descended.

[E31] This hymn-tune is still in use in the Danish Church.

[E32] Dr. Otto Sperling, the elder, is often alluded to in the Autobiography of Leonora as 'notre vieillard;' he was a faithful friend of Ulfeldt, and in 1654 he settled in Hamburg, where he educated Corfitz's youngest son Leo. He was implicated in Ulfeldt's intrigues, and a compromising correspondence between them fell into the hands of the Spanish Government, which placed it at the disposal of Hannibal Sehested when he passed through the Netherlands on his way home from his mission to France in 1663. In order to obtain possession of Sperling's person, the Danish authorities used the ruse of sending a Danish officer to his house in Hamburg, and request him to visit professionally a sick person just across the Danish frontier, paying in advance a considerable fee. Sperling, who did not suspect the transaction, was arrested immediately on crossing the boundary, and brought to Copenhagen. He was condemned to death July 28, 1664; but the sentence was commuted, and he died in the Blue Tower December 25, 1681. Otto Sperling, jun., to whom Leonora sent the MS. of her Autobiography, and who often visited her at Maribo, was his son.

[E33] The name of this judge was Villum Lange, and it is a curious coincidence that a letter from him of a somewhat later time (1670), has been found in one of the archives, in which he speaks of this very affair, and in which he expresses himself very much in the sense here indicated.

[E34] The words 'under the bottom … to … Auguste,' inclusive, have been struck out in the MS., and it has been impossible to read more than what here is rendered. In the Autobiography, where the same occurrence is related, Leonora says that she put on it the names both of the King and of the Queen; that on the bottom she wrote to the Queen, and that it was the Queen who discovered the inscription; from which it would appear that the Queen at all events was included in her ingeniously contrived supplique.

[E35] This book was doubtless the German translation of Conr. Lycosthenes' work, 'Prodigiorum ac Ostentorum Chronicon.' It is an amusing illustrated volume, much read in its time. The translation in question appeared in Basle, 1557.

[E36] This custom of congratulating persons who intend to communicate, or just have done so, is still retained by many of the older generation in Denmark.

[E37]
[E37b] It was a Colonel Hagedorn that entrapped and arrested Dr. Sperling, and Jäger played only a subordinate part in that transaction. He is stated to have been a cousin of Gabel, and to have been formerly a commander in the navy. He was appointed prison governor on June 12, 1665, and Balcke therefore doubtless only held the appointment provisionally.

[E38] 'Anno 1666, soon after Karen, Nils' daughter, came to me, we first discovered that there was a stone floor to my prison chamber, as she broke loose a piece of rubbish cemented together, and the stones were apparent. I had before thought it a loam floor. The former Karen, Ole's daughter, was one of those who spread the dirt but do not take it away. This Karen tormented me unceasingly, almost daily, that we must remove it everywhere, and that at once—it would soon be done. I was of opinion that it would make us ill if it was done all at once, as we required water to soften it, and the stench in this oppressive hole would cause sickness, but that it would be easier and less uncomfortable to remove one piece after another. She adhered to her opinion and to her desire, and thought that she could persuade the prison governor and the tower-warder to let the door remain open till all had been made clean. But when the tower-warder had brought in a tub of water, he locked the door. I went to bed and covered my face closely, while she scraped and swept up the dirt. The quantity of filth was incredible. It had been collecting for years, for this had been a malefactors' prison, and the floor had never been cleaned. She laid all the dirt in a heap in the corner, and there was as much as a cartload. It was left there until evening at supper-time, when the doors were opened. It was as I feared: we were both ill. The woman recovered first, for she could get out into the air, but I remained in the oppressive hole, where there was scarcely light. We gained this from it, that we were tormented day and night with numbers of fleas, and they came to her more than to me, so much so that she was often on the point of weeping. I laughed and made fun of it, saying that she would now have always something to do, and would have enough to beguile the time. We could not, however, work. The fleas were thick on our stockings, so that the colour of the stockings was not to be perceived, and we wiped them off into the water-basin. I then discovered that one flea produces another. For when I examined them, and how they could swim, I perceived that some small feet appeared behind the flea, and I thought it was a peculiar kind. At last I saw what it was, and I took the flea from which the small one was emerging on my finger, and it left behind evidences of birth: it hopped immediately, but the mother remained a little, until she recovered herself, and the first time she could not hop so far. This amusement I had more than once, till the fleas came to an end. Whether all fleas are born in this manner I cannot tell, but that they are produced from dirt and loam I have seen in my prison, and I have observed how they become gradually perfect and of the peculiar colour of the material from which they have been generated. I have seen them pair.'

It is scarcely necessary to say that, as far as natural history is concerned, Leonora has committed a mistake.

[E39] Leonora alludes to an anecdote told by 'Cicero in Tuscul. Quæst. lib. i. c. 43.' He recounts that the cynic Diogenes had ordered that his body should not be buried after his death but left uninterred. His friends asked, 'As a prey to birds and wild beasts?' 'Not at all,' answered Diogenes; place a stick by me, wherewith I may drive them away.' 'But how can you?' rejoined these; 'you won't know!' 'But what then,' was his reply, 'concern the attacks of the wild beasts me, when I don't feel them?'

[E40] This sister was Hedvig, who married Ebbe Ulfeldt, a relative of Corfitz Ulfeldt. He was obliged to leave Denmark in 1651, on account of irregularities in the conduct of his office, and went to Sweden, where he became a major-general in the army. He is the person alluded to in the Autobiography. Several of Leonora's children lived in Sweden with their relatives after the death of Corfitz Ulfeldt; but in 1668 the Danish Government obtained that they were forbidden the country.

[E41] The title 'Herr' was then only given to noblemen and clergy. Master means 'magister,' and was an academical title.

[E42] The original has here an untranslatable play upon words. *Leth* is a family name; and the woman says 'I am one of the Letter (the Leths),' but laughter is in Danish 'Latter.'

[E43] The newspapers in question were probably German papers which were published in Copenhagen at that time weekly, or even twice a week; the Danish *Mercurius* (a common title for newspapers) was a monthly publication.

[E44] His name was Torslev; see the Introduction and the Autobiography.

[E45] The name is in blanco; she was probably the Catharina Wolf which is mentioned in the Preface.

[E46] Walter's participation in the plot of Dina is mentioned in the Introduction. He was then ordered to leave the country, but afterwards obtained a pardon and permission to return. He does not seem to have availed himself of this till the year 1668; but his conduct was very suspicious, and he was at once arrested and placed in the Blue Tower, where he died towards the end of April 1670.

[E47] Leonora alludes, no doubt, to the Queen Sophia Amalia.

[E48] The song of St. Dorothea exists in many German and Danish versions.

[E49] The feast of St. Martin is supposed the proper time for killing pigs in Denmark. It is reported that when Corfitz Uldfeldt, in 1652, had published a defence of his conduct previously to his leaving Denmark the year before, he sent a copy to Peder Vibe, one of his principal adversaries, with this inscription:—

> Chaque pourceau a son St. Martin;
> Tu n'échapperas pas, mais auras le tien.

[E50] This Knud was the favourite of King Christian V., Adam Levin Knuth, one of the many Germans who then exercised a most unfavourable influence on the affairs of Denmark.

[E51] Hannibal Sehested was dead already in 1666, as Leonora was no doubt well aware. The whole passage seems to indicate that he is supposed to have had some love-intrigue with the duchess. Nothing has transpired on this subject from other sources, but it is certain that her husband, Duke Ernst Gynther, for some time at least, was very unfriendly disposed to Hannibal Sehested.

[E52] The Martilegium was probably a German history of Martyrs, entitled 'Martilogium (for martyrologium) der Heiligen' (Strasburg 1484, fol.). The extracts to which she refers were no doubt her earliest collections for her work on Heroines.

[E53] 'Hours of Spiritual Refreshment.' This very popular book of devotion was first published in 1664, and had an extraordinary run both in Germany and, through translations, in Denmark. The last Danish extract of it was published in 1846, and reached the third edition in 1856.

[E54] It was a common superstition that persons who understood the art of showing by magic the whereabouts of stolen goods, had the power, by use of their formulas alone, to deprive the thief of an eye.

[E55]
[E55b] Griffenfeldt, who was then at the height of his power, was the son of a wine-merchant, by name Schumacher, but had risen by his talents alone to the highest dignities. He was ennobled under the name of Griffenfeldt, and was undoubtedly the ablest statesman Denmark ever possessed. Eventually he was thrust from his high position by an intrigue set on foot by German courtiers and backed by foreign influence. He was accused of treason and kept in prison from 1676 to 1698, the year before he died, to the great, perhaps irreparable damage, of his native country. The principal witness against him was a German doctor, Mauritius, a professional spy, who had served the Danish Government in this capacity. The year after the fall of Griffenfeld, he was himself arrested on a charge of perjury, forgery, and high treason, and placed in the Blue Tower; he was convicted and conducted to Bornholm, where he died. But Griffenfeldt, who had been convicted on his false testimony, was not liberated. Griffenfeldt's ability and patriotism cannot be doubted, but his personal character was not without blemish; and it is a fact that in his prosperity he disclaimed all connection with his earlier friends, and even his near relations.

[E56] The MS. itself is bound in a very primitive manner, which renders it probable that Leonora has done it herself.

[E57] It appears from the State accounts that ever since the year 1672 a sum of 250 dollars a year had been placed at her disposal. It would seem, therefore, that somehow or other a part of them had been unlawfully abstracted by someone during the first years.

[E58] The acts of this famous trial are still in existence. Originally the quarrel arose out of the fact that the Countess Parsberg (born Skeel) had obtained a higher rank than Lady Grubbe, and was further envenomed by some dispute about a window in the house of the latter which looked down on the courtyard of the Countess's house. Regitze Grubbe (widow of Hans Ulrik Gyldenlöve, natural son of Christian IV. and half-brother of Ulrik Christian Gyldenlöve, as well as of Leonora Christina), persuaded another noble lady, Agnete Budde, through a servant, to poison Countess Parsberg. Miss Budde was beheaded, the girl Lucie was exiled, and Lady Grubbe relegated for life to the island of Bornholm.

[E59] This tune is still in use in Denmark; it is known in the Latin church as 'in natali Domini.'

[E60] 'I have in my imprisonment also gained some experience with regard to caterpillars. It amused me at one time to watch their changes. The worms were apparently all of one sort, striped alike, and of similar colour. But butterflies did not come from all. It was quite pretty to see how a part when they were about to change, pressed against something, whatever it might be, and made themselves steady with a thread (like silkworm's silk) on each side, passing it over the back about fifty times, always at the same place, and often bending the back to see if the threads were strong enough; if not, they passed still more threads round them. When this was done, they rapidly changed their form and became stout, with a snout in front pointed at the end, not unlike the fish called knorr by the Dutch; they have also similar fins on the back, and a similar head. In this form they remain for sixteen days, and then a white butterfly comes out. But of some caterpillars small worms like maggots come out on both sides, whitish, broad at one end and pointed at the other. These surround themselves with a web with great rapidity, each by itself. Then the worm spins over them tolerably thickly, turning them round till they are almost like a round ball. In this it lies till it is quite dried up; it eats nothing, and becomes as tiny as a fly before it dies. Twelve days afterwards small flies come out of the ball, and then the ball looks like a small bee-hive. I have seen a small living worm come out of the neck of the caterpillar (this I consider the rarest), but it did not live long, and ate nothing. The mother died immediately after the little one had come out.'

It is perhaps not unnecessary to add that this observation, which is correct as to facts, refers to the habits of certain larvæ of wasps which live as parasites in caterpillars.

[E61] It has been stated already that a copy of the first part of this work is still preserved. Amongst the heroines here treated of are modern historical personages, as Queen Margaret of Denmark, Thyre Danobod who built the Dannevirke, Elizabeth of England, and Isabella of Castilia, besides mythical and classic characters, as Penthesilea, Queen of the Amazons, Marpesia, Tomyris, Zenobia, Artemisia, Victorina, etc. There existed not a few works of this kind—we need only mention Boccacio's 'Donne Illustri,' in which many of these last personages also occur.

[E62] The Peblingesö is one of three lakes which surround Copenhagen on the land-side, in a semicircle.

[E63] The Lutheran Church has retained the division of the Commandments used in the Roman Church; and the Commandment against murder is therefore here described as the fifth, whilst in the English catechism it is the sixth.

[E64] The name of this governor, which is not mentioned by Leonora, was Jörgen Iversen, the first Danish governor of St. Thomas. In 1682 he returned to the colony from Copenhagen on board a vessel which was to bring some prisoners over to St. Thomas. Very soon after their departure, some of the prisoners and of the crew raised a mutiny, killed the captain and some of the passengers, amongst them the ex-governor Iversen. But one of the prisoners who had not been in the plot afterwards got the mastery of the vessel, and returned to Copenhagen. The vessel struck on a rock, near the Swedish coast, but the crew were saved and sent home to Copenhagen by the Swedish Government, and the murderers were then executed.

[E65] The Queen's church was a room in the castle where service was held according to the Calvinist rite.

[E66]
[E66b] This poem still exists, and is printed in the second volume of Hofman's work on Danish noblemen. It is intended to convey an account of her own and her husband's fate.

repeated note.

[E67] This picture is still preserved at the Castle of Rosenbourg, in Copenhagen.

[E68] The Excellency alluded to is Ulrik Frederik Gyldenlöve, a natural son of Frederik III. Anna Catharina Lindenow was daughter of Leonora's sister, Elizabeth Augusta, who married Hans Lindenow.

[E69] This Husum is a village just outside Copenhagen, where Leonora remained for some months before she went to Maribo, as is proved by a letter from her dated Husum, September 18, 1685. Of course the last paragraphs must have been added after she left her prison, and the passage 'This is finished in my prison' refers, at any rate, only to what precedes.